Lucky Baby

Lucky Baby

MEREDITH EFKEN

HOWARD BOOKS
A DIVISION OF SIMON & SCHUSTER, INC.
New York · Nashville · London · Toronto · Sydney

Published by Howard Books, a division of Simon & Schuster, Inc.
1230 Avenue of the Americas, New York, NY 10020
www.howardpublishing.com

Lucky Baby © 2010 by Meredith Efken

In association with the Steve Laube Agency

Library of Congress Cataloging-in-Publication Data

Efken, Meredith
  Lucky baby / Meredith Efken.
    p. cm.
  1. Adoptees—Fiction. 2. Intercountry adoption—Fiction. I. Title.
  PS3605.F57L83 2010
  813'.54—dc22
                                            2009039529

ISBN 978-1-4165-9550-2
ISBN 978-1-4391-7070-0 (ebook)

10 9 8 7 6 5 4 3 2 1

Manufactured in the United States of America

For information regarding special discounts for bulk purchases, please contact:
Simon & Schuster Special Sales at 1-866-506-1949 or business@simonandschuster.com.

Edited by Dave Lambert and Alton Gansky, Gansky Communications
Interior design by Kate Moll

The Simon & Schuster Speakers Bureau can bring authors to your live event.
For more information or to book an event, contact the Simon & Schuster Speakers Bureau
at 1-866-248-3049 or visit our website at www.simonspeakers.com.

*For my daughter Jessamyn Zhu-Chun. Every word in
this book was inspired by my love for you, sweetheart.
Everyone told us you were a lucky baby, but I know
in my heart that I'm the lucky one
to be your mom.*

ACKNOWLEDGMENTS

This story could not have been written without help from some amazing people. I am especially grateful to the following:

- Dr. Jeanne Prickett, superintendent of Iowa School for the Deaf, for helping me create a realistic diagnosis for Wen Ming and helping me see the world through that little girl's eyes;

- Dr. Weixing Li for helping me with the Chinese phrases in my story;

- Jeff Gerke, Brian Stuy, Jason Efken, Randy Ingermanson, and Maureen Lang for answering various research questions ranging from bosons and nanoparticles (Jason and Randy) to life in Chicago (Maureen) to current info about adopting from China and life in the orphanages there (Jeff and Brian);

- Tim Dickmeyer for helping me choose a good instrument for Meg, the Lincoln Symphony Orchestra in Nebraska (where he plays bass trombone) for letting me sit in on a rehearsal, and Clark Potter for explaining to me why violists are superior creatures to violinists;

- Jessamyn Efken for helping me understand the mind-set of an eleven-year-old girl and for brainstorming Eva's character with me;

- Todd Compton, fifth-grade teacher at Omaha's King Science and Technology Magnet, for letting me borrow his name for Eva's teacher;

- Brant and Katy Robinson for introducing us to the amazing world of Argentine tango and for helping me with my tango scenes;

- Jason Efken for being my key brainstorming partner, as well as a wonderfully supportive husband who cooks and cleans and taxis children so that I can write;

- Amy Bettis, Maureen Lang, Randy Ingermanson, Natalie Gillespie, Sharon Hinck, and Tosca Lee for being my fresh sets of eyes, reading the manuscript in its various stages of development, and for being a support system as I struggled to write this book—without their help and encouragement, I think I would have given up on the story; and

- Judy Duenow for being an amazing creativity coach—I could not have overcome the writer's block I had with this book without her insightful and encouraging coaching sessions

PROLOGUE

Wen Ming, April 2001

The woman of my earliest memory has no body. Just a round face with skin like a plum. Smooth and tight. Firm. A smiling plum with dimples. She is not my mama. I don't remember my mama.

Many years later, now that I am nearly grown, there are other things I remember. They are only pieces, like torn bits of a blurred photo. Sometimes I don't know what is real memory and what my mind has filled in for me, but I think most of our lives happen in our minds, so it doesn't bother me.

I remember a misty rain that smelled like the ocean and dead earthworms; massive concrete steps and the ache in my legs as I climbed them; the fuzzy nubs of my blanket, and its unchanging odor of old sun-dried sheets, steamed rice, and sour water. The blanket corner caught a step and I tripped. The woman grabbed my hand tighter and told me, "You should be more careful. Now hurry."

We did.

Not the hurry of going to the park for tai chi. Not the hurry of getting to the market before all the best fish were taken. Not the hurry of peeling off my many layers of clothing to squat over the toilet. Those normal sorts of hurry never turned my fingers into clammy, day-old rice noodles, never set an eel to swimming in my stomach. This hurry was the nightmare that chased me down dark alleys in my mind and swallowed me with its nothingness.

I was too small to fight it, but I did drag my feet. She tugged my arm. I shuffled after her. I had no choice.

Lots of hallways. Dim and musty, damp. The voices of a man and a woman—this woman with the perfect plum skin.

"You are not allowed to leave a child here. This is a police station, not an orphanage. She cannot stay. It's against the law."

"She isn't my child."

"She has been living with you?"

"I . . . took her in when her mother . . . actually, I don't know her parents."

"This was how long ago?"

"She'll be three in July."

"What sort of mother would give up her child after almost three years? She is that much trouble to you?" The man laughed and ruffled my hair, as if I were nothing more than a dog to be scratched behind the ears. Sharp teeth bared in my heart, and I pulled away from him with a silent growl. The woman jerked my hand and made me stand closer to her.

"I am not her mother!" Her anxiety flowed from her hand through mine, up my arm and to my heart, leaving a trail of numbing coldness. "It isn't that I don't care for the child. But she is not registered, she has no *hukou*. She is going blind . . ."

I felt the man's hand under my chin. He lifted my face, his touch more gentle than before. He was a towering shadow of dull greens and grays. "You should have gotten a *hukou* for her. You should not have been so foolish."

The woman said nothing. In my mind, now, I am sorry for this memory woman. It is a shameful thing to give up a child, even one who is not your own. She could not save face. Not when she'd taken me in illegally. Not when she was too poor to care for a child going blind.

"I could have left her in a restroom. She doesn't talk yet. I brought her here because she would be safe. You think I'm a bad person?" Her voice sounded like the never-ending shrill of Shanghai traffic. "I'm not a bad person. My husband's parents—they are the ones who went back on their word. Our parents think a girl with poor eyesight is not worth it. So how can I afford for her to go to a doctor? Am I to lose my job and do nothing but care for a blind child? Who will pay for that? Would you have us all end up on the streets? I'm a good person and a hard worker. My husband is also. We want a healthy child, just like anybody."

Her words made me thin, translucent, a sheet of paper about to be crumpled and thrown in the trash. A sheet of paper scribbled with unwantedness.

The man did not speak right away. Maybe he did not agree with the woman. Maybe he did not find me unwanted. But if he disagreed, why did he not speak?

I held tightly to the woman's hand. I do not know if I loved her, but if she let go, if she left me, I'd be alone in my world of shadows. Already, the dark seemed to creep under my skin, separating me from my own body. I wiggled my fingers and toes, but they didn't seem to be mine to control.

"Please," she whispered. "I was going to register her when we took her in, but we never had enough money. My husband's parents promised to help pay for the *hukou*, until they found out she was a girl. Now they are angry because we have a girl who is going blind. And who else will take her? You can understand."

I squeezed my eyes shut, willing the man to be unmoved by her pleading. To be untouched by her humiliation. To not understand.

After many moments, when he tried to speak, his voice sounded choked and thick like old sesame oil. "On her papers, I will write that you found her and brought her here. I won't say anything about the rest."

For the first time, the woman's hand slackened. She let go of me and opened her purse. "Thank you. I have her birth date too, for her papers."

My breath came in tiny pulses, like the throb in a chicken's neck the moment before it snaps.

Shadowed paper yuan traveled from her purse to his hand. He had shielded her not only from shame but also from legal trouble. That was worth a monetary gift, even from a woman who could not afford it. She knelt in front of me, a wide, forced smile stretching across her smooth skin.

"You're going to a good place. Lots of other children. They'll help your eyes there. It's really the best thing for you."

A tear on her cheek caught the light. I touched it and her smile wobbled. She laughed a little. "I wish I could go too! Lucky baby. You'll have so much fun."

I threw my arms around her and pressed my face against her neck, where her skin was softest and smelled like soap. She held me, and a sob ripped through her, through us both.

She tore herself from me. Disappeared into shadows. I heard the rapid squeaking of her rubber-soled shoes echoing down the corridor as she made her escape.

I lunged to follow. The man's arms snapped around me and I screamed. I kicked and thrashed, but he was so much stronger than I. He told me not to be a naughty baby, to hush and be good. I don't think he meant to be unkind. He held me against him, rubbing my back and bouncing me. His heart beat very fast. And his hands trembled. For his sake, I tried to stop crying. I wanted to be good.

The aunties who work at the Shanghai Children's Welfare Home think I was too young to remember this. They say I made it up. A child of two and a half years could never have such a memory, they insist. But this I remember—I know it happened, not just in my mind. I know it was real.

Is this a thing a child could forget?

Part One
LADYBUGS

"Do we really know our poor? Do we really know the poor in our own house, in our own family? Maybe we are not hungry for a piece of bread. Maybe our children, our husband, our wife, are not hungry, are not naked, are not homeless, but are you sure that there is no one there who feels unwanted, unloved?"

—*Mother Teresa*

O
N
E

Meg Lindsay

I watch her sleep. The turbulent energy of day has given way to the Elysian simplicity of night. I brush her pink lips with my thumb and her still-childish cheeks with my fingers. Her skin is the softness of every gentle memory and warm sensation I have ever known. It's all there, in touching her. She will never know how many nights I've done this—stolen into her room to watch her—hungrily, desperately trying to fill the hole inside myself with her. I can't love enough, can't want enough, can't get enough of her. The little hands; the messy, sweaty hair; the delicate skin of her eyelids. I never asked for this love, never expected it to be such an unsatisfied pain inside. But now I crave it, no matter how it devours me, no matter if it destroys me, I need to love her. I want to love her.

I never wanted this.

I never wanted to be a mom. There's the cold, hard truth of it. Lots of people thought it was because I'm self-centered and too career-focused. Lots of people thought it was because I didn't like children. Lots of people thought it was because I must be infertile.

Lots of people were wrong.

From my earliest memories, "mother" has meant the woman who criticizes, who critiques my every move, who is never satisfied or totally pleased. A mother is someone who loves only if you do what she wants. With a mother, you're always one step away from emotional abandonment, from becoming an orphan of the heart.

So why would I want to become that person? Why would I want to do that to an innocent child? I don't dislike children. I dislike mothers.

Why would I ever choose to become what I dislike?

And yet, that's exactly what I did. I'm not saying my motives were right. I know they were not. But every revolution, every paradigm shift has a catalyst. A shove. A compelling reason to risk everything to find a new path, to change.

My shove, my catalyst, was my mother.

March 2005

"Tell me again why we're doing this." My husband, Lewis, guided our car into my parents' driveway and shut off the engine.

I stared out the window at the prosy March Sunday, pedestrian as a Schoenberg string quartet. "Because I haven't seen my sister in two years?" She'd been in France and had only returned home two days ago.

Lewis lifted his eyebrows in an is-that-the-best-you-can-come-up-with expression.

"I know, I know." I leaned my head against the back of the seat. "How about this one? We're doing this because I still harbor the thoroughly unrealistic hope that my parents will change if I do the good-daughter thing long enough."

He opened his door and ducked out of the car. "Give you points for honesty, anyway. Let's go do this."

"Besides, I'm going to talk to them about the savings account. I want to use it to pay off my grad school loans."

He stopped in the middle of the driveway, bringing me to a halt behind him. "Seriously? You're going to bring that up today?"

"Why not today? I've chickened out for six months. I'm disgusting myself."

"I've told you, we don't need it. If you bring it up, it will be wedding mess Act Two. We're fine."

"It's my debt and it's hanging over both our heads, and that's not right. They created a savings account for me, and there's no reason why it can't go toward something as responsible and practical as paying off debt. It's not like I want to blow it on a cruise or something."

Lewis put his arm around my waist. "I just don't think it's worth the trouble. You can't bring it up without reminding them that the money was supposed to pay for your wedding—to Adam, not to me. They've only been talking to us again the last six months. And if you screw it up, I don't think I'll be able to fix it with another sob-story letter."

"So it was my fault?"

I started to pull away, but he tightened his grip on me and pressed a kiss against my temple. "That's not what I meant. I just don't want you hurt again."

"Me neither."

My mother eased open the door and watched Lewis and me make our way up the brick walk to the trilevel suburban house where I grew up, her smile so warm and hospitable, I once again believed in it for a second. For one blinding, glorious, faith-filled second the world in my heart seemed to match the world outside.

"Meggie!"

She waved at me and I headed for her warmth like a kid goat tottering toward its dam. My mom. Mine, mine, mine. Finally I was close enough to touch her. I leaned into the doorway to fill my arms with mother love.

She gave me a one-armed hug, the other arm holding open the beveled glass storm door. "I was hoping you were Beth."

Of course she was. "She's not here?"

"She went to pick up a . . . friend." My mother suddenly looked like she'd secretly eaten an entire bowl of brownie batter. But she didn't elaborate as she let us through the door.

We trudged up four carpeted steps and into the living room, where everything was cloyingly symmetrical and perfect in shades of rose, peach, and wine. While my dad gave me an airy hug encompassing all the empty space of the issues we never spoke about, my mom wrapped her arms around Lewis's slim waist as if he was the best son-in-law a mom could ask for.

He patted her on the back. "Hi, Karen." Looking over my mom's head, he nodded at my dad. "Doug."

My mom stepped away, and no one but I caught the subtle glance of distaste she shot at my husband. She smoothed her palms down the skirt of her Sunday best, wiping away the touch of him. "Watch out, Mom," I wanted to tell her, "atheism is catching." But I'd never dare. She and Dad turned their backs on me five years ago when I married Lewis instead of Adam. Lewis's letter to them had been a masterpiece of pleading and scolding and negotiation—their letting me back into their lives in exchange for his backside in a pew at our church every week. The ultimately ironic sacrifice of love. It had purchased a fragile reconciliation for me, and I wasn't about to throw it away.

"Aunt Meg!" The screech accompanied a thud against the backs of my knees.

Lewis steadied me. I glanced over my shoulder and down at the brown-haired preschooler pressing his face between my legs. "Hi, Jakey. Where's your brother?"

He tipped his head up to shrug at me. "Sammie's playing. I told him to come say hi but he didn't listen."

"Little brothers are like that."

"Like what?" My little brother sauntered into the room, towering over my own five feet nine inches. He barely nodded at Lewis.

"Pesky. Annoying."

He jabbed my arm lightly, grinning. "If so, we learned it from our older siblings."

Jakey transferred his grasp to my brother's left leg. "Dad! Come see my Lego tower."

Joe hoisted the three-year-old into his arms and smiled at me. He loved being a dad. He was the hero, the king, and the object of his sons' worship. There was triumph in that smile. Invincibility too, as if he half believed the mythology his children had created.

A part of me wanted to punch him. Just to remind him that not all of us adored the very air he breathed. To some of us, he would always be a loved but pesky little brother who had been anything but heroic when his big sister needed it.

"Come on, Grandpa!"

My dad trotted after the duo. My mom had already bustled back into the kitchen, where my sister-in-law, Ellie, was helping get dinner ready. A big banner stretched above the dining table, reading, "Welcome Home Beth and Congratulations!"

Congratulations? For what? Surviving a two-year missionary tour of duty in southern France? Yes, she suffered so much. The Riviera Missionary—poor baby.

That was unfair of me. Maybe she didn't suffer physical deprivation, but some of the French could be terribly unfriendly, especially to Christian missionaries. She'd been lonely, judging from her e-mails and phone calls to me.

"Meg!" my mom called. "We could use your help out here."

I winced at the faint accusation. Lewis gave my hand a squeeze, and I leaned in for a kiss. Fortified, I left him standing in the living room, alone, looking as misplaced as he always did in my parents' home.

Entering my mother's kitchen, I saw Ellie whisking around, efficiently skirting my mom, as they performed the sort of ritualistic, meal-preparing dance that I had never quite mastered.

I stood on the threshold, trying not to feel the awkwardness welling inside me. "What can I do to help?"

I should have known the dance by now. Ellie didn't have to ask. She just did. And whatever she did was usually right.

Mom handed me a bowl and a short "Here, grate cheese." I shuttled off to a corner of the island counter, feeling like an inept eight-year-old. Grating cheese is what you make kids do when they can't be trusted to do anything else. Everyone knows that.

If a stranger were to walk into our kitchen at that moment, he would have thought Ellie was the daughter of the house, and I was a newly minted in-law. Ellie and my mother laughed and chatted together about the clever things her boys said and made plans to go shopping.

"We'll have lots to shop for," my mom told her, "especially now that Beth is home."

I supposed they meant for Beth's apartment. At twenty-eight, she'd hardly want to live with her parents for long—even if she had the sort of cozy relationship with them I could only dream of.

Ellie grinned. "Thanks for including me in all of it."

"Well, of course. You're family." She gave Ellie a hug.

My sister-in-law caught my eye, and her smile grew plastic and pinched. At least she was nice enough to look uncomfortable on my behalf. She pulled back from my mom. "So Meg, how's the symphony going?"

The Nouveau Chicago Symphony—a rebel ensemble of musicians wanting to play crowd favorites and new composers instead of the "moldy oldies." I was a charter member on my viola, eking out a meager salary as a principal player. My parents had never attended a performance, but Ellie and Joe liked it on occasion, if the tickets were free.

"Great. In fact, I was going to see if either of you wanted a season pass for next fall."

Ellie shrugged and nodded. "Have to ask Joe, but I think that would be fun. If we can find babysitters."

I took a breath. "Mom? You interested?"

She had to be interested. Just for once, be interested in something I did.

She reached into the fridge to pull out a fruit salad. "I doubt it, honey. We have some serious reservations about that group."

Even Ellie looked startled. "About the Nouveau Symphony? Why?"

"They play music from movies we don't approve of. And I read that their guest composer this year was Sam Chesterfield."

Oh, she was upset about dear Sam, was she? "Sam's a terrific composer."

"He's a gay activist."

"That doesn't have anything to do with his orchestral music."

"Of course it does! There are evil spiritual forces that attach themselves to the music while it's being composed. I just don't think it's right for someone claiming to be a Christian to support gay music or music from rated-R movies."

Ellie wouldn't look at me. She and Joe would still probably take a season pass, but she wasn't the sort to get between my mother and me in an argument.

"Okay, whatever. I was just offering. It'd be nice to actually have some support from my parents."

"I'm not being judgmental or anything, Meggie, but I'm right— these things do have an impact on us. Look at you—I really do think that if you had directed your musical interest in a more God-honoring direction, you wouldn't have rebelled like you did and ended up in a godless marriage. You should have stuck to playing on the church worship team."

Ellie bit her lip, glancing at me with pity in her eyes. "I think I hear Jakey calling for me." She rushed from the kitchen.

"Could we maybe not have these conversations in front of Ellie?" I handed Mom the bowl of grated cheese. "She shouldn't be dragged into it."

"You're the one that asked about tickets. I was just explaining why I said no." She set the bowl on the counter and then stirred the gravy simmering on the stove.

What had I thought? That I could soften her up by offering season passes to something she'd never had any appreciation for? She'd always suspected anything beyond hymns and gospel music was the realm of the devil. If it hadn't been for my dad's mother, I would have grown up plinking out "Faith Is the Victory" on the piano instead of falling in love with the viola and the world of the symphony. Grandma was the only person who could intimidate my mother. She paid for my instruments and my lessons, and attended all my recitals and performances until she became too sick to leave the nursing home. She died two years ago. There was still an emptiness inside me where she ought to have been.

There'd be no softening of my mother. If I said I wanted my savings account to pay off graduate school debt, she'd respond that if I hadn't gone to grad school in the first place, there'd be no debt to pay off. And if I'd married Adam Harris the Future Pastor, as I'd been engaged to do, instead of Lewis Lindsay the Atheist Physicist, as I'd done five years ago, then I'd have received the savings account money and wouldn't have to be asking for it now.

No, there was no scenario in which this was going to go smoothly. Might as well just jump in. "Hey, Mom? I was wondering about my savings account. How much is in there these days?"

She stopped whisking the gravy and stood motionless at the stove, her back to me. "Why are you asking *now*?"

I swallowed hard, my mouth dry. Brazen it out. "Just curious. I'd like to talk to you and Dad about transferring it into my name."

The whisking started up again. Her voice sounded deceptively cordial. "Why?"

Arms crossed, I pinched the soft skin on the insides of my elbows. The sharp pain stopped my heart from racing and cleared my head. I kept my voice calm and low. Respectful. "You had a savings account set up for each of us kids. The last I knew, we each had over twenty thousand. For when we got married. Joe got his. I'm married now. I'd like to have mine. Please."

My mother was silent for a moment. The whisking stilled again, and then resumed more briskly. I saw the tension in her shoulders and neck. "I'm sorry, dear"—still the same cheerful tone—"we had to use that money for other things, since you didn't need it for a wedding."

The sound of the front door opening choked off my bitter reply. Mom pushed past me and hurried toward the entryway, calling a greeting to my sister. I followed her into the rush of voices and movement at the door.

It was all I could do not to shove my way forward to grab my baby sister in a hug. The five years that Mom and Dad had refused to speak to me, she'd never disowned me. She'd been the sole family member to defy them and attend my wedding. As the baby of the family, she'd gotten away with it. My brother and Ellie had been too scared to try. But Beth—she'd actually been happy for me. Relieved, even. As if she'd known how unhappy I was with Adam.

"Meg!" she squealed, lurching forward and catching me up in her arms.

I squeezed her tight and closed my eyes. "I missed you!"

"Not as much as I missed you!" She turned her mouth toward my ear to whisper, "I'm so glad you're here."

I opened my eyes and looked over her shoulder at another person standing behind her. It was his hair I saw first. That dark, nameless sort of blond that I would have taken great pleasure in calling "dirty dishwater"—except that my real hair color was similar and I hid it with light ash color and golden lowlights. A hot-cold, sick sort of shiver sped through me.

I hated that hair, always cropped and styled so neatly, so rigidly. Countless times, I'd run my fingers through its thick softness only to be told I was messing it up and that there shouldn't be much touching until we were married. To this day, I'm convinced Adam Harris loved his hair far more than he loved me—which would not have been a problem if he had been engaged to marry his hair instead of me.

And now the hair—and presumably the man beneath it—was standing in the entryway of my parents' home, its presence stripping away the years. It seemed so natural, so right, so obvious for him to be here as he had been so many times before. The here-and-now was suddenly anachronistic—he'd apparently been the "friend" Beth had brought—and Lewis and Ellie were within the family circle while Adam hovered on the fringe.

I stepped back from my sister. The room grew stiflingly quiet. Adam's lips scrunched into a tight smile. "Hello, Meg."

"Hi?" I hadn't meant for it to sound like a question, but it was all I could manage beyond blinking at him.

My mother pushed past me. "Move out from the middle of the walkway, Meg." She touched Adam's arm, drawing him farther into the room. "It's so wonderful to see you, honey. We would have had you over right when you got home, but Beth said you were sleeping off jet lag. Are you feeling better now?"

"Much better, thanks." He had the chutzpah to walk right up to Lewis and extend his hand. "Lewis, right? I don't think we ever formally met. I'm Adam Harris."

Lewis shook his hand, his face carefully blank. This was a farce, a nightmarish farce.

Was no one going to explain why my ex-fiancé was standing in my parents' living room? I felt like a cork that had been shoved down a wine bottle's neck, the only way of escape now too small for me to fit through. The smell of those memories, aging for more than five years, was the worst sort of wine—the sort that swallows the air and makes clear thought impossible.

Lewis walked to me and slipped his arms around my waist. I felt tension in him, but he kissed my ear and whispered, "Do you want to leave?"

I shook my head. There was something important happening and it seemed I ought to understand what it was, but my mind had become a stray dog—matted, trembling, and futilely chasing its tail.

Everyone started talking at once, but none of it made sense. The sound pressed hard around me, saturating the air, filling all my pores, heavier and heavier—

"Someone tell me what he's doing here!"

My shout cleared the air, silencing the noise. I hadn't meant to yell. It was all making me crazy.

My sister sidled up to me and took my hand. "He's not a bad person." Her voice was soft, pleading, like when we were young and she was trying to talk her way out of having broken the headphones for my Walkman.

"I know."

"I always liked him. You knew that, didn't you?"

"I guess so. I suspected. But—"

"We were on the same team in France."

"I thought he was in Haiti."

Adam just watched the two of us, shifting on his feet.

"He was, until after you . . ."

Broke up with him. "And then?"

"He went to France, and I followed him there."

She shot him a look of pure admiration, and suddenly I knew exactly what she was going to say next.

"We're getting married, Meg! You have to be happy for us."

"I . . ." I wanted to say the words she needed from me. There was so much hope and trust in her eyes. But a spiny knot twisted in my heart. This was why she'd been so supportive when I'd married Lewis instead of Adam. It hadn't been about me at all. It had been about her. "Congratulations, sis." I tried very hard not to spit out the words.

Suddenly the banner made sense. Everyone else already knew, except Lewis and me. It was hard to breathe.

Beth threw her arms around me. "I knew you'd understand. Mom didn't think you would, but I knew you couldn't help but be happy for us! I want you to be my matron of honor, okay?"

"When?" I hadn't meant for it to sound like an assent, but she gave me another happy squeeze.

"Thank you!" She grabbed both my hands. "Mom and Dad have been great about the whole thing. Just wait till you hear! They talked the church board into hiring Adam as associate pastor. And they're paying for the whole wedding, *and* our honeymoon, *and* a down payment on a house! I had no idea we had that much in our savings accounts, did you?"

I met my mother's eyes and read the heartless truth in them. *"Had to use that money for other things,"* did they? Like securing the only son-in-law they'd ever really wanted. Like rewarding Beth for being the kind of daughter they approved of. It wasn't the money itself. If they'd asked me if they could use it to help Beth—and even Adam— I'd have readily agreed.

It was the coldness of it all. The spite and spark of glee in my mother's eyes. I couldn't look away. She was relishing it—this moment when she got to stick it to me in front of everyone. I'd embarrassed her horribly when I'd thrown over the seminary graduate for the scientist. And she was going to make sure I got my punishment at every opportunity.

I stumbled down the steps to the front door. My hand grasped the knob.

"Meg!" My mother's voice froze me. "If you leave now, you will *never* come back. Do you understand?"

I squeezed the doorknob, leaning my weight against it, my breath coming in heaves. My family or my freedom? Inclusion or self-respect? Why did I even have to choose?

A touch on my arm. I looked up into Lewis's brown eyes. They were soft, glimmering with concern. He gave me a tiny shake of his head. He knew what it was like to have almost no family. It was why he'd been willing to do anything to help me reconcile with mine. I couldn't throw that away.

I let go of the doorknob. For him. He put his arm around my waist and led me upstairs. I wouldn't look at my mother. I didn't want to see the triumph in her smile.

Wen Ming, January 2004

L ucky girls live with their families. Lucky girls have good eyesight. Lucky girls have beautiful black hair and round cheeks, and their heads are flat in back because their mothers know this is the most flattering shape for heads. They have their own rooms full of books and toys that do not have to be shared. They have cute milk names and grandparents and aunties, uncles, and cousins. Lucky girls are not abandoned.

I was never a lucky girl. I had weak eyes, a round head, flat cheeks, and mud-puddle hair. I had no books, no milk name, no family. But I had a mind not lacking in cleverness and a spirit not wanting for stubbornness. They told me that I could not be like other girls. I was too unlucky.

I knew about those other, lucky girls. They walked to school past the Children's Home, giggling and eating their breakfast of *danbing* from the street vendor. The smell of the egg pastry—rich with frying oil and the pungent tug of cilantro and scallions and *zacai*—filtered over the courtyard wall, scenting the air just enough so that for a second, my hungry belly quivered with anticipation of finally being filled. I could almost taste the comfort of fried dough safely cradling pillowy eggs that would give me strength all day long. Breathing in, I could almost feel myself wrapped in spices, their warmth like arms around me. But no matter how deeply I breathed and how hard I imagined, the *danbing* belonged to those other girls, not me. They walked on, taking their enticing fragrance with them, and my belly still remained as it had before—empty.

And no matter how much I envied those lucky *danbing* girls, I always reminded myself that I would never be one of them. I knew much more than they did, even though I was so young. I knew that outside the bubble created by the wonderful aroma of their meal, there was a dangerous and lonely world where adults did not buy *danbing* for children. I knew, though they did not, that in a world like this, there was only one way to survive:

I must be strong. I must not trust. And most important—

I must not love.

I don't know how I knew this, and I could have never put it into those words at the time, but the knowledge was there inside me, and I can still feel the ache of it today.

I sat by myself, away from the other children, in a primary room that felt like the inside of an ice cube, all soft blue and white and hard. I bent over a scratched and gummy wooden table, listening to an auntie read a story about a dragon who was cast out of heaven and the kind villagers who saved its life. I shifted my wobbly metal chair so that it kept time with the rhythm of her reading. Though my toes were clammy, my waist itched from sweat and the bulk of the four layers of clothing we all were required to wear. In my hand, I worked a ball of red craft clay. It was supposed to be a dragon, but it stubbornly refused to look like anything but a lumpy snake.

Picking clay from under my fingernails, I slid a glance at the auntie. Perhaps if my dragon made her smile, she would place it somewhere safe so it could dry, and then I would have my very own dragon. We orphans owned nothing ourselves. Even our clothing circulated between us every day. We had to warn one another about new holes or seams that chafed. So the chances of making a dragon I could keep were not great—they never let us dry the clay because it was too expensive to keep replacing. But this auntie was new, so maybe she didn't know the rules. If the dragon pleased her enough, maybe just this once she might be persuaded.

I squinted at her until her eyes appeared haloed like the streetlamps at night. Between her front teeth lay a dark gap—like a mail slot for envelopes the size of a grain of rice. It would be fun to be able to eat rice without opening my mouth. I meant to ask her sometime if she had ever tried it.

She was ruining the story. Grown-ups always thought they must read each word so that it plopped like an egg into boiling soup. Boiling soup that was always cheerful, bubbling, no matter if the story was sad or scary or suspenseful. I could never depend on grown-ups to do anything correctly. But I listened carefully anyway, so I could memorize it and tell it to myself the way it should be told — so that I could taste and chew and swallow each feeling and each exciting moment until they piled up in my stomach like a feast.

"Thunder shook the tiny village. The villagers had never seen so much rain," the auntie read in her egg-plopping voice. "Surely the Emperor of Heaven was angry! And so he sent rain dragons to shake the heavens and pour upon the earth his anger."

Something like thunder shook the floor. The sound of feet, like many raindrops, pattered down the hallway, punctuated by children's shouts and chatter.

I raced to the doorway and watched other children blur past me, catching joyous words blown to me by the wind they created. "Crane! In the courtyard. A real crane!"

A *danbing*-laden shiver slammed into me. I didn't stop to find a jacket. I leaped into the stream of bodies hurtling toward the courtyard. It was a sign, a lucky sign. Long life, blessing, good fortune. I would find a way to see the crane, eyesight or no. I could not miss something so wonderful.

The doors to the courtyard were blocked by a hundred straining orphan bodies clamoring for a sight of the rare bird. The word that filtered to those of us in the back was that the aunties and teachers were not allowing us to go into the courtyard because we would frighten the creature. Director Wu, we were assured, would take pictures and pass them around so we all could see. The children around me groaned and shouted protests.

I felt a falling, a stumbling forward into the last sniff of a promised treat that had been snatched away. Photos? She thought photos could replace a real experience? What was a photo to me but blurred bits and splotchy sections of someone else's memory? It was nothing more than bland, watery congee.

No. I wanted the *danbing* this time. Wanted it for myself.

If all the teachers and aunties were guarding these doors, then it was likely no one guarded the courtyard entrance from the director's office. But could I? Did I have the courage to trespass in Director Wu's own office? We children were never invited to enter there. The only reason I knew the north courtyard door led to her office was that I had asked an auntie about it during playtime last summer.

My feet twitched, shifting and edging away from the other children, begging me to follow their lead. My ears locked onto the sound of Director Wu's voice. Should I mind the rules, or feed luck to my soul?

The director was strict, but kindness glinted from her sharp eyes. She never beat us or denied us supper. The worst that could happen was that I'd be banned from the preschool story and craft room for a few weeks. I wouldn't get to keep my half-finished red clay dragon.

Seeing a real, live crane was better than having a lumpy, poorly shaped clay dragon.

A lucky omen was better than any personal possession.

I slipped past the other children lining the walls and crept through the deserted corridors toward the director's office. The darkened room seethed, outraged that an orphan trespassed. Its disapproval pressed against me, and I felt that at any moment, it would clamp down around my wrist and hold me trapped until Director Wu could hand down punishment.

I shuffled forward, and my knees rammed into a metal desk. The room echoed like a giant gong sounding an alarm.

Even my heart stopped thumping.

But after seconds of crushing silence, when the office had seen that it had failed to stop me, my heart began to tiptoe once more. I felt along the desk, lightly trailing my hand over papers and folders.

I jostled a photo frame and it clunked flat on the desk. The sound shot from my head to my toes, leaving a dizzying trail behind it. I seized the frame and squinted hard at the photo. It was difficult to see in such dim light, but it looked like it was the director and a man—her husband—and in front of them, a small boy. Her son.

The director had a family. This was unfair. She ought to have been an orphan like me. I did not like having my life controlled by a person who did not know what it was like to be unlucky. She could not understand.

I set the frame back on the desk, hoping I'd arranged it like it was before. Then I shuffled toward the door behind the desk. I'd have to be quick. It would be hard for me to spot the crane, and it would likely fly away as soon as any of us made too much noise. Plus, I was surely going to be caught and punished.

I held my breath and eased open the door. Daylight and a cold breeze greeted me. I blinked, urging my eyes to cooperate for once, and stepped into the courtyard.

At first, I could see nothing but bright gray and white glare. I didn't hear any sounds, so I must not have been spotted yet. I scanned the courtyard, hardly daring to hope.

My vision became shadowed, and then—

There it was. Looking at me. I saw it clearly, though everything else was a hopeless mash of color and shadows. It was about my size, and on the top of its head, between the eyes that were locked on mine, was a red patch of feathers that seemed to glow with joy and blessing.

I could not look away. I wanted the moment to soak into my mind the way ink is absorbed into rice paper, words and fiber inseparable. My feet moved forward, almost without my consideration. My hands stretched out.

If I could just touch it. Even one feather.

It didn't look away or move. I was wrapped in its gaze, drawn toward it. It wanted me to come.

Only a few steps more. It dipped its head toward me, like a bow, welcoming me.

"Wen Ming!"

The director's screech exploded through the air. The crane lurched toward me, wings unfurled. My vision blurred once more, and the last clear image I had was of a tangle of feathers and a piercing set of eyes that no longer looked so welcoming.

Warm body and the breeze of wings, it flew over me to freedom. I screamed, covering my head with my arms.

Something warm and gooey and wet plopped on my head and on one hand.

More shouting, and the slap of feet running on concrete. An angry hand grabbed my arm. I didn't even bother to listen to the director's tirade. The crane had flown away, scared of me. Shame dripped over me like the wet substance in my hair.

"What is on your head and hand?" The auntie who had been reading to us held up my hand. She wrinkled her nose. "It's poo! The crane pooped on her."

The teachers and aunties laughed, and the director joined them. She could hardly speak for a moment, then she gasped, "Let that be a lesson—for scaring off such a beautiful bird. I had no chance to take even one picture. You ruined it for everyone."

The auntie pulled me toward the door where the other children crowded around, listening and watching. "Cranes are very lucky," she said loudly to the other adults. "So having one fly at you is a good sign."

"Yes, flying at you. But pooping on you?" someone else said.

"It comes from a lucky bird. Maybe it's lucky poo."

They laughed at this. "Do you feel lucky now, Wen Ming?" and "Lucky poo should not be washed off" and "Maybe we can scrape some into a painted bottle and you can wear it as a charm around your neck."

The poo slid down my neck. It did not feel lucky. It did not smell lucky. I dipped my head, not wanting to face the entire Children's Home witnessing my disgrace.

The auntie dragged me through the crowd of children, who held their noses and pointed at my hair. She took me to a washroom and pushed my head until I was bent over the sink. She poured water over me. It was cool, and all I could see was a large stain in the ceramic that looked vaguely like a brown dog. Even the dog seemed to laugh at my foolishness.

Anger poured into my upside-down head, until it felt tight enough to burst. I had not done anything so terribly wrong. Yet these grown-ups, these lucky ones who had money and family and their own homes, they mocked me for trying to grab a bit of luck for myself. They laughed.

This is why they would never have my trust.

After the auntie scrubbed and soaped my head and hand, she rubbed me with a towel and took my soiled shirt and sweater. She pointed to an old metal chair.

"You sit here. I will get you some different clothes." She left, and the room pulsed with my silent outrage.

I shut my eyes and pictured the crane again, its peaceful eyes locked onto mine. They could laugh, but they would never be able to take that moment from me. I knew it was the power and love of the crane that had allowed me to see, for even a few seconds. It was worth the price of humiliation.

"Are you all right?"

The soft voice, the breath puffed into my face, made me jump. My eyes flew open and I saw a face. Her upper lip was cruelly split into two rounded, rosy humps. I gasped. I'd seen cleft lips before, but never so close. Never so clearly. Part of her nose was missing, and a knob of pink flesh, like a small toe, protruded from the hole.

I pitied her. But she should learn to mind her own business. "I'm fine. You shouldn't be here." I tried to make my voice stern and un-caring. "Go away. You'll get in trouble."

"Nobody gets in trouble here." Her mouth twisted into a grimace that I took for a smile. A smile that filled the air with the scent of the very best *danbing*.

My stomach felt like a big hand, grasping and reaching, and I grabbed little gulps of air, trying not to notice. "I just got in big trouble. You are too stupid to understand."

The hand in my stomach punched me for being so cruel. But it had to be done. She had to be made to go away. I had to be alone.

She crossed her arms and did not look like she was going away. "That was not trouble. Not like my old orphanage."

She had more fight in her than I'd guessed. "You're new?"

"Yes." Her words sounded slurred and distorted. I could tell she worked hard to pronounce each one.

"Did you see what happened to me, with the crane?"

"Yes."

I wrapped the towel around my chilling body. If this wonderful, persistent, delicious-smelling girl did not leave soon, the ache in my stomach for her would tear a great hole through me. "Go away. I am very unlucky. You should not talk to me."

"I don't think so."

"I was pooped on!"

"You're lucky just because you live here."

"You really are stupid! We are orphans. This is an orphanage. And you and I will never be more than unwanted, unlucky girls who will never eat *danbing* or have a crane's good fortune." I panted for air and forced tears a safe distance from my eyes. "Go away. Just go away."

I squeezed my eyes shut and buried my head against my knees. But I still felt her standing beside me, still smelled her gentle, enticing scent.

"It's pretty here. Lots of toys, and bright colors on the walls. And every bed has lots of blankets. Everyone gets enough to eat."

"Just congee, every day." Watered down, cabbage flavored, absent any spices. It kept me alive, but it didn't make me live.

"Better than nothing every day."

Her arm crept around my shoulder. I never let anyone hug me. It felt like burning soup thrown across my bare skin. I screamed and shoved her. "Don't touch me! Don't you dare touch me!"

She huddled on the floor, arms over her head, shivering. Crying.

And still she would not leave. Why wouldn't she leave?

Her little sobs pushed into my lungs, squeezing them shut. I wanted to hold her, take care of her, hide her from anyone who might hurt her. I didn't want to care. But everything about her shoved and pushed, crept and trickled into me. Taking me over. Forcing me to open to her. To feel things I did not want to feel.

I reached a shaking hand to her and helped her up. "I am sorry. Don't be afraid. Please, don't be afraid of me."

She leaned toward me, and her small hand snaked into mine. The trembling spread from my hand to my whole body. She climbed onto my lap and I could not stop her. She wrapped her arms around me and I could not stop her. Her warmth seeped into my chilled body and I could not stop her.

I cried, and I could not stop myself. She was breaking into me, and I wanted to hide from the terror of all the feelings she was freeing. But she was so warm and smelled so good, and I was so very hungry.

"Did they beat you at your other orphanage?"

"Sometimes. If anyone noticed we were bad. But there weren't enough aunties even to beat the naughty ones."

A burning slid down my throat. I could not let myself picture her being beaten. I would feel it in my own body.

"Why did they send you here?"

"I don't know, but I am very lucky." She found my hand and squeezed it. "You are lucky too, even if the crane pooped on you."

She kissed my cheek. A kiss. No one had ever kissed me before. Soft, moist, accepting. The two humps of her lips and the tiny toe that should have been her nose left a print in my skin, as if I was the dough and she was shaping me, leaving her mark on me.

It was *danbing*. I tasted it, not just in my imagination but for real. The flavors coated my tongue, blanketing it in love. I sank my teeth into the egg and dough, as if they were deep pillows. It squashed around my gums and mashed against the roof of my mouth, warm and soft, filling all the hidden empty spaces in my head with steamy, spicy moisture. My tongue rolled in it and rolled it around and around, and I never wanted to stop tasting and tasting and tasting, until it all slid down my throat, a gentle caress, and settled in my stomach, where it seemed to say, "Hush, I am here now."

With a great clenching pain, something hard and sharp collapsed inside me. I leaned on her shoulder, shuddering.

And then, it hurt a little less. The hunger was a little less than before. The need had changed—less desperate, more in control. I felt a faint warmth in my belly.

I touched my fingers to her mangled lip, gently. "Does it hurt?"

"No. Only when people laugh at it or run away from me. Then it hurts. Do your eyes hurt?"

I shook my head. My eyes were never what hurt.

She wriggled off my lap and faced me. I missed her warm weight.

"You are very lucky, Wen Ming."

"Why?"

She took a step back and put her hand into the pocket of her pants. "Because the crane left something for you."

"More poo?"

She didn't answer. Just held out her palm. There in the middle was a wispy bit of red. She pinched it with her other hand and put it in front of my face.

A small, rumpled, fluffy red feather.

She handed it to me, and the world swam with my tears. I clutched the feather in my hand, the first possession I'd been given since arriving at the Children's Home.

"What's your name?"

"Zhen An."

I grabbed her into a hug. The crane had brought her to me. Given her the strength to force-feed me her love. The feather was beautiful and rather made up for the poo, but the real gift was this girl. A friend. I had a real friend. And it was frightening and wonderful, and I felt like I might devour her in my hunger, but still I was satisfied.

The auntie found a tiny bottle to put the feather in. We put it on a string so I could wear it like a necklace—just like they'd teased me about doing with the crane poo. Everyone wanted to see my red crane feather, but Zhen An was the only one I let wear it.

They all called me Poo-Poo Head for weeks. They weren't trying to be mean. They were just envious because even with poor eyesight, even being an unattractive orphan, even while exiled from story time for a month, I, with my crane feather and new best friend, was the luckiest girl in China.

Meg Lindsay, March 2005

I wedged my viola between my chin and my shoulder. I crushed the bow against the strings, the pungent smell of rosin escaping in a cloud around my head. I didn't need to look at the music; the song exploded from my fingers—brazen, rebellious, and defiant as it always was in the privacy of the study.

I pushed the notes harder, faster, digging deep into each string to punish it, almost beyond its ability to endure. My viola became my voice, screaming out all the words I wished I'd been able to say to them. It became my legs, so I could outrun the hurt. It became my fists, to attack when I was too weak to defend myself.

My viola became my spirit. Its rage wet and hot, a geyser bursting through a crust of earth that could no longer contain it. No more. No more pretending it didn't matter. No more pretending I didn't care. That it was only my imagination.

My arms shook; the bow slid up the strings in a shriek. I yanked it back, dominating it like a wild animal I would wrestle into submission.

The voice of my mother echoed in the shudders of my viola; her words cut across the years and vibrated through the glossy wood, into my body. Into my soul.

"You've always been such a disappointment, Meg. We expected better from you . . ."

"Meg?" I felt Lewis's voice more than heard it. Felt his body next to me. Lewis—whom I loved so much and paid for so dearly.

"*How could you turn your back on your upbringing, on your faith? How do you think God feels about this . . .*"

"Meg, stop. Come on, honey."

"*Rebellious. Selfish.*"

I didn't want to stop. Not until I could silence her voice. My fury would continue its tempest until I found a way to rid myself of that unrelentingly judging voice. Until I found a way to be free.

"*You might be part of this family because you were born into it, but the decisions you've made and the life you live are not what this family stands for. You can't expect to throw our values and beliefs in our faces and still have the sort of close relationship you seem to expect from us . . .*"

"Put the viola down, sweetheart."

"*If you leave now, you will never come back.*"

His hand curled around my upper back. He was trying to connect to me, but I didn't want to be connected. I needed to disconnect from all the years of trying to make myself into what they wished me to be. I would never be that person. She didn't exist, and trying to make her real was killing me.

My playing slowed, quieted. I heard a faint buzzing, bumping sound on the ceiling. Looking up, I saw a ladybug crashing uselessly against the textured surface. It was too early in the season for insects to be out, and I felt empathy for the tiny creature that had somehow found itself trapped in a place where it didn't belong.

"I don't belong, Lewis. With them," I whispered.

"No."

"All these years—why have I been trying so hard?"

His body tensed, and his face became like stone. He looked away from me, at the tiny ladybug now crawling up the windowsill. "Because she's your mom. And you never outgrow that."

"Does she love me?" I leaned my head on his arm.

He turned back to me. I looked into his eyes and saw a desolate echo of my question.

"Sure."

But there was no conviction behind the word.

"You think? Was that why she called my music a waste of time?

Why she avoided every recital I was in? Or what about the time when I was in high school, when I wore a miniskirt—just once—and she caught me and made me copy all the verses in Proverbs about harlots, ten times each? Or how about when she told Adam that he was going to have to watch out for my 'rebellious attitude' once we were married? Is *any* of that your idea of love?"

I ground a tear into my cheek, determined not to waste any more on her. She'd already been the recipient of far too many.

"At least she never left you."

"She did! She and Dad both did. When I married you."

"I seem to have that effect on parents."

I put my arm around his shoulders and leaned against him. "I'm tired of it. I don't want to care anymore. I don't want to hurt anymore. I don't want to wait anymore for her to love me."

"I don't think you have a choice."

He was right. I couldn't break away from her, any more than that ladybug could break through the walls that confined it. I'd tried. Tried to live my own life. Tried not to care about the broken mess that was my relationship with my mom. A choking dampness surrounded me. I wrenched from Lewis's hold, panting. I played faster, grinding the notes into mist that whirled around the room in angry eddies, making it even harder to breathe.

Lewis gripped me by my upper arms. "Stop it!"

I looked up into his face, my breath coming in little gasps.

He touched my cheek. "I'm sorry. You play so beautifully. But . . ."

"It's because I'm angry."

"This isn't good for you."

He eased the viola from my grasp and placed it and the bow back in the case.

"Did I ever tell you about the first time I saw you?" He pulled up his office chair.

"Well, sure. I was there. You were sitting in the back of the re-hearsal hall at the university during my orchestra rehearsal—when I was a grad student. And I wondered who that geeky-looking guy was, and my stand partner told me it was this crazy-smart physics prof who had a habit of sitting in on orchestra rehearsals to work on his research. We all thought you were good-looking, but a bit odd."

"No, that was the first time *you* saw *me*."

I frowned. "So you saw me before then?"

"Yeah. A few days before that, you were in a practice room, and I walked by and heard the most amazing music. So I looked in the window, and I saw you. And I knew I had to meet you and convince you to play for me forever."

I scooted closer to him, the reckless anger seeping away. "You never told me."

"It's not something a geeky physicist admits to. Ruin my reputation for having no romantic instincts." He smiled and dropped a kiss on my cheek.

"Well, you got lucky. You're the only one I can play for. Just the thought of a solo in front of anyone else makes me feel like my heart is being shoved into a blender going at full force."

He winced. "That's an effectively graphic description. I wish you hadn't dropped out of counseling. I worry about you."

"I know. I'm sorry I disappointed you. I don't want to have performance anxiety." But I hadn't wanted to follow the shadowed threads that bound my ability to perform. They led into a forest where every tree was carved with my mother's name, and I was too scared to journey there. It was easier to sit in my chair and enjoy making music with the group.

"I'm not disappointed. I just wish we . . ." He trailed off and reached for me in a playful hug. "Everyone's a bit cracked, right? Why should we be any different?"

"*Viva la* dysfunction?"

"Exactly."

He grinned at me, and I giggled, but the humor felt hollow. Lewis knew all about dysfunction. His father was a workaholic, his mother left when he was seven and he never heard from her again. We both needed to break free. Stop waiting for those shadowed threads to lead us out of the dark. Stop expecting our parents to be who they could never be. Stop hoping for the family we'd dreamed of.

The ladybug landed on my knee. It rested, flexing minute black wings beneath its red casing.

We needed something new. Something pure. Something that belonged only to us. That wasn't tainted by either of our families. We needed something that would let us begin again and get it right this time. And as I watched the tiny beetle, a glimmer of an idea flicked to life in me. I didn't know what—only that it fizzed and tickled, like hope.

"I need to go for a walk." I grabbed my jacket that I'd flung on the floor of the study.

"Now?"

"I won't be gone long."

"You want me to come too?"

"No, no. I just need some fresh air."

Fresh air. Fresh ideas. A fresh start.

On the street outside our apartment, I discovered the ladybug had hitched a ride to freedom on my shoulder. It took to the air. I blew a good-luck kiss as the dark dot became smaller and then vanished. The chill of Chicago in March gave way to the warm glow of the new song forming in my heart. I listened to it for a minute, until the notes became clearer. Then my steps picked up its rhythm, blending with the driving beat of the city.

Wen Ming, June 2004

It is a powerful thing to love. It fills up the hungry emptiness inside and makes me strong. I thought I could be strong by not loving, by being all alone. But I discovered by loving Zhen An that the tired, always starved ache inside me went away. It was like having the very best food to eat, as much as I wanted.

I did not have much interest in loving grown-ups. They did not need me, they did not need my protection or care or love. But children — the little ones — they needed me, and their need and their love filled me. I wanted them, very much.

Every week, I found new babies, only weeks old, in the blue metal-barred cribs of the Infant Room. I used to sneak into the sparse, wood-floored room when the auntie on duty wasn't looking. I pushed my face as far between the crib bars as it would go and made funny faces at the babies I found. My poor eyesight made them look fuzzy and framed in an odd black shadow, like I was peeking at them through a keyhole, so I put my hand through the bars to stroke their soft cheeks and thick hair. Their little eyes and perfect round faces fascinated me. My belly squeezed with want. I needed more. Needed them to rely on me, to love me, to want me. I needed to love them.

When Auntie Yang, the one with the gap between her front teeth, would catch me, she always scolded me. "You can't come in here with dirty feet and unwashed hands!" She scooped me up and set me down outside the door. "Go play with your friends. You're too little to help with the babies."

"I'm not too little! I can help!" I jammed my fists on my hips. "If you let me play with the ones in the cribs, they won't cry so much."

"Why don't you play with the children your age?"

I scowled. "They are such babies!"

The auntie laughed. "If they are babies, you should enjoy playing with them." She gave me a little shove. "Go! Keep *them* from crying. It will be so helpful."

I trudged away, looking over my shoulder and sticking my tongue out at the dark form of the auntie. She laughed again and walked back into the Infant Room.

But the next time I wandered past the door to the Infant Room, listening with longing to the crying and babbling inside, Auntie Yang caught me by the arm. "Wen Ming, I have told you not to come in the Infant Room with your dirty feet!"

"I wasn't! I was outside."

"Oh. So you were." She gave me a hug that smelled of rice cereal and laundry bleach. "Here, I've brought you something."

She knelt and lifted my right foot. It threw me off balance, and I had to hold her shoulders to keep from falling over. She slipped a lightweight canvas bootie over my sandal. Then she slid another one over my left foot.

"They're too big, but they are the smallest I could find. Your feet are so tiny."

I reached down to feel them. She'd tucked the extra fabric around my sandals, which was not comfortable. But as I traced the shape, I smiled. "They're just like yours, Auntie!"

She slipped a hairnet over my head and tied the extra netting in a knot at the base of my neck. She gave me a worn green tunic that puddled on the floor around me until she tied it up with a strip of cloth. She rubbed my hands with funny-smelling antiseptic. "Now you can come in without getting the room dirty. Babies get sick if there are many germs." She stood and took my hand to place it on a box hanging outside the door. "The used coverings go in here. I'm going to give you a whole bag of the small ones. Then you can come for a visit whenever you like. But you have to obey your aunties."

"I will." I threw my arms around her waist. "Thank you."

From then on, I was a junior auntie for the Infant Room. At first, I shuffled in my new foot coverings, and I often tripped until I got used to the extra fabric around me. The adult aunties found me useful for fetching and toting, as well as for cuddling the weepy babies who couldn't be consoled by anyone else.

My supreme joy was sitting in the wood rocking chair clutching a warm little body to myself. The aunties piled me with cushions to support the baby because I was so small. I turned the chair toward the plaster wall so I could push against it with my foot. There I would sit for an entire morning or afternoon, calming one baby after another.

One by one, I held them, and as I did, they turned into huge, hand-painted cloisonné vases that I poured all my love into. I rocked and poured, rocked and poured, until they were so full of my love that they could do nothing but sleep. My love was a great power—I was Wen Ming, Calmer of Babies. My love gave them good, wonderful dreams. The kind of dreams only I could give them.

As they slept, I felt their heat, their peace, seep deep into my being like hot black tea. Sometimes I wanted to squeeze them, squeeze all that warmth into me, but that would make them cry more. The aunties would frown at me.

They were so much more than just warm bodies to me. I came to know their moods, how they liked to be touched, and even what songs were their favorites. They were *mei mei* and *di di*—little sisters and little brothers—to me.

And then they would disappear.

The first time it happened, I had arrived for an afternoon of helping in the Infant Room, and I skipped down the rows of cribs to greet each of "my" babies by name. But instead of a welcoming coo, I was met with silence.

"Where is my *mei mei*?" I pointed at an empty space in a crib. It was useless for me to search the room to see which auntie had her. I could barely make out the form of her crib mate only inches from me.

The aunties were silent.

"Where is this *mei mei*?" I squinted into the next crib. "And this one?"

I ran from crib to crib. Ten little sisters, missing!

I rushed to one auntie, standing by the bathing table. I could see enough to know she wasn't holding a child in her arms, but I reached for her and felt along her body anyway. Maybe one was hiding. Maybe my eyesight was getting worse and I could not see.

No *mei mei*. This was not right. Babies were missing, and the aunties didn't seem to care. My heart pounded, and I felt a lump in my throat. Still the aunties stayed frozen. "Where are they?" I wailed. I grabbed the auntie's tunic in my fists and shook it.

"Stop it, Wen Ming!" She held my arms and crouched down to put her face near mine. "Come here."

The other aunties suddenly seemed quite busy with other duties. She led me to a rocking chair and settled me on her lap. It seemed strange to be the one being held instead of the one doing the holding. "The babies have gone to live in America. With families. You should be glad for them. They have a mama and a baba now."

I could hardly breathe. Auntie expected me to be happy at this news, but my heart had been ripped away. "What is America?" I put my hands to her face and stared hard at it, trying to make the fog clear from my eyes and from my mind.

"It's a country far away, across the ocean."

She confirmed my worst fears. An ocean? It was like saying they had died. They could never return from a distance so vast. My throat tightened. "No!" I scrambled off her lap, though she tried to hold me back. My tunic tangled in my feet. I fell to the floor, my chin smacking the wood. The radiating ache left me dizzy and breathless, but I struggled to my feet with little more than a moan. "No!"

I ran to the nearest crib, one whose occupants had both disappeared. I felt hot inside, and strong—a strength that I couldn't control. I put my hands on the bars and shook the crib until it thumped on the floor. "I want my babies! I will hold my babies! They will come back!"

The aunties pried me away from the crib. One picked me up and shouted in my face. "Stop it, Wen Ming! Stop, or you will never come to the Infant Room again!"

I screamed harder. The remaining babies joined me. Auntie Yang took me from the other auntie. She carried me out of the room. I kicked at her and flailed my fists, but she did not shout. She paced the corridor until I relaxed against her, whimpering.

"Who will hold them?" I coughed, my throat raw from screaming.

"Their new mama and baba will."

"Will they have a big sister?"

"Some."

Another tear slid from my eye, down my cheek, and onto her neck. The thought of another sister holding my babies made me want to scream again, but I was too weary. "Why do they need America and a mama and baba and sister? I love them. I was their big sister."

She kissed me, just under my ear. "I know, my precious Wen Ming. I know. This is how I too feel. But it is better for the babies to have families."

I shuddered. It didn't make sense to me how a family could be better. Didn't they have aunties? Didn't they have a big sister to hold them and fill them with love so they would have the best dreams as they slept? A mama or baba from across the ocean could never love my *mei mei* like I did. I knew nothing about this strange place called "America" that stole my little sisters.

But I hated it.

F
I
V
E

Meg Lindsay, March 2005

The Dragonfly Tea House in Hyde Park is located in the corner of an old brick storefront, and even from outside the battered wooden door, the smell of tea and coffee filled my nose, my mouth, my throat, easing muscles in my neck I hadn't realized were tense. I reached to shove open the door, but stopped. For a moment, the air seemed to quiver, sending a mirage of ripples up the brick wall. I knew the feeling—it was that sense that what I was about to do would change my life forever. I'd felt it in the seconds before I accepted Lewis's invitation to go to the tango lesson and the moment before I took off Adam's engagement ring. But it was silly to feel it now. It was just the Tea House. My oldest and closest friends were inside. But something in the air had changed, like the scent of the wind before Mary Poppins arrives.

I shook off the absurd feeling and yanked open the door. It sticks terribly. You can sit at any of the jewel-toned tables and watch customers lurch their way in. Cinnamon, the owner and one of my best friends, says she won't fix it because it's an equalizing force in the world—not even Audrey Hepburn could have walked through that door gracefully.

I recovered my footing and sidled up to the purple counter beneath a copper and stained-glass dragonfly sculpture suspended from the open ductwork. The shop smelled like possibility. Like miracles.

A new beginning.

Cinnamon glanced over her shoulder and gave me a lazy wave. Palms pressed on the cool granite surface, I leaned forward, feeling flush with awareness and wonder. The world was a mysterious pool and I would plunge into it headfirst. "I want a baby."

There. I'd said it. Was I the only one who felt the crackling power of that word? My head felt airy, as if it could float with the dragonfly above me. A sharp, clarifying joy shot through me, making it hard to breathe.

New. Mine. A fresh start.

Cinnamon whirled to face me, sending the pencil behind her ear flying. The pencil clattered to the floor. "Baby?" The shock in her face scurried behind a professional mask of teasing detachment. "Sorry, honey, we're fresh out."

She disappeared behind the counter to retrieve the errant pencil and popped up a moment later to secure it again, this time wrapping her dark, glossy hair into a bun and shoving the pencil through it like a chopstick.

"Why do you wear a pencil? It's so cliché. You don't even use it."

"I might. And it matters to you . . . how?"

"Point taken. So? What do you think?"

"About?"

I stifled a growl. "About a baby!"

She grabbed a mug. No need to ask my order. Always rooibos chai latte, skinny. Always and forever. "You know I love you, but do you think we're ready for that step?"

My lip curled. "You're so funny."

She tossed a grin in my direction and reached for the soy milk. "Shouldn't you be having this conversation with Lewis?"

I shrugged. "I'm having it with you."

Audra, my friend who teaches high school English, left her laptop and scattered pile of student essays to come lean against the counter, clutching the mug that contained her latest fix of Cinnamon nirvana. "What are you having with Cinnamon?"

Cinnamon raised her voice over the whir of the milk steamer. "A baby, apparently!"

"Oh, shut up." I rolled my eyes and tried to hold in my laughter.

"I'm going to sit down." I yanked a chair up to Audra's table and cleared a space for myself.

Cinnamon joined us.

"Don't you have a tea shop to run?" I plucked a petal off the live carnation in the vase on our table. Now I'd said the word, and they were expecting an explanation for it. It was going to sound so foolish. So inane.

Selfish.

Dumb.

Absurd.

I pulled more petals off the carnation. One. Two. Three. They lay on the table, mute testimony to the dismantling I was doing to my self-confidence.

Cinnamon slapped at my hand. "You just stormed into my shop using the words 'I' and 'want' and 'baby' in the same sentence. I think my vast hordes of customers can wait."

In the end, I pushed aside the rush of fear. I told them about the welcome-home party for Beth that had turned into an engagement party. About the savings account that now would not be mine. About Adam.

It sounded like so much whining, except that they'd been with me through all the difficult years that had gone before. They understood why I'd dithered for years before accepting Adam's proposal. They'd stood by me while I worked my way through graduate school after graduating from the Bible college where I'd met Adam. They hadn't judged me when I met Lewis and began to fall in love with him, even though I'd been engaged. They knew about the past five years of si-lence and the fragility of my reconciliation with my parents. They knew all the little ways I'd angered my family too—the tango dancing, the political rebellion, the symphony. They'd been there for me when I'd cried over the countless jabs and criticisms from my mother, the subtle ways she had cut me out of her life, the horrible distance that had grown between us. What had happened today was simply the final raindrop that caused the dam to overflow and send muddy floodwaters raging around me. They would know it was more than whining.

"Lewis and I need our families, but you can't force people to be a family. So . . ." I plunged into the conclusion I'd reached. "We need to start over. Create a new family that's just ours."

"But I thought Lewis didn't want children."

I looked away. It was a problem, to be sure, but I didn't need to have an answer for it yet. The world was trembling with miracles—I could feel it. "I'll talk to him."

"So you want to get pregnant?" Audra frowned. She knew how I felt about motherhood. I couldn't blame her for being confused.

"No. I don't." I didn't know where the ideas were springing from. It was like I'd pushed a single button and an entire contraption was unfolding before my eyes. Thoughts, desires I didn't even recognize as being mine, were pouring out of me before I could form the words. "I want to adopt. And not exactly a *baby* baby. Not like a newborn or something. I want someone older—someone nobody else wants."

"Why?" The word burst from both of them at the same time.

I didn't know. "I—we . . ." The answer blossomed in my mind. "We need to start over. Anything that comes from us will end up with the same baggage we have. I just want a family that isn't connected to anything that has gone before. Something totally different. Someone who needs us as much as we need her."

My words faded into uncertain silence. I waited for their verdict. Their images seemed to pulse in time with my heart rate, and my mouth felt dry. I took a sip of tea. Wished it had been water. I couldn't look at them anymore.

Why didn't they speak?

"What sort of an adoption?"

I hadn't thought that far. I'd been like a child running through the streets, utter faith that someone greater and wiser than me would keep me from getting lost. Would lead me home.

The tea shop door lurched open and a decidedly un-Chicagoan, moist breeze fluttered in, swirling around me. An Asian woman tripped across the threshold. She looked tired, and there were many more years in her eyes than I was sure she'd actually lived. A small black mole rode the left side of her chin. Cigarette smoke tainted the air around her.

Before the door closed behind her, I caught a glimpse through it of rice paddies and bamboo-covered hills. I heard the Oriental ripple of an ancient zither, the tones bending and sliding around the woman. I saw a child standing across the street, dark hair shorn and dark eyes locking with mine. Then a city bus barreled through, whisking away both the scene and the sounds. The door rattled closed.

The air shimmered with something greater and wiser than me. I smiled at my friends.

"China. I want to adopt from China."

Cinnamon nodded distractedly and moved to serve the woman who had entered, but the woman waved her back to our table, saying she needed to make a phone call first. Audra shook her head and looked at the ductwork, as if asking it to blow some sanity down on me. "It doesn't make any sense! You've always thought that it would be better to help lots of orphans by sponsorship programs or relief organizations instead of spending all that money to just adopt one."

"Well, yes—if the goal is to rescue an orphan. I still believe that. But I'm not trying to rescue an orphan. I want to start a new family."

"So you're using a conveniently orphaned child to thumb your nose at your mother?"

Cinnamon gasped.

"No!" The protest burst out louder than I meant it to. I took a swallow of tea and then a deep breath. "No. I want to make a family and I want that orphan to be part of it." A new thought unfolded, stretching and tearing its way out. I didn't know if I could say it. "I want . . . I want . . ."

"What do you want, Meg?" Cinnamon took my hand.

It couldn't be true. Couldn't be what I wanted. And yet there it was. I blinked, but it wasn't enough to hold back the tears.

"I want to be a mom."

Audra took my other hand, and the two of them watched me silently. It was true. I didn't want to be a mother like my own. I wanted to be different from her, as different as possible. But if I couldn't know what it was like to be loved by my mother the way I'd always dreamed, I'd create the chance to give that love to someone else. I'd be the mother, the one who loves, the one who accepts and is delighted by her child. And in doing so, I'd receive a different love, one no less powerful, I knew, because I'd felt it surging within me for years—

The love of a daughter.

S
I
X

Wen Ming, August 2004

Zhen An loved cherry blossoms. There was a large old cherry tree in the courtyard of the orphanage, and in the spring, she would fill my ears with her exclamations about it. Her hands full of tiny blooms, she would creep up behind me and toss them into my hair. The crushed sweetness stayed in my nose and mind for weeks.

I was more practical. Blossoms were useless without fruit. The tree at the orphanage gave us no cherries, only pretty flowers. What good is that? Empty, fragrant pleasure for a few days—but no lasting benefit.

I learned much about adoption in the weeks following the day in the Infant Room. Chinese families rarely adopted from the Children's Home. It was too expensive and only the Americans were wealthy enough to afford it. Chinese families who did adopt only took the prettiest babies because they wanted physical perfection. They also wanted to keep the adoption secret. Americans seemed willing to adopt any child, but they preferred healthy babies too.

That meant I was safe from being adopted. At six years old, I was surely too old, and my eyesight was growing worse. No one would want me. I was glad for it.

But Zhen An wasn't yet safe. She was four, but some four-year-olds were adopted. Americans didn't seem to mind cleft lips, and they were all rich enough to pay for surgeries to fix the lips. She would have been beautiful were it not for her mouth. Some wealthy American was sure to want her.

Being friends with Zhen An was like being covered with cherry blossoms. But I needed to think like a tree that wanted more than just blossoms.

I wanted cherries.

I wanted a family.

I wanted Zhen An—with me, forever, my *mei mei*.

I didn't need a mother or a father. I—Wen Ming, Holder of Babies and Possessor of Crane Feathers, Best Friend of Zhen An—I would be Zhen An's mother, sister, auntie, friend, and all the family she needed. Already, we'd asked to have beds next to each other, and it was a good thing. Many nights, she cried in her sleep, troubled by nightmares about her former orphanage. I would crawl into her bed and hold her close so she would go to sleep. Finally, we pushed our beds together. As long as I was there to hold her, she had no nightmares.

And when we were grown, I would become the director of the Children's Home, and I would have no family picture on my desk but the children. They would be the only family I would want.

I suspected that the aunties and the director would not believe that I could be Zhen An's mother, since I was so young and nearly blind. I would have to lead them to believe it was they who were taking care of us. But I had a plan, and I would succeed. I would make my own family and no one would take them from me again.

The first step was to show the director we had no need for American parents. In my eavesdropping and questioning the previous weeks, I had learned what a foster parent was. If Zhen An and I had a foster family, then it would be clear that we did not need to be adopted. And I already had the perfect foster mother chosen. All I had to do was convince her.

I'd already tried the direct approach. "Auntie Yang, Zhen An and I would like you to be our foster mother. Please?"

She laughed at me as if I were a trained animal at the Shanghai Wildlife Park, performing for her amusement. She kissed my head and waved me away.

I waited a few days and tried a different technique. "Auntie Yang, if Zhen An and I were your foster daughters, we would pack you a delicious lunch every day for you to take to work. And we would sing to you in the morning."

Her mouth curved in the superior way adults had when they thought they knew so much more than me. "Perhaps I enjoy packing my own lunch. And I like my mornings to be quiet."

The appeal to money: "Auntie Yang, did you know that foster parents get money each month for every child they care for?"

She looked displeased. "I don't wish to discuss my finances with you. And where did you learn about the foster family stipend anyway?"

"I asked and listened."

"You should spend more time asking and listening to your teachers so you will do well in school, not prying into grown-up business."

I wanted to tell her it was not just grown-up business. It was my business too, because I was the one who needed a foster family. I *would* convince her!

I sulked and was short-tempered for nearly a week before I found the courage to try again. This time, I held nothing back.

I had the rare opportunity to catch her while she was sitting down. There were no babies in her lap, and she was not reading to a group of children. I eased myself onto her lap and snuggled close. When I felt her muscles relax, I launched an attack full of sweetness and innocence. "Auntie Yang, why do you not want to be our foster mother?"

"Why do you want me to be?"

"Because you are kind and good to me."

"Thank you. But I can be kind and good to you here. You don't need to come to my home for that." She rubbed her hand up and down my arm. She seemed to be thinking. I sensed a weakening in her. "Are you unhappy here, little bird?"

How to answer that without hurting my cause or giving insult to the orphanage? "I think Zhen An and I would be even happier if we had a family."

"Perhaps I should speak with Director Wu about putting you into the International Adoption program?"

"No! We want to stay here. We are Chinese. We want a Chinese family. We want you."

"It's not so simple, little bird." *Xiao niao.* Little bird. She'd called me that twice now. Almost like a milk name. That had to be a good sign. I wrapped my fingers around the bottle that held my crane feather and asked the crane to give me luck.

"What is not simple? You have no children, and we have no mother. Is your husband not as generous and kind as you?"

She tensed and didn't speak for a moment. Maybe I had hit upon a truth I would regret learning. But then she relaxed. "My husband is even more generous and kind than I am. But how will we know what to do with two of you at once? We haven't been parents to even one child."

I knew I had won at least a partial victory. I sat up and put my face close to hers so I could see it more clearly. "Then at least take Zhen An home with you. She needs a family. She cries at night because her dreams frighten her. I always sleep with her so she won't be scared. But in your home, I'm sure she would be the happiest girl."

"You would miss her."

"I want her to be happy."

I held my breath, hoping.

Auntie Yang's arms tightened around me. "You are more generous than I or my husband. It would be unfair to separate you and Zhen An. I will talk to my husband about taking you both."

I wrapped my arms around her neck, my heart thudding with joy. "Thank you! Thank you!"

"I can't promise. It's only talking."

But I knew talking would lead to doing. I knew.

And I was right. By the time the school year began, Zhen An and I were living with Auntie Yang and Uncle Zhou in their flat in a high-rise not too far from the Children's Home. It wasn't cherries yet, but it was definitely more than mere blossoms.

SEVEN

Meg Lindsay, April 2005

I fell in love with Lewis Lindsay at my first Argentine tango lesson. I'd been placidly engaged to Adam for over a year, and he had stormed off on a three-year missionary trip to Haiti, angry that I hadn't been willing to quit graduate school to go with him. Lewis and I had formed a strange sort of friendship—I think we intrigued each other. The analytical, godless scientist and the sheltered evangelical embracing her artistic side. It should never have worked, but it did. I'd never met someone who so totally accepted me for who I was.

He cornered me after my last performance with the university orchestra, three weeks before I graduated with a master's in viola performance. "Great concert! What are you doing on Friday?"

"I should be practicing or studying. My graduate recital is next Wednesday, and I have an oral exam the following Friday morning."

His eyes narrowed. "How are you feeling about the recital?" He knew about my performance anxiety.

"I'm trying not to think about it. I get ill if I do. My doctor finally agreed to prescribe a beta-blocker for the performance, but I don't like relying on drugs."

"I'm sorry. I wish I could help."

"You're coming to the recital—your support is help enough." I smiled into his eyes, and the answering warmth there grew uncomfortably pleasant. I looked away. "So, what's Friday?"

"Um . . . Argentine tango lesson?"

My head whipped back to stare at him again. "You want to take dance lessons?"

He laughed, looking thoroughly embarrassed. "I've been dancing tango for over ten years. I thought maybe you'd like to learn."

"I had no idea." For years, he'd been just Lewis, the cutely geeky physics guy, but now he seemed to be something more. There was a whole world about him I didn't know. Intriguing. "I'd love to. What time?"

"Well, it's probably not a good idea. You should practice or study. I don't want to interfere."

"No, I want to. A tango lesson is just what I need—too much preparation is just as bad as too little."

His smile was Christmas joy and look-at-my-art-project pride. "Okay, then. Meet me at El Bailongo at six o'clock."

The minute he pulled me into the full-body embrace of an Argentine tango, chest to chest, my arm around his neck, I felt as if he'd stripped me of not only my personal space but the barriers guarding my innermost secrets. And with a surge of guilt, I realized I liked it.

It was heady and exciting in a way Adam's few embraces had never been.

"Maybe you can teach this to Adam." His words tickled against my ear. "And dance it at your wedding." The tone was soft, but there was a bite to it, especially the word "wedding."

I choked back a laugh. "On Adam's list of deadly sins, dancing is right up there with premarital sex and voting Democratic."

"His loss." His arms tightened around me, and I felt the tension in his neck. "Why did you ever agree to marry him?"

"He . . . well, I love him." I realized that didn't sound very impassioned, so I hurried to explain. "I mean, we're past all that romantic infatuation. But that never lasts anyway, so I think it's good that we've known each other for so long because once we do get married, there won't be a big crash after the honeymoon period."

"Sounds thrilling." He pushed me back to stand on my own. He looked grim. "And will he support your musical career while he's preaching to the natives?"

"He's going to come home and be a pastor."

I hadn't answered his question. He shook his head and tugged me back into the dance embrace. "Don't throw your talent away, Meg. You've worked too hard."

I twisted my head to look at his profile. He glanced sideways at me, his brown eyes round and somber. I turned back to gaze over his shoulder. "Easy for you to say. You're not the one inconvenienced by my auditions or my rehearsal and performance schedules. Marrying a musician is tough. We're an eccentric and moody bunch."

I felt his lips against my ear, his breath tight and frustrated. "I'd be supportive. You're worth it."

And that was it. The timing couldn't have been worse. I should have handled it better with Adam. I wish I'd been more honest with myself and him. But the truth is, at that second, the world changed. I fell in love.

With Lewis.

We honeymooned in Buenos Aires at a little, quirky hotel where we took private tango lessons every day and attended *milongas* in the evenings. We took walks down cobblestone streets shaded by towering oaks, and kissed on the Bridge of Woman at sunset—with the water turned to fire beneath us—in Puerto Madero, where all the roads are named for suffragettes.

I went with him on a silent pilgrimage to stand at last in front of the stately home where his mother had grown up. Her parents were Italian, and her father had worked for the government. They had lived in Buenos Aires for years. He wouldn't tell me anything more about her—I wasn't sure how much he really knew. She'd left the family when he was only seven. But this piece of her childhood, for Lewis, seemed to be some substitute for the woman. Intimacy, acceptance, friendship, love—this is what Argentina meant to him. Once I realized that, I came to love it too. Not that it was difficult—the country shimmers "love me" and only the hardest heart could resist its appeal.

At home in Chicago, we fell into a pleasant routine. Friday nights belonged to tango and drinking the pungent Argentine mate tea, which Lewis elevated to the level of sacred ritual.

One gourd, a shared drink. One *bombilla*, its drinking-straw shape hiding a grate that filters out the dried yerba mate leaves. My mouth sipping the hot liquid that produced clarity of thought and brought strength.

His mouth taking the place of mine.

Sharing not just the beverage, but a part of ourselves as well. Trust. A willingness to take a risk in order to be close to your friend.

Intimacy.

This Friday, it was more than a ritual. More than a reaffirmation of our acceptance and love. This Friday, I had to find the words to convince him that our little circle of two should be expanded to three. That we needed a child who needed us too.

The plaintive swell of a *bandoneón* greeted me when I walked through the door Lewis held open for me. The first time I ever saw a *bandoneón*, I made the mistake of calling it an "accordion."

Lewis was horrified and told me so.

"What's the difference? They both look the same."

"That's like saying there's no difference between Britney Spears and Luciano Pavarotti!"

That was the last time I made *that* mistake.

El Bailongo, more than just a "place to dance" as its name suggested, also served Chicago's best Argentinean empanadas—at least in my opinion. The pastry's beef filling and spices scented the air with warm acceptance and welcome, like home cooking that doesn't expect anything from you except happy consumption. Suddenly, the gnawing in my belly had little to do with physical hunger or even with my own nerves. The hostess showed us to our table in the balcony overlooking the dance floor, and it struck me again—my fondest food memories were created by a restaurant.

Even Lewis would have to see how pathetic that was. How much we both needed to change. He hated change. It was a battle to get him to buy new socks when his old ones had holes.

Our mate arrived in a gourd-shaped container made from stoneware. The dry yerba mate had already been shaken and was strategically sloped in the gourd, and a stainless steel *bombilla* protruded from the middle of it. Our waitress set a teapot of steaming water and a bottle of honey next to the gourd before taking our orders for the empanadas.

Tonight, I needed to leverage every bit of intimacy from our mate drink that I could. If I didn't take charge of the conversation, we'd end up spending the whole evening discussing the many virtues of fermionic and bosonic fields. Like any hot-blooded woman, I find a rousing conversation about superparticles to be the ultimate aphrodisiac, but one must occasionally sacrifice pleasure for the greater good of humanity.

I reached for the gourd and teapot just as his fingers touched them. He drew back, eyebrows raised. Normally I let him serve. Not tonight. Tonight the mate belonged to me. I'd be in charge.

I poured a little hot water in the gourd, just enough to moisten the yerba mate. "I got an e-mail from your cousin today."

He snorted. "Which cousin?"

"I don't know. Jessie Bao. Who does she belong to?"

"I think she's Deng's wife, which would make her my second cousin, in-law." He surveyed the gourd. "You should add the rest of the hot water now."

"Yes, I know." I poured hot water over the soaked mate. "So Jessie—"

"Aren't you going to add honey?" Poor Lewis, I'd disrupted his ritual. But it was necessary. For a good cause.

"No. I don't feel like having it sweet today." What could he say? It's the server's choice. "Jessie said your grandma might have to have an angioplasty?"

I took a sip through the *bombilla*, letting the pungent power of the drink seep through me. Normally, I didn't get the first drink, since the server takes this responsibility—to make sure the mate tastes right. The bitter jolt, somewhere between strong coffee and green tea, tasted of boldness, and as it welled in me, the restaurant doors opened and three families entered. The couples were Caucasian, and each had at least one Asian child with them. The hostess led them to a large table to my right, where they scrambled noisily for seating.

I motioned to Lewis to look, but he didn't appear to see anything significant. One small Asian girl stood to the side of the table, watching me, a small smile on her face. She had terribly cropped hair, and her dark eyes seemed familiar to me. But I couldn't think why. But when I looked at her, I felt courage well up in me. As if she were cheering me forward.

"So about this e-mail." I swallowed more of the drink.

"I got one too." He watched me, eyes narrowing. "I hope Nai nai is okay. Heart surgery at her age is tough."

"We should visit her. You never spend enough time with your family. You hardly even talk about them."

"There's not much to say."

"They're your family."

For a second, his eyes closed. "I don't fit in their world—you know that."

"But you could." I finished off the mate and refilled the gourd with hot water. I handed it to Lewis. "You love Argentine culture, and you're not even Argentinean. Why not Chinese culture?"

His lips closed around the *bombilla,* still moist from my mouth. He sipped, then glanced at it and up at me, eyebrows lifted. "Good job." He drew more of the drink into his mouth, observing me as if I were one of his experiments. He swallowed, and I could almost sense the heat spreading through him. I couldn't read the expression in his eyes, and a stinging point of nerves knotted in my belly.

I glanced at the little girl at the table next to us. She looked over her shoulder at me, and I saw a little ladybug land on her hair. Red peace washed over me, and I turned back to Lewis. "Why aren't you interested in Chinese culture? Those are your people."

He nearly choked. "My what?"

"The people of China."

He shoved the gourd back toward me. "I'm supposed to immerse myself in Chinese culture simply because I'm one-quarter Chinese? I'm more Italian than I am Chinese."

I took Lewis's hand, rubbing it with what I hoped was a soothing rhythm.

"All your living relatives are Asian. At least the ones we know of."

"I'm not Chinese. Okay?" He didn't speak for some time. "I never belonged in their world. No matter how hard I tried. I was just too different. You don't know what it was like."

I probably understood better than he thought, but it would do no good to say it. I refilled the gourd and slid it back to him for one more round. "So explain. Help me understand. Talk to me."

His shoulders slumped. He ran his finger along the rim of the gourd. "When I had to stay summers with my grandma, she and all my other relatives would only speak Chinese to me. They knew I didn't understand the language, so they took it as their duty to immerse me in it for the two months I stayed with them. I know they meant well, but it always seemed like a punishment. Their way of reminding my dad that he'd failed in passing on his heritage to me."

I felt his isolation streaming from him, surrounding me with a bitter strength. "Why haven't you told me about this?"

He shrugged. "I tried to pick it up, but it's a hard language. The summer I was eight, I asked my cousins for help." He pointed at his water glass. "I asked them, 'What's that?' And they told me, 'Chi shi.' So the next time I wanted a drink, I went to my aunt and said, 'Chi shi.' She slapped my face and yelled at me."

My mouth dropped open. "Why?"

"It's a pretty obscene way to say 'Eat crap.'"

Tears pressed against my eyes. "Couldn't you tell them what happened?"

He took a small sip of tea. "I tried, but they said if I could learn to swear in Chinese, I could learn to justify it in Chinese too. It was the sort of prank they expected from their own kids, so they suspected I'd done it on purpose. I was grounded to my room for a week. My cousins thought it was a great joke. I never asked them for help again."

"How awful."

He shook his head. "They're good people. But there were just so many unwritten rules. Things I didn't know were wrong. And there were happy things too. Things they enjoyed, but that I didn't understand and couldn't appreciate." He twisted his lips into a mocking grin and leaned back in his chair. "Sorry I never told you—figured it wasn't worth talking about. Big deal. No worse than being shipped off to some wretched summer camp every year, right?"

He wasn't fooling me. "I'm sorry, love." I reached for his hand. "I wish I had been there for you."

He squeezed my hand and gave me a small, but real, smile. "Me too."

The mate had grown cold. Our empanadas arrived, but I'd lost my appetite—for food anyway. My only desire now was to erase that horrible emptiness from my husband's eyes. How could we have been married for five years without my knowing this part of his life? Was I really so self-centered that I'd failed to notice yet another closed door on his past?

I envisioned him as that eight-year-old, slight and wiry, freckled nose and big, lonely brown eyes framed with glasses too large for his face. He never fit in with his family, any more than I fit in with mine. My breath quickened, and a weight pressed on my chest. This was why we had to do this! We found someplace we belonged—with each other. Shouldn't we offer the same chance to another unwanted child?

I picked at my food, my stomach uneasy. Lewis ate most of his in silence. Finally, I gave up the pretense and set down my fork. "I wonder how many other kids tonight feel just as unloved as you did."

He stared at me, hard. His eyes narrowed, and their intensity made me shiver. "Don't do this."

"Do what? I just think it's sad. Don't you?"

"Of course. But people don't want to become projects, Meg. They don't want you to fix them."

"No. But don't you think we have a moral responsibility to help where we can?"

He pushed his plate away. "I think we have a moral responsibility not to make things worse."

"How could we possibly make things worse?"

"Well-intentioned people tend to barge into things without understanding what they're doing, and then they cause more harm than good."

Somehow, despite my best efforts, I'd lost control of the conversation. "What does any of this have to do with your *nai nai*'s surgery?"

He stood abruptly. "I don't know. You tell me." He held out his hand. "Let's tango."

I thought we already were.

I followed him onto the dance floor. His right arm enfolded me, giving me no choice but to curve myself against him, my left arm around his neck, my lips not even an inch from his ear. I knew he could feel my heartbeat increase. The satisfied tightening of his fingers against my lower back proved it. I rolled my eyes. Not a dance floor in the world is big enough to contain the ego of a man.

My attempt at dinner to talk about what lay heavy on my heart had been an abject failure. But maybe once our bodies began moving together, our hearts and minds would follow.

The *bandoneón* opened the song—a haunting, sensual melody. Stringed instruments and guitars soon joined to create a misty atmosphere, languid and suggestive. I waited for the signal from his body—a tensing of muscle, an intake of breath, a pressure against my torso.

Tango is a "little walk" done cheek to cheek, the two dancers offset, looking over each other's right shoulder. I couldn't see his face, but I felt the tension in his body. When he finally stepped forward, pressing me back into the flow of other couples, his fingers bit sharply into my shoulder. I winced. He muttered a brief "Sorry" and loosened his hold.

I knew this song. One of my favorites because the rhythm of it slid deep into my soul and made my heartbeat conform to it. Throbbing drums intensified the music. Lewis's hand pressed against my back, commanding my every move. I would have enjoyed the sensuality of it, but there was such unease, a lack of peace, in his touch that I felt like ending the dance.

I couldn't, of course. It would ruin the dance not only for us but also for the other dancers on the floor. He spun me around and snapped into a tighter *abrazo*. I felt his breath on my neck. The dance was not a fast one, but he was breathing hard. For a moment he clung to me, rocking with the throb of the music, his face almost buried against my shoulder.

"Are you okay?" I whispered the question against his coarse, dark hair.

"Just dance."

I hooked my right leg around his. Normally it would be as fluid as a satin ribbon whipping around him. But our timing was wrong. I nearly tripped him, and his fingers dug into my back when he kept both of us from falling. We'd never been so clumsy, even when I was just a beginner. I blinked back a film of tears and tried to snuggle closer to him.

He didn't let me stay close for long. Brushed my foot with his and stepped away, forcing me into the *carpa*, or "tent," in which the top half of my body leaned against him and my legs slanted away. Then he dragged me several steps and lifted me.

I answered by sliding my leg up the outside of his, and then flicking it between his legs. I couldn't tell if we were trying to work together or fight each other, but I thought he looked angry.

Our disagreement at dinner? We'd had sharper discussions before without this result. I pulled my hand from his and flicked a tear from my eye. He saw the movement but looked away.

On the last note, he leaned me back in a dip, finally meeting my eyes. It was hurt I saw there, not anger. For the space of a breath, he looked almost betrayed.

He pulled me to a standing position, and we hurried off the dance floor.

I grabbed his hand and pulled him to a deserted hallway by the banquet room. "Well, that was a disaster."

He nodded. "Not our best dance, was it?" One corner of his mouth drooped, and he looked away from me again.

Something prompted me to wait, to not speak. I eased myself against the wall and watched him, my hands cushioning the small of my back. He took off his wire-rimmed glasses and cleaned them on his shirt. Then he put them back on. He leaned his right side against the wall, close to me, looking into my eyes.

"Meg . . ." His voice sounded choked. He swallowed hard but didn't look away. "When were you going to tell me you've been thinking about adopting from China?"

E
I
G
H
T

Meg Lindsay, April 2005

There was a time when I couldn't imagine having a fight with Lewis. When everything about him was to me like a penlight to a kitten. A voice lacking even a trace of judgment, eyes that looked at me with desire and appreciation instead of with ownership, hands that touched in order to please instead of . . . just not touching at all.

I don't think I ever stopped to wonder, in my mad plunge into love, if it would be possible to sustain a marriage at that feverishly harmonious level of perfection. I didn't expect it, but I didn't expect anything about Lewis. So maybe I hoped. Or maybe I just hurtled my bridal-gowned self down the aisle without thought, without analysis, without even dreaming—for once in my life—because who needs to dream when reality is so unbelievably perfect?

And strangely enough, I don't remember our first fight. I think it came on by degrees—a snipe here, a snark there—until at some point we probably had a "real" fight. But it didn't make a big impression on me. No trauma, no drama, no oh-my-goodness-how-did-we-get-to-this-point introspection born out of insecurity and false guilt.

I do remember feeling, at some point in our second year of marriage, a sense of amazement that I could actually feel anger at someone I loved and admired so much. And even more amazing that I could feel that anger without despising him or his despising me. I remember sitting in a practice room at the university, warming up with a C-sharp major scale, when the realization hit me. Lewis was safe to be angry with, and safe when he was angry. No guilt trips, no grudges, no icy silences. We fought with honesty and directness, and I think we even admired each other's sparring skills. The scale halted on G sharp and I cried for a full five minutes. Somehow, despite my impetuosity and inexperience, I'd managed to help create a relationship where we could fight, grouch, whine, and be as flawed as can be—and it was so unimportant to our love and our friendship, to respect and loyalty, that we were barely conscious of the friction.

That's grace, because God knows I didn't deserve it.

I floundered as I searched for a response to my husband's question. For the first time, warm fear shuddered through me. Maybe this time, I'd gone too far, demanded too much. More than he could give. Maybe now we were about to have the sort of ebenezer-raising, epoch-marking fight that would divide our marriage into BC and AD and take us into a place we never dreamed we would find ourselves.

He'd been honest and clear from the start. Physicists, he said when we were dating, made horrible parents. The research, the intense focus, the utter absorption in his work signaled disaster to any child looking to him for guidance and love. And since he had no intention of giving up his career, he refused to chance ruining a child's life by being an absent father.

I never saw the justification for blaming it on physics. True, his own father had been that way, but Liam Lindsay was no scientist. But considering I'd been running away from motherhood to avoid becoming my mother, I couldn't criticize Lewis for doing the same in response to his father.

But we could choose—to be different, to start over, to break away from that past.

"How did you know?" I whispered, my words nearly lost in the tango music that had begun again.

He wouldn't meet my eyes. "Temporary Internet files and search history. It wasn't difficult."

"So you were spying on me?" I edged toward the dining room, trying not to look upset. Public scenes tended to make me crazy. I couldn't handle it.

Lewis hurried behind me, speaking over my shoulder, into my ear. "I don't blame you for being mad about it. But I was worried. You've been acting strangely ever since that Sunday at your parents' house. And you wouldn't talk to me."

I grabbed my coat from my chair. Lewis glanced at the bill and tucked two twenties neatly into the pocket of the check holder. There was no sign of the Asian children or their parents. The little girl with the chopped hair was gone. "Maybe you just should have asked."

"Maybe you should have just talked. Keeping secrets is what your parents do—I thought you didn't want to be like them."

The truth doesn't just hurt. The truth is like that South American ant that screams before it attacks you—its venomous bite a paralyzing bullet of unabated, throbbing pain. Pleasant fellow.

"If you weren't so anti-kid, I wouldn't have to keep secrets." I stalked toward the door, but I felt the radiation of confusion and shock coming from my gentle husband and I knew my unjust rebuttal had hit its mark.

It was like falling through ice. Thrash against the numbing embrace, and the ice breaks further, isolating you from any solid grip of safety. But if you don't fight, you sink down into dark depths that leech the warmth of life away.

I didn't want this! But there was no way of escaping it. Even the desperately launched prayers for wisdom seemed to fall like weights on my feet. I was not wise, and my foolishness was going to drag me under.

Just outside the door, Lewis grabbed my arm, and I felt in his touch the frustration and mounting anger at my hit-and-run attack. We were like two dogs, all bared teeth and ugly snarling. This wasn't going to be a fight with logic and calm respect. The emotions were too deep, too tangled. We were about to damage each other, and that made me ill.

"I've never been 'anti-kid.' You know that. You know—"

I cut him off with a trembling wave of my hand. To my left, leaning against the building, was the same Asian woman I'd seen in the tea shop the day of that dinner at my parents' house. A thin stream of smoke curled up from the cigarette she balanced in her left hand. She didn't look any more rested than she had that afternoon in the tea shop.

She stared into my eyes and pointed with her cigarette toward my feet. Following the gesture, I saw a narrow, gleaming scarlet ribbon tied around my right ankle. It loped across the uneven pavement and curled around Lewis's ankle too. I felt the pulsing connection between us, that soul-deep certainty that we were God's gift to each other. Soul mates whose lives had been connected from the moment of our births, that red string shortening and tightening over years until it brought us together and made us one. The ribbon tightened around my leg and his, pulling us back from the edge, straining to protect us from ourselves. Reminding us that nothing—not even this current conflict—was important enough to damage that precious, miraculous bond we had with each other.

"I'm sorry." I grabbed the back of his head and put my mouth on his. I wound my leg around his, like a tango step, until my ankle brushed his. The thread connecting us exclaimed its joy in a shivering jolt of heat that said everything else could be worked out, but this—our togetherness—was right, and true, and good.

He kissed me back, his hands sliding up my cheeks and into my hair. We pressed against each other, coming back to a sense of ourselves, of the best and truest part of who we were—as a couple and as human beings.

And I knew—this was the moment our fresh start had begun. With each other. In making the choice to honor the bond instead of tearing it apart. The realization stole my breath—it should have been obvious, but I'd almost missed it.

I heard a rustling and flapping, and I opened my eyes. I caught a glimpse of great wings and a slender white body, a red patch on a crane's head glimmering in the light of the streetlamp as the elegant bird disappeared into the night sky. I pulled back from Lewis. The woman was nowhere to be seen.

A small red feather circled down an invisible spiral of air and landed on my coat sleeve like a promise. I pinched it between my fingers and held it up to Lewis, who frowned at it in scientific puzzle-

ment. I brushed it against my lips, inhaling the faint scent of tobacco
still clinging to its tiny, downy vanes.

"I'm ready to talk now," I said. We linked hands and walked, the
red thread snapping and tugging between us.

He listened to me, putting aside his justifiable annoyance at how far
I'd developed my adoption fantasy without ever involving him. He
asked the sort of intelligent, logical questions you'd expect from a
scientist—how does the adoption process work, how do the parents
know there's no corruption involved, how are the children and
parents matched? Scientists love to know the "how" of something—
it's observable, understandable, controllable. And if we don't know
the "how," we can research it, study it, experiment with it, and find
out. It may take a while, but "how" has an answer. "How" assures you
that eventually it's all going to make sense, that it will all work out at
some point. There's a hope in the "how" questions.

It's the "why" that is full of dark uncertainty and helplessness.
Even when you know why, it doesn't change a thing. Doesn't make
it better, doesn't make the way forward any clearer. The "why" of
something is elusive, transient, coy. It beguiles us, building in us an
obsessive desire to capture it, hold it close to our hearts. It extends to
us the promise of satisfaction, calling to us in a sweet echo of dreams
and desire.

We stumble after it like half-mad addicts, and when we do finally
catch it by its gossamer wingtip, it crumbles like an illusion made of
spun sugar—glimmering and ultimately unsatisfying.

And yet, even the scientists can't resist its song. Why China? Why
were the children abandoned there? And more painfully intimate—
why did I want to adopt? Why did I want to be a mother? Why wasn't
I satisfied anymore with our family of two?

Why wasn't his love enough for me now?

"It's not about your love." The chilly winds of April swooped down
around us and whisked my words away.

"Is it about your love, then? Are you tired of me?"

"No," I said hastily, hating to see the childlike fear and pain in
his eyes.

How to explain the "why" this time? How do you tell the little boy in that man's heart that even though you adore him and always will, there are some wounds that not even your love for each other can heal? Why was that so? Why couldn't God, who gave us to each other, make that enough? For that matter, why wasn't the love between my God and myself enough to ease the ache inside? What was wrong with me that I was seeking someone else?

I didn't want to peer too closely into that. It wasn't a question I could talk about with Lewis, who respected my spirituality but felt no need for it himself and had no desire to understand it.

I wrapped my arms around his waist and settled my head against his shoulder. "I don't know. I can't tell you why. It's not because I don't love you or you're not enough or anything like that. I just know that I need this. We need this. I don't know why."

His arms tightened around me, but it didn't signal agreement. Just acceptance.

Next came the "what" questions—spear-tipped arguments. What about our jobs? What about our apartment? What about our child-unfriendly lifestyle? Those sorts of questions have no ending. They aren't meant to resolve anything or create understanding. They only wear you down until you surrender out of exhaustion. I'd expected this assault, and I gave good answers.

But in the end, I could see I'd failed to win him over. When we'd reached the entrance to our apartment building, and he'd opened one of the great glass doors for me, I could feel the barrier encasing him, the impenetrable shield of resistance. A trembling pressure built inside me—a churning mixture of tears and wild-eyed pleading and the choking knowledge of failure and dreams struggling for one more breath, and more than just a touch of anger born from the helpless understanding that I could not do this without him. I clamped my lips together to keep it all from bursting out while he made a detour to our mailbox. No public scenes. Ever.

From the antiqued bronze and black cubicle, he pulled several envelopes and two packages. One was a manila envelope addressed to him. He studied the return address for a moment with a frown before smiling. "It's from Chase Littleton—we were in grad school together.

He's at the University of Washington now. Haven't heard from him in a couple of years. Wonder what he sent me?"

He flipped to the second package—a cardboard envelope addressed to me, from Red Thread China Adoptions. The agency's graphic logo of a ladybug on a scarlet ribbon adorned the top left corner. He handed it to me, his face carefully blank.

"I e-mailed them on Monday to request some information. That's all." I didn't mean to sound so defensive.

He was quiet for several moments, like the hush of a balance scale in the act of weighing, measuring, vacillating. Finally, "My mother left when I was seven years old."

"I know."

"My father was too busy to spend time with me."

"Yes."

"If they couldn't love me, their own flesh and blood, how do I know I could love a child that isn't mine?"

"Love isn't limited by blood."

"You don't understand. I won't make a good father. I know this. Why would you even think about putting a child in that situation? Knowing her dad didn't—couldn't—love her? That's the Hell I believe in, Meg. I've lived it nearly my whole life, with both parents. I won't do that to another child."

He held out the cardboard envelope to me. I snatched it and walked to the elevator, the spiked heels of my dancing shoes sinking into the richly padded carpeting. He followed. Neither of us spoke. The hows, whys, and whats swirled around us, but we had no answers. There seemed to be nothing more to say.

Wen Ming, October 2004

My days were full of sounds curling and floating like rice noodles in soupy shadows. Auntie Yang sent me to the local school where the other children from the Home attended, but there wasn't much for me to do there. I could only read the largest and darkest characters in the books, and even then, I had to turn my head from side to side to see the whole character. Writing was nearly useless. My teachers lamented that if they only had the right computer programs, maybe they could teach me to type and use voice recognition software. But I'd have to attend a special school for blind children to have access to such wonders. So I used my ears and mind instead.

I listened and remembered. I also begged and bullied Auntie Yang and Uncle Zhou to read to me. I did not care what, as long as it was words that taught me something. The newspaper, television, radio—they were like the choicest morsels of duck and pork that had begun to appear in my bowl at mealtimes now that I had my foster family. Uncle Zhou spent many meals reading to us from the newspaper about the great deeds China was doing. His voice grew deep and full of pride about the wondrous progress our nation was making, and how we were about "to take our rightful place as the most prosperous and influential country in the world." He explained the mysteries of science that he taught to his students at the university. There was nothing he didn't know about the ways of nature. I soon knew more about nearly everything than my schoolteachers did, even though I could not read. But I tried not to show it—it would shame them to realize how much smarter I was.

And there was touch. Zhen An's arms around me, her hand in mine. Auntie Yang's hugs and Uncle Zhou's pats and tousling. Zhen An was even trying to learn to read so she could snuggle in my lap in the evenings and open the pages of the world for me. I knew each of them by their skin, by their smell, by their voices. I loved them all.

My days were dim, but beautiful, misting together like the very best dreams and giving me a reason to wake each morning.

If days were shadowed, nights were utter darkness. Once the sun had set, only the brightest indoor lights were enough to throw off the black veil flung over my head. I hated going outdoors, where even the light from streetlamps faded into the blackness gobbling up my sight.

Uncle Zhou used thick construction tape to fasten a rope to the floor, making a path throughout the flat. Once I found the rope, I could be assured that there would be no obstacles in my way, nothing to stub my toes on or trip over. I slid my foot along the ridge on the floor and traveled on my track from one room to the next like a train.

I felt proud that I could survive so well in my ever-darkening world. Zhen An was afraid of the dark, but I was fearless. Night held no secrets from me. It was an old friend, begging me to help it reconcile with my beloved *mei mei*.

She was my only worry. She'd been transferred to our Children's Home for a reason. Grown-ups were always coming up to her, their voices big and cheerful, talking about how beautiful and sweet she was. And then they'd confer with each other in low tones so I couldn't hear, but I knew anyway. They were trying to put her up for adoption in the International Program—to be taken from me.

One October night, I lay in bed, her body pressed against me, her steady breathing assuring me that her dreams were peaceful. It was I who could not sleep. In the morning, we were both to visit a doctor, to determine what could be done about our deformities. Why? To make us more presentable for American families?

I lay on my side, curled in a tight ball, trying to still the aching shivers in my throat and shoulders. I reached to pull Zhen An against me, but a sickening doubt made it hard to breathe against her silky hair. Could I really hope that my thin arms could keep her with me?

A glowing shape tore through the blackness. A great bird of prey, with a white head and brown wings that spanned the entire room, talons that clutched pointed arrows, and a curved beak like a knife. Eyes so dark it made my night seem like day, it swooped over us with a screeching cry.

It shot its arrows toward my Zhen An, my sleeping *mei mei*. I threw myself on top of her to keep her safe. I raised my crane feather bottle toward the bird, and its power made the arrows glance harmlessly off my body. The creature dived toward me, its eyes enflamed, its talons cruel and sharp.

"You can't have her!" I screamed. I stood on the bed, straddling her, and swung my fists at the attacking bird. It screeched again, its rage heating the room. I held my bottle in my hand and punched the creature. It cracked against the wall and slid to the floor. I scrambled off the bed and threw myself on top of the bird, hitting and kicking and screaming until my hands were slick with feathers and smeared blood. Still the beast struggled, inching closer to the bed, determined to take my Zhen An. My crane feather gave me strength, and I wrapped my arms around the bird's neck and squeezed. My body ached, and the room smelled of sweat and blood and death, but I would not let go.

The bird rolled, pinning me under its great body. I couldn't breathe. My grip loosened, but the bird was weakening too. If I could just hold on longer . . .

A trembling talon clamped around my neck and the room spun and I spiraled with it until my body became one with the darkness and gave up the battle. My last thought was for Zhen An and the hope that I'd been able to save her from the evil bird.

"Wen Ming!" Auntie Yang's voice, full of fear, her hands shaking, as much as they were shaking me.

My body returned to me, and I found I was on the floor in my room. I tried to sit up, but there was a pain in my shoulder and my leg. Zhen An was crying. I struggled to stand, fear ripping through me like the talons I could still see in my mind. "Zhen An? Are you all right?"

Uncle Zhou caught me in his arms. "She is fine. It's you we're worried about."

I struggled against him, trying to force my eyes to work properly. "The bird! It is still here?" It was still night, and I could see nothing.

"Hush, little one. There is no bird." Auntie Yang held my hand to her mouth and kissed it. Her face was damp with sweat. "You had a nightmare and fell out of bed. And it looks like the bed table and the lamp fell on you. The lamp is broken and there is glass on the floor. You're bleeding. We will have to reschedule the doctor's appointment for another time. Instead, we will have to take you to the hospital. You might need stitches."

"You frightened me, *jie jie*," Zhen An whimpered. "You never have nightmares. Only me."

I clutched Uncle Zhou and buried my face against his chest. Zhen An was right.

I never had nightmares.

Meg Lindsay, April 2005

There's a sort of not-speaking that is comfortable and even draws you closer to another person. Lewis and I often experienced that kind of silence—meditative, seeping into the cracks and roughness of the soul like massage oil, intimate and binding, a sacred vow.

But then there's the not-speaking that is like approaching a light switch on a cold, dry winter day. You know there will be a spark, a shock, and even as you try to avoid it, you know it's coming. Sometimes the silence is like that—a buildup of static waiting to discharge at the slightest touch. Avoidance only means the shock will hurt worse. Still, we try everything we can to keep it from happening.

We were in that sort of not-speaking when we reached our apartment. We couldn't bear to look at each other as Lewis unlocked the door and held it open. I clutched the agency envelope tight against me and watched him retreat into the office. If I'd said anything, if we tried to talk about it right then, the shock of pain would be sharp, intense. The surge would come, like it or not, but we sought to avoid it a little longer.

I slumped on the couch, my knees pulled nearly to my chest, with the envelope resting against them. I wanted the information it contained. But what good would that do? Why torture myself with what I couldn't have?

I leaned my forehead against the stiff cardboard and two tears slid down my cheeks. They fell on the envelope and suddenly a sweet, smoky fragrance of incense engulfed me. It swirled around me, calling me, and I could no longer resist. I opened the package and removed a DVD.

I watched my dreams coalesce in the images that silver disc contained. They joined the longing in my heart and took shape in tangible colors and sounds, drawing me in, surrounding me, transporting me. And always the smell of incense. Of faith. The fragrance of the hand of God.

I saw a deep river valley, afloat with fishing boats; a woman singing a traditional Chinese song. She stopped her singing and looked into my eyes. I saw a small mole on the left side of her chin.

I couldn't breathe. Smoke swirled around me, the pungent sweetness reaching into my lungs, becoming my breath, opening my eyes. Making me see and smell and taste and hear and touch a nation a half world away from my own. The smoke filled every crevice of my body, the essence of China that I would carry inside me for the rest of my life.

I saw rice paddies and high-rise cities. I danced with a street performer selling flutes in front of a world-class hotel. I stood with a well-dressed businessman at a bus stop, surrounded by concrete rubble.

I sank my hands into the thick fur of a panda. I bowed to an ancient emperor. I knelt before the homeless huddled in alleyways, and let myself be carried by the crush and noise of humanity in an upscale nightclub.

I saw the most populous nation on earth trying to cover her nakedness with the tatters of national pride and bind her wounds with soiled rags that had been painted white. I looked into her face and it was my own gazing back at me.

The fragrant smoke drew me in, relentless and restless. I saw the children. They toddled around the patchy grounds of an orphanage, their brown bums peeking through split crotch pants. A row of children sat at a low table, eating rice with wide, shallow spoons. Toddlers reclined in playpens and rested passively in walkers. Their expressions were so old, as if they'd already lived far longer than any human ought to be forced to live. In a world no child should ever experience.

Out of the haze swirling around me appeared a toddler with shorn hair crouched by a metal crib. She raised a half-empty bottle of formula to her mouth and sucked it, staring at me with somber, unfocused eyes. I reached for her, but she turned and retreated into a stark, sterile room jammed with cribs. No toys, no teddy bears. Two or three infants in every crib.

The smoke became a wall between us and I beat my fists on its insubstantial surface, helpless to find her. Helpless to heal, but how could I heal when I was so broken too?

I don't know when the weeping started. I grabbed a tasseled satin throw pillow and clutched it to me. I was a rice paddy, the images and sensations like water flooding me. The souls of the children sprouted in my soul, their roots going deep and tangling in my heart. In so many ways, I was one of them. If not in circumstance, at least in spirit; in the living-out and knowing of rejection. In the experience of being found wanting, of being found unacceptable by the very ones who should accept and want no matter what.

I swiped a hand across my eyes, the mascara leaving a long black streak on my palm. The floor creaked. I saw Lewis leaning against the doorway into the living room, watching the television. He drew the smoke into his nostrils with each breath, and I saw the glow of the incense filling his eyes. It spilled fragrant drops of oil down his cheeks.

He looked at me, and finally the charge had built high enough that we couldn't escape it. Electricity arced between us, sending a fiery stake of pain zigzagging through me. I smelled burning flesh mingling with the incense, the acrid stench of sacrifice and atonement.

He choked on a cry and staggered back, disappeared into the office. In the opposite direction, I saw the unseeing child, older now, crouching under a half-collapsed wall of concrete. Her grief screamed to me, and I knew if I walked toward her, this time she would not turn away.

The competing pain tore at me, ripping a valley of lifeblood down my middle. I heard his cry, heard her whispered screams. They merged together into one song of sorrow.

And I saw, finally, the poverty in my own home. The hunger and nakedness of a million orphans was mine. If I wanted to ease the pain, I had to stanch the wounds closest to me.

Clenching my hands together to stop their shaking, I turned my head away from the little girl. I left her behind, in the smoke and heady fragrance, and made my feet carry me to the person I still loved most in the world. A person who was far more broken than I'd realized, but who was still mine. Mine to hold, mine to love, mine to heal.

Lewis almost never drinks anything harder than a glass of vintage port with dessert, but once in a while, when something has upset him, has stirred the darker memories he keeps jailed in his mind, he pours bourbon into a snifter and carries it to the desk in our office. He never closes that door—he only bars the doors to his soul. I sometimes walk past the room and peek in, hoping he will glance up at me with need and invitation, but his eyes are trained on a framed photo of his idol, the world-famous physicist Dr. Naomi Ricci, as if he can mine the depth of her brilliance and find a solution for whatever is churning inside.

He sips at the bourbon, letting its darkness drag him down into a slow and gentle embrace. Sips and stares, and every so often a muscle in his neck tenses. His jaw hardens. A fog of old pain swirls like the liquid in his glass. Soft and bitter. Smooth and burning.

It's all I can do not to grab his shoulders, shake him, try to make him see what I see. I want to tell him, "As much as you adore her, as much as she is the air you breathe and the food you eat, she can't help with this. She doesn't have the answers. No matter how many times you search, you won't find what you're looking for. You won't find what you need. It's not there in her eyes or in her face or in her mind."

But I can't say all that to him. Can't say any of it. Naomi Ricci is only the high priestess of the goddess he adores. As demanding and tempestuous a deity, she seduces his mind and enraptures his heart. And his love is so loyal, I don't think he can see her limitations for her beauty.

Someday, he will realize that she has no answers for his questions. No nourishment for his emptiness. No balm for his pain. He's strong, but I sometimes wonder if he will survive the moment when his goddess is revealed as mortal.

Fallible.

When it comes, and I know it will, I want to be there to hold him. To let him cry. To lay his head to my chest so he can feel my heart. To finally help open those locked doors and let the light into the dank and rotting places inside. To show him we're not all a bunch of I-told-you-so finger-pointers. To make him smile again. It's all I've ever wanted.

And it's why I never say a word.

That's where I found him this time, the forgotten bourbon gleaming like amber in a chalice. He glared at Dr. Ricci's photo, and heat poured from the room. The photo sweated, dripping tears from its metal frame. The manila envelope lay on the desk partially obscured by several pages torn from a magazine and stapled together.

He didn't acknowledge my presence, so I crept into the room and picked up the magazine pages. I scanned the first few paragraphs. An interview with Dr. Naomi Ricci, from *American Science News*, dated October 1983. A handwritten note was scrawled across the top.

> *Was cleaning out boxes of old journals and magazines and found this. Don't know if you ever saw it—came out during your first year of college, I think. But I know you're a huge fan of hers so thought you could add it to your collection.*
> *—Chase*

Lewis didn't move. I finished reading the article. It talked mainly about Dr. Ricci's 1979 breakthrough, something about bosons and subatomic particles that was hopelessly beyond my comprehension. Much was made about her contributions as a woman physicist, in a time when many female scientists were still unwelcome and pressured to become high school educators or homemakers. She spoke of her unwavering dedication to her work and brushed off the questions of her struggle to be taken seriously as a woman. Said she had made some sacrifices for her career, but that they paled in comparison to the thrill of her research. And that as soon as her male colleagues had seen the quality of her work and the level of her focus and commitment, they had accepted her without question.

As a feminist, I wasn't impressed by her obvious kowtowing to the male establishment, but that was the way the world worked more than twenty years ago. I had to admire her determination and her accomplishments in what had to have been a hostile environment.

"Interesting article." I set the pages back on the desk in front of him. The moisture on the photo wisped into scorched tendrils of steam. "Lewis?"

"She didn't have any children." Each word slid from his mouth, soft and dull like drops of melted lead.

"What?"

Without shifting his eyes, he handed me the article again. "Read it, page two."

I thumbed through it until I found the quote he was referring to. "So?"

The fire inside him flared, making his body glow like it was built from embers. "She didn't have any children, Meg!"

The room was hot with his anger, and the edges of the magazine pages curled in blackened ash.

"You've had too much to drink."

He grabbed the snifter and downed the rest of the bourbon in one swallow. "She didn't have any children!" He screamed the mantra at the photo. Snatched the magazine pages from my hands, crumpled them, and hurled them at the photo. The rage-hardened ball of words and soot shattered the glass of the photo frame. A shard sliced across my cheek and I felt the warm trickle of blood and a sting of fire.

"Lewis!"

He tore himself from the trance and met my gaze. The fury eased, replaced by concern and contrition as he gently caught the blood from my cheek on his trembling fingers. The room gradually cooled, and he held a tissue to my face and kissed my forehead.

"Scientists don't make good parents," he whispered against my neck.

"You will."

"Those kids on the video—they need someone who won't leave them."

"We won't leave them."

"How do you know? Do you think our parents intended to leave us in the ways they did?"

"We know what it's like. That's why I know we won't make the same mistake. We can't fix what's happened to either of us. But we can fix it for a child—they still have time."

The room filled with the fragrance of incense and pulsated to the beat of Chinese drums. We stood silently in the midst of it, lost to any sense of time. Lewis held me against him, his hands buried in my hair.

Finally, the surrender came. "Okay."

"As in 'yes'?"

I felt him nod.

"Are you sure? It's not just because . . . I don't want you to feel forced into it."

"I've known you were thinking about it for weeks. So I've been thinking too. I'm scared. I think it could be a huge mistake. So no, I'm not sure. But I'm saying yes, anyway."

"Thank you."

"Don't let me leave, Meg. Whatever happens, don't let me abandon you or her. Promise me."

"I promise." As if I held that much power in anything but my prayers. "You are going to be a great dad."

"You think?"

"I know."

He pushed against me in a tango walk, until I backed into a filing cabinet. "We're going to be parents." His voice was hushed, wondrous.

I smiled at him. "We're going to be parents."

Smoke surged through the room, enveloping us in a sweet-smelling column of whirling images and voices. I saw the child lift her unseeing eyes to the sky and smile. I saw the woman with the mole and cigarette bow to me with the grace of a queen. I saw yards and yards of scarlet ribbon fluttering in a festive breeze, ready to lead us a thousand footsteps to our future. A crane's wings brushed my cheeks. And sailing past us, joining in a dance of surrender and hope, were hundreds and thousands of tiny, ruby-colored ladybugs.

Part Two
FIRECRACKER

"It is easy to love the people far away. It is not always easy to love those close to us. It is easier to give a cup of rice to relieve hunger than to relieve the loneliness and pain of someone unloved in our own home. Bring love into your home, for this is where our love for each other must start."

— *Mother Teresa*

ELEVEN

Wen Ming, February 2005

After the broken lamp incident, which earned me five stitches and much admiration at school, Auntie Yang never rescheduled the doctor's appointment. It seemed I had won that battle—for the time being. After a while, the stitches came out, leaving only a small white scar. Zhen An stopped fretting about my "nightmare" and everyone else stopped talking about it. But sometimes, when I was playing with Zhen An, Auntie Yang would sigh or "hmm" to herself. She was thinking something, I could tell.

She began telling me I was like bamboo—slender and flexible, but with hidden strength. I would bend and not break. Zhen An she likened to a porcelain vase—beautiful, but would shatter if dropped. I didn't know then what she meant by this, but significance weighted the air whenever she said it.

She said it particularly often after New Year's Eve, my seventh and the very first one I could remember spending with a family. We were to travel to the home of Uncle Zhou's grandparents. All his relatives would be there—aunts and uncles, brother and sister, cousins and nephews and nieces and in-laws. It was beyond my ability to imagine such a wealth of family, and we, two deformed orphans, were to be included. For weeks it was all we spoke of. The excitement and thrill and honor robbed us of several nights' sleep, until we were so overwrought and exhausted that we fought like two stray cats. Auntie Yang, who rarely became cross, said children who did not sleep and who were naughty were not invited to the New Year's Eve reunion dinner. After that, there were never two such sleep-loving children in all the world. We would have strapped ourselves to our bed for a week if it meant being able to be part of our foster family's New Year celebration.

Finally, the morning of New Year's Eve came.

"Zhen An! Wen Ming! I have something for you."

We found Auntie Yang standing with Uncle Zhou in the family room. I tilted and turned my head, scanning her until I could tell she was holding something behind her back. Her face was blurred, but the sparks from her smile skittered across my skin like tiny firecrackers.

"*Hong bao, hong bao!*" Zhen An bounced, shaking the floor with each syllable.

"No, goose." I gave her a playful shove. "Red envelopes come later, at the party."

"She's partially right." Auntie Yang held out a shopping bag toward us. "It's something red."

We surged toward the bag. Presents were nearly unheard of, even in our foster family. There were too many medical and other expenses, and we were only foster children, after all.

We shoved our eager hands into the bag and I touched fabric, cool and smooth and soft. I pulled it out and held it close to me so I could smell and see it. The brilliant red of the brocade pierced through my shadows. A dress. A beautiful red Chinese gown.

I held it in trembling hands, staring at it. How could this be? I'd never touched anything so wonderful in my life.

"It's for you, Wen Ming. Zhen An has a matching one. You will look as fine as all the other children there, and red is festive and lucky."

Zhen An was already twirling around the room and showing Uncle Zhou her new dress. I heard his indulgent voice cooing over the treasure. But I couldn't speak. I scanned for Auntie Yang and stared up at her blurred form, hoping my face could say what my mouth could not.

Then her arms were around me and mine around her neck. "*Xie xie,* Auntie," I whispered against her shoulder. She hugged me even tighter and I knew she understood.

Later in the afternoon, we wriggled into our new dresses, complete with white tights and shiny black shoes. I twisted and turned and squinted, trying to see how I looked in the mirror. But I had to be content to smooth my hands down my body and feel how nicely the silky fabric slid against my skin. Auntie Yang brushed my hair and pulled part of it into a high ponytail and said she'd tied it with a gold ribbon.

I ran my fingers along the smooth strands of my hair. Last New Year seemed so long ago—in the orphanage there were no new dresses or gold ribbons for hair. My hair had been cropped short so that when there was a lice or scabies outbreak, it was easier to treat. But it had grown several inches, and Auntie Yang had faithfully trimmed it until it was nearly all the same length.

"My turn!" Zhen An nudged me aside, comb in hand. "Will there really be *jiaozi*?" Her favorite food was the pork-stuffed dumplings that made an extra-special appearance on New Year's Eve.

Auntie Yang grunted as she tried to comb through Zhen An's wispy, easily knotted hair. "Hold still! Yes, there will be plates and plates full of *jiaozi*. Auntie Fang makes the best you've ever tasted."

"Not better than yours."

Auntie Yang gave another tug. "You are very sweet. Now hold still."

Zhen An's prattle lasted all the way through our ride on the subway to the old part of Shanghai, where Uncle Zhou's baba, mama, and *nai nai* lived. The weather was chilly, but I barely noticed. The flame of family warmed me, even if it was a borrowed family.

I held Auntie Yang's hand tightly and stumbled when the concrete pavement gave way to stone blocks. The sun had set, and I was in my world of darkness. Zhen An slid closer to me and described what she saw.

"This street is so narrow, a car or bus would get stuck if it tried to come here. And there is laundry hanging above our heads."

I had a sudden flash of familiarity. Somewhere, sometime, I had lived where the streets were narrow and the laundry crisscrossed overhead. That thought blocked out the rest of Zhen An's description. Soon I felt Auntie Yang tug on my arm to lead me around a corner.

"Did you live here when you were a child, Uncle Zhou?" Zhen An left my side. I heard a knock on a door, and Auntie Yang and I stopped walking.

"Yes. My great-grandfather bought this house, and our family has lived here ever since. When my *nai nai*—" He cleared his throat. "Someday, my brother and his family will probably live here too."

I knew why he'd changed what he was going to say. He meant that when his *nai nai* died, his brother would move into the house to take care of his parents. But it is very unlucky to talk about death during New Year celebrations.

I heard the door open. Zhen An said it was a very pretty red door with peach blossoms and bamboo shoots and a spring couplet poster. Auntie Yang let go of my arm, and the night turned cold and menacing. I couldn't go into that home—the home of Uncle Zhou's ancestors—the home of strangers. I wouldn't know my way around. There was no rope on the floor to guide me. Auntie Yang and Uncle Zhou couldn't hold my arm the entire evening. I would be lost.

The flutter in my stomach spread throughout my body. I heard the grown-ups talking, but it was like a buzzing in my ears. My heartbeat sounded louder to me, and I opened my mouth to gulp much-needed air, but all I could get was a stream the size of a rice noodle.

A warm body pressed against me. Zhen An. She wrapped her thin arms around my jacketed waist and took a step forward, coaxing me to follow. "We'll stay together," she whispered to me. "I will see for you, and you can talk for me—since you understand me better than anyone else."

I squeezed her and nuzzled her cheek. It seemed strange to be dependent on her. I was supposed to be her mama, after all. But she was right; we needed each other. "Are you nervous?"

"Not with you," she said.

Auntie Yang's voice came closer to me again. "Come, little birds! We don't want to stand outside all night."

She introduced us to Uncle Zhou's mother, who had opened the door. She greeted us with a cheery "*Gong xi fa cai!*" and ushered us into the house. A warm rush of smells greeted me. Dumplings, rice, fish—it was the smell of plenty. Of a feast like I'd never had before.

I heard many voices, muffled and distant.

"It's a beautiful house," Zhen An told me, her voice hushed and reverent. "The floors are shining wood, and there is a real chandelier hanging above us."

Uncle Zhou's mama took our jackets, and we slipped off our shoes. Auntie Yang helped me put on a pair of guest slippers. Brand-new, she said, so that they would step on any gossips during the coming year. I didn't know what a gossip was and there was no time to ask. I imagined it must be a tiny lizard or beetle, but why on earth anyone would want to step on them, I didn't know.

Zhen An led me down a hall and to the left, into the room where all the voices were coming from. I felt a thick carpet beneath my slippered feet, and the cozy glow of radiant heat added to the warmth created by a crackling fireplace. I'd never dreamed any place could be so perfect. So perfectly home.

And yet not my home.

We were guests here. And as introductions were made, and voices mixed like soup around me, I remembered that I did not belong. Zhen An pressed closer to me and I knew she felt it too. We were introduced to six other children. Zhen An told me they all nodded respectfully to us, and we did the same in turn. The youngest child was only two years old, and when he saw Zhen An, he started to scream. His mama was very apologetic and took him to a different room.

One of the other boys, older than me, said loudly, "He was scared of that girl's face. Look at her mouth!"

The grown-ups hushed him and slipped us some candy to make up for their embarrassment.

The other children scampered in and out of the rooms. They called out "Auntie" and "Uncle" and "Cousin" and even "Mama" and "Baba" with a sort of confidence we had never seen before. A confidence they had because those family titles were true and would last forever. Would Auntie Yang and Uncle Zhou always be our auntie and uncle? I could not believe that.

We found a recliner in a corner and squished into it together, so Zhen An could tell me all her eyes saw, and I could tell her what my ears heard that hers had missed.

"Does anyone even notice us?" I asked her.

"They give us some looks, and then I see them whisper to Uncle or Auntie. Then they nod." She was quiet a moment. And then, "I wish the other children would play with us."

"They all know one another. They are family. But we could try to join in with them."

"No! They are already scared to look at me because of my face."

"Well, soon it will be time to eat *jiaozi*, so maybe we should just watch until then."

She snuggled a little closer to me and we let the party spin around us, pretending they were all actors and we had front-row seats at the movies.

I had to admit—Auntie Fang's *jiaozi* was a tiny bit better than Auntie Yang's. But I would never say it out loud. And there was *niangao*—a sticky, sweet fried rice cake that Zhen An liked much better than I did. I loved the chicken—I never tired of having meat. The texture, the smell, the flavor. It made me feel full and sleepy. Satisfied. When I grew up and became director of the Children's Home, I would feed my children meat every day. As much as they wanted, until all their little bellies were round and their chins doubled up against their necks.

During the reunion dinner, I tried not to listen to Uncle Zhou's mama as she spoke with him and Auntie Yang. They sat several seats to my right, and they did not realize my hearing was very sharp. They were talking about me and Zhen An in quiet, private tones, but I heard anyway.

"So how long are you planning to keep these . . . foster children?"

A long pause. "Why do you ask, Mama?" said Uncle Zhou.

"They cannot be cheap, especially with their disabilities. You should be saving your money so you can start a family of your own."

"We told you," Auntie Yang said in a respectful voice, "the foster program is sponsored by an American aid organization. We receive a stipend each month for their care."

"So you are helping America pry into Chinese private matters instead of having a good Chinese baby of your own."

"We are helping take care of Chinese orphans, Mama." Uncle Zhou's voice was quiet and full of honor, but I could tell the conversation embarrassed him. It didn't seem that anyone else at the table was listening. Or if they were, they pretended not to listen.

The *jiaozi* felt thick and suddenly sour in my throat. I did not want Uncle Zhou and his mother to have an argument because of me and Zhen An. I didn't mean to bring trouble to his family, after he and Auntie Yang had been so kind. It was dishonoring and ungrateful.

I clenched my hands in my lap under the table. Zhen An slipped her hand into mine and whispered, "Are you okay?"

I nodded, even though it wasn't true.

The grown-ups were still talking. Uncle Zhou's mama sounded even unhappier than a moment ago. "I am the only one of my sisters who is not a *nai nai* yet. And why? Because you have not made me a *nai nai*. And why have you not made me a *nai nai*? Because you are spending all your time caring for orphans! I might be old and getting around with a cane by the time your brother and your sister find people to marry. I do not understand any of you. All your cousins found good spouses and have children now. What is wrong with the three of you?"

"There's nothing wrong." Uncle Zhou sounded as if he had more to say, only his mama had more than more. She talked faster.

"Oh, yes there is. Your minds must be dull-witted or crazy to treat your loving mama this way. No grandchildren? Whoever heard of such a thing?"

"We do plan to have children, when the time is right."

"When the time is right? When is that? Never. That's when. You keep waiting for the right time and you run out of time. I know older parents are best, but too old is as bad as too young. And here you are spending your precious time on orphans"—here her voice dipped to a whisper, but I heard it like a shout—"deformed orphans, instead of giving me grandchildren of my own. What did I do to deserve such a son? That's what I'd like to know. What did I do wrong to be repaid like this?"

Uncle Zhou sighed. Tears leaked from my eyes, much to my horror.

Zhen An on the other side of me gasped. "You are crying, *jie jie*! Are you sick?"

"Crying?" Auntie Yang's words caught the attention of the rest of the family and their conversations stopped. "Wen Ming?" I heard her chair scrape across the floor, and then she was beside me, feeling my forehead.

"I am not sick." I tried to say more, but my words were choked by tears. I hid my face against her. I could feel everyone staring at me, their gazes hitting me like slaps. "I am sorry."

"Shh, my *xiao niao*. Did you hear our conversation?"

I nodded. I hadn't meant to admit it, but the weight of shame and hurt was too heavy for me.

"She heard you!" Auntie Yang turned her head, and I assume it was to glare at her mother-in-law.

Uncle Zhou's mama groaned. In a second, she joined Auntie Yang beside me. "No crying! No crying. Here, have some candy. I didn't mean to hurt your feelings. You weren't supposed to hear. I am glad to have you in my home, and I am glad my son and daughter-in-law are caring for you. Someday you will understand." Then she hesitated. "Well, maybe you won't understand. But when you grow up it will all make more sense. Here, dry your tears. No crying on New Year's Eve, yes? You don't want to bring bad luck to the New Year, do you?"

One of Uncle Zhou's other grown-up relatives filled the silence left by my sniffles with a booming "We were done eating anyway. Doesn't anyone want a present for the New Year?"

I was quickly forgotten as the other children clamored for their red envelopes. The uncle (whose name I could not remember) quieted them and said, "I think the first *hong bao* should go to our young guests."

Auntie Yang urged me to my feet, and Zhen An gripped my hand hard. The hurt I'd been feeling didn't go away, but it went to sleep for the time being. It was hard to cry when I was about to receive my very first red envelope. Would there be a very great amount of money in it? Probably not, but any amount seemed a fortune to me. Maybe Auntie Yang would take us shopping to spend our money. Maybe I could buy something of my very own that I could keep forever.

Auntie Yang held out my hands, and the uncle said *"Gong xi fa cai"* in his cheerful but loud voice. The envelope slid into my hands and I said *"Xie xie"* and nodded my head as solemnly as I could. Zhen An said thank you as well. I felt my envelope. It was bulky, with several thin, round shapes in it. Coins! My very own coins.

It would have been very poor manners to open the envelope right then. But I fingered the coins through the paper, my heart beating hard and strong. The envelope was not heavy, but it seemed to hold a great many coins. How much could I buy for that amount? Auntie Yang would have to help me count them.

After the envelopes were all handed out, someone turned on the television. They said the CCTV New Year's Gala would be starting soon. I didn't know what that was. Auntie Yang said it was a huge show with comedy skits, dancing, songs, and other performances to celebrate the coming year. Everyone seemed excited about it, but I knew I would only be able to really enjoy the singing.

Somehow, Zhen An and I found ourselves in a smaller room with three of the children.

"Let's open our *hong bao*," said a boy Zhen An told me looked a little like a giraffe. "Zhou Wei and Zhou Li, you go first."

The other two agreed with him and we heard the crackling of envelopes being torn open. They were exclaiming about their money, but it didn't sound like either of them had received coins. Theirs were brand-new paper bills, and they all seemed very happy with their gifts.

"Open yours!" commanded Giraffe Boy. (I could not remember all those names!)

I thought it could not be wrong to do so since they had opened theirs. So I felt along the envelope for the flap.

"Are you blind?" a girl asked me.

"Mostly," I said. I found the flap and ripped it open. The coins slid into my hands and I held them carefully. I wasn't sure I could trust the children to find my coins and return them to me if I dropped any.

"It's chocolate!" Giraffe Boy said.

I frowned.

"You can't even see, can you? They are chocolate coins."

"They're not real money?" Zhen An's voice trembled.

"Of course not! Why would my baba give real money to orphans?"

No shopping with Auntie Yang. No buying anything of my own. The truth hurt—why *would* anyone give orphans a present of real money? But these children would not see how I felt. I'd already cried once this evening. No more. "Chocolate, Zhen An! Isn't that wonderful? It will be so much fun to eat."

"How do you eat with that mouth anyway?" asked Giraffe Boy.

Zhen An stiffened but didn't say anything. A black mist swirled across the already dark shadows. I glared through the mist toward his voice. "Leave her alone."

Giraffe Boy walked closer to me. I could feel the smug heat of him. "It's good she is here. She looks like the monster Nian, with the lion's face." I felt him pacing around us, felt the mix of horror and fascination as the other two children watched their naughty cousin, uncertain whether they should join in or tell their parents. I put my arm around Zhen An, who was trembling. Giraffe Boy stopped right in our faces. "Do you eat little children, Nian? Shall I scare you away with firecrackers? I will catch you!"

Zhen An whimpered and hid her face against my chest. Rage made me strong and bold. "You are a very bad person. I will tell your baba you are being unkind to guests."

"He won't believe an orphan. I will tell him we were just playing a New Year's game. He will believe me and take back your *hong bao*."

Zhen An clutched her envelope tighter. I felt huge inside, and tight, like something was trying to burst out of me.

And it did. A black and red dragon shot from my chest, glowing in light that made me able to see. It curled around Giraffe Boy (who really did resemble that animal), wise and calm, and it winked at me.

Its strength brought peace to my heart. I glared at Giraffe Boy. "Why don't you open your *hong bao*? We want to see what's inside."

He grinned at me, so full of himself he could not see the dragon breathe across the envelope. He ripped open the envelope and pulled out a single sheet of paper with a poem written in beautiful calligraphy on it.

Giraffe Boy frowned and read the poem out loud.

Once a boy
Whose neck was like a giraffe
And who had the face of a horse
Dishonored a guest on New Year's Eve.
This foolish boy
This unwise giraffe
Could not see
That he had acted like a monster
And angered the Dragon
Who brings justice and protects the innocent.
So this foolish boy
Received no present for the New Year.
If he becomes wise this year,
Perhaps the next there will be a gift for him.
What a pity to be such a boy.

The boy's cousins giggled. Zhen An drew a sharp breath, and I could feel the radiance of her smile.

I put a confused frown on my face and shrugged my shoulders. "At least we got chocolate."

"Baba!" Giraffe Boy yelled, running into the other room. The rest of us laughed and laughed. The dragon nodded in an elegant bow and disappeared in a puff of red mist.

The other children were very kind to both of us the rest of the evening. They even helped us light firecrackers at midnight. I didn't know I had a dragon living inside me, but it made me feel brave and strong. That's something a nearly blind orphan needs.

Zhen An did not have a dragon inside her. She hung her head, letting her hair fall over her face, and would not speak or look up the rest of the evening, no matter how I pleaded.

The Giraffe Boy and the other children had broken my fragile *mei mei*.

Two weeks later, after Auntie and Uncle had many private talks, Auntie Yang took us to the finally rescheduled doctor's appointment at the orphanage. I didn't see why we needed to go, but Auntie Yang said it was because I was bamboo and Zhen An was porcelain. It was the sort of grown-up remark I hated for its complete nonsense.

The doctor was confident that Zhen An's mouth could be repaired, but he said that there was no money to pay for it. He said her best chance was to be adopted by a foreign couple. Zhen An hung her head and let her hair fall across her face and would not look up again until we left.

After examining my eyes, the doctor muttered big words like "retinitis" and "pigmentosa" and said there was nothing he could do, and that I'd probably be completely blind before I was grown up. Auntie said that maybe someone from America would want to adopt me too, but I knew better. Nobody would want a blind child. I'd be a burden to any family, even a wealthy foreign family. They would want Zhen An, who could be operated on and made into the perfect, beautiful child.

What kind of life would I have as a blind orphan? Teased and looked down upon like I was at the New Year's party? Or worse—a beggar on the streets? Auntie Yang assured me that would never happen. I was resilient and resourceful, she said. I'd find my way. But there was a note of worry in her voice that she couldn't hide from me.

And what about Zhen An? If she stayed, she would be tormented by people like Giraffe Boy for having a deformed face. She would be broken, just like Auntie Yang feared. Delicate, beautiful, flawed porcelain. But how could I let her leave me? Some things even bamboo cannot withstand.

I pulled her aside the next day and made her promise me that she would not let anyone adopt her.

"But Auntie says they could fix my face."

"Yes, but we will never see each other again!"

"I wouldn't go without you."

"You won't have a choice."

I could sense she was torn by the two choices. I hugged her tight. "When I am grown, I will earn money and take care of you. I'll pay for your surgery and give you the prettiest face in China."

"You will?"

"Of course! You are my *mei mei* for always."

Still she hesitated. Then she hugged me and said, "Then I will stay with you for always."

And so we vowed by all the ancestors we never knew that we would refuse to be adopted and that we would be each other's family forever. And I promised the dragon that lived in the wide expanses inside me that I would protect my *mei mei* from all those who would hunt her like a monster for nothing more than being imperfect.

They were beautiful vows. But what if they were broken? What if she left? I tried to remind myself that I could bend and not break. I was strong. I would find my way. I was bamboo. Dragon bamboo.

But still, the worry hung in my heart, darker than the shadows that were eating up my vision. A porcelain vase could be shipped all over the world. But bamboo had to stay rooted to the earth or it would die.

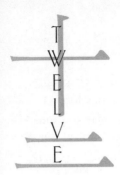

TWELVE

Meg Lindsay, September 2005

"Meg! Just put it all in the envelope. Come on." Lewis tried to take our completed dossier out of my hand, but I held on.

"I want to check through it one more time." I flipped through the home study, and all the other documents, along with their layers of notary certificates and letters of authentication. "I don't want the adoption agency to have to return it because we missed something. If we get it to them now, in about two weeks, it should be logged in China. I don't want any delays."

"Everything is perfect. You've checked it six times this morning. We need to mail it."

My hands stilled on the dossier. "You dragged your feet for five months. You can give me a couple more minutes."

"How did I drag my feet?"

My dramatically patient sigh didn't seem to impress him. "The questionnaire that took you weeks to complete. How you couldn't find time to go with me to the notary. Stalling on making the appointment for your physical. We could have had this done two months ago if I hadn't had to prod and push you every step of the way."

"That was thirty-six essay questions!" He had that pinched look around his mouth, like he was about to whip out his calculator to prove his statement. "Maybe you don't mind writing paragraphs about your sex life and your financial situation and your philosophy of child rearing for total strangers to pore over and judge. But I do."

"It shouldn't matter—helping a child is more important."

"You didn't tell me that I was going to have to be picked over and examined like some data from an experiment. There are subatomic particles with more privacy than what I have left."

I couldn't help but crack a smile at that, but it disappeared just as quickly. "I didn't know it would be so invasive. I'm sorry."

He shook his head at my apology and crossed his arms. "My dad didn't even seem to care when I told him we were adopting. Too busy making his investments and financial deals. My California relatives are worried about us ignoring the child's culture and heritage. You seem to think this is some sort of grand adventure. You haven't even *told* your parents yet."

I didn't know how to respond to that. It was quite true. Something deep inside me didn't want to tell my family. It wasn't that I thought they'd disapprove—just the opposite. I feared it might actually be one of the few things I'd ever done that would meet with their approval. And I didn't want to have my new beginning tainted with their involvement. I wanted this to be something between just Lewis and me . . .

. . . and the social worker, and adoption agency, and U.S. Immigration, and the Chinese government, and the notaries, and all the other officials, of course.

"It *is* an adventure. You don't think so?"

"So far, it's been a tedious pain in the butt."

I fuzzed up like a cat, claws out. It was all I could do not to hiss. "Is that how you're going to feel about being a dad?"

He looked like he'd been slapped. His face turned red. We stared at each other, and I knew I'd gone too far.

"I'm going to work." He grabbed his jacket and strode toward the door.

"Wait. Lewis. I'm sorry. That was low." I hurried to the door and wedged myself between it and him. "I don't want you to leave angry. I am sorry—I didn't mean it."

His expression softened a little. "What is your problem anyway? All I did was try to hurry you up this morning. You're making a huge deal out of it."

"I didn't want to hurry. I wanted to savor the moment. This should be a landmark day. We're sending off the paperwork to become parents. It's like—going off the pill and coming home at noon to have sex because my temperature is up. I just wanted it to feel important. Something more than just tossing the papers in a mailbox and running on to the next chore. I wasn't trying to pick a fight."

He looked at the ceiling, then back at me. "Sometimes, I really don't get you." His lips turned in a half smile, still tinged with frustration. "To me, these are just hoops to jump through. I'll get excited when there's a child with our name on it. I don't need to make an occasion out of every step."

"But I do. Maybe not every step, but at least the big ones. I know a completed dossier isn't as exciting as sex at noon, but it's still important. To me, anyway."

He studied my face a few moments longer and then stepped away. He tossed his jacket over a kitchen chair and pulled out his cell phone.

"What are you doing?"

"I'm calling in and taking a personal day. Then I'm going to check the dossier myself, put it in the envelope, and seal it—even if I have to lock you in the bathroom to keep your obsessive hands off it. And then, we're going to mail it together, and go to Chinatown and sample every single sort of dim sum they have."

"Why?" I breathed.

He grinned at me and dialed his work number. "Prove to you I can make an occasion out of it. Though, it would help a lot if we came home at noon and pretended your temperature was up."

My arms around his neck, I gave him a quick kiss. "I think that's a deal I can agree to."

October 2005

Our dossier had been logged in China for about a month, and already the wait felt intolerable. It could be well over a year before we got a referral, but even so, I'd wheedled Lewis into helping me redecorate the second bedroom in girly shades of hot pink and lime green.

I hated the idea that somewhere across the ocean was a little girl, my little girl, who was spending one more day without her family. There was a restless anticipation building in me, like the shaking of a soda bottle until the plastic walls are taut and convex. Waiting over a year was unacceptable. There were children now—this very minute—who needed families. My daughter was out there, and I wasn't going to spend the next year painting her bedroom.

I was going to find her.

Her voice came to me on the October breeze, smelling of peonies and cherry blossoms. "Mama," it said. A word that speaks love in almost every language on earth. A word I never thought I'd hear applied to me. And yet the whispered scent followed me. "Mama," it said. "I am waiting."

I saw her eyes in the clouds, in the falling leaves, in every shadow and sunbeam. I knew her eyes, knew the shape and exact color. I'd seen them before, and they lived in my dreams.

I had to find her.

I am waiting.

Waiting. A waiting child. The phrase jumped at me from my e-mail inbox. "New waiting children." A link. My fingers flew, entering the log-in information to give me access to the parents-only part of the agency's website.

The list. I stopped. Was I ready? What if she was here, on the list? My life would change. I wanted it to change. But was I ready?

And what if she wasn't there on the list? Would I be ready for that too? My mouth felt like it was stuffed with socks. My hands trembled.

I started scrolling through the photos. Those who waited on lists like these usually were older or handicapped. Lewis and I had already discussed what sort of conditions we felt able to handle. I hurried past several that were too severe for our comfort level. I was afraid to look into their eyes, in case one of them would happen to be her. Better to never see her on the list than to see her and know she couldn't be ours.

The computer screen froze on the photo of a little girl, forcing me to look into her eyes.

Eyes I knew. Beautiful, dark, gentle eyes full of sadness and a knowledge of the world's cruelty. Hungry eyes that had watched me from outside the tea shop; somber eyes that had challenged me as I drank the mate with Lewis the night I told him about wanting to adopt.

Her eyes held the promise of kind laughter. Traces of childhood innocence clinging stubbornly in a heart that had to grow up too soon. A spark of fire, a hope of wholeness and life. Energy and grace. Intelligence, and even a glimmer of fun.

My heart thudded in my ears and my hands lost their strength. I tilted my head back and let joy rain down on me, tears of cherry blossoms falling on my face. Their sweet fragrance filled my spirit as the pink petals fell around me in drifts on the floor. They slid down my cheeks, fluttering across my eyelids like the curious fingers of a child—my child. My daughter.

She was here. I'd found her. She existed, right now. Not just in my dreams and hopes and wishes. But in a real world, a real city made of concrete and bricks and glass and wood. She had substance, flesh, bones, and muscle. She cried real tears, ate real food, and in her soul she held all the real mysteries a human heart carries.

I stared at her, and in her eyes I saw not just her need, but also a promise—of purpose and potential, of strength, of the contribution she had to make in this world. And I knew this wasn't—couldn't be— merely about me and what I needed. She was destined for something, and we would be just one part of making it come true.

I hollered for Lewis, and he rushed in. I pointed to the computer screen. "I found her."

"Found who?"

Didn't he know? Couldn't he feel it? Smell the cherry blossom scent of her? "Her!" I tugged him to the computer monitor and pointed to her picture.

He frowned at the monitor. "What? Who is . . . Oh! You mean—"

"Yes!"

He adjusted his glasses and leaned in to read the information. "She's the one? Are you sure?"

"Hey, you told me you'd be excited about this."

"When she has our name on her."

"You can't see that she does?"

He looked suspiciously like he was biting his tongue. "Give me a chance, okay?"

I scooted my chair over to let him lean in. He studied the information without speaking, the same intense look on his face as when he was studying his physics journals.

I nibbled on my thumbnail and watched him. "She's not perfect."

"Mmm." He didn't blink.

"But neither are we."

He nodded without breaking concentration.

"But she is perfect. For us."

"Meg, shut up and let me read."

"Sorry."

The silence was torture. At last, he leaned back and turned to me. "She needs surgery."

"That won't be a problem . . . will it?"

"Are you positive she's the one?"

"I feel like I've always known her. Like she's already part of me. Yes, I'm positive."

"You are incomprehensible, you know that?" But he was smiling when he said it. He touched the screen with his fingertips. His fingers lingered on her lips, and his face became troubled and soft. "Poor little thing . . . So have you picked out a name for her yet?"

His words were a jolt of espresso to my heart. "A name?"

"Yeah." He winked at me. "You know, the word we use to call her when she's in trouble or we want her to clean her room." At my blank stare, he laughed. "Don't tell me you haven't chosen a name? Or are we keeping her Chinese name?"

I jumped off my chair and nearly knocked him over, squealing. I couldn't stop kissing him. He didn't even try to stop me, either.

Truth was, I hadn't chosen a name yet. It took me another couple of weeks to figure it out. But finally it came to me.

Eva. Life.

We would name our daughter Eva Zhen An Lindsay.

T
H
I
R
T
E
E
N

Meg Lindsay, January 2006

We were expecting the referral package that day. Our agency had called two days ago to say they'd received the referral information from the China Center of Adoption Affairs. Eva Zhen An was ours. Or would be as soon as we received the referral packet, signed the documents, and faxed them back to the agency. Since Eva had been on the waiting child list, and because she needed surgery, the CCAA had expedited things for us. Guilt tinged my euphoria— many families who had gotten their dossier to China earlier than we did were settling in for a wait of eighteen months or more for a referral. It hadn't always been like that, apparently, and I didn't understand all the reasons for the slowdown. Some people said it was because fewer children were being abandoned. Others blamed the recent baby trafficking scandal in Hunan that had resulted in the closing of that province to international adoption. Still others insisted China was hiding thousands of healthy orphans from the rest of the world—a proposition I couldn't quite accept.

Regardless, things were changing rapidly in the Chinese adoption program. I felt like we'd gotten in at the end of a golden age. And feeling that way disgusted me. Who could think of something as tragic as abandonment and overflowing orphanages as a golden age? But on one level, it felt that way: thousands of orphans being matched with loving families; a program that was stable, low on corruption and scandal, and predictable. Happy endings everywhere.

I'd get one of those happy endings and make it into my new beginning. A family. Me, a mother. It still seemed like this must be happening to some other lucky person. Not me.

The day they called us, I phoned Lewis right away to tell him the good news. He was working hard on his upcoming experiment, but when he got on the phone, I said, "She has our name on her."

"Really?"

"Yep. She's ours!"

I wasn't sure what to expect. He'd promised to be excited, but when he spoke, his voice became husky and choked. He said, "Meg, thank you for talking me into doing this. I just wanted you to know I'm really glad."

Lewis doesn't get emotional often, so I didn't know what to say. Finally, I fell back into the safety of humor. "Yes, but are you *excited?*"

"When I get home, we're going to go out and I will eat the equivalent of her weight in dim sum. Will that convince you?"

"Absolutely."

I wandered around the city afterward, wrapped in the euphoria, a snowy mist propelling me to Chinatown. I was looking for something—something special to give my new daughter—but I didn't know what. My childhood teddy bear sat on the bed waiting to go to China with me. It would be Eva's first toy. I wasn't searching for a toy now. But I was searching.

I ambled along the sidewalk with the flow of shoppers, stopping to study the displays in the shop windows or to enjoy the smell of food in the restaurants. But a restless energy drove me forward, until a woman stepped in front of me. She had a mole on the left side of her chin.

"Hello," she said, her voice soft and low-pitched. "You looking for something?"

I frowned at her. "I know you . . . don't I?"

She smiled a secretive smile. "You are going on a very long journey."

"Yes. My daughter is in China."

"Not that journey."

"Then what do you mean?"

She pulled out a cigarette. It lit by itself and she took a drag. "You think you are a mama now, don't you?"

I didn't know how to respond. So I said nothing.

"You not a mama because of phone call. Just like I not a mama because of birth. You become mama through journey. Very long journey."

I nodded. "That makes sense. But I'm very anxious to get started." I took a step to move past her.

She grabbed my arm. "Where you going?"

"To look for a gift for my daughter."

"Okay. But where you going?"

I looked down the street and pointed at a random shop. "There."

Still, she did not release me. "You not find what you look for in that shop. Come. I show you." She dropped my arm and started down the street.

Intrigue battled with impatience and won. I slid through slush and eased over icy patches on the sidewalk until I caught her. "This isn't anything illegal, is it?"

She looked offended. "No."

"Sorry."

She rolled her eyes and took another drag on the cigarette. Shook her head and started walking again.

I had to hurry to keep up with her as she led me past streets and down alleys, twisting and turning into more byways than I knew Chicago's Chinatown had. I felt like we were going in circles, but the tourists thinned out and the merchants faded until she and I were the only ones, meandering down a passage so narrow that two bicycles would have had trouble passing each other.

"A journey, see?" she hollered over her shoulder.

"Where are we going?"

"Not where you thought."

Tall, decrepit brick buildings towered on either side of me, and laundry crackled on frozen lines suspended over my head. The alley was clean, far cleaner than a typical Chicago street, and it smelled different—like cooked rice and sesame oil.

She stopped at a tall, black iron gate. It swung open and she gestured for me to enter before her. I stepped into a dark corridor, like the space between two brick buildings. Green vines meshed overhead, sending tendrils to dangle down the brick. A warm breeze curled around me, bringing a pleasant, earthy fragrance with it.

The woman nudged me to move ahead, so I followed the brick walkway toward the source of the fragrance. The walls gave way to an open courtyard, where the air was warm like early summer. Large boulders and smaller rocks framed the centerpiece—a pond of soft green water floated with lilies and lotus. A willow draped itself along one side, and a footbridge invited further exploration.

It was quiet, except for the rustle of leaves and the frothing of water. I followed the path to the edge of the pond. A black and orange koi slid past me under the surface of the murky water. A flash of pale green around its tail caught my eye.

I turned to the woman, who was watching me and breathing out a thin trail of smoke.

"Journey is surprising to you? Took you someplace you did not expect. But this place is better. Look at the fish again."

I did, and he swam past me once more. I saw that the green around his tail was a bracelet of jade. Without thinking first, I reached into the water and snagged the bracelet with my finger. The koi somersaulted in the water and slipped away. I drew the bracelet out of the water and held it to the sunlight. Droplets of water glimmered and splashed to my feet. The bracelet was carved to look like a slender dragon. A round ball, representing a pearl, separated the head from the tail.

"Thank you," I told the fish.

A dark shape dove above me and landed on the pond. A Mandarin duck, with brilliant patches of white and orange and brown. It paddled over to me and dropped a second jade bracelet from its beak. This one was carved to resemble a circlet of cherry blossoms and Chinese knots.

"And thank you," I said to the duck.

The woman laughed lightly. "Much better than you get in the shops, yes?"

I smiled at her, nodding. "They are breathtaking. Do I . . . need to . . . pay or anything?"

She snorted. "Do duck and fish need money?"

I started to reply, but a noise distracted me. It was the sound of a child. Weeping.

"Who is that?" I asked the woman. The sound poured loneliness and despair into my heart until I thought it would overflow and spill my blood into the pond. I tried to spot the child, but I couldn't see anyone. All I knew was that it was not Eva. That made it worse because I knew we would have a chance to comfort her. This other child was out of my reach.

The woman looked sad. "Some journeys are not so easy. Please remember that where you going is not always where you think you go." She tilted her head, studying me around the edge of her cigarette. "You will become very good mother, I think."

I couldn't speak for a moment. It felt strange and wonderful to have her affirmation. "Thank you," I finally managed, my voice thick and my throat raspy.

She was looking restless suddenly. I held up the bracelets. "I only have one daughter."

"Keep other for yourself. You will know who to give it to." She took a step back.

I wanted to stall her, but I didn't know why. "Who should I tell Eva the bracelet is from?"

She looked mystified. "Her mother, of course. Didn't you want to give gift to your daughter? Here is gift. Just need daughter."

I bit my lip and smiled at her. She obviously wasn't going to tell me her name or anything else. But in this place, it didn't seem very important. "Thank you."

She took another step away. I could still hear the child crying.

"Wait!" I walked toward her. "How do I get back to the street?"

She turned to walk back into the dark, vine-covered corridor. I tried to follow her, but there were too many boulders and bushes in my way. By the time I reached the corridor, I couldn't see her anymore. I stifled a groan and took a final look back at the idyllic garden. So much peace there, marred only by the child that had been crying.

Whoever it was had quieted now. I looked at the bracelets I clutched in my right hand. I slid the dragon one over my hand—a tight fit, but it was just the right size for my wrist. The other I slipped into my purse for safekeeping. It seemed right that Eva should have the cherry blossoms.

I wished I could stay. The bridge beckoned to me, but whoever owned the garden would not want me intruding any further. Wistfully, I turned to enter the corridor.

When I opened the black gate on the other end, I found myself on the same street I'd started from.

Journeys, indeed.

Lewis had promised to go home during his lunch hour to check for the package from the adoption agency, so when he showed up at the Nouveau Chicago Symphony rehearsal, I nearly knocked my music stand over in my haste to get to the door. We were just getting back from our own lunch break, and Maestro Don Chelsea was chatting with our bassoonist, to my left. He caught my music stand and righted it with a bow.

"Thank you, Don."

"My pleasure to help a lady in distress." He kissed his fingers toward me. I grinned. That was just how Maestro Chelsea was. He couldn't help it. Most of us women found it endearing. Most of the men found it annoying.

"Is everything okay?" My stand partner and good friend Li Shu frowned toward Lewis.

"Everything is wonderful! I'll be right back." I swam upstream against the flow of musicians heading back to rehearsal and grabbed Lewis's arm. "Did you get it?"

He held up a manila envelope and grinned. I shrieked and bounced on my toes. I dragged him to a few plastic chairs at the end of the hall so we could open it together.

The gold color of the envelope—holding within a vast treasure—lit the hallway. The air smelled of ink and adhesive, of paper and post office. The smell of important news. The rending of the seal vibrated my body and its sound created a pillar to mark the moment in my heart.

We put our hands into the envelope together and pulled out the sheaf of documents. There was a cover letter, but we skipped it. What we wanted was the photo.

There. A tiny picture stapled to the document. It was a different photo from the one on the website. It was our photo. Ours and no one else's. Nothing more than an ID-style photo, and not a good one at that, but when I looked at Lewis, tears had collected at the corners of his eyes, threatening to slide down his nose.

"I'm going to be a dad."

"A great one."

He crushed me against him, the papers sandwiched between us.

Finally, we thought to look at the documents.

Lewis scanned the cover letter and his elation drained out of him. "Um, Meg? This says we might have to travel in February."

I looked over his arm at the paper he was holding. "Is that a problem?" Then it hit me. "Beth and Adam's wedding. And your experiment!"

He nodded. "If we have to travel during the run of the experiment, I won't be able to go with you."

"You would miss adopting your daughter? For a work project?"

"It's not just a 'work project.' It's one step closer to making scientific history."

"Can't you have a grad student handle it?"

"Would you hand off your seat in the symphony to a high school substitute? Look, we're expecting some landmark results. If I missed it, I'd never forgive myself. Please, Meg. This is everything to me."

I didn't see how anything could be more important than becoming a father. But I didn't want to fight with him at my job. "Can they move the date?"

"This project involves more than five different universities and fifty scientists from around the world, not to mention the Fermilab staff. No, it can't be rescheduled."

"I think we should talk about this more later."

He took me by the arms. "Listen to me. I know what you're thinking—that I'm a selfish, horrible person. Maybe I am. All I know is that this is every bit as vital to me as adopting is for you. I'm not expecting you to understand. But please don't judge me. And give me a chance—I want to be a good father every bit as much as you want to be a good mother. I can do that, even if I don't travel with you." His eyes filled with self-doubt. "Please believe in me. I need you to trust me."

I slumped in my chair. I couldn't refuse what he was asking of me. If I didn't believe in him, trust him, he wouldn't be able to do it for himself. But not once had I ever contemplated the idea of traveling to China by myself. This journey was already starting to take an unwelcome turn.

"Hey." Lewis rubbed my back and dropped a kiss onto my head. "Don't worry about it. Everyone says travel is slow right now. And Chinese New Year is coming up. So we probably won't get to travel until March. It'll be okay. Let's don't freak out about it until we find out if we have to, okay?"

"Ever the voice of reason." I stood and kissed him. "No matter what, she's ours. Where are the papers we have to sign?"

When I returned to the rehearsal room, I brought the photo with me to pass around to my colleagues. They fussed over it and congratulated me. Except for Li Shu. She politely peered at the photo, gave me a tight smile, and opened her music folder, the Nouveau Chicago Symphony logo on the front scratched and marred by a coffee ring. I saw a photo taped to the left pocket. It had been there for as long as I could remember, but I had never taken an interest in it.

"Taping the photo to your folder was a good idea. I think I'll do the same with mine."

She gave me another superficial smile but said nothing. It was odd. We'd become friends over the past three years that we shared a music stand. She was a naturally warm and lively person. This reticence was unusual.

It was the adoption. It had to be. She was far too polite to criticize me for it, but ever since I'd told my coworkers two weeks before, there had been a tightness in her. A wall between us. I didn't know what the problem was, and I wasn't sure how to find out. She was a Chinese national, not Chinese-American, and sometimes I didn't know how to relate to her without treading on cultural toes.

I leaned closer to get a better look at her picture. The photo was dulled and worn. Marks around the edge attested to the many times it had been retaped to her folder. It was a snapshot of a toddler boy sitting in front of a plum tree loaded with blossoms, surrounded by mounds of flowers in pinks, reds, and yellows. He was bundled up in a winter coat and hat, even though the weather couldn't possibly have been very chilly. He looked up at the camera with a wide grin that poked dimples into each cheek. A couple of thick locks of black hair determined to find the sun stuck out from under the hat. He gripped a blue toy elephant in his hand with fierce, joyful possessiveness. My breath caught.

"Who is that?" I pointed to the photo, being careful not to touch it.

Li Shu had been in the process of pulling her music from the folder. She froze, hands still on the sheets of music, and shot a sideways glance at me before frowning at the photo. She gathered her music and set it in her lap. "That is my best friend's child."

A very *good* friend for her to have the son's photo taped to her folder. "What's his name?"

She riffled through her music like she was looking for something. She'd always been good at not showing her emotions, but I thought maybe I'd made her angry. Was there some Chinese taboo against asking about family photos? Finally, she looked over at me and smiled, shrugging her shoulders. "I am sorry. I don't remember."

She snatched the folder off the stand and shoved it under her chair. Then she retrieved her viola from its case and started to tune it with such focus, I didn't dare ask more questions.

Wen Ming, January 2006

It was Auntie Yang who told me about Zhen An. Uncle Zhou took Zhen An to the park and Auntie Yang fixed some tea for me. She made it the way her British coworker at the Children's Home did—with milk and sugar in it—because she knew I liked it that way. She sat next to me at the table and prodded me to drink my tea.

Whatever she had to say hung heavily on her body, like bags and bags of groceries she was trying to tote through the bustling crowds on the street. I did not think I would like what was in these bags, though. If it was something good, she would not be so reluctant to say so.

I sipped at my tea, but the treat I usually loved crawled around in my stomach like a beetle trying to escape a glass jar. I set my cup down and waited for her to speak.

She was silent. And after moving my head around so I could study all the different parts of her that didn't fit into my vision, I was pretty certain that she didn't want to look at me. Had I done something bad? Maybe she didn't want me anymore because I was too much trouble. Maybe she and Uncle Zhou were keeping Zhen An and sending me back to the Children's Home.

It was like the air was being sucked from the room. My joints ached flulike, my vision darkened even more, and my heartbeat quickened, thudding in my ears like a drum through a stack of blankets. It was going to explode if she didn't say something soon.

She took my hand and stroked it, then touched my cheek with her fingers. "Wen Ming, you are such a strong girl. I need you to be brave now."

"You are sending me back to the Children's Home, aren't you?" My chest felt like a bus had parked on top of it.

"No! No, darling. We want you here. It's . . ." She bowed her head and squeezed my hand. "It's Zhen An."

I don't remember the words she used to tell me. I banished them from my mind and from my soul. I just remember the way my body quivered, as if it had become waves on a lake, and the terrible crushing pressure on the sides of my head, like an egg being squeezed until it shatters.

I saw the shadow of the monstrous bird of prey, hovering, flapping its wings in victory. "She promised me," I gasped. There didn't seem to be any more air to breathe. "She promised she wouldn't let them . . ." I couldn't say the hated word.

The pressure increased. I would die if it didn't stop. Something in me was trying to get out, but I fought it back. It wasn't a wise dragon this time. I wasn't sure what it was, and I did not want it to escape, for fear it might destroy me.

But it was stronger than me. With a scream and a great ripping sound, a many-splendored bird tore from my throat. It had double pupils in its fierce eyes, and a long plumy tail like a rooster. But even its threat of ill luck could not frighten away the shadow of the great predator that lurked to take away the only person I had ever really learned to love.

It shuddered with its cries, and its cries were pulled from my heart. Its cries were my heart, and together, we filled the room with a rising flood of grief.

I could not feel my own body, only the body of the many-splendored bird—a body full of the deepest kind of sadness, the kind that makes people afraid because when you sink down into it, it is so deep you can never again reach the surface. A sadness that surrounds so completely there is no room for any other feeling. Everything else flees, leaving only the sorrow.

"You adopt her!" I pleaded.

A wet drop landed on my hand. Auntie Yang was crying. "We can't. She needs surgery, and it is too expensive for us."

"Then let me go with her too."

But I knew without being told that this could not happen. Auntie Yang held me, but I could not feel her anymore, only the emptiness of my own loss. Finally the many-splendored bird, the double-pupil bird, shook off its white feathers of death and flew off on fleshy wings. My throat was raw and sore from where it had clawed its way out of me. The shadow had hidden itself, but I still felt its presence.

"I tried so hard." Now I started to feel Auntie Yang's arms around me. The skin on her neck was smooth and soft. "I knew they would want her, but I thought if she had a foster family, it would be enough to make her stay."

"I am sorry, little one."

"She promised."

"It wasn't a promise she could keep. Did you think a little girl like you could stop her future from happening? She was transferred from her old orphanage to the Children's Home for just this reason. It took longer than what anyone expected, but it was bound to happen."

"So she was meant to be adopted? Why not me?"

Auntie Yang caught her breath and did not move. "You were! You were meant to be adopted too. But you weren't meant to know this. You mustn't tell anyone I told you. Your adoption file was sent to America." She stopped speaking.

"What happened?"

She kissed my forehead. "My dearest little bird. It . . . came back. The files only stay active a certain amount of time."

The truth slapped me, making tears spring to my eyes. "Nobody wanted me."

"That may not be true. We don't know what happened or why."

I swiped the tears from my eyes and lifted my chin. "I didn't want to be adopted anyway."

"Well, it will be the best thing for Zhen An. She needs that surgery."

And there was nothing that anyone could do for my eyesight.

I knew she was right, but the truth made me angry anyway. "Being taken from her family is the best?"

Auntie Yang pulled me back so I had to look at her. "We are not her family, Wen Ming! She is not losing a family. She is gaining one. Do not be selfish and wish to keep her for yourself. She needs this."

I yanked myself from her grasp. "They are not her family. They will never be her family! I am her family. I'm her family. I am! I"—I couldn't breathe again—"am."

"You will always be her friend. But she needs more than what you or I or Uncle Zhou can give her. And she needs your love and good wishes for success with her new parents. I told you—you must be brave."

Yes, I would be brave. I would find a way to bring her home to me. Maybe I was not wealthy like the Americans. Maybe I could not pay for her surgery. But I loved her like they never could, and my love made me strong. Someday, somehow, I would best them, and then—

I would bring *mei mei* home and keep her with me forever.

FIFTEEN

Meg Lindsay, February 2006

Never try to reassure someone by saying, "We probably won't have to worry about that." It's a sure way of making whatever it is happen.

We spent the two weeks after receiving the referral falling in love with our daughter-to-be. I cradled her photo in my hands, holding it under different lighting, staring at it, touching it, until I could paint her picture with my eyes on the canvas of the world around me.

But when we received our travel approval, we saw that I would, indeed, be traveling to China by myself. Adopting Eva, by myself. Becoming a parent, by myself. The date of Lewis's experiment fell on the very day we were scheduled by the Chinese government to adopt Eva. What to do? We were caught like a bug between two elephant-sized government agendas. Neither was going to budge just because we had logistical problems. There were power-of-attorney papers to sign, and other hoops to jump through, but I'd be traveling alone.

I liked being alone, but not this way—not under these circumstances. The knowledge sucked the air from my lungs every time I thought of it. But for Eva, I would do it. I could be strong for her.

Beth and Adam's wedding was also happening, six days into the itinerary. I'd be a mother for two days by the time my sister married my ex-fiancé. She'd had the nerve to ask me to be her matron of honor. I hadn't had the nerve to say no.

Now I wished I'd told my family about the adoption months ago. Beth and my mother were going to be furious when I told them I'd have to bail on the wedding.

I agonized over how to phrase it, how to break the news. I practiced in front of my mirror, like a teen preparing for her first date. I discussed possible scenarios with Lewis until he fled to the study, claiming work to do on the experiment.

And in the end, it all just came tumbling out, clumsy and tactless, at the first Sunday dinner I'd been to at my parents' house since New Year's.

"I have an announcement!" I said over the din of after-dinner conversation.

"You're pregnant!" My mom grinned triumphantly.

"No . . ."

"Oh. Maybe you've just gained weight, then. Must be the holidays. Partying too much? You know alcohol is loaded with calories."

"Don't start with me, Mom." A year ago, I'd have cowered in silence and then ranted all the way home. Now I was getting closer to ditching the cowering entirely and skipping straight to the rant. But not quite. I sat up straighter and thought of Eva, my daughter, the one who was going to replace all these unhappy family moments with new joy. For her, I could be strong. I could be brave.

"I'm not starting anything. But I do wish that—"

I cut her off before she could start haranguing me about drinking. "We're adopting a child from China. She just turned six years old, and she has a cleft lip and palate. We're naming her Eva."

Nobody spoke. I don't think they were even breathing. My eyes met Adam's, and he raised his eyebrows in what almost seemed like a tiny salute of respect. I would have liked to believe that it was because I was taking charge of my own life, but I suspected it was more because I was finally "settling down" and having a child—even if it was in an unconventional way.

Then the silence exploded into a cacophony of exclamations and questions. For a moment, I soared on the rush of my family's excitement. A grip of irritation at myself dragged me back to earth. I didn't want to be so satisfied by their approval. I wanted not to care. It was easier that way.

Then my mother asked, "So when is all this happening?"

I looked to Lewis; he grabbed my hand and held it. I turned back to my mom and tried to keep my voice steady and confident. Eva. Just think of Eva. "We're leaving February 19."

"Wait—so soon? I thought these things took months." Beth frowned. It wouldn't be long now. Where was your friendly neighborhood natural disaster when you needed it? I'd take just about anything else—tornado, blizzard, earthquake, hurricane. Random spontaneous combustion. A stampede. Even a plague of grasshoppers.

I pictured my daughter's haunting eyes and the universe in them that I was waiting to explore. "They, uh, do. Take time, I mean." I dug my fingernails into Lewis's hand until he winced. I shot him an apologetic glance. "We started last April."

"And you are just now telling us?" My mother gave me the young-lady-you-are-in-big-trouble look that always made me feel fourteen years old. "It's a good thing you'll be back for the wedding."

"Yeah. About that . . ." I willed my breath to become steady and my heart to stop racing.

Beth leaned forward on the table. "You will be back for the wedding, right? We can let your child come, you know. Maybe she'd even like to be a second flower girl. I'll get her a dress."

That was sweet of her. Naive, but very kind. Drat. Why hadn't I told them earlier? "I won't be home until March fourth. I'm sorry. We didn't have any control over the timing."

Beth's eyes widened and she slumped back in her seat with a wail. "My wedding! What am I supposed to do? Why didn't you tell us sooner?"

"We just got the travel approval yesterday. I didn't have any say in the schedule. It's set by the Chinese government. I have to go."

My mother turned so cold, she had icicles dangling from her hair. "This is so like you, Meg. I'd been hoping maybe you'd changed, but you haven't. Same old self-centered behavior."

"Oh, like I planned for this to happen just to ruin Beth's wedding?" Usually, her icy blasts froze me and I couldn't think. But now, strength seeped into my bones. I stood up. "No! I'm not accepting that this time, Mom. I'm not the selfish one here. You're mad because I'm going to miss a wedding? If I was pregnant and went into labor the day before the wedding, would you be angry at me? I don't have any more control over this than I would if I were giving birth. So don't throw the 'selfish' label at me. I won't take it!"

My sister slammed her hands on the table. "You did the same thing to Adam!"

I snapped my gaze to her. "Yes, I know—it's Adam's wedding too. And I'm really sorry, okay?"

"No. That's not what I mean. This is exactly what you did when you broke up with him. You didn't even give him a chance. You didn't tell him you had feelings for anyone else. You didn't try to work it out. You waited until it had already happened and then you just dumped him."

Adam's face had gone a sickly blush, like a tomato caught between green and red. "Beth, that's enough."

A buzzing started in my ears, and my heart pounded. Beth had always been my one constant, my support.

"No, it's not enough. Someone has to make her see why everyone in this family is mad at her." She glared at me. "You love being the martyr. But we're not the villains here."

Not even thoughts of Eva were enough to clear my mind this time. Funny speckles of black and white floated across my vision, and the sound of my heartbeats was louder to me than the voices of my family.

Lewis guided me down to my chair. He took my hand. "This family is the worst advertisement for Christianity there could possibly be." He sounded calm, clinical, like he was commenting on a mathematical formula.

"You stay out of this!" my mother snapped.

"I've only really been around you guys for a little over a year now. But I've seen the effects of how you treat each other. You judge me for not believing in God—I know you do. But I'm judging you for saying you believe in God and then not acting like it."

"You have no right—"

Lewis cut off my dad's objection. "I'm not saying that the way Meg and I got together was the right way. But I do know that the thing between her and Adam was broken before I met her. And it's time you all stopped punishing her for being honest and putting an end to it."

"Who are you to tell us what to do?" my mother asked in her most frigid tone.

"Unfortunately, I'm part of this family. And I'm going to be the dad of a little girl—your granddaughter. And I'll be hanged if I'm going to let you hurt her and criticize her and control her the way you have your daughter. If you want Eva to be part of your life, then things between you and my wife have to change."

"You can't keep our granddaughter from us!" My mother's face had gone an angry white. Beth was crying, and Dad looked like he wanted to spank both of us. Adam looked like he might be sick.

Lewis glanced grimly at me and then back to my mother. "Try me."

No one said anything. I hung my head and tried to focus on keeping my breathing even and my hands from shaking.

Finally, Beth grabbed some more salad, dumping the lettuce on her plate before slamming the bowl back to the table. "Anyway, where am I supposed to find a maid of honor at this point?"

I tried to feel some sympathy for her—I remembered how stressful a wedding could be, especially when family couldn't, or in my case wouldn't, come. But the sting of her earlier accusations hadn't yet faded.

I tried to summon up Lewis's bold courage. My voice was trembling and high, but I forced myself to look at her. "I don't know, Beth. I should have told you no from the beginning. I wasn't comfortable with it, and I'm sorry I didn't tell you that when you asked. But now I'm going to China and adopting a beautiful little girl. You'll have a great wedding, and I'm sure you'll find someone to take my place."

Lewis nodded at me, a tiny smile voicing his approval.

We'd done it. We had stood up to them and survived. For Eva.

For Eva, I'd do anything.

SIXTEEN 六

Meg Lindsay, February 2006

My bed was a landscape—mountains and plains of clothing, pools of papers, a wasteland of shoes, a lake of socks, caverns of suitcases. It was a wilderness, hostile and confusing.

"I think you're overpacking." Lewis picked his way around random piles until he reached me. He massaged my shoulders.

"They gave me a packing list. At least I could cross off the diapers and formula. But I still have to bring her clothing and first aid supplies and things to keep her busy on the airplane." I sank down into a hill of underwear and pantyhose. "I don't even know what she likes to do! How am I going to keep her happy for a twenty-four-hour flight?"

He flopped on his stomach beside me, two of my bras falling across his back. When he tried to move them, they got tangled on his arm. He shook them off, smiling. "Not my style, I'm afraid. Weren't you telling me that a lot of parents buy clothes for their kids once they get to China and then donate them to the orphanage when they leave, to save space in their luggage?"

"Yeah, but I wouldn't want to leave any of her clothes. They'd be hers."

"It's just clothes. You're not going to keep every outfit she ever wears, are you? We'll need a bigger place."

"It's just that each outfit will have a story with it." I held up a soft pink chenille sweater and a pair of jeans I'd purchased at Gap

Kids. "When I look at this one, I might remember how she wore it to the Hard Rock Cafe in Guangzhou. Our travel group already has that planned." I rubbed my hand across a purple blanket sleeper with glittering silver stars stamped on it. "This will be what she wears the first night in the hotel. And this"—I laid a red Valentine's party dress across my lap—"is what she'll be wearing the first time she meets her daddy."

Lewis rolled onto his back and a stack of jeans fell on his head. I heard his laughter under the pile of denim. "We really will need a bigger place! Why don't you buy *your* clothes in China then and leave them?"

"I'm only taking a few pieces with me. I'm going to mix and match."

He shoved the jeans off and looked around. "A few?"

"I'm narrowing it down."

He raised his eyebrows. "Could you use some help?"

I plunged back into the swath of clothing. "Please!"

He held out his hand for the packing list and studied it with analytical efficiency. He was the yang to my yin, the reality to my fantasies, the practicality to my whimsy. How was I going to manage for two weeks without him? Become a parent without him? Be strong without him? I bit the inside of my cheek, forcing myself not to say anything. I'd already done enough whining. It was time to be resolute.

He set the list down and turned his dark brown eyes to me. "I'm wishing I'd decided to go with you."

"Me too." It wasn't a show of weakness to say it since he said it first.

"Or at least that you weren't going alone."

None of my family could have gone, because of Beth and Adam's wedding, even if I'd wanted them to. Cinnamon had the shop to run, and Audra had to teach school. There wasn't anyone else I was close enough to whom I'd want to travel with for two weeks and share the sort of intimate experience that I assumed would come along with becoming a mother to Eva. One of Lewis's cousins had offered, but I barely knew her. I had a feeling I'd want my privacy before this trip was done.

I gave Lewis a kiss. "I'll be fine. I'll have the rest of our travel group, and there'll be an agency representative with us the whole time. Even at the hotel. I won't be alone."

"I feel bad for staying home."

I nuzzled his neck. "I know. It's okay."

He picked up the Chinese-English Bible I had placed on my pillow. "You're not taking this, are you?"

"Yes. It's for Eva. I know she can't read much yet, but I want to see if they'll put her footprints in there when they take the footprints for the adoption certificate. And since we're putting her in Chinese school when she comes home, I hope someday she'll be able to read either version."

His grip on the book tightened, and so did his face. "Isn't it illegal to take Bibles to China?"

"Not your own personal copy. I suppose if I had a whole suitcaseful, they might have a problem with it."

I knew he wanted to say more, and I was pretty sure I wasn't going to like whatever it was.

"But this Bible is for Eva. Right?"

"Yes . . ."

He set it down and sat on the edge of the bed.

"What's wrong?" I sat next to him and rubbed his neck with one hand.

"We didn't really talk about this part. Religion."

Oh. My hand stilled on his neck. Then I started rubbing again. "Do we need to?"

"Yes. But I guess the night before you leave isn't the best timing."

I took his hand. "It's okay."

He rubbed his thumb on the back of my palm. "I respect your religious beliefs, but I don't want Eva brainwashed into being religious."

"Brainwashed? That doesn't sound respectful of my beliefs to me."

"I'm sorry." He closed his eyes a moment. "What I mean is that you were raised to believe a certain way. You didn't really have a choice. And when you grew up and decided you wanted to live your life differently, your family punished you for that. I don't want Eva to feel that sort of pressure—from either of us. I want her to be free to choose her own beliefs and her own path in life. And if that ends up being your religion, then I'm fine with that. But if she decides that's not what she believes, then I want you to accept that too."

A thin stream of air whooshed from my lips. How had I not seen this moment coming? I could almost hear my mother's voice: "This is what happens when you marry a nonbeliever—an atheist. He'll corrupt your children and encourage disbelief."

But was my faith that fragile? If my relationship with God was real, shouldn't it be able to stand up to scrutiny? To doubt? And Lewis had a point. Too many children in Christian homes weren't given the opportunity to choose faith or unbelief for themselves. Their only options were to ascribe to their parents' beliefs or to rebel. I didn't want to force Eva to make that choice.

I needed to proceed carefully. I couldn't handle fighting with Lewis on this last night before our lives would change forever. "So what do you want to see happen?"

He was being careful too. "I'd like to not have her go to church with you."

"And no Bibles? No Bible stories? No Christian stuff at all?"

"Well . . ."

I took a deep breath to slow myself down. "I don't want to hide my faith from my own daughter."

"I don't want to hide my beliefs from her either."

"And I don't want us to be in competition with each other—trying to win her over."

He winced. "Definitely not."

I huffed another sigh. "Why didn't our social worker discuss this with us?"

"Like she'd be able to work it out for us?"

I smiled at him. Then I kissed him, because he needed it. And I needed it. Needed to be reminded of our oneness, our intimacy, our love—despite the very deep differences between us.

He placed a soft kiss on my forehead. "I'm sorry. I just don't want her forced to go to church. Or to read the Bible."

"You think that's what happened to me? That I was forced?"

"Yes."

"There were a lot of behaviors—like going to church or not drinking or dancing—that I didn't have a choice about when I was growing up. But that's not faith. My faith is real; it's my choice. I jettisoned a lot of those rules when I met you, but my faith didn't go anywhere."

"I don't really see the difference. You just adjusted your beliefs to match how you wanted to live your life."

Was he right? A shiver of doubt raced through me. I turned my head and caught sight of a glass goblet full of bloodred wine and a plate of bread that looked like focaccia. I took the cup and the wine went down with a burst of heat and the sweetness of assurance and love. I offered it to Lewis, but he held up his hand and shook his head.

"There's more to this life than what you can see or taste." I swirled the wineglass and held it up to the light. The reflections in the wine broke into colors and images. Images of Lewis, of me, of Eva. Pictures of things that hadn't happened yet. Things that only God could know, and that I could only hope and pray he would make reality. "I think faith is being willing to look past what your senses tell you is true, so that you can find what is even more true." I watched an image of Lewis for a moment. "What's the name of that physics thing you're trying so hard to discover?"

"The Higgs boson?"

"That's it." I shook the glass, and the image of Lewis stumbled a bit and glared at me. I smiled apologetically. "I have faith that you'll find it. It's there, somewhere."

"You're just saying that because you know I want it so badly."

"You believe it exists, right?"

"Yes. Very reliable math points to it."

"You believe you can find it?"

"I hope very much that I'm part of the team that finds it. But that's just my hope."

"No." I watched Lewis in the glass walk to a podium to speak before hundreds of scientists. "Hope comes from faith. If you had no faith, you'd have no hope. You wouldn't be giving up going to China if you didn't believe deep down that you could do this—that you have to do this. That it's why you're alive, why you exist."

"I don't believe in faith. I don't like it. I like what I can prove. What I can see."

I gripped the glass tighter and stared at it, asking God to help me not lose my temper. He answered with more pictures. "Faith sees too. I see Eva hugging another Chinese girl, a friend, in high school maybe—she's going to have a normal life, full of love and laughter."

Lewis gave me a sort of indulgent, wouldn't-that-be-nice smile. He didn't look angry. So I told him all the other pictures in my heart, the things I could only trust God to make true—orphanages transformed into places of love, laughter, and sunshine; Eva with her face whole and unscarred. Families that weren't broken anymore. Dark, old wounds healed.

My own mother and father, holding me, smiling.

My voice broke and I couldn't continue.

Lewis slipped his arm around me and pulled the cup out of my hand. He stared contemplatively, gently at it and swirled it around. "You make me almost wish I had faith too. But I think it's too late for me."

I wanted to argue with that, but instead I wiped a stray tear off my cheek. "That's why I want Eva to come to church. I want her to be able to have faith. To be able to hope."

"You think a church is the only place to learn to hope?"

"No, but I do think it's one of the best."

He set the glass on the end table, next to the focaccia bread. "What about taking her to different churches, exposing her to a variety of religions?"

I grabbed a shirt off its hanger and folded it vigorously. "You think religions are interchangeable?"

"You are biased toward your own religion. I don't want her to be biased. You know how much hatred is stirred just because one religion thinks it's better than all the others."

I took a slow breath, willing myself not to show my frustration. "That would be very confusing for a six-year-old. How about if I just teach her about my faith for right now and when she's older—say high school—I promise to go with her to other religious services so we can talk about them together?"

"You think you can do that without criticizing the other religions?"

"Lewis! Do I ever criticize anyone else for their beliefs?"

"All right. I'm sorry. I just . . ." He took the shirt that I'd been wadding out of my hands and smoothed it on the corner of the bed. "Promise me you won't start acting like your parents, okay? Promise me you won't indoctrinate her."

He didn't understand what he was asking of me. I looked at the cup again, and this time in the jeweled red glow of the wine, I saw centuries of men and women and children loving one another when it was impossible, facing death with courage, filled with peace in the midst of chaos, giving, sacrificing, patience and quiet wisdom and strength in their eyes. "I promise—to teach her only the very best of my faith. The kindness and gentleness, respect and peace. I will do everything I can to show her what it means to love no matter what, and to serve generously, and to care about people who are broken and hurting, regardless of their faith or actions. If that's indoctrination, then so be it."

Lewis caught his breath, and I waited motionless for his response. Finally: "Could you at least find a different church? I hate the idea of her growing up in your parents' church. I know you have friends there and that your parents will be mad if you leave, but since this is all about a fresh start, could you give Eva one at church too?"

I wrapped Lewis in my arms, breathing my gratitude into him. My parents would be very angry, and I would miss my friends. But since Adam had begun preaching there, it hadn't felt like home to me anymore. It was time. Time to show good faith to Lewis. Time to show that faith could be good. Time to put our family ahead of the one I'd grown up in. Time to start fresh.

"You drive a hard bargain, mister," I murmured.

He kissed me. "Thank you."

I'd been a fool to think that the differences in our beliefs could remain in the background forever. I looked at the wine cup again, trying to see in it a reflection of the three of us attending church together. There were no such reflections, but I did see one of Lewis and me, holding hands and looking down at a sleeping Eva.

I could accept that. We didn't have to have it all worked out and be in total agreement. We just had to be willing to work together and find ways to love each other no matter what. And judging from the reflection in the wine, I could have faith we'd do exactly that.

Wen Ming, February 2006

S he was taken away from me on a rainy, cold Thursday in February. I had barely slept that night, just holding her close to me, trying to memorize the shape and feel of her. The smell and sound of her. Another *mei mei* stolen from me. But this one was the most beloved of all. A true sister, my only real friend.

A hard tangle of anger had been growing in me since Auntie Yang had given me the news. It scared me. I was not yet eight years old, and my feelings were dark and powerful. They were much more than I knew how to handle. But Auntie Yang wanted me to be brave. I was afraid that if she knew how angry and fearful I felt, she would send me away. She had said she wouldn't, but I was beginning to doubt if anyone could be trusted to keep her word.

My *mei mei*'s hair was done up in pigtails, and Auntie Yang dressed her in a warm sweater and cute jeans. She was adorable, and my heart and stomach hurt when I looked at her. Even if I ever saw her again, I might not be able to *see* her.

I couldn't eat breakfast. I couldn't speak. I followed her around the flat, touching her however I could until she protested to Auntie. Then I followed her, the best I could, with my eyes, squinting and straining to create as many images as possible to hold on to.

It hurt to breathe.

Auntie was watching me. I felt it. Felt her concern and sadness for me swish around me like warm bathwater. I didn't want to cause her to worry, but I could not think about that. Couldn't think about anything beyond the very next second.

It hurt to think.

I don't think she understood what was happening. She'd been told, and she said she wanted this, but she didn't seem to be very sad about leaving me. She prattled on, asking Auntie Yang questions about America, about her new parents, about the airplane ride.

Why didn't she feel sad? I wanted her to hurt as much as I did. I wanted her to cling to me and kick and scream that she would not go without her *jie jie*. Instead, she seemed excited.

It hurt. Everywhere.

Auntie Yang would drop me off at school and then take her to the government offices to meet . . . I couldn't bear to think about it. While Auntie finished getting ready, I sat with Zhen An on our bed, holding her hand and swinging my foot against the side rail.

"You seem sad, *jie jie*."

"I will miss you very, very much."

She put her hands on each side of my face and leaned close to me so I could see her. "Don't be sad."

I bit my tongue to try to stop my eyes from filling with tears. I could not speak. I flung my arms around her and held her tightly. For a moment, our hearts beat together, in unison, and our souls spoke to each other.

Don't love them, mei mei. *Love me. Just me. Keep me in your heart*, mei mei. *Only me.*

Only you, jie jie.

My arms convulsed; the air choked in my lungs.

Don't forget me, mei mei.

Never, jie jie.

Auntie Yang called to us and I drew back, wiping my face. It was time to go.

Too soon, we reached my school. I did not see how I could learn anything today, but Auntie said I could not go with her and Zhen An. Our paths had to part here, in front of my school. I thought I would never love school again because every time I came here, I would remember this is where I lost her.

"Here," I said, lifting my crane feather bottle from my neck. I put it around her neck. "I want you to take it."

"I shouldn't take your feather."

"You found it, remember? It is good luck for your surgery and new life."

She nodded, suddenly formal with me. "Thank you."

Auntie Yang patted my shoulder. She wanted me to hurry.

It was time. I grabbed Zhen An to me, the end of her ponytail whipped wet against my face. My body shivered, but not with cold.

"Wen Ming, darling . . ." Auntie Yang was crying. I heard her. "We have to."

"I can't! Don't make me." I knew I should be stronger. My tantrum was scaring Zhen An. Her breath was coming in quick pants, and she was restless against me. "I can't let go." I leaned my head on her shoulder and sobbed.

Auntie Yang knelt beside us and put her arms around both of us. I couldn't understand whatever she was murmuring. Then she lifted her head and spoke to someone behind us.

It was one of my teachers. She put her hands on my shoulders and gently separated me from Zhen An. My hands trailed down Zhen An's arms to her hands.

"Wo *ai ni, mei mei.*" I love you, little sister.

"Wo *ai ni, jie jie.*" Her face was wet too. With rain or tears or both.

The teacher took one of my hands and tugged slowly, kindly.

Our palms slid against each other. My fingers held hers, which were warm and damp, smooth, soft. I tried to make that moment of final contact last forever, but finally, a sliver of cold air pierced the connection. Separated us. I held my breath so I would not scream.

She smiled a little at me and waved. The teacher led me one step back. And then another. And another. After only a few steps, I could not see her anymore. I was glad my last image of her was a smile.

I do not remember anything about school that day. I only remember the hurt that nothing could relieve.

And that is how I lost my little sister.

EIGHTEEN

Meg Lindsay, February 2006

The day I received my daughter, the skies rained, as if they were mourning for someone else. And I supposed they must've been — it was a day of rejoicing for me, but somewhere that day, someone had died. A marriage had fallen apart. A dream had been dashed. And so the heavens cried, reminding me that not everything centered on me and my happiness.

As I dressed, alone for the last time in my Shanghai hotel room, it was hard to remember that everyone in the world was not as gloriously giddy as I. I looked out my window across a sleek and exotic skyline that wore a gray cloak of rain, and the rhythm of the city beat out a chant, "At last. At last. At last."

My fourth day in China, and it still seemed like I'd set foot in a fantasy realm. The twenty-four-hour flight from Chicago to Beijing had been my initiation into this journey. It had stripped me of all that was familiar until even my language was torn away. All around me were faces darker than mine. I remember how we chased the sun, and how its face glittered off miles of frozen plains for hours until time ceased to have meaning. Finally we tackled the sun and sent it spinning over the horizon to give welcome to the endless starry darkness.

My old life had fallen away somewhere over the ocean, and I emerged from that flight like a phoenix, reborn, anonymous, voiceless, invisible — in a land where I was as helpless as a child. I became part of the stew of humanity, mashed against strangers, becoming a stranger to myself, without identity, without a name, herded through immigration checkpoints like livestock. I could only hope that the crowd was headed to the baggage claim.

When I saw a handsome man waving a flag with our adoption agency's logo on it, I was tempted to throw my arms around him and sob. I was, he informed me, the last of the travel group to arrive. He hurried me to the hotel, a grand edifice, far more elegant than anything I'd stayed in before. He and a smartly uniformed bellboy deposited me in my room. I had barely enough energy to phone Lewis to tell him I'd arrived before diving into one of the narrow twin beds.

I spent two whirlwind days in the murky coldness that was Beijing, dodging bicycles and scooters and trying to avoid being run over by pedestrians or vehicles. Our agency sent us there first, to recover from our trip, and to experience the capital city of our child's country of birth. Standing on the Great Wall and walking the grounds of the Forbidden City, shivering in my light coat and my breath steaming before me, I felt the presence of thousands of years and millions of bodies across the ages, pressing and shaping me, entering my heart and taking pieces of me to keep as their trophy. But beneath the wonder, my heart beat with impatient rhythm. These ancient glories would always be here, waiting for me. I had come for my little girl.

I'd arrived in Shanghai the day before, when the skies had been bright—at least more so than the dim haze of Beijing. This flight, I'd sat with others in my travel group, getting acquainted with the families with whom I'd be spending the next week and a half. With them, it was easier to block out the strangeness around me, to feel less strange myself—until a group of giggling young Chinese women ran to me in the Shanghai airport, cameras in hand, wanting a picture of me. Our agency representative said it was because of my blond hair and height. I tried to take it in stride, tried to have fun with it, but my insides trembled, and my fingers were numb by the time I waved good-bye to them. I wished I had a hat or had dyed my hair. I didn't like drawing attention to myself.

I dined with two other families in my travel group in one of the hotel's four restaurants. This one had three small Chinese junks moored in a pool in the center of the dining room, which looked like a dockside boardwalk. We ate pigeon and duck in one of the boats, the waitstaff surreptitiously laughing at our poor attempts to use chopsticks to cut the meat into bite-sized pieces. They might not have laughed if they'd noticed the lettuce leaf one of my travel mates slapped over the duck's head so it would not stare at us while we ate it.

I longed to discover Shanghai, find its heart, memorize it, eat it, drink it in. I wanted to store as much of it as I could fit into my heart, so that in later years, when Eva's memories of her homeland had blurred with time, I could be her memories, I could give Shanghai back to her. I could not do all that in only one week, but I would do what I could.

But there'd be no time today to eat or drink Shanghai. Today was all for Eva.

I couldn't eat. The hotel tried too hard to offer a "western-style breakfast" anyway. Runny yogurt in small glass jars, brown hard-boiled eggs (precracked), lumpy oatmeal, bacon and sausage, a huge array of pastries and breads. The fruit looked beautiful — bright, glistening, seductive. But we'd been warned to stay clear of fresh fruit — since we didn't know what sort of water had been used to wash it. So I looked longingly at the only thing I might have been able to force down and decided breakfast wasn't a good idea this morning. Tea was good enough.

I wasn't the only one who looked nervous. Several in my travel group eschewed breakfast, and we huddled in knots in the hotel lobby, waiting for the tour van that would take us to the government offices for the adoptions. We alternated between fitful, jagged conversation and restless, apologetic silence. We attracted curious gazes from the mix of strangers in the lobby. The intensity and intimacy of our emotions clouded the lobby in a quivering, shifting mist. Several couples offered their condolences again that I was making this trip solo. They offered their help, but hesitantly — afraid I would actually take them up on it. We were all afraid. Ecstatically terrified of the great unknown we were plunging toward with every second.

Even the death-defying traffic of Shanghai wasn't enough to jolt me out of the kaleidoscopic swirl of fear and anticipation, regret for

Lewis's absence, and pride that I'd successfully survived four days in China on my own. Every second was bringing me closer to her, to my future, to motherhood, to the love of a child and the greatest responsibility I would ever know.

The gray government office building loomed over our heads as we hurried through the rain to get inside. None of us spoke much now. We had each retreated inside ourselves, a last few moments of introspection, our emotions contracting into tight, heavy, trembling spheres inside us.

I tried not to envy the couples who clutched each other's hands and drew their strength from the other. We were led to a cheerless waiting room: wooden floor, worn carpet, with several faded chairs. I settled down beside a single woman named Dee with whom I'd made acquaintance in Beijing. She was traveling with her mother, and they sat together, fussing over the most well-stocked diaper bag I'd ever seen. I had a small bag too, but just a few things I thought might help Zhen An warm up to me. I pulled out my teddy bear and held it on my lap.

"How old is your child?" I asked her.

"Thirteen months. Do you want to see a picture?" She had the photo out before I could point out there was no need. I'd see her new daughter very soon.

The thought made my heart skip and my breath stumble. Soon. Very soon.

I studied the photo. "Beautiful."

"What about yours?"

"She just turned six. She was a waiting child—cleft lip."

Dee smiled at me and turned back to check her diaper bag again. "Are you nervous about getting an older child?"

"I'm just nervous, period."

Dee laughed—too loud and high-pitched for the level of humor. She was nervous too.

Then something in the air changed, tilted, wavered like a mirage on a summer highway.

She was here. I felt her presence. Blood pounded in my head, but not enough to keep pace with my need for air.

An adoption official burst into the room and called for our attention. In broken English, she explained the procedure and handed out yet another round of documents to sign.

"Are the babies here yet?" someone called out.

She nodded. "You see them soon. Papers first."

The signing took on a party feel with that. The babies were here in the building, breathing the same air, standing on the same floors. Within reach. Almost ours.

The official collected from each of us the mandatory "donation" of three thousand dollars that would go to the orphanage to help provide care for the orphans remaining at the Home. I tried to remember to hand it to the official with two hands—a one-handed pass would be disrespectful. I almost forgot, and pulled the envelope away from her to put both my hands on it. Her eyes widened, and she gave me a little look that seemed to say, "Americans really are strange." But she smiled and nodded anyway, and handed me more documents to sign. It seemed the paperwork would never be completed.

Finally, a hush fell over us. She marshaled us into the Chinese idea of a line—a crowded mishmash of anticipation. We pressed around her as she led us to another room. The children were there.

I'd read on my adoption e-mail loops that there was usually some sort of little official giving-and-receiving ceremony. If our orphanage had such a thing planned, it was somehow thwarted, because the next we knew, our children's names were being called and parents were pushing through to get to the auntie holding their child.

One by one, the room sorted into trios or pairs, video cameras flying and still cameras snapping. Hushed exclamations and gentle cooing. Tears. Reverent touches of a tiny finger. Caressing a nose, cheeks, hair.

The air filled with the fragrance of motherhood and fatherhood blooming—a salty, tear-laced perfume of unutterable sweetness and poignancy.

But where was she?

Finally, I heard her name called. I edged around the newly united families who were blissfully unaware of my last struggle to reach the object of my desire. I wished I'd had someone to video this moment for me, to capture it in a photo, but it would live in brilliant color in my memory forever.

At last, I reached the auntie whose voice had said my daughter's name. She was much shorter than I, and her face was round and kind. Her eyes looked tired, reserved, like she'd already had a difficult morning. She studied me, measuring me. I tried to hold steady against her prodding. Her approval seemed very important to me. She nodded and smiled, a gap showing between her front teeth.

She squatted beside a tiny form next to her. "This is Zhen An," she said, looking up at me. Her words were precise and clear, but her voice trembled slightly.

This was it. I took a quick, steadying breath and knelt beside the child. I looked into those eyes that had filled my dreams for months. I saw the poor, deformed mouth. It didn't look grotesque to me. I'd never seen a more beautiful child. My throat tightened and I heard again the delicate melody that had called me to China to begin with.

I blinked back tears. I didn't want my crying to be her first memory of me.

I handed her my teddy bear. She looked at it but would not touch it. "Hello," I choked out. *"Ni hao."* The Chinese phrase felt awkward on my tongue. We'd been studying as much Chinese as we could, knowing we would have to be able to communicate on at least a basic level with her until she started picking up English.

She just stared back at me, somberly. Unresponsive. Her only movement was to grab her auntie's hand more tightly. I glanced at the auntie. She grimaced and said something in Chinese to Zhen An.

Zhen An's eyes widened and she shrank back, shaking her head. She hid her face against the auntie's shoulder. The woman closed her eyes, her face tightening with pain. Then she looked at me again.

"You take her now."

Something was going wrong. I felt it. I wanted nothing more than to pull this child into my arms, to feel her body against me, but it didn't feel right. Didn't feel safe. Not yet.

I curled my fingers around Zhen An's free hand. At the same time, the auntie slipped from Zhen An's grasp and stepped back. I heard a crack like loud thunder coming from the auntie, and I knew that the one step she'd taken had required great effort. Something had broken just now. Something in that Chinese woman.

I swallowed hard and smiled at Zhen An. I pulled on her hand, willing her to take a step away from the auntie.

A piercing wail exploded from her. It knocked me back, but I still held her hand. I yanked her toward me without meaning to, and she became a whirlwind of screaming limbs and thrashing cries.

I felt the energy of all the room directed at me. Everyone's attention rooted on the drama we were enacting on the office floor. A surging wave of numb coldness washed over me as I tried to calm the frantic child in my grasp. I wanted to scream, "Don't look at me! Don't watch me!" but all my focus had to be on containing Zhen An.

She stomped and swung her free arm, smacking me in the cheek. Her panting screams battered my mind. I didn't know what to do. Let her go? Hold on? No one had ever told me how to comfort a hysterical child. No one said it would be like this. They never warned me she'd be terrified.

I was terrified too. I wanted to run away, out of the room. I wanted to hide.

I wanted to go home.

The auntie finally crouched beside us, crooning in Zhen An's ear. The child clung to her, gasping and shuddering. A jealous shiver sped through me. This woman obviously had Zhen An's trust and affection. I wanted it. I knew it would take time to build that relationship. I had tried to stay realistic about that.

But nothing had prepared me to fail. To be rejected. I choked back a sob. "I'm sorry."

The auntie watched me over Zhen An's head. Tears streaked her face. "I am sorry also." She heaved herself to her feet, carrying Zhen An. She spoke with an adoption official, who nodded at her.

I had one moment of wild fear that they were going to take Zhen An away again. But then the auntie gave me a grim smile. "Come. More quiet room."

I followed her out of the room, away from the stares of the other parents. They all looked so happy, so idyllic with their new babies. My failure tasted acrid.

We settled in a nearby office, but the auntie kept Zhen An on her lap.

"My name is Yang Hua."

"I'm Meg. Meg Lindsay. Or just Meg."

"I am pleased to meet you, Meg." She spoke in Chinese to the girl and pointed at me, smiling encouragingly. But Zhen An only pressed herself tighter against Yang Hua. The auntie sighed. "Is very difficult for her."

"I know."

"Difficult for you too?"

"Oh yes." Dream-dashingly, heart-slashingly difficult. "I am so sorry I scared her."

"Not your fault." Yang Hua rubbed Zhen An's back slowly, in a figure eight, with the confident manner of a familiar caregiver, someone who knew exactly what Zhen An's preferences were, knew what would give her comfort. It made me feel sore and hollow inside.

"Are you her foster mother?"

"Yes. For about one year or more."

I knew she'd been in foster care. The information had said so. But nobody told me I'd be meeting the foster mother. In my arrogance, I had assumed that a foster family would not have a close bond with the child. But here we were, with Yang Hua, the loving foster mother, and Zhen An clinging to her on one side of the room, and me, the scary, foreign nonmother on the other side.

My tears started again. I brushed them away with a muttered apology. Yang Hua politely looked away, down at Zhen An, whose breathing seemed to be more steady now.

"Meg, is not your fault. Is my fault." Yang Hua gave me a small, pained smile. "I should have prepared her better. It is my first time as foster mother. I did not know what to expect."

"She loves you." The words hurt me, like crunching on a handful of straight pins.

"She will love you too. She need time."

"I know." I was silent for a moment, watching the love flow between her and Zhen An. It was a deep red, glowing and sparkling in a silent stream of understanding, passing through Yang Hua's hands and into Zhen An and back again.

"Yang Hua?"

She looked over at me again.

"You love her."

Her eyes slid back down to Zhen An. "Yes. Very much."

I didn't want to pry, but I had to know. "Then why are you letting her go? Why didn't you adopt her?"

She clamped her lips shut, and I worried that I'd offended her. But then, "She need operation. Is too expensive in China."

I squeezed my eyes shut. Tried to steady my breathing. I knew I had to say my next words. My conscience demanded it. My God asked it of me—like Abraham of old. He wanted me to give her up.

"If I paid for the surgery, could you adopt her?"

Yang Hua froze, staring at me. "You would do that?"

I nodded, unable to say more.

The questions and amazement in her eyes shamed me. I was no hero. It killed me to contemplate returning home with empty arms. But I couldn't be the one to tear apart a family. I couldn't live with myself.

Finally, she stammered a reply. "You are very kind. But . . ." She looked away again. "Chinese see adoption different. It is not same as America. Adopt child is . . . embarrassing. Many parent don't tell child he is adopted. They pretend he is their own. They want only a baby. That way no one know."

"But you don't feel that way."

"No. But my husband and I . . . we want to have a baby. Our own baby. And we have a second foster daughter. She is almost blind. Very expensive. We cannot adopt only Zhen An and not Wen Ming. They are like sister. Best friend. We can't take both."

I wish I could say I didn't feel relieved when she told me this, but relief rushed through my bones. "I am sorry. I didn't know I was separating Zhen An from a family."

"Wen Ming is very sad. Hard to make her let go this morning. Her teacher had to help. This is why Zhen An probably so upset. She doesn't know what this mean."

Now I felt even worse. There was a second brokenhearted child involved. I was a monster. A greedy, wealthy, foreign monster that tore apart happy homes.

Yes, I know that's unfair, but the bleak, hateful description swept down on me like bone-chilling rain.

"Zhen An is a good girl. She just need time to know you. She will get better soon."

I rummaged in my bag for my notebook and a pen. I needed to stay in contact with this woman. It was the right thing to do. She seemed gladdened by that suggestion, and my heart clenched again at the thought of the horrible pain this separation would cause—that I would cause.

I had to win Zhen An's heart. Somehow, I vowed to myself, I'd make her life happy again. I'd make up for everything she was losing. I'd shower her with so much love that she wouldn't be able to help but love me back.

"She is asleep, I think," Yang Hua whispered. "You come take her and I will leave."

I wondered if that was a good idea. Wouldn't it traumatize her further to wake up with her foster mother gone? But the trauma of Yang Hua escaping while she was awake might be even worse. There would be pain, no matter what.

Was this what becoming a mother was like? This bladelike certainty that—no matter your best intentions—you were going to cause your child pain?

I drew a slow breath. "Okay."

Yang Hua dipped her face and rested it on Zhen An's head for a moment, her eyes closed. I saw more moisture collect on her cheeks. My heart clenched at this final good-bye. I didn't yet know how she was feeling, but someday, I was sure I would understand.

She raised her head and nodded at me. "Please write to me. Or call. Anytime. I want to help. I do love her."

"Thank you." I slipped across the floor toward her. "I am glad I had a chance to meet you."

"I am too."

I sat next to her and she slowly shifted toward me.

We stared at each other for a moment that seemed to hang suspended in time. I saw trust and acceptance reflected in the black depths of her eyes. In a soft flash, I saw the rest of her day. How she would return to work at the orphanage, with her grief bottled inside her, how she would pick up that other child from school and travel silently home. The somber dinner. The quiet sobbing late that night as she was held in her husband's arms.

I saw it all, and I loved her for it. Certain I was breaking a million cultural taboos, I leaned forward and kissed her forehead.

"Here," she murmured, not looking at me. "Take her. I leave quickly."

The transfer was smooth. Zhen An barely stirred. Yang Hua stood with silent grace, laid her hand on Zhen An's head for one more moment, and then bolted out of the room.

I held my sleeping daughter a few minutes more, until the adoption official entered the room and quietly informed me there was more paperwork.

Always more paperwork.

The rest of the day was full of Zhen An's screams and cries, broken only by minutes of shuddering, sniffling quiet in which it seemed her spirit turned inside itself, lowered the shades, shut the doors . . . so it could grieve alone.

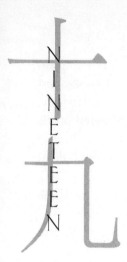

NINETEEN 九

Meg Lindsay, February 2006

Zhen An—my little Eva—had finally fallen asleep on the twin bed closest to the window. Her face was still flushed and sweaty from crying, and every two or three breaths shuddered from her, aftershocks of having the foundations of her world heaved around her this morning.

I cradled her small hand in my palm. I lowered my lips to it and brushed them against the soft skin. It seemed a strange liberty to take, and yet she was my daughter now.

"I'm sorry," I whispered. The agency had warned us that the transition would be difficult. But I hadn't thought that the pain would begin so soon.

What had I thought? That she'd throw herself into my arms crying "Mama" with tears of joy?

Mama . . . I was no mother. I was a thirty-two-year-old career musician sitting alone in a Shanghai hotel room with a strange child in my bed. A child who seemed to hate me. It felt like legalized kidnapping, not parenthood.

I'd wanted the tears of joy so very badly.

I looked at the clock. Eleven o'clock in the evening; nine in the morning in Chicago. Lewis would be at Fermilab doing whatever it was that they did to coax the universe to give up its secrets.

He should have been here with me. Should have been snuggled with me in the ridiculously narrow twin bed, looking out across the skyline of Shanghai that winked at me through the window. He should have been here to explore every tiny finger and her nose and her perfect ears.

But I was alone. Alone with a child who was terrified and heart-broken.

I hated the universe and its secretive ways. Despised the hold it had over my husband.

This was not what being a mother was supposed to be like. A smothering restlessness pressed around me. I was exhausted but the bed promised no rest, only an endless dance of the questions and doubts in my mind.

I shoved one of the upholstered armchairs to face the window. I sat and leaned on the sill to press my forehead against the cool pane.

God help me, what had I done? I couldn't possibly be ready for this—for being a mother. It was too late now. The fees had been paid, the papers signed, the deed done.

Her footprint had been stamped in ink the color of blood.

But none of that could make me truly this child's mother. What would, I didn't know. They didn't cover that part in the adoption workshops. Nobody ever explained how the hearts of two strangers could join in that most intimate of bonds.

Mother. Child.

What had I been thinking? How naive.

I stared at the Shanghai night sky. It was black. The brassy glow of the city shielded the stars from my view, the man-made collud-ing with the natural to keep yet more secrets from me. If I could peel back the sheen, I would polish the blackness until the stars shone like metal studs in leather. I would force the sky to yield its secrets.

A faint glimmer of light. And then another.

The stars grew bigger, brighter, greater in number, until a trail of them stretched across the sky, more pure and more vivid than the paltry lights crafted by human hands.

Like a rose in time-exposed photography, each star unfurled into a human form. Women, beautiful Chinese women, promenaded across the sky. Their faces, etched in starlight, were like calligraphic scrolls singing the poetry of poverty, struggle, and the fire of hope and dignity that no hardship can extinguish.

The women joined hands, and as I studied their faces, they began to look familiar. A curve of an eyebrow, the arch of a mouth, the glow of an eye.

Somehow, even after only a day, I knew these features. I recognized them, and they sparked a hot, possessive joy inside me.

My daughter. Mine. She had those hands, and that chin, and hair with the same gloss and texture. My child. My little girl.

The unbroken line of ancestors stretched from one horizon to the other, east to the dawn of civilization and west to the present, curving above my window, so close the city pigeons could have landed on their shoulders. Some wore the clothing of peasants, others the gowns of nobility, but all of them were strong, graceful, wise.

All of them were Chinese.

They stared back at me, and in their eyes a myriad of emotions swirled—apprehension, curiosity, even envy. They turned their heads to the west, and I followed their gaze. Closest to me, where the past met the present, there was an empty space. A space where the mother ought to have been. It was a space that waited for something. Someone.

For me?

They looked back at me, and I understood now the questions in their eyes. How could I fill that space? How could I make the lineage whole and unbroken? How could I even dare to try?

They challenged me with their questions, with doubt and disapproval in their eyes. A defensive something reared in me. Was I not as strong, as hopeful, as resilient and dignified? Did I need to be Chinese to join my hands with theirs? Must their blood flow in my body?

"I love her," I told them, and somehow I knew it was true. She was a stranger to me no longer. I put my hand across my heart. "I promise you this, with my life—I will always be encouraging. I will accept her just the way she is. She'll have my trust, my patience, my forgiveness. I'll always be there for her, I'll put her first. This is love. And I will teach her to love you and respect and honor you. But she belongs to me now too."

My heart creaked open, a jeweled box with rusty hinges. The inside was raw, torn, unbearably sensitive. I lifted Eva and placed her inside, where she curled like a kitten that had found a warm cushion near a fire. I held open my arms to invite the others, those ancient and seeing others, to enter as well. Letting them in hurt, like touching a broken blister, but I felt full and protective with the new burden I now carried in my heart.

Slowly, one by one, the disapproval faded from their eyes. One at a time, they smiled at me, acceptance in their faces, pride, and even relief.

They held out their hands to me and I reached for them, not quite touching, but I felt a connecting surge flare between us. It wrapped around me and spread to my sleeping Eva, pulling us into the line, which was no longer a line but a circle where past and present danced together. And I was part of them, and they of me. And we were all within Eva, her heart, her blood—it was us. Together, joined by a bond that could transcend time and distance.

And without words I vowed to them that the one whose place I was usurping would not be forgotten. She would be included in this circle, somehow; if not in this lifetime, then in eternity. I loved her because she was part of Eva, and she was part of me.

And these women understood. I felt their peace and satisfaction. Embracing, yet releasing. Sending me out, yet holding me close.

I stared at them for a timeless moment, until, like candles burned to stubs, they flickered and shrank and faded into the glowing lights of Shanghai.

TWENTY

Meg Lindsay, February 2006

I'd never known true exhaustion until I became a mother. That soul-deep weariness that comes not just from lack of sleep, but also from the stress of all my senses being sharpened, heightened, and the knowledge that there was an innocent life in my hands, dependent on me for everything. How could I sleep? I lay in the darkened Shanghai hotel room night after night, tossing on the hard, narrow bed in half wakefulness, wondering if she would be all right, if she'd still be there in the morning, if she'd ever accept me.

There were no tantrums after that first day. No screams, no tears, no thrashing or flailing.

No anything.

No smiles, no words, no attempts to communicate. No eye contact.

Just a shuttered stare and compliant passivity—the world's best-behaved doll. I'd never seen anything that frightened me more.

Despite the small fortune I would face in international phone bills, I called our adoption agency. I called our pediatrician. I called my therapist. They all said that it was part of her grief process, that this happens sometimes. That she'd come out of it when she was ready.

I couldn't accept that. I knew in my mind that what they were saying was true, that it wasn't a personal rejection of me. I'd read about it, Lewis and I had discussed the possibility that she could respond this way. I hadn't gone into this ignorant of what could happen.

But nothing can really prepare a person for the reality of it.

I took her on all the tours our agency provided for us while we were in Shanghai waiting for her passport to be processed. I saw a real panda for the first time in my life—smaller than I'd expected, slow and gentle, easy to love. I tried to commit to memory what it felt like to walk down streets crowded with humanity—so many people, most of them faceless in my mind. So close to me. Brushing up against me, heedless of my American sense of personal space. But the women! Whether they were dressed in black business suits and high heels or wearing hooded jackets and clogs, walking, riding bikes, stepping into a bus—I couldn't help but follow them with my eyes and wonder . . .

Was this one the mother of my child?

We ate at a corner restaurant—a true-to-life Chinese fast-food-style café crowded with busy employees on their lunch hours. The delicious smells had lured Dee and me, and two other couples, to stand outside and study the pictures on the menu placard, debating whether to go in and try to order, until finally a restaurant employee noticed us American stragglers and came outside to help.

Through all of this, my little Eva followed me like a flesh-and-blood specter. She complacently trudged through gardens and parks, museums and zoos—and only the smallest occasional flicker of interest revealed that she was even aware of her surroundings. She ate rice, if I placed it in front of her, but she ignored any other food. When she had to use the restroom, she stood silently, legs pressed together, and waited for me to take her.

Some of the other families were having similar trouble with their babies, but most of them were already happily engaged in the process of bonding with their new children. They sent me sympathetic, pitying looks, but then they'd turn back to their own child and coax another smile or giggle out of her. And each time that happened, it felt like my heart was being dipped in acid.

I tried to keep a steady flow of cheerful chatter, using as many of the Chinese phrases as I could.

"*Ni zhen piao liang.*" You are so beautiful.

"*Dao shang dian guang yi guang.*" Let's go shopping.

"*Wo hen gao xing zuo ni ma ma.*" I am happy to be your mama now.

"*Rang wo gei ni shu tou.*" Let's brush your hair.

"*Gai chi fan le.*" Time to eat.

But her face remained impassive, except for the occasional confused quirk of an eyebrow that I attributed to bad pronunciation or my atrocious accent.

When I ran out of things to say in my mangled Chinese, I switched to English. "Just wait until your baba meets you. He's going to adore you. Who wouldn't? I just talked with him last night on the phone, while you were asleep. I miss him so much. But it sounds like his experiment is going great! I'm so proud of your baba, aren't you? I thought you would be. Okay, kiddo, let's take a look at the schedule for today. Hey, look here, Eva! We're getting your passport today. That means we will be set for Guangzhou tomorrow. Won't that be nice?"

And when my manic, frantic monologue wound down into silence, I would think all the things that I couldn't say aloud—in any language.

Please, darling Eva-girl. Please love me. Let me be your mama. Let me into your world. Don't be empty anymore, don't be sad. Please. I can't stand the thought that maybe I've broken you—when all I wanted to do was help you heal. Help us all heal. I have to make you happy, don't you see?

I must.

And my thoughts would finally disintegrate into fragments of prayers and disjointed pleading that only God could understand.

Once we received our children's passports, we relocated to Guangzhou for the final week of the trip—to keep our appointments with the U.S. consulate there and get the kids' American visas. Eva handled the plane ride with stiff stoicism. I tried to pull her close, to reassure her, but she didn't respond. We hit some turbulence, and I saw the flash of fear in her face, but still she wouldn't let me comfort her. She gripped the armrests with fingertips pressed white, and when I tried to take her hand, she slipped it from my grasp and returned it to the armrest, staring straight ahead the entire time.

I set my teddy bear on her lap. I'd tried to give it to her several times, but she had ignored it. This time, she grabbed its frayed ribbon and trapped it between her fingers and the armrest.

It was better than nothing.

Going from Shanghai to Guangzhou was like traveling from New York City to the Deep South. The air was warmer than in Shanghai, and humid. Rainy. We boarded a bus that took us through the narrow, winding Guangzhou streets to Shamian Island, where our hotel was. The U.S. consulate used to be nearby, but it had moved to a different part of the city a few months ago. The island had a quiet dignity and time-worn grandeur that Shanghai's slick, modern buzz could never duplicate. Still the crowds, still the traffic and endless buildings, but for some reason, I could breathe there.

Our hotel was the legendary White Swan, where adoptive families had been staying for almost a decade. I'd seen so many pictures of it that when I finally set foot in the lobby, it hardly seemed real.

"Look!" I said to an unimpressed Eva. "There's the waterfall with the pagoda on top! And look at the jade ship sculpture!"

I was still exhausted, still heartsick about Eva's emotional block-ade, but for the first time since receiving her, I felt a stirring of hope. Thousands of other families had come through this lobby, sat by the waterfall, and toured the shops. The hotel had extra amenities specifi-cally for the families adopting Chinese children. I was not alone, and I was not the first to have the kind of challenges I faced with Eva. These other children—they'd had problems too, and they survived. They healed. They became true families. We would too.

I took one last look at the waterfall and then wheeled our luggage around to head for the elevator. "Come on, Eva," I said, not expect-ing a reply, but feeling for her hand anyway.

I couldn't find it.

I couldn't find her.

A bucket of icy fear dumped over my head, the shock robbed me of breath, a cutting numbness made it hard to think.

I gasped for air, forcing my body to come alive. "Eva! Zhen An!"

The others in our group scrambled to look for her. The agency representative spoke with the concierge and soon the entire hotel was shut down and the doors guarded by hotel staff.

Everything around me sped up, turned into a blur of lights and voices and movement, whirling around me. My soul exploded in a wordless, voiceless scream for my daughter. My heart shook my body with each thunderous pulse, until—for one moment—it stopped entirely, and the world was silent.

The waterfall was the only movement—its veil of water plunging noiselessly into the pool below. And behind that veil, a woman—a Chinese woman holding a cigarette, and bearing a familiar mole on the left side of her chin. Our eyes met. She nodded her head slowly, regally.

The world burst into motion once more. My heart crashed in my chest, and air forced its way into my lungs. Noises returned. I shoved through the people and ran down the path, behind the falling water.

Eva was there, crouching in a dark corner. A strange, wild sort of possessiveness surged through me. I never knew anger and joy could be twins. I grabbed my girl and crushed her close to me. I couldn't get enough of the warmth in her soft little body. "Don't you *ever* run off from me again! Do you understand? That was naughty. Very, very naughty! You scared Mommy very much."

She pulled away from me and ran to the edge of the path. "Wen Ming!" she hollered, whirling around frantically.

Wasn't that the name of the other foster child? The one she was friends with? She seemed to be looking for her. Maybe she'd seen another child who looked like her and ran after her.

I wanted to grab her again, but something warned me not to. I waited, watchfully, and after a moment, she stopped and looked back at me with disappointment and hurt.

"You poor darling. She's not here, is she?" I knelt down and held out my arms.

She came to me. Her arms slowly wound around my neck. She was shaking. But she was holding me.

I rubbed her back and took a deep breath. "I'm sorry. I didn't mean to yell. I was just worried. I didn't want to lose you, darling." I rocked her back and forth, then picked her up and hurried back down the path to let everyone know I'd found her.

We somehow retreated to the safety of our room without further incident. Once there, Eva floated wraithlike to the window to look out over the Pearl River.

I dropped the rest of the luggage in the middle of the room and sank to the edge of the rocklike twin bed closest to me. I gripped my head in my hands and let out a small moan.

The stress, the anxiety, the loneliness of the past week and a half crashed down on me. The fear, the pain—everything I'd been trying so hard to ignore. It would not be ignored any longer. I rolled to the side, drawing my knees up to my chest, and gave way to racking sobs.

I felt a warm, small hand on my cheek. I sniffled and opened my eyes. Eva stood in front of me, tears on her face, her eyes wide.

"*Dui bu qi,*" she said. It was soft, garbled, her cleft lips and palate getting in the way of clear speech.

I mentally rifled through my Chinese phrases, trying to find a close match. *I'm sorry.* That's what she'd said. She'd apologized.

I choked on another sob and sat up to pull her into my arms. This time, she climbed on my lap on her own and put her arms around me. I didn't care what the phrase was—she had finally spoken to me, and that was all that mattered.

We cried together for several more minutes, purging the dark emotions and clearing away the fear. A tap sounded on the door, and I wiped my eyes and stumbled to open the door.

Dee was on the other side. She gave me a soft, sympathetic smile and held up a bag from an American-style fast-food place. "I know, I know. It's not very healthy. But I thought you could use some comfort food."

Normally, I hated fast food. But the greasy, overcooked smell was a bit of home that I desperately needed. I let her enter, and I pulled a cheeseburger out of the bag.

"Eva, you want a French fry?" I held up a long, soggy one.

Her eyes lit with more animation than I'd seen since that first day. "*Mai dang lao!*"

I handed it to her and watched her munch it. "Enjoy it now, kiddo. It's fruits and veggies and multigrains for you at home."

I bit into a cheeseburger with guilty pleasure. "I don't deserve this, Dee. I handled the whole thing in the lobby so badly. I panicked."

"Anyone would have panicked."

"And then, when I found her, I yelled at her. Yelled!"

"Yeah. I know. You sounded like a mom to me. A worried, relieved mommy."

"I did?"

"Totally."

How had that happened? But she was right—something had risen up inside me and out had poured mother-angst.

"So when does it get to be fun?"

Dee smiled at me and shook her head. "Beats me. This has been the longest, hardest week of my life."

"Yeah." I felt a twinge of guilt—I'd been so engrossed in my own troubles with Eva that I hadn't really paid attention to how Dee was doing. I encouraged her to talk about it while I finished eating.

When we were done with our artery-hardening snack, Dee stretched out on my bed. "You want to go do some shopping? My mom is taking a nap with Callie, and you two look like you could use some fun. I've been looking forward to the Shop on the Stairs and Jennifer's Place and all those other adoption tourist traps they have around here."

"What about it, Eva? *Dao shang dian guang yi guang.*" I held out my hand to her.

And this time, she took it.

A lifetime happened on that trip to China. Pieces and flashes come to me when I least expect it, a montage of color and emotion. A smell puts me back on the streets of Shanghai, or the expression on a stranger's face lands me back in Guangzhou.

I remember the Shop on the Stairs near the consulate in Guangzhou—the most straightforward name for a shop I'd ever heard. On a set of narrow steps between two buildings, built into an enclosed shop, is a vast collection of knickknacks and tourist gifts. A Chinese woman with the English name Sheri runs the shop. She also does foster care of Chinese orphans.

She took one look at Eva and understanding sparked in her eyes. She leaned close to study the tiny painted bottle on a string that Eva wore around her neck and showed me the red feather inside.

"That's strange," I told her. "I have a very similar feather." I pulled mine out of the baggie in my backpack where I'd stashed it.

"Crane feather. Very lucky," Sheri said. "You want to wear it in a bottle like your daughter?"

"Please."

I couldn't wait for the time when I'd be able to ask Eva where she'd gotten that feather and bottle. I could have asked Sheri, but I wanted to experience the story myself, not secondhand through a translator. I would wait. Sheri found a small bottle, painted inside with a crane. It had a cork and a tiny handle. We placed the feather inside the bottle and threaded a ribbon through the handle.

"Now we each have one."

Eva almost smiled. But her face dimmed again.

I glanced at Sheri and shook my head. "She isn't handling this very well."

Sheri sat several steps above where Eva stood, so they were eye level. She said something in Chinese, and Eva responded with a flood of words that made me envious.

"She is sad to leave China and a little scared," Sheri told me.

"I believe it. I would be too."

"Come with me." She motioned to both of us, and we followed her up the stairs to a little door at the top. Beyond the door were more stairs, like those in an attic. We continued up until we came to a storage room. Sheri went to a corner, set aside a few boxes, and pulled out a dusty brocade box. She opened it to reveal two chime balls.

"You see Baoding balls before, yes?"

I nodded.

"But you not see them like this. Look." She took one out of the box. It was enameled with a cloisonné design of a dragon in a stand of bamboo. The other showed a woman with a beautiful vase sitting under a blossoming cherry tree. She rolled them in her hand and they made the chiming sound I was accustomed to hearing. Her hand stilled, but the chime continued, and grew and changed until it filled the room with the sound of a woman singing a Chinese lullaby. She rolled the balls again, and this time the chime became the sound of children laughing and shouting in Chinese. A third time and the sound became an ocean echoing with a Chinese flute melody.

Eva gazed at the balls with longing. Sheri set them back in the box and handed the box to me. "This is for when she needs to hear China speaking to her. Is okay with you?"

"Yes," I whispered. *"Xie xie."*

Another memory that shines in my mind like the soft glow of a dying fire is the evening our travel group took our new children to the Hard Rock Cafe in Guangzhou, our last night in that city. We had a birthday celebration for Eva, and I gave her the carved jade bracelet I had gotten for her in Chicago.

"This is for you. Happy Birthday. *Sheng ri quai le.*" I handed it to her with two hands and a formal little bow. Her eyes grew wide, and she traced the carvings reverently.

"Xie xie," she said, sliding it onto her wrist. It was too large, of course. So she took the glass bottle from around her neck, untied the knot, and slid the bracelet onto it. Then she held it out for me to retie. I tied it securely and then placed it back around her neck. She gave me her first smile.

And later, we all danced on the dance floor—new parents and their children, the stress lifted. This part of our life's journey was nearly complete; we had one foot in the East and were stretching the other back toward the West. We had been through a profound experience together, and there was a bond connecting us. I didn't know if it would last, but that evening, we felt we were one. I even coaxed Eva into dancing with me, and soon she twirled around on her own and doubled up with some other children in crazy, heedless moves that showed me that there was still an innocent child somewhere inside her. I picked her up, set her on my hip, and we danced—as tired as we were, as new and strange as we still were to each other, in that moment I had hope for the first time that we might make it and become a family.

The plane ride home was grueling. As I watched Asia fade away, I felt a surge of excitement to be going home. Home to Lewis. Eva, though, spent hours staring pensively out the window. I understood a little of what she felt. I'd been in a similar position two weeks ago, only I had the promise of returning to the familiar. She would have to learn a whole new familiar. I hoped we'd be able to help her learn.

We landed in San Francisco, and as we did, I hugged Eva and told her, *"Ni shi Meiguoren."* You are American. Since the adoption was final in China, all she had to do was set foot on American soil and she was automatically a citizen. She still had to go through immigration on a Chinese passport, but it would be her final act as a Chinese citizen. The thought made me sad as much as it brought me joy. We were asking her to give up so much of who she was. I hoped what she'd gain in her new life could balance what she was losing with the old.

I never did change Eva into the special coming-home dress I'd bought for her. We were too tired to bother. We staggered from the plane, and since we'd gone through immigration in San Francisco, we were able to head straight for baggage claim. I wanted my husband and my bed and my shower—though not necessarily in that order.

We wove around knots of travelers and past happy scenes of re-united loved ones. And there he was. Looking as tired as I felt—and no wonder, since he'd been working nearly around the clock on the experiment. But he saw us and a light came into him. He walked toward me, and soon I was in his arms. Too tired to cry, I let him kiss me and I savored that soft pressure of his mouth. I'd missed him so much.

We stepped back and I looked down at Eva. *"Zhe shi ni baba."* This is your daddy. I had been practicing that phrase and how to say it for weeks. But now, my exhausted mouth and overwrought emotions stumbled over the simple phrase. It didn't matter. She knew who he was.

He knelt down, a hopeful question in his face. She studied him for a moment and then stepped close to him and laid her head on his shoulder. He looked at me, his eyes wide. For a second, a rush of envy twisted through me. For ten heart-wrenching days, I'd worked and struggled and prayed for the very thing he got from her with no effort at all. What had I done wrong?

And he just sat there, looking a bit frightened. I nodded at him and waved my arms in an embracing motion. Awkwardly, he patted her shoulders and twisted his head to look down at her. I saw him breathe in the scent of her.

She was barely awake. He picked her up, and she slumped even more heavily against him.

I blinked back tears. I didn't want to ruin the moment with my petty jealousy. But seeing them together hurt worse than I'd ever imagined. As if the last two weeks had meant nothing to her.

I knew better. The reasonable part of my travel-addled brain knew that in Eva's version of the world, I was the Big Mean Stranger who had taken her away. She was mad at me, even if she couldn't express it. But the knowledge didn't stop the tears. I choked on a sob, and Lewis looked from the sleepy child in his arms to me. For the first time since we'd met, he couldn't comfort me. His arms were full.

"I'm sorry," he whispered.

"It's not your fault." I smeared some tears onto my palm.

He shifted her onto one arm and drew me close with the other. We stood there, looking to the rest of the world like a family of three. A unit.

But it couldn't have been farther from the truth.

Meg Lindsay, April 2006

I n the weeks that followed our return from China, Eva blanketed my world with herself, like a snowstorm that rages and consumes with silent grace, transforming everything I knew into unfamiliar wonder. Things I never thought about before, things so mundane they passed by me in robotic anonymity, became miraculous because of her. The first time she fed herself with a fork, the curve of her fingers and the soft pinkness of her bottom lip stole my breath. The first time she ate Lewis's special black-bean-and-cheese enchiladas—how strings of melted Monterey Jack cheese draped between her plate and her fork like suspension cables on a bridge, and her giggles as she stretched them and twirled them around her fingers before dropping the whole succulent mass into her open mouth. The way she lined up all the stuffed animals and dolls we'd filled her room with and then counted them—*yi, ar, san, su, wu, liu, che, ba, jie, shi*—all the way to twenty-three, slowly, spinning around at the end until she plunged down in the middle of them all and scooped them into her arms to hug them all at once. Then lining them up to do it again, as if she couldn't believe they all really belonged to her.

She loved when I played my viola. She dragged her pillow and a blanket from my room and curled up on the floor, sucking her thumb, while I practiced. And when I looked at her, when I played for her, I never felt anxious. My music flowed out to her, smoothing her hair, patting her cheeks, tickling her tummy until her eyes sparkled and her body glowed with a golden light. One afternoon, I unlatched my viola case and she came barreling toward me, glee in her face.

"Music!" She clapped her hands. "Music!"

The accent was thick, and her lips distorted the sound, but I knew what she'd said. Even though she still stiffened anytime I tried to hold her, her first English word was to exclaim over something I'd done. A delight I'd given her with my art. Her first steps into her new language, and they had been for *me*.

After that, stepping turned into running. Every day brought more new phrases, new words. But with that blossoming came a sort of death. We played a game of "What's that in Chinese?" and once when we were playing it, after about a month, I pointed to her shoe.

"What's that in Chinese?"

She opened her mouth to respond, then stopped, looked at her shoe, and frowned. She lifted her foot and twisted it in the air, glanced back at me, and shook her head slowly. "I don't know."

I turned away to hide sudden tears. Why was it that in order for her to come fully into her new life, the old life had to die? Something infinitely precious was slipping away from her. Would she someday come to resent that? I'd have given anything in that moment to be fluent in Chinese. I vowed that we'd get her into a Chinese-language school as soon as we could.

Everything wasn't joy—there were still tantrums and nightmares and uncertainty and fear, but for those few weeks, the energy of her explosion into our lives outshone the lurking darkness. We were together nearly every minute, she and I. There were books to be read, songs to be sung, games to be played. Shops to be shopped, treats to be eaten, pictures to be colored, and stories to be told.

One day, she even let me hold her hand.

A few days later, I hugged her, and she didn't pull away.

And even though she wouldn't yet call me "Mama," I could see that the doors of her soul were slowly swinging open, and I felt that Lewis and I soon would be invited to enter.

Eventually we had to go back to "normal" everyday life, right? The honeymoon must end. The holidays can't last forever. Sunday always gives way to Monday. At some point in every vacation, after the photos have been snapped, after the souvenirs have been purchased, after the sightseeing is done, you have to return home. You just have to.

We tried to prepare Eva for her first day of kindergarten. We had even toured her new classroom together and met her teacher, a gentle young black woman with a smile as radiant as Venus when it dances with the moon. I thought Eva seemed excited about the prospect of going to school, but there was still so much I didn't know about my daughter. When it came to understanding Eva, I was still a kindergartner myself.

We arrived at the school early, Eva looking like a delectable cupcake in brown jeweled pants and a pink sweater. I put her hair in high pigtails tied with orange and pink ribbons, and it was all I could do to keep my mouth and hands off her—she looked so kissably and huggably sweet. It was almost frightening to me how very much I adored her already.

Her teacher welcomed us into the classroom and showed Eva where to put her jacket and the little lunch I'd slaved over the night before. There was a desk with her name on it. "Eva Lindsay." I realized with a small twinge of guilt that her Chinese name was absent. We'd kept it as her middle name, and I kept meaning to call her Zhen An. But I'd thought of her as Eva for so long, and her Chinese name brought a sad hollowness into her eyes. So we took the easy way out and called her Eva. She seemed to have accepted it, but I couldn't help feeling bad anyway because I knew part of my motivation was that I wanted her to be Eva. I wanted her to belong to me, wanted to have the mother's privilege of choosing her name and the joy of seeing her respond to it.

Then the moment came for me to leave, to walk away, to let the process of growing up and growing away begin. Already? I wanted to hold on to the seconds a bit longer. I'd only had her to myself a few weeks. Could this teacher, as kind as she seemed, really appreciate the miracle that was my daughter? Would she notice all the tiny, amazing achievements Eva accomplished every day? I didn't see how it was possible. She would sit, surrounded by the wealth of all that was Eva, and not understand how precious it all was.

And I'd miss out on it all.

For a moment, I thought about quitting, about snatching Eva up in my arms and running back to the apartment, where I could keep her to myself. But it wouldn't be good for either of us. I couldn't hold her back, and I didn't want her to hold me back.

Didn't want her to hold me back? I couldn't feel that way. It wasn't right. Wasn't motherhood all about being selfless? If I gave up my career, I could keep her with me. Home-school her or something. But I couldn't bear the thought of giving up my music. I didn't have the courage to throw myself on that altar.

So I kissed her good-bye and told her I'd see her after school. I turned to leave, determined to save my tears for after I left the building.

"Don't leave!" The tiny voice was a whispered wail. Then it grew louder, pleading. "Mamaaaaa! Don't leave!"

I whirled around. Had she really called me that? The joy stabbed me in a fierce thrill and I gasped from the force of it. I flew back to her and knelt beside her, folding her in my arms. She wrapped her arms around me and clung to me.

"It's okay. Mama will be back. I'll come back when school is done."

She'd said "Mama"! I kissed her again and forced myself to stand. She grabbed my jacket.

"No! Don't leave. Don't leave me!"

"Eva, darling. I have to. Mommy has to go to work. It's okay. Mrs. Jacobs is right here. You'll have a great time, and you can tell me all about it at supper, okay?"

I took a step away, and simmering rage and terror conflagrated, engulfing her in their flames. She screamed and wrapped her arms around my legs, begging me to stay in a broken mix of English and Chinese.

I picked her up and held her against me, tears distorting the image of her teacher, who was watching us with a pained expression. Other children were arriving, and the room was filled with an uneasy anticipation and the sounds of my daughter screaming.

The teacher held Eva's hand. "Hey, Eva, would you like to feed our pet bunny? His name is Squeakers, and he's so soft." Eva pulled away, shaking her head and crying harder. The teacher looked worried. "Mrs. Lindsay, I think you should just put her down and leave quickly. She'll settle down as soon as you're gone."

I had a searing vision of Yang Hua running from a government office in Shanghai. My stomach lurched. "I don't think that would be a good idea. The last time someone left quickly, it was her foster mother, and it took me weeks to help her get over that and to trust me. I think I'd better just keep her with me, and we'll try again tomorrow."

She didn't understand. I could see that clearly. She shrugged doubtfully and said okay. She retrieved Eva's coat and lunch and gave her a falsely cheerful good-bye. "See you tomorrow, Eva, okay?"

Eva wouldn't look at her. She pressed close to me and shuffled out the door. Her shuddering sniffles didn't subside until we reached the apartment.

I was going to be late for rehearsal, my first day back. And what was I supposed to do with Eva? I pictured her lying on the floor, listening to me practice.

"Eva, go get your pillow and blanket, darling."

I didn't have any other choice. I'd take her with me. Just for today. Just this once. We could figure out kindergarten tomorrow.

"So how was the first day back?" It was the first question Lewis asked me when he came home that evening, after leaning in for a quick kiss.

"Don't ask." I peeked at Eva's bedroom door. Closed, and quiet inside. She must still be sleeping. At least one of us wouldn't be tired and grouchy all evening. I walked into the kitchen and yanked a pan onto the stove, then dumped some olive oil into it.

"That good, huh? Don't worry, you'll get back into the swing of things soon, I'm sure."

"Oh, you're sure, are you? Why don't *you* try getting her to go to kindergarten tomorrow, and we'll see. Better yet, when she throws a Shanghai-sized screaming, kicking tantrum, why don't you take her to work with you and see if you can get 'back in the swing of things,' okay?"

He blinked at me, his mouth open. "She did that?"

"Yes!" I slapped two zucchini onto a cutting board, then slammed the knife through them so hard that Lewis twitched. "So I took her to rehearsal with me. Everyone loved meeting her, but then there was the constant stream of 'I go potty' and 'I'm bored' and 'What's that?' I brought a bag of things for her to play with, and it lasted all of fifteen minutes! Maestro Chelsea finally told me to leave early because she was such a distraction."

"I'm sorry."

I threw the zucchini into the skillet. "Me too. It was humiliating! And unprofessional. I think Li Shu was really annoyed. Barely said hello to Eva, and hardly talked to me all day. I bet they would never take a child to work in China. She probably thinks it was insulting."

"What else could you have done? I think you made the right decision not to force her to go to school today. That could have really traumatized her."

I snatched a tomato and chopped it. "Thanks. When I get fired for being late to rehearsal and bringing my kid with me, it'll be a huge comfort to know you approved."

"Hey, why the sarcasm? What did I do?"

I whirled around, knife in hand, to face him. "You didn't do anything. That's the problem! I had to handle this all on my own."

"What was I supposed to do? Walk out of my class? Bring her with me? I don't have the flexibility you do."

"You think just because it's a symphony job, it's more flexible? Or is it because it's 'just' a rehearsal? Or because it's not forty hours a week? What if that had been a performance today? What would I have done?" I minced garlic and diced carrots and sent them winging into the skillet.

"It wasn't. And it was just this first day. I don't understand why you're angry at me."

I slammed my hands on the countertop and leaned hard on them. "You weren't there for me. You took a whole week off when we got back from China, but since then, it's been me dealing with Eva. And even when you are home, it's still me. I get her dressed, I wake up when she has a nightmare, I feed her, and I read her bedtime stories. It's like being a single parent, except that no matter what I do, all she wants is you. And most of the time, you aren't there."

He stared at me without speaking, and I felt ashamed. I'd been unfair.

"I told you it might be like this. I warned you. It's not that I mean to be uninvolved."

He ran both hands through his hair, suddenly looking young and old all at once. His cell phone rang before I could reply.

While he walked to the living room to talk to whoever it was, I studied the skillet, trying to figure out what I'd been intending to make. It looked like the start of a good stir-fry, but I'd been chopping out of a need for catharsis and not to make dinner.

This conversation with Lewis was not finished. He had to be made to see that we *needed* him.

My knife stilled.

I was kidding myself. The problem wasn't with Lewis.

It was me. This was about me being mad at Eva and Lewis for creating such a cute daddy-daughter bond and leaving me to handle all the mother responsibilities with none of the emotional benefits.

If I really loved Eva, why didn't she respond to that love? Why was it always Lewis she wanted? Why not me?

I chopped through a head of broccoli, the knife making satisfying hits against the granite.

She didn't recoil from me anymore. And she did call me "Mama" today. Shouldn't that count for something? I was too selfish. Too impatient. I needed to give her more time.

It shouldn't be about my needs and wants. That was the way of my own mother. I was supposed to be different.

I continued lecturing myself in this way for several more minutes, until I felt adequately chastened. Lewis was still on the phone. I set down my chopping knife and grabbed a towel, wiping my hands as I went in search of him.

He was sitting on the couch in the living room, slumped over, elbows on his knees, one hand curled into his hair. His voice was flat, tight, and controlled. "Yeah. Okay. No, that won't be a problem. The university will give me bereavement leave."

Bereavement? "Lewis?"

He looked up at me, his face grim. "*Dad,*" he mouthed.

I shut my eyes and caught my breath. He and his dad had never been close, but I knew from my own experience that the wishing for it never goes away. To have that wish denied, to lose even the chance of it coming true, to have the hope of a good relationship taken away—no matter how unlikely that hope was—is an especially cruel pain.

A few more murmured words, and then Lewis clicked his phone shut. He didn't sit up, just stayed hunched over, flipping the phone from hand to hand. I sat next to him and put my arm across his shoulders and waited.

"Dad died . . ." he finally told me. "Heart attack, this afternoon. Gone before they could get him to the hospital."

"I'm sorry." I kissed his shoulder through his shirt and leaned against him.

"He was never there for me. And now I wasn't there for him."

I'd never heard him use this sort of monotone voice before. He was in shock, of course, but it still frightened me a little.

I leaned over him, rubbing his arms in a slow, soothing motion. "There wasn't anything you could have done. I'm sorry. I'm so sorry, love."

"Baba okay? Baba sad?" Eva stood behind us, looking sleepy and worried.

I held out my arms to her. "Yes, your baba is sad right now. His baba died today."

She came to stand in the nook between Lewis and me. She put her hands on Lewis's face. "Where your mama, Baba?"

Lewis's face tightened to the point that I thought it might shatter.

"Baba's mama isn't here, either." I put my arm around her waist.

"I'm an orphan now, I guess. Just like you, Eva-girl."

She lifted his face so he had to look at her. "We no orphan, Baba. We got us."

"And Mama," Lewis added.

He pulled her close to him, and once more, I envied the bond that seemed to strengthen between them every day, but at the same time, I was glad for it this night. He needed it. He carried her to her room, whispering something in her ear that made her giggle.

Late that night, after we'd been in bed for hours, I woke to muffled, hoarse sobbing. There's something horrible about a man crying. It's rusty and awkward, and always violent—too many years of holding it all in, and when it finally explodes, it's ugly and heart-wrenching.

I gave him my body in as complete an embrace as I knew how to give. He took it, grasping me to himself, curling his hand into my hair, his tears burning holes through my T-shirt.

"I'm sorry." The words groaned out of him. "I'm sorry I wasn't there for you today. For any of you."

I held him against me, trying to absorb his grief into myself. "I was wrong earlier. I shouldn't have said any of that. You are here. And we're here. We're all here for each other. We're doing this differently. None of us will ever leave each other, no matter what. I promise."

TWENTY TWO

Wen Ming, May 2006

Sometimes, in the middle of the day, I could hear her crying. My *mei mei*. Crying the night cries of fear as she ran from the darkness in her mind. I felt her tears on my skin and her tremors in my chest. It did not surprise me to feel such things, for wasn't I her *jie jie*?

Her new "mother" would not be able to feel Zhen An's heart and mind. Her new "mother" would try and fail to comfort her. Her new "mother" would someday realize that Zhen An's love belonged only to me, because her heart was locked inside mine and not even powerful grown-up Americans could separate us.

And what does a mother know of fear in the night and the longing to take it away and the anger that comes when you must stand aside and do nothing for the child you love?

Mother—what nonsense. Was it a mother that held Zhen An when she was sad or scared? Was it a mother who told all the other children to stop teasing Zhen An about her mouth? Was it a mother who held Zhen An's heart in her own and shared every hurt and every happiness?

No. I did that. Wen Ming, the *jie jie*. The one who did not need a mother. The one who was a better mother than either of ours. I was not the one who left. I was not the one who didn't want her child.

And now I was the one whose arms were empty and whose soul felt like a sky that was always ready to rain.

Nobody understood. They thought I should put a smile on my

face and be a happy girl. They told me to be thankful that I had a foster family. That I could go to school even with my poor eyesight. That I was so smart.

I didn't want to be smart. Or happy. Or thankful. I wanted to rumble like thunder and pound like the rain. I wanted to split the earth like a lightning bolt and sweep away all the mothers in America in the green waters of my flood.

"Wen Ming," Uncle Zhou said at the table after dinner. A rainstorm battered the windows and shook them. Our tall building seemed to sway in the force of the wind. "We have to talk about your marks at school."

I picked at a dried bit of rice on the table. "I don't want to."

"Wen Ming!" Auntie Yang's voice scolded me. I felt ashamed. It was wrong to dishonor parents—even if they were only foster parents.

But I had thunder in me. And that cannot be silenced by shame.

"You have poor marks in math. You are a good student. Is there a problem?" Uncle Zhou spoke with patience and kindness to me, even though I had been rude.

"I don't like math."

"That is no excuse," Auntie Yang said. She too sounded patient.

I didn't want patience. I didn't want kindness. I wanted a storm and noise and crashing and yelling, just like the chaos inside me. "Don't talk to me about math. You aren't my parents."

There was a shocked pause. Then Uncle Zhou said, "We are your foster parents."

A crash of thunder. I jumped to my feet and shoved the chair backward. "Not real parents! I don't have to listen to you. And I don't have to talk about math with you."

"Is that a way to talk to us? So rude?" Auntie Yang stood as well.

Thunder rolled from my mouth and I ran to my room and slammed the door. I pressed my face against my window and let the damp coldness of the rain-soaked glass cool my face.

After a few minutes, my door opened. "Do you want to be adopted? Is this why you are angry and unhappy?" Auntie Yang's voice was gentle but cool. The mattress creaked, and I knew she was sitting there.

I turned toward her voice, and my own felt sharp, like driven rain. "No. When I am grown, I will become the director of the Children's Welfare Home. I will take all the orphans in the whole world and love them. And I won't let any of them be adopted, ever. I'll keep them with me, and I will never send them away."

"My little bird."

The pity and sadness in her voice angered me. "I'm not your little bird. I'm no one's little bird."

I heard her sigh. The mattress creaked again, and I heard her walk across the room. "Very well. Good night, Wen Ming." She closed my door quietly.

I threw myself on my bed and beat my pillow with my fists. When I was too tired to continue, I curled up as small as I could and pretended that my pillow was my little sister, sleeping next to me. And I wondered if she could feel my pain in her heart too, or if I felt it all by myself.

TWENTY THREE

Meg Lindsay, July 2006

I don't think I expected to actually hear from Yang Hua. I'd given her my contact information in a burst of adoptive guilt, hoping to ease the pain of giving up a child she cared about. In the months following Eva's homecoming, I admit I nearly forgot about the sweet-faced woman who had been a devoted caregiver for more than a year. I wanted to believe she'd moved on, taken in other children, or finally succeeded in having her own.

She called on a Sunday morning, while we were getting ready to go to a picnic. "Mrs. Lindsay? This is Yang Hua—your daughter foster mother in China."

I stumbled out some greeting, then waited through a nakedly awkward silence. Eva was watching a movie in the living room. I slipped into the study and eased the door closed.

"How is Zhen An?"

I couldn't miss the wistfulness in her voice. "Eva is fine. Good. Doing great." And she was mine, I wanted to add, even though I knew it wasn't necessary.

"How her mouth?"

"Okay. She had surgery a month ago."

"Pardon?"

"Surgery. Operation."

"Oh! Sorry to trouble you."

"No, it was a month ago. She's doing fine now."

"Good. I am sorry to ask, but I call for other foster child. Wen Ming."

Oh, yes. The best friend. I waited for her to continue.

"Wen Ming miss Zhen An very much."

Eva. Her name was Eva now. "Eva speaks of Wen Ming sometimes. She cared very much for her." Why did I put that in the past tense?

"Wen Ming is having difficult time. She is having trouble with school. I am sorry to bother you, but I want to know if okay with you for Wen Ming and Zhen . . . E-va to correspond. Phone call is expensive, so only once in a while. But we have e-mail too."

Why hadn't I seen this request coming when I gave her my contact information? It wasn't that I minded, exactly, but it seemed like Eva was just starting to adjust to her new life. I didn't know if I wanted her old life intruding too much right now.

"Eva is already starting to forget how to speak Chinese. And of course she can't write in Chinese. How would e-mail work?"

"My husband speak very good English. He write for Wen Ming and translate E-va e-mails for Wen Ming. Please? Wen Ming . . . she need her *mei mei*."

I just didn't want to share. How was this going to help Eva bond with me? If she could keep running back to her foster family, how could I get her to think of us as her real family?

But just as I was about to say no, Eva pushed the door open, the Baoding balls in her hands. "Mama, listen!"

She rolled them in her hands, and I heard the voice of a child, weeping in a way that made me think I'd heard her before.

"It's Wen Ming. She need me. Maybe can I write a letter?"

My shoulders slumped. How selfish was it to wish Eva cared about what I needed? I didn't want to answer that question. I shooed Eva out of the room, not wanting her to know who I was talking to. I just needed some time to get used to the idea. "Yang Hua? Yes. E-mail and phone calls would be fine with us."

"Thank you very much, Mrs. Lindsay."

It seemed strange to stay home from church so we could make the ninety-minute drive to the Families with Children from China's annual Fourth of July picnic. Living up to my agreement with Lewis, I'd found a new church that Eva and I both liked. I didn't actually miss the people at my old church as much as I thought I would. I definitely didn't miss the awkwardness of seeing Adam and Beth every week, or the unpleasant chill of my parents. They were mad at me for making the change, but after piling on so many offenses, I was beginning to grow numb to their displeasure. I told myself it didn't matter anymore anyway—I had Eva.

"And there will really be other China children?" Eva should have been buckled into her booster seat, but somehow she'd come loose and was now bouncing on the edge of her seat, poking her head between Lewis and me like a puppet peering over the top of a stage.

"From what I understand," I told her, "there will be more children than you've ever seen in one place—even more than the orphanage." And more parents, more people who understood what we were going through, people who had been there and were there yet. All three of us needed that. It wasn't that our friends weren't understanding or supportive, but there were things about this adoption journey they couldn't relate to, even though they tried.

Eva grew suddenly sober, and with a lurch of my heart, I thought maybe I'd upset her with my reference to the orphanage.

"My scar is very ugly." She touched her mouth where a shiny new pink scar marked the operation she'd had a month ago to repair her lip.

Her comment was a relief. Body-image worries I could handle. "Your scar is so much better than it was, and your lip looks much nicer than it did. And your speech is already improving."

"They will tease me. They will call me . . ." She frowned. "Call me . . . there is a name for it. It is a monster in China, but I not remember."

"Did children tease you in China?" Lewis's eyes narrowed to sharp blades.

"Not at the orphanage. It was a party with my foster family."

I half turned to smile at her, but tears rained down my throat, like a downspout on a house. No little girl should ever be called a monster. "You listen to me, Miss Eva Zhen An Lindsay. You are a beautiful girl, and no scar in the world can change that. Besides, I bet you'll see other children there with repaired cleft lips. You won't be the only one."

The bounce returned and so did a smile. I smirked at Lewis—I was getting pretty good at this mom stuff.

When we arrived at the park, Eva scrambled from the car and cast a skeptical eye toward the gloomy clouds. "It will rain maybe. On my first picnic ever!"

"I don't think so. It wouldn't dare." I reached my arm around her shoulders, but she ducked from my grasp. "If it does rain, we'll just tell it: *Rain, rain, go away, come again some other day.*"

She made me repeat the rhyme again, and then skipped around the car chanting it while Lewis and I unloaded our supplies.

This was how it was supposed to be, childhood. Chanting silly rhymes, skipping, with no greater care than whether rain will spoil the picnic. This was what I'd been longing for—to give her a childhood full of carefree innocence. I was doing it. Doing it the way I wished it had been done for me. There was no one to tell her she was skipping wrong, or that she didn't pronounce the letter *r* correctly, or to warn her how much trouble she'd be in if she got her shoes muddy.

It was just Lewis and I, watching her fondly and with indulgent enjoyment, with patience and understanding, as it should be.

The overcast clouds grew darker. Rain, rain, go away.

We shuffled with our picnic supplies to the covered shelter where the FCC group was supposed to gather. It spread out before us like a buzzing, bustling Brigadoon that would only exist a few hours before disappearing into the mist. Children scampered everywhere, their parents alternating between standing around like afternoon cows alongside a pasture stream and rounding up strays like so many sheepdogs.

Somewhere in this barely controlled chaos was a place for me. I was sure of it. I scanned the crowd, not even certain what it was that I was looking for.

A dragonfly with wings dipped in fairy dust zipped past my ear. It circled my head and zoomed into the throng of families. I followed its wispy trek, a glow and glimmer of crystal sea foam, until it hovered above a family just staking out their claim with a red and orange vinyl tablecloth and a purple blanket spread under an arching oak. I studied the mom—short, spiky black hair, tight-fitting T-shirt and jeans, and the right sort of body for tight clothes. Abundant smiles. She moved about with a loose, careless rhythm, like a jazz song whose restless energy still cools the humid afternoon. The dragonfly circled them three times, then zinged like an arrow back to me before veering off into the overcast sky.

I pointed toward the family under the oak tree. "Let's try over there."

So many social niceties—Do you mind if we join you? Of course not. We're Lewis and Meg Lindsay, and our daughter, Eva. They say they're Bree and Jordan. Nice to meet you.

Names and occupations, area of town, and adoption stats—all the little gates adults must go through and footbridges they must cross in order to form an acquaintance. I plunged ahead through each successive threshold, knowing that if I let myself stop, if I let myself think, I'd freeze up and not go another step.

Meanwhile, Bree and Jordan's two Chinese daughters and two natural-born sons as well as our own Eva had, in the way children do, leaped past the formalities and were already engaged in a game of Spaghetti and Meatball that involved long foam noodles and a soccer ball. When had connecting with people stopped being so simple? Why couldn't I be like those children and just jump right into a relationship with no more complexity than what is required to play a child's game?

Patience, I told myself. No need to push or try to force it to happen.

Lewis headed back to our car to unload the rest of our picnic supplies. Jordan took one of his sons to the restroom. Bree pulled out a glass bottle full of red, murky liquid and popped the lid off. "Want some? It's Kombucha—fermented tea. Totally organic and raw. Way healthy."

I thought of myself as something of a health foodie, but even I'd never heard of fermented tea. But I wasn't going to turn down the friendly offer, so I took the bottle and sniffed the odd drink.

"Just try it. That one has blueberry and acai juice in it. Superfood!"

I took a sip—it was tart and fizzy, like champagne punch. "Thanks!"

"They seem to be hitting it off. Look at them." Bree pointed toward our children with her tea bottle. *Our* children. She leaned back on her elbow, swigging the Kombucha with her other hand. "They make it look so simple."

"Make what look simple?"

"Friendship."

Our eyes met, and there was a strange sort of understanding that flared between us. I sucked in my lower lip and nibbled it, then smiled at her.

Eva and Bree's older daughter, Jolie, ambled back toward our blankets, arms around each other's neck. "We are the same age!" Eva shouted, even though I was within feet of her.

"And we like princesses!" Jolie, the taller of the two, wrapped her other arm around Eva's waist and tried to pick her up. They stumbled backward, and I lurched to my feet just as they caught themselves. They staggered in a three-legged turn back toward the other children.

I sank to the ground, my embarrassment a ballast weighing me down. Bree grinned at me. She hadn't even twitched. "Give it a while, and you won't be so jumpy."

The two girls burst into a sprint of tag lasting all of ten seconds. They collapsed on the ground, giggling and whispering. A fiery hope burned against my eyes. This was everything I wanted for Eva. This was everything I longed for myself.

She needed a friend here. Someone she liked well enough to distract her from Wen Ming. I didn't want her to forget Wen Ming, but her importance to Eva seemed like a morning glory vine—something beautiful, but it could take over an entire garden and choke it in a matter of weeks. Eva needed her own life, apart from the little girl back in China. Maybe Jolie was the answer.

Our husbands returned, and we marshaled the children back to eat. The Cayhills were vegetarian, but still impressed with our little gourmet-styled, health-conscious lunch. I wasn't about to tell them how simple our meals normally were or that I'd taken extra time to make this lunch especially attractive so everyone could see that I was a good mom.

Lewis and Jordan, an electrical engineer, bonded over an arcane discussion of the ethical implications of nanomachines—whatever those were.

Bree's eyes flattened into sly, laughing slits. "Isn't it wonderful being married to a geek?"

"I heard that!" Jordan flicked a leaf at his wife.

"Then you heard me say it was won-der-ful." She tilted toward him, hanging her arms around his neck, and kissed him.

I leaned against the tree and wrapped my arms around my knees. This was good. This was how I wanted life to be. Maybe I belonged here.

After we finished eating, the children begged to play along the lake. I glanced at Lewis. He shrugged. I held Eva's hands and looked up at her. "You can go with the other kids, but stay out of the water, okay?"

"Okay."

They sprinted off to blend in with the other children, and in a way, it hurt a little to see her go. She was already growing up, and I had missed so much. I never wanted a baby, but at that moment, I wished I could wave my hands and turn back time until she was an infant sleeping in my arms. I wished I could see her first tooth, her first haircut, her first steps, and all those other firsts that mark the passage of time and whose importance signify that this child was loved and valued.

Two other couples drifted over to us, and the talk turned to adoption. We shared our travel stories and tales of the rude, ridiculous, and outrageous comments people made about our children.

"My grandma," said Lewis, "told me that we ought to have had our own children first before adopting anyone else's."

I'd turned away to whisper something to Bree, but Lewis's words snapped me to attention. "When did she say that? You never told me."

"At Dad's funeral."

A hushed, awkward pause froze us, then Jordan clapped his hand on Lewis's shoulder. "That's really rough. I'm sorry."

Bree offered him another organic brownie. "Maybe she just isn't comfortable having a grandchild of a different race."

Lewis chuckled. "She's Chinese. Emigrated to California when she was nineteen. She's hung up on bloodlines. In her mind, you don't count as family unless you're related by blood or by marriage—and sometimes not even then."

"Negative family reactions are the worst," said one of the other guys who joined us.

His wife offered M&M's to the rest of us. "Any new developments with the baby-trafficking scandal in Hunan?"

Bree shrugged. "I heard they arrested a huge ring of people and are investigating what happened. They claim none of the trafficked babies were adopted internationally. A lot of them were boys who were taken to other Chinese families who wanted them. But I just wonder . . . how do we know?"

"Know what?" another woman said. I think her name was Leslie.

"How do we know that our children were really abandoned? How do we know their parents truly gave them up?"

Jordan folded his arms and rolled back onto their blanket. "You've been on that for weeks, Bree. Chinese adoption is one of the least corrupt and most stable international programs. The Hunan thing was an aberration. Jolie and Julianne were not trafficked!"

"Have you seen some of the recent posts from Rumor Queen?" Leslie grabbed a handful of M&M's. "On the increase in wait times? I am so glad we got our adoption done last year. They're expecting it to go as high as eighteen months."

"I didn't see that post," said Bree, "but I saw the big debate on her site about why the wait is increasing. One blog says it's because there aren't as many babies being abandoned and even couples in China who want to adopt are being turned away because the orphanages are putting all their kids into the international program. He says domestic families are being denied a child because the orphanage can make more money off the donations we foreigners give when we adopt."

"That's ridiculous." Leslie's husband tossed a twig away from our blankets. "China just doesn't want to look like they're exporting kids to America. It's because of the bad press they got from Hunan. Made them look bad."

Lewis put his fingers to his chin. "It's possible. From what I know of Chinese culture, they hate to be embarrassed. But I've been reading that other guy's blog too, and there might be some truth to it."

"Impossible. China has thousands of orphans. Only a third of orphanages even participate in the IA program. Where are the rest of the kids in the other two-thirds?"

The discussion roiled around me, matching the uncomfortable rhythm inside me. What was true? Was China suppressing adoption just to save face? Or was our demand for children keeping Chinese families from their dream of adopting a child?

I looked into the leaves of the oak tree and saw Yang Hua's face, the way it looked the last second before she'd left me alone in the government office room with Eva. She'd said they hadn't wanted to adopt her. But what if she was saving face too?

"He acts like he feels guilty for adopting from China. All this talk about the loss of birth culture and those poor, waiting domestic families." Leslie's husband jabbed his finger into his palm to emphasize his words. "Birth culture is important. We are all for teaching our daughter to love and respect her Chinese heritage, but I don't think we should feel guilty for bringing her here. She's got a great life and a loving family."

I edged farther back against the tree. I felt that guilt, and it didn't seem right. But Leslie's husband's attitude didn't seem correct either.

Yang Hua was the living embodiment of this conundrum. I had deprived Eva of a loving foster family, but I'd given her a loving permanent family. We took her from China, but we gave her America. Was the trade-off fair? Was it just? Suddenly, I didn't know. It had all seemed so simple at the beginning, but the farther I traveled in this journey, the more I realized that there wasn't a single thing about any of it that was simple.

Children's shouts and someone crying halted the discussion and my private questioning. Bree's sons ran to us. They were carrying a muddy, sobbing Eva.

"She fell in the lake!" The older boy set her down and she tottered toward me.

A picture of a drowning Eva flashed through my mind. I shuddered and gripped her shoulders. "You weren't supposed to go near the water! You knew that!"

"I didn't mean to." She looked miserable, and for a moment my anger wavered.

But the crushing image of what could have happened flared in me again. "You never mean to. Why can't you just do what I tell you? Why don't you listen to me? It's not hard."

My words collapsed in my mouth, and her sobs grew louder, hanging in the humid air.

A sharp pain shot through my skull.

I sounded just like my mother.

Impatient. Accusing. Disdainful.

Had she felt the way I was feeling—this anger born of terror?

I didn't want to think of her that way, didn't want to feel sorry for her. I didn't want to feel sorry for me, either. I'd just behaved abominably. I'd acted like my mother, and that was unforgivable.

The drowning image flickered to life again. I reached through it to cup her dirty face. "I'm sorry, honey. You scared me . . . again. Are you hurt?"

She shook her head, her body still trembling. I pulled her close to me, but she only tolerated my touch, not relaxing into it. My breath quivered from me.

The group stared at us. I felt the familiar tightening of my chest, heard the faint buzz in my ears. I whipped my head to Lewis and pleaded with my eyes for help.

He nodded and took Eva's hand. "I think it's going to take both of us to get you cleaned up, toots."

He supported my arm with his other hand and helped me to my feet. "You're going to be okay," he murmured in my ear.

I cleaned her up as best I could in the park restroom. She skipped happily back to her friends, the ugly incident apparently forgotten. Lewis walked me to our car so I could berate myself in private.

"What kind of mother doesn't even find out first if her child is okay before scolding her?" I balled a tissue in my fist and scrubbed at my eyes.

"You were scared. It's okay."

"I should be more patient with her. But instead, I acted just like my mom."

He handed me another tissue. "That's not all bad, you know. Your mom has issues, but she's not an evil person. She did some things right. Look at you."

"My mom doesn't deserve any credit for how I've turned out! I did that in spite of her. You weren't there; you don't know what she was like. The criticism, the constant blame, the never-ending disapproval. I did that to Eva! In front of everyone. I'm ruining my daughter and killing whatever chance of friendship I had with those people."

Lewis tugged me close to him, slipping one arm around my shoulder and using the other to cradle my face against his chest. "Shh. That's not true. Not at all. So you lost your temper. Frankly, Eva sort of deserved it. She didn't listen to what we told her to do."

"She didn't deserve it. And I don't deserve her."

"Don't go there, Meg. Not today. I don't think any of us really deserve most of the good things that come our way. But Eva's here and you are a great mom to her. You're her good thing."

"I don't feel so good for her. I feel sort of toxic."

He kissed my forehead. "I know. But I'd have given anything to have a mother who loved me enough to panic and lose her temper when I did stupid things. It's love. Maybe she won't appreciate that for years, but trust me—she will someday."

"I don't think I like what motherhood is doing to me. This was supposed to be a fresh start. I was supposed to do things differently."

"You are, already."

"How?"

"You care. You care intensely about the impact your words have on Eva. I think that will make all the difference in the world between you and your mom. You care."

Maybe he was right, but as a light rain fell from an ever-graying sky, I wondered. I'd always thought I was so different from my mom.

I wanted to be different—as far apart in temperament and action as humanly possible. I'd thought that an adopted child would help me be different, be better. Clean out whatever bits of my mother were infecting my soul. But she was still there, in me, like a weed whose roots were entangled hopelessly deep in my mind and spirit.

She was there. And I didn't know how to tear her out and throw her away.

Meg Lindsay, September 2006

The empanadas at El Bailongo had missed me. I knew this because when a plate of them was set down on our table, they wrapped fragrant fingers of steam around my head and blew spicy kisses at me. I breathed them in. "I missed you too."

"Talking to the food?" Lewis's mouth quirked in a smile. "I knew you needed to get out, but I didn't know how badly."

"Do you think I should call Krista, just to check how Eva is doing?" I had my cell phone out before he could reply.

His hand covered mine. "You called when we got here—all of a ten-minute walk. That was twenty minutes ago. She's fine. She's in bed. Probably asleep by now."

"We've just never left her with a babysitter before."

He picked up an empanada and held it in front of my face. "Eat, and stop worrying."

"How can I not worry? Krista is only fifteen. What do fifteen-year-olds know about taking care of a child?" I bit the proffered pastry, and for a moment, my worry was smothered in beef and flaky, fried breading.

"You babysat when you were her age, didn't you?"

"Yes! And that's why I'm worried."

He laughed. "You are such a mom."

That stopped me midbite. Such a mom. Me? I grinned an empanada-happy grin. "Yeah, guess I am."

"Sorry we're late." Hands clapped me on my shoulders from behind.

"Bree!" I stood to hug her and Jordan. Lewis hurried around the table to kiss Bree's cheek and shake Jordan's hand.

Jordan helped seat his wife. "Beckham just turned thirteen, and it's hard for him to find babysitting jobs because he's a boy. So he's taking care of the other three, and we had to have a last-minute haggle on the price."

"Plus, we got lost—but Jordan's too much of a guy to admit that part. Right, sweetie?"

"I blame construction."

Lewis and I grinned at each other. Bree and Jordan's constant banter was like our own private floor show. I shoved the plate toward them. "You're just in time for an empanada. Grab one now because I haven't had any in over six months—since we got Eva—so I'm not feeling too much like sharing."

"First date since becoming parents?" Bree speared an empanada, and as it traveled to her plate, I gazed after it with great regret.

"Pretty much," said Lewis.

"I hope we aren't intruding, then."

"No. Of course not. We've been looking forward to this for weeks."

Jordan cut his empanada in precise sections before poking his fork into a bite. "So are you going to give us a dancing demonstration? Bree is threatening to make me take lessons."

Lewis smiled, shaking his head. "An opportunity, not a threat." He touched my wrist. "Would you like to dance?"

I flipped an empanada onto my plate. "Sure. But note the contents of my plate. They had better be exactly the same when we return. Understand?"

"Ooh," Bree said. "You've gotten the mother-eye down very well, Meg! I'm scared."

Lewis tugged me away, chuckling. We weaved through the tables and down the steps to the dance floor. I waved to Bree and Jordan, who were standing against the balcony railing to watch us.

Lewis put his arm around my waist and led me onto the

floor. "Enjoying our adults' night out? Just the two of us and our friends?"

I wrapped my arm around his shoulder, into the full embrace I knew so well. "Yes. Only she's still with us, you know? I don't think it will ever be just the two of us again."

"I know."

The music began, and Lewis pressed us back into the flow of the other dancers.

His hands tightened on me. "I have missed dancing with you," he murmured against my ear.

"I feel so rusty."

"You're doing beautifully. Backward *ochos*, now."

He pressed me into the twisting figure-eight-styled steps, and by the second one, my muscles remembered what they were about and I enjoyed the sensual slide of my body through the steps.

He reclaimed me into his arms. "Lovely, Señora Lindsay."

I turned my head just enough to nibble his earlobe. And somewhere over my shoulder, I heard my little girl's voice. "Ew, Mom, that is so disgusting."

Giggles rippled through me. This was a tango for three, apparently.

"Hungry, are you?" Lewis shifted me into a turn and then back against him and I giggled harder. "What's funny?"

"Nothing," I gasped. "Just that it's *really* not just the two of us anymore."

Before I drew another breath, blackness engulfed me. A terrorizing aloneness separated me from even myself. My limbs were torn from my body, and a burning hand twisted off my head and threw it into the blackness. For a moment, my face leered back at me, but not my own.

Eva's.

"Eva!"

My shout cleared the evil darkness, and I stumbled in the still-going tango. Lewis steadied me. "Are you okay?"

"It's Eva. We have to go." I dragged him through the other couples, destroying the flow of the dance, but I didn't care.

"What are you doing?" He stumbled after me.

Bree met me at the steps and grabbed my hand. "Your phone rang so I answered. It was your babysitter's mom, and she said that Eva was having a terrible nightmare. They can't wake her up and she's screaming."

Lewis muttered something unrepeatable and pushed past me up the stairs. "If Jordan will stay, can you drop us off in your car?" He threw the plea over his shoulder as he raced to our table. He grabbed his sport coat with his wallet in it and tossed my purse to me.

"Sure." Bree snatched her purse from her chair and we followed her to her car.

It was a short ride home, but every second seemed like an hour.

"Does she have nightmares a lot?" Bree said.

"Usually one or two a week." I rammed my head against the back of the seat. "I knew we shouldn't have left her."

Bree let us off in front of our building, saying she was going to find a place to park and join us. We dashed through the lobby and caught the elevator just in time. Soon, we were by her side in her bedroom.

She had wakened by then, but was still crying. I pulled her against me. "Shh, darling. Mommy's here. Mommy's here, baby."

But I hadn't been there. That was the whole problem. I should have been there for her.

What sort of mother love was this?

She pushed me away. "Baba!"

Hesitantly, Lewis crept forward. She lunged at him and he wrapped his arms around her, staring at me with wide, uncertain eyes. I motioned for him to continue and then scooted off the bed. She'd chosen him, chosen her daddy to comfort her. Not me.

Bree waited for me on our sofa. I slumped beside her, and she eased my head onto her shoulder.

"She didn't want me. She never wants me." I brushed aside a tear. "I know it shouldn't matter, especially not right now, but I want to be the one she needs."

Bree smoothed my hair. "It's okay to feel that way. Our agency always tells parents that every institutionalized child has special needs. She's got more scars than the one on her mouth."

"I just wanted to help her. I want to make it better."

"And you are. She's making great progress."

"Is she? I can't take this roller coaster, Bree! Some days, things are great, and I get fooled into believing it's getting better. And then, everything goes crazy again. Up and down, day after day. It's making me sick."

Bree made a soothing, cooing sound. "That's how it's been for our Julianne too. It's terribly hard. Attachment is rougher for some kids than others. But you are making progress. You have to remember where you started and how far you've come."

"They don't warn you about this part when you apply to adopt."

Bree snorted. "Of course they don't. They're not stupid." She propped me up to turn my face to her. "Look, some things with our kids are so broken that we can't fix them on our own—no matter how much we love them. No matter how great of parents we are. You *are* a good mother. You are!"

A dull hopelessness settled inside me, like a rock sinking to the bottom of a lake. "But it's not enough. I'm failing her."

Bree sat up straight and took me by the shoulders. "You have not failed her! You've given her a second chance at a life full of love and security." She glanced around the room. "Got a piece of paper? And a pen?"

I brought them to her from the study. She flipped open her phone, pressed a few buttons, and then scribbled something on the paper. She handed it to me. "That's the name of our psychologist. Jolie didn't need her, but Julianne does."

"You think Eva needs therapy? Lots of kids have bad dreams."

"This goes beyond bad dreams, and you know it. She needs help. You're her mother. It's your job to help her, and sometimes, you need a support team to do that. You can't do this by yourself."

I heard Eva sniffle from the other room. Heard the murmur of Lewis's voice. I glanced at the paper in my hand. I wanted to be in that room so badly, but maybe it was supposed to be this way. Maybe this was how I was to help. To be there for her. She did need me, even if she didn't know it. I hugged Bree. "Thanks. I'll give her a call."

TWENTY-FIVE

Wen Ming, September 2006

Some nights, as I lay in my bed trying not to think about how I missed Zhen An, trying not to worry about how empty my life would turn out when I was blind and alone without her, I heard thumping and bumping coming from the bedroom of Auntie Yang and Uncle Zhou. Something large was hitting their wall, and from the squeaky, rhythmic sound of it, I guessed it was their bed.

And they always told *me* not to jump on my bed!

I thought it was very unfair. And why must grown-ups jump on beds anyway? They were not children. Jumping on beds was a child thing to do. They did not do it every night, but it was often enough that I was just about ready to bring it up to them and see about re-negotiating my own bed-jumping ban.

One night, I faintly heard them talking.

"Your mother asked . . . baby . . ." Auntie Yang sounded sad.

Baby? What was this?

"I'm sorry. I'll talk to her."

". . . always talk. She doesn't listen."

There was some rustling, and creaking, like one of them had sat on the bed.

". . . try tonight?" Auntie Yang said.

"And if it doesn't . . . disappointed." Sadness flavored Uncle Zhou's voice.

"I'll be fine."

"You don't fool me . . . want this very much."

It was quiet, and then, "Yes, I do."

Uncle Zhou laughed low and soft, in a way I'd never heard before. It made me feel strange—curious and embarrassed and oddly safe. ". . . not what I meant."

"Please?"

"As if I'd say no."

I didn't hear much more for several minutes. Then the thumping began.

We were definitely going to have to have a talk about this. Rules were rules, after all.

About two weeks later, during which time they'd jumped on their bed almost every night, I found Auntie Yang crying while she made breakfast.

"Are you sick?" I asked her.

"No." She sniffled. "Just tired." She set a hot bowl of sweet soy milk in front of me and guided my hands to it. I could still see it a little, but I was glad for her help. "And Uncle Zhou bought deep-fried devils from the vendor early this morning. And there's pork dumplings. So eat."

I loved the fried strips of dough. I tore one in half and dipped it in my soy milk. "Maybe if you didn't jump on your bed so much at night, you wouldn't be so tired."

She dropped something. I heard it crash to the floor and heard her say some very bad words that I was never to say. Water ran in the sink, and then I made out her shadowed form on the floor, wiping up the spilled milk. "I thought you were asleep. You shouldn't still be awake that late."

"And you shouldn't jump on the bed. You always tell me not to. It's not fair."

She started crying again. I felt my way to her and hugged her.

"I'm sorry. You are the grown-up. It is your bed. You can jump on it if you want."

She hugged me back, but she was still crying.

Then I remembered the sad-sounding voices I sometimes heard at night. "Are you crying because you don't have a baby?"

She stiffened, sighed, and then muttered something about having her room "soundproofed"—whatever that meant. "You need to eat your breakfast, Wen Ming."

"You don't need a baby, you know. You have me."

She patted my back and kissed the top of my head, but didn't say anything. And I think I heard her still sniffling while I ate my pork dumpling and drank my soy milk. A cold twist of worry curled up my spine. I was better than a baby.

Wasn't I?

TWENTY SIX

Meg Lindsay, February 2007

"Clean your room, Eva." It slipped off my tongue with hardly a thought from me. I was working on the grocery list to give to Lewis once he returned from the exercise center.

Thousands of mothers say it every day, and their children offer up various degrees of compliance. I remember being given that command. I remember the unreasonable surge of anger and despair that always confronted the task of putting my room in order. It wasn't that I wanted my room to be messy. I loved it neat and orderly, but having to create that order overwhelmed me.

So I get why children dislike it. I don't enjoy it either, even after years of being an adult. But this is what we did on Saturday mornings, especially on Saturdays when I had a performance in the evening. After a year of Eva living with us, I thought it was a well-established routine.

It wasn't until I noticed the silence of noncompliance that I looked up. She stood in the entryway to the kitchen, unmoving, a dark light glowing in her face.

"I don't have to."

The words were soft, incredulous. As if the thought was a revelation to her. As if she had surprised herself with her own defiance.

I set my pencil down with a click. "What did you say?"

Stronger now. "I don't have to."

"Eva . . ." I tried to send her the Mother's Stare of Doom. She shifted and looked away, but there was still a stiff, unyielding jut to her stance.

Then a black mist poured from her, like a car engine that had just burst its head. She turned back to me, her eyes swallowing the light. "You aren't my real mom! I don't have to do anything you say! And I'm not cleaning my room! I hate cleaning my room!"

My body lurched hot, then cold, and I couldn't feel the table anymore under my fingertips. This could not be happening. What had I done to trigger that anger? I tried to think of what the therapist would say, tried not to let her words pierce me—but they did, carving out huge holes that let the black mist seep into the pores of my skin, choking my thoughts, and filling my blood with a bleak sense of destiny, as if this script had been written from the beginning of time and we could do nothing but recite our given lines.

"Don't you dare take that defiant tone with me. I *am* your real mother. I'm the only mother you have, and you'd better not forget that!"

I wasn't sure she even knew the word "defiant."

"I never wanted you for my mom!"

Her words formed into a silver lance that plunged through my chest. My heart thudded and I fought for air. The mist looped around my throat, squeezing. Then it was in my throat, in my body, churning up all my own inner darkness, calling it out of me. I fought to keep it in, but the pain grew too intense. I let go, and it burst from me in a putrid stream.

"You think this is what I wanted? I thought I'd be getting a daughter who would love me. Instead, I got one who's rude and unkind."

My words slapped her, and she jerked back from them, her eyes filling with tears.

The rage drained from me. What had I done?

I was her *mother*. I, of all people, was supposed to accept her just the way she was. Problems and all.

Why had I said that? Why couldn't I have just helped her with her room?

I choked back a sob of self-hatred.

I'd thought that I could become a mother without becoming the person I detested. But there was no such thing as starting over. There were no fresh beginnings. There was only me—carved with the sharpest of knives into a bleeding, infected image of my mother—now wielding those same knives on my own daughter.

I wanted to scream, wanted to fall on my knees and fling my arms over my head and ask God to make the world collapse on us both so that we would not do further harm.

But then, I saw a silvery shape slide through the mist. Myself—or at least a reflection. It was not the carved mother-image I saw in my own heart, but a whole, intact me. Scarred, but somehow beautiful, in a way I'd never thought myself to be.

This silvery reflection knelt beside Eva, took her in her arms, and said, "I am sorry, darling. I said things I didn't mean. I want you—no matter if you are angry or happy, no matter if you love me or not. Let's try this again, okay? How about if I help you clean your room."

It was me—the way I dreamed of being. Gentle and soft, accepting, full of love. I didn't know if she could ever be more than a dream, but something inside me propelled me off my chair. If I could just catch the image, hold her tight, maybe she'd stay—maybe she'd become me, and I could become that person I wanted to be.

She shimmered, and I do not know if she disappeared or if she vanished into me, but I grew a little stronger, a little less dark. A little more hopeful.

I'd taken her place with my arms around Eva. She stiffened, but then collapsed into my embrace, sobbing and shuddering. "Why did she leave me? I want my China mom! I don't want to be adopted. I want my mama. I just want her. I want to live in China and be with her!"

Each word ripped the flesh from my bones, and the wounds stung with the salt from my tears. I had known that eventually this moment would come. We'd been warned that it might. But who could put into words how much it would hurt? I grabbed her tighter and cried into the soft hollow where her neck and shoulder met. We sobbed together our grief and pain.

What do you say to your child when her soul has already been so crushed and battered by realities no child should face? We talk about it in adoption seminars, we discuss it on e-mail loops and parent support groups. But there's a careful layer of distance laid over the gaping, exposed hearts that are bleeding underneath the questions. You can plan and practice what to say, how to cope, but in the dark moment of that reality, you have nothing left but a desperate cry to God for strength and wisdom. You have no choice but to forget about how your own spirit is lying weak and bloodied. Somehow, you find a way to lift your child in your broken arms and carry her, because you know your own pain is nothing compared to her suffering.

I let her talk to me about her China mom. I encouraged her to tell me her fantasy of how life would be if she were with her birth family, if she'd never come to the orphanage, if she'd never come into my life. I listened, even though every word made me want to grab her and scream, to hold on and never let go.

I loved her. I couldn't help it. Even though she couldn't love me in return right then. Even though she might never be able to love me, I loved her with a love so deep and wonderful and powerful, it was a barely dormant volcano inside me.

So why wasn't that enough? Why wasn't I enough for her? I knew that her fantasy of the perfect China mom wasn't true. I might be flawed and fighting against my own inner darkness, but I hadn't abandoned my daughter. I'd taken her in. I was loving her even when she didn't love me. Why couldn't she see that? Why did she want the woman who had left her? Why wasn't I good enough?

I was never good enough.

I had never been good enough.

Later that evening, at the University of Chicago's Mandel Hall, where the Nouveau Chicago Symphony performed, that knowledge curled and flopped inside me, like a flesh-eating fish. Backstage, I took my viola out of its case, and the fish inside me attacked. It bit into my lungs with a savagery that left me shaking and unable to stand. It devoured my stomach and bile crawled up my throat.

I couldn't speak. The viola slipped from my numb fingers, and only Li Shu's quick reaction kept it from splintering on the floor. She guided me to the restroom and held my hair while I vomited. She brought me some bottled water, breath mints, and something in a thermos and then sat with me while I huddled, gasping for air.

"I . . . can't play tonight."

"Yes you can."

I curled into a tighter ball. She rubbed my back. "Here, try this." She poured steaming liquid from the thermos into a cup and handed it to me. "It's Chinese medicine tea. Helps you relax. I always have some before a performance."

I sipped it, and the warmth flooded my body and brought back feeling to my hands and lips. "I had a horrible fight with Eva this morning."

"I'm sorry."

I drank more tea. It loosened my tongue. "She doesn't want me for her mother. She wants her China mom. I'm failing her. I wanted to help her, and I'm making her life worse."

Li Shu drew a slow, deep breath through her nose. Her jaw clenched. I felt a struggle in her, but then it calmed. "You shouldn't feel inadequate. You are a much better mother than her birth mother." Her face hardened. "You are a much better woman than she is."

"You can't say that. You don't know what she went through that made her do what she did."

"A mother never gives up! A mother would fight for her child. That woman is not a mother."

Her words sliced the air with a harsh blade. I wanted to put my arms around her, but her body was serrated and sharp and I didn't want to cut myself. She was wrong—sometimes a mother had no choice but to give up. A mother didn't always have the strength to be what she should be.

Yet, her confidence in me, as misplaced as it was, gave me a measure of peace. And the brittle hollowness in her eyes gave me strength. I stood and held my hand out to her.

And like so many other musicians before us, we bled our pain through our instruments, turning it for our audience, who would never know the sacrifice, into a thing of beauty and pleasure.

TWENTY SEVEN 七

Wen Ming, April 2007

B efore the New Year comes, we clean the house. We sweep every
floor and carry the dust and dirt of the old year away to make room
for the New Year. We light firecrackers to chase away the old year and
welcome the new. At midnight, we open our doors and windows, so
that the old year will slink away into the night, and the New Year will
fill our houses with fortune and happiness.

The old cannot stay with the new. We never hold on to the old.
It is banished. It has served its purpose, and there is no room for it in
our hearts or homes. The old has no promise. It either has fulfilled its
promise or brought us disappointment. But the new is yet to come.
It has not caused us either joy or pain, so we embrace it because we
have hope that it will live up to all we imagine it to be.

I used to wonder what happened to the old year. Sent away, un-
celebrated, chased out, without being thanked for the memories it
gave us, for the growth it prompted in us, for the love it provided.

On a warm evening in April, when I was months away from turning nine, my auntie and uncle sat with me on a sofa in our living
room and gently explained to me that I was their old year.

"We are having a baby!" Auntie Yang held my hand, and though
I could not see her smile, I felt the radiance of it. She had wanted
a baby for so very long. I was glad her dream was finally coming
true.

"We are? When?" I bounced a little on the cushion. "The baby can sleep in my room, and then I will comfort it when it cries, so you won't have to wake up at night."

The silence that followed drained me of my excitement. Something was very wrong.

Finally Uncle Zhou patted my knee. "You are a smart girl, almost grown-up. So I know you can understand."

"Understand what?"

"We love you very much, Wen Ming." Auntie Yang's voice didn't sound right. It was higher-pitched than usual, and restrained. "But a baby is a big responsibility. It means we have to make a lot of changes."

"So, you don't want me to hold the baby at night? Is it because of my sight? I understand. Maybe I will just creep to its crib and hold its hand. That would be safer."

"That's not what I mean!" Auntie Yang sounded like she was going to cry. Why would something as wonderful as a baby make her cry?

"Auntie Yang is trying to say that . . . we need to put all our effort into caring for our child."

Something didn't make sense.

"We love you, but . . ."

There is something awful about the word "but." It has a way of canceling whatever good has come before. I felt that word ramming against the foundations of my life, making my world shudder around me.

"But what?"

Uncle Zhou sighed and shifted next to me. I put my hands out and felt his back curled, hunched over. I traced down his arms where he'd rested his elbows on his knees. "We have to send you back to the Children's Home. We are sorry. But it has to be this way."

The world fell down around me, its dust choking my lungs. I swallowed rocks and pebbles from the rubble. My foster parents didn't want me anymore. "Why?" I whispered.

They said it was because they did not have room enough for me and the new baby. But I knew the truth. It was expensive, even with the foster stipend, to care for me. And in many ways I was as depen-

dent as a baby—they had to take me everywhere and help guide me.
I tried to be good, but since Zhen An had gone, I'd felt naughty and
angry even though I didn't wish to be. I'd made Auntie and Uncle
tired of me.

And I remembered what Uncle Zhou's mother had said at that
long-ago New Year's party.

*"You are spending your precious time on orphans, deformed orphans,
instead of giving me grandchildren of my own."*

Mothers were powerful. They could control even the hearts of
their sons. This mother did not approve of me. I felt sure she would
not want me to stay here once this house held a grandchild of
her own.

"When are you sending me back?" I didn't recognize my own
voice. It sounded so cold and calm. I did not feel cold or calm inside.
I was too full of the stones of rubble from my collapsed world.

"In one month."

Auntie Yang squeezed my hand. "It's not that we don't love you.
And I'll still see you every day. And we've already made sure you
can still call and e-mail Zhen An. Director Wu promised us. One
of the aunties from Great Britain will help you with the English.
So it's—"

"Take me tomorrow."

"What?"

My mouth was full of stones that I spit at her. "I don't want to wait
a month. I want to go back tomorrow."

"But we were going to take you shopping for new clothes and
some things to take with you."

"I don't want them. I'll wear what all the other orphans wear."

"Wen Ming . . ."

The stones had filled up my insides, hard and heavy. I was cursed
to be unwanted—three times now I had been sent away. I could not
give in to the pain. I must be strong. I must be hard like a stone so I
would not be crushed. "I don't want your gifts! I don't want anything
from you. You say you love me, but you don't. I don't want to talk to
either of you ever again."

And I didn't. The next morning, they took me to the Children's

Home and I did not say good-bye or even thank you. After all, the old year does not say thank you when we sweep it away or chase it from the house. I held my head high, my hot stones bold and stubborn in my stomach. I would not be chased. I would not slink away. I would be like a great boulder—hard and strong and immovable. A constant reminder that a child is not like an old year. You cannot throw her away.

TWENTY
EIGHT

Meg Lindsay, March 2008

There were so many good days. So many that I didn't always
remember to be thankful for them. Then a dark day would take
me by surprise, and I'd be shaken by how fragile the peace in our
family was.

A day like today.

I picked Eva up from school, a dull ache along the back of my
head numbing my good sense and my restraint. "You are in big trouble, young lady."

She hadn't even gotten her seat belt on. "What did I do?"

I jerked the car out into traffic. "I got a phone call today from your
teacher. You are failing second grade—at least for this report card!
You haven't been bringing home your work, and you were mouthy to
your teacher."

She didn't say anything. Just stared out the car window like she
hadn't heard me.

"Eva!"

"What?"

"Did you hear me? Do you want to flunk school?"

"I hate school."

"Too bad. Learn to like it. You are not allowed to fail, and you are
definitely not allowed to be disrespectful to your teacher."

I wanted to bite off my tongue. She'd only been in the United
States for two years. She'd made amazing progress. I should have
been proud of her, not scolding her.

I missed a stop sign and nearly collided with another car. So I held my tongue until we were safely in the apartment. She threw her backpack on the sofa and started for her room.

"Get back here. You are not going anywhere."

"Can I have a snack?"

"No!"

She slouched to the armchair and flung herself across it so her legs hung over the arm. I had a sudden glimpse of what life would be like when she was a teenager, and it made me run to the kitchen for a glass of ginger ale to settle my stomach.

The critical, disappointed words were there, in my mouth, waiting to be let out. But I saw the dull glow of shame behind the defiance in her eyes. A little of my anger left. I knew how she felt.

I forced an encouraging note into my voice. "What's going on with school? Your teacher says it's mostly reading. I thought you were doing okay with reading?"

"I'm not the reading type. It's too hard for me." Her chin wobbled.

Lewis walked in the door. Home early for some reason. I gave him a quick synopsis of the story, and he gave a helpless shrug and sank onto the sofa.

"You are most certainly the reading type." The urge to criticize was an animal caged inside me, gnawing its way to freedom. "You are a very smart girl. You shouldn't be having problems."

"It's hard!"

Her wail grated on me. The animal in me struggled harder. "Lots of things are hard in life. It doesn't mean you don't have to do them anyway. And it doesn't excuse your behavior to your teacher."

"I'm tired of her. She treats me like I'm stupid."

"Well, maybe if you didn't act—" I clapped my mouth shut. Lewis gave me a sharp glance. He knew what I'd been about to say. The animal had almost gotten free. "Maybe if you acted more respectful, she would show you more respect too." I was proud of delivering the chiding line in a calm, pleasant voice.

"You can't sass your teacher." Lewis leaned toward Eva, and I envied his low, authoritative voice. "Not for any reason, no matter how hard school is."

Eva's eyes filled with tears. "I don't mean to be sassy. I don't mean to do badly on my work. I'm trying really hard."

My heart twisted, choking off that beast inside me. I was supposed to love her, to encourage her. I wanted to, so why was it such a struggle? "I know you are. Why didn't you tell us that you were having a hard time reading? We could have helped you. We can't help if you don't tell us."

Her lower lip jutted forward. "I told Wen Ming! She said—"

That was too much after the day I'd had. What I'd gone through for her. "Wen Ming is not your mother! I don't care what she said! She's a child with just as many problems as you, and she can't help you. I'm your mom! You talk to me. Not her."

A tear slid down her cheek. "I like talking to her. She never gets mad at me."

Would this bizarre competition between me and that far-off Chinese child ever stop? I started to answer, but Lewis shook his head.

"Eva, if your grades and your attitude do not improve at school, and if you do not start telling us what is going on, then you will not be allowed to e-mail or talk to Wen Ming anymore. Do you understand?"

She stared at him with her mouth open, her face reddening with tears. I could feel her pain and fear. "Lewis, I think that's a bit harsh."

"No, it isn't. School comes before friends. Good behavior comes before friends." He glared at me. "Eva, why don't you go to your room and *read a book*."

As soon as she was gone, he motioned for me to follow him into our bedroom. He closed the door. "You didn't back me up. I was trying to support you, and you didn't return the favor."

I paced between the bed and the dresser. "I'm sorry. I don't know if threatening to cut her off from Wen Ming is a good idea."

"I think Wen Ming is a bad influence on her. She has more nightmares after she hears from Wen Ming. And she is sassier to you after she talks to Wen Ming. I don't like it."

I sat next to him on the bed. "I don't like it either. But I'm afraid she'll hate us if we take Wen Ming from her. I couldn't stand that."

He pulled me against him. "I know." He rubbed my arm. "So what's the real problem? Something is bothering you."

I snuggled into him. "The school called me during my symphony leadership meeting. I had to step out of the meeting, and after I got off the phone, Maestro Chelsea was waiting for me in the hall. He's 'concerned' about how much time I've been missing from rehearsals and meetings because of Eva. He says I'm spread too thin and he wants me to cut back."

Lewis was quiet a moment. "I'm sorry. I haven't been as much help as I should."

"You can't. I was a fool to think I could manage it all. Don's right—I need to cut back."

"What are you going to do?"

"I'm going to let Li Shu have my chair and my spot on the leadership committee. If I'm not the principal violist, I can cut my hours to three-quarters and have more time to spend working with Eva. Maybe I can find her a tutor, or volunteer at her school."

"But that symphony is your baby! You built it."

"There was a group. It wasn't just me."

Lewis pushed me away so he could look at me. "The Nouveau Chicago Symphony exists because you and the other charter members pushed for it and got funding for it. You poured your hearts into that group."

"It couldn't last forever, honey. Eva needs me more than they do."

"Music is your life, Meg. I don't want you to give that up."

"I'm not giving it up entirely. But you and Eva are my life now. And she has to come first. That's what a mom does."

"That's not what my mom did. She chose her career over me."

I reached across his back and laid my head on his shoulder. "You aren't your mom."

"I might be." He made me sit up to look at him. "I got home early today because I had some news."

I raised my eyebrows, waiting.

"I've been offered a position on a team that will be working on locating the Higgs boson."

"That's great! I thought that's what you were already doing."

He laughed. "Well, indirectly. But this team—Meg, we might actually do it. We might find the Higgs."

There was a catch somewhere. I could feel it. "And . . . ?"

He hesitated. "Our work will be conducted at the LHC at CERN."

"In English, please." I shoved him lightly.

"Sorry. It's a huge accelerator at CERN—the lab in Switzerland."

"Oh. So you'll have to go there for the experiment?"

He winced. "Not that simple. I'll be in charge of building a certain component of the experiment. It has to be constructed on-site at CERN. So I'll have to travel to oversee the construction and testing of that piece."

"How much travel?"

"Weeklong trips, not a lot at the beginning—once during the first six months or so. But the second part of the year, it will be once every month and then I'll have to stay in Switzerland for an entire month while we run the experiment."

"Oh my goodness."

"Plus, there will be a lot of prep work done here at the university."

"No! I don't like this. What's wrong with working with a team at Fermi?"

"Fermi is dying. The cutting-edge stuff has all moved to CERN. Meg, this is what I've worked for my whole career. This is everything to me."

There was something more to it. A fire, a passion that meant more than a step up for his career. "It means more than your family? I need you. Eva needs you."

"I'll be home more than I'll be traveling."

"Yes, but where will your heart be? And your mind?"

He rolled off the bed and to his feet. "I have to do this!"

"I don't like it." The drive in him frightened me. There was something he wasn't telling me, something important. Something that went to the core of his being.

And he was shutting me out.

"I don't want you to go to Switzerland. I don't want you to work on this team. I want you to say no. For us."

"You can't ask me to do this."

"I'm taking a demotion in my career! For Eva. She deserves the same commitment from her dad."

He convulsed as if I'd shot him. With carefully shuttered eyes, he glared at me. "We'll talk about this later."

We never did.

Three days is a long time to be frightened. Three days is plenty of time for the imagination to concoct scenarios of every sort as to what secret your husband is keeping from you. Three days is a torturous amount of time to worry that you might be losing him. Three days is an eternity when you are barely speaking.

Three days is what I gave him. He didn't leave me a choice.

But at the end of three days of private tears, of long phone conversations with Bree, and tea therapy with Audra and Cinnamon, I was done. He'd had three days. It was time for him to talk.

So after we tucked Eva into bed, and after we'd rushed into her room to calm her after a nightmare, and after we gave her a drink and reassured her that "Mommy and Daddy were okay" . . .

After we'd silently loaded the dishwasher, checked our e-mail, put away some laundry, and paid a few bills . . .

After I couldn't stand the wall between us anymore . . .

I closed our office door. I cleared away the papers. I leaned against the door and faced him, my arms crossed.

"We need to talk. No—*you* need to talk."

"About?"

"About the thing you never talk about. The thing that's making you want to ditch your family and run away to Switzerland."

"Don't be so dramatic. I told you—it's for my career. You're the one not being supportive. You should be talking about why."

"It's not just about your career. There's something more. I can feel it. It's in the way you talk about the Higgs. It's always been there, and I've tried my best to respect your privacy and not ask. But I can't do it anymore. Not now."

His face paled when I said the word "Higgs." I hooked my arms around his neck.

"Lewis, please. You have to tell me. What's going on?"

He stepped away from my embrace and stood in front of his desk, looking at the photo of Naomi Ricci hanging there—like a shrine.

"Naomi Ricci is the descendant of Gregorio Ricci-Curbastro, an Italian mathematician who invented tensor calculus." He sounded like he was reciting from one of his textbooks. "She is a brilliant physicist who was one of the first to work on $N = 4$ supersymmetry phenomenological calculations. She wrote a seminal paper on $N = 4$ Yang-Mills supersymmetry back in the late seventies. A real breakthrough. But even before that, everyone knew she was destined to be one of the greatest physicists of her generation. Even more impressive—she's female. At that time, female physicists were rare and not well respected. But it's her life, her one driving passion. She forced the science community to respect her, on the basis of sheer intellect and drive."

I stared at the photograph, and as Lewis spoke, it began to glow. A shot of light burst from it and engulfed me in a veil of mist and stars. It drew me toward the photograph and pulled me in. For an awful moment, I felt like a coin dropped down one of those funnels set up by charities. I spun around and around, pulled toward the center of a deep hole, powerless to resist.

It shot me out through the hole into a world colored like a faded photograph.

I am in a house decorated in midseventies style. I cower on green shag carpet between the back of a yellow floral sofa and a wall the color of an overripe peach. I hear voices arguing. A man and a woman. My parents—only not *mine*, Meg Lindsay's, but the parents of this person I have become. They are yelling at each other, again. And in my seven-year-old body, every word lodges deep and burning, like lead shot.

"I never wanted to marry you, Liam!" the woman says. "I only did it because you got me pregnant. You did this to me! I wanted to give him up for adoption, but you wouldn't let me. I'm not going to let you ruin my life anymore."

"Please, honey. You're too worked up. I'll cut back my hours. I'll do whatever it takes. Just don't leave. Don't leave me alone to raise our child. All I ever wanted was you. Please."

"Stop whining. You didn't want me. Your family hates you for marrying an Italian instead of some Chinese chit. They despise me. They've made me miserable. And for what? So I could spend the past seven years being your babysitter? You don't want to raise a kid alone? What do you think I've been doing?"

"But you're his mother!"

"And that means what to you? That I should give up my career? Stay home and be nothing more than a housekeeper and nanny? I would go insane! I never wanted to be a mother. I never wanted kids. I was forced into it and it's killing my career. I'm leaving, and you can't stop me."

The terror rises in my heart. This is it. They've argued many times before, but there is a finality to this one. All he wants is her. All she wants is her career.

Neither of them want me.

I hear a suitcase clicking shut. The sound thunders through the house, jolting me to my feet. "Mommy!" I scream, running into their bedroom, even though she's told me to never, ever go in there.

Naomi Ricci stands there, suitcase in hand, dressed in one of her work pantsuits. I launch myself at her, grabbing her legs, pressing my head against her tummy.

"Don't go! Don't go, Mommy. I'll be a good boy. I'll be a good boy. I promise!" I am choking on tears and phlegm, and I rub my runny nose on my sleeve.

She pinches my arm and yanks me away from her, holding me out from her body as if I am a dirty towel or rotting fruit. "You're going to have to make that promise to your dad. I'm done. I'm absolutely done."

I stop screaming and crying. A heavy calm presses on me. She means it. It's over. I am going to lose my mother. I am shaking, and I might wet my pants. I try to hold it because if I have an accident now, she will hate me for it. "When can I see you again?" I don't call her "Mommy" this time. Somehow, I know it will only make her angrier.

She gives me an annoyed scowl, but I think something in my tone touched her, because she drops my arm and takes my chin in her hand. "You want to see me again? Then do something useful with your life. Find me the Higgs particle. Bring me the Higgs, Lewis, and we'll talk. Unless I find it first."

She doesn't even look back as she walks out the door. I know I will never see her again.

Unless . . .

The Higgs. "Bring me the Higgs, Lewis, and we'll talk."

I have no idea what that means, but that word brands me. Higgs. I will find it, even if it takes my whole life. And when I do, my mommy will love me again.

If I find the Higgs, I'll get my mom back. And this time I will never let her go.

My father spins toward me, rage distending his body, making it loom above me. He grabs the object closest to his hand—a large glass perfume bottle of my mother's. "This is your fault!" he shouts, his voice growly and scary. He throws the bottle at me. I duck, my arms over my head, and the bottle crashes through the bedroom window. The sidewalk below will smell like my mother for weeks, and I will lie on it and breathe her in until the next rain washes her away. But for now, I skitter toward the door. My father slams it behind me. "Stay out of my room!"

I collapse in the hallway, the walls turn to Jell-O, tumble down on me, and the world goes black. I am alone, and the only thing I hear is the sound I make crying.

When I opened my eyes, I was crouched on the floor, holding Lewis as if he were a little boy. He was crying, the sobs shaking him. "I want to find my mom." The words were almost unintelligible. "I know it's stupid. All these years, everything I've done. For her. She probably doesn't even remember. I hate her!"

But I knew he didn't. Not really. I'm not sure it's possible to ever truly hate a parent. No matter the rage and the pain, underneath there is still a nugget of love, and it chafes and rubs and refuses to go away. It leaves blisters and sores on the heart no matter how we try to protect it. He'd turned her into a hero, a mentor of sorts—wanting to follow in her footsteps and yet terrified he'd become just like her.

No wonder he'd been so frightened about having children.

That reminded me . . . "She said in that article you showed me that she didn't have children."

"I know." His voice was choked, barely audible.

I cried with him then. CERN, Switzerland, experiments . . . the Higgs. It was all okay. I would support whatever he felt he needed to do. Anything. Anything at all to help him ease the decades of pain and loss. Of rejection.

"Why didn't you tell me?" I kissed him above his ear and smoothed his hair. "All these years, I never knew. You had to know I would have been sympathetic. I would have been more supportive. Why didn't you trust me?"

"I trusted you. You're the only one in my world I really trust. I just didn't want to talk about it."

"Why not?"

He lifted bleary eyes to mine. Eyes full of the red emptiness of abandonment. "Because talking about it makes it real."

TWENTY-NINE

Wen Ming, September 2008

Zhen An was gone, though we still talked and e-mailed with Auntie Helen's help. Auntie and Uncle had deserted me. And though I had returned to my old job as a junior auntie in the baby room, there were fewer babies now, and they almost always were adopted before they were old enough to speak. I knew better than to become attached to them. I held them, but I didn't fill them with beautiful dreams or give them my love. They would take what I gave them and leave me, like everyone else had done.

So all that was left to me was my old dream of finishing my education and becoming the director of the Children's Home, so I could keep all the children to myself forever. School was what I lived for. I studied every moment I could—begging one auntie after another to read to me and test my memory of my lessons.

My eyes ached from the strain of trying to read. I shone a bright, hot lamp on the book and then leaned my face to the book until my nose mashed against the page. I'd move my head around in a circle trying to piece together the images that were too big to fit into the shrinking circle of my vision. And still, it was not enough. Ten years old, and though I could calculate math problems in my head and remember all the Chinese dynasties in order, with dates, I could not read or write.

I couldn't walk to school with the other orphans. At first, they tried to lead me, walk with me, but they soon lost interest and ran off. They were in great trouble over that, and from then on, one of the aunties escorted me to and from school.

I was a terrible burden. I had to be led everywhere and there were few activities at school I could participate in. I was so hungry—starving, really—for information, for learning. The less I was fed, the poorer I behaved. I knew I should do better, but there was such anger and restlessness in me. I didn't know how to contain it.

When the school's director told Director Wu and me that since they weren't equipped to deal with my vision problem they could no longer let me come to school, I should not have been surprised.

And I wasn't. Everything else had been taken from me, why not this too? I didn't even have the fire in me to be angry. There was a hole where my heart should have been, and all my feelings escaped through that hole.

I was never hungry. I hadn't been eating well since Auntie and Uncle sent me away. The orphanage food revolted me compared with Auntie Yang's cooking and Uncle Zhou's treats. But they were getting ready to cook for and treat their baby. And I was back to eating congee and limp vegetables. Now that the world of learning had been closed to me, now that I could not feed my mind, I could find no reason to feed my body.

Director Wu would not let me lie in bed all day—even though that was what I wished to do. She made me help in the baby room and do chores around the orphanage. I could tell she was worried. I smelled the worry on her skin and heard it in her voice. Auntie Yang offered to read to me and tutor me at the orphanage, but I would not speak to her. What she had done to me was unforgivable. And besides, I had no desire to be around her as she became large and round with her baby.

Her baby!

And when they ran out of chores for me to do, and when the babies were asleep, I felt my way out to the cherry tree in the courtyard. I sat at its base, leaned against the trunk, and lifted my face to feel the warm sun and to memorize the play of light and dark that still remained for me. Sometimes I would close my eyes and think of Zhen An, imagining what life would be like if she had stayed and been my little sister forever.

Auntie Helen found me there one afternoon in September. She was from England, which I didn't hate quite as much as America, but they took away my babies too, so I held no love for the country. I knew who it was because she smelled different—like a foreigner. And I could still see some color—she had blond hair.

"Sulking?" Her accent was terribly strong, but she spoke fluently. Sometimes I didn't understand her, but she was always good-natured about repeating herself for us.

"I am not sulking. When you sit under a tree, do people ask you if you are sulking?"

"No, because I eat my meals and don't avoid other people."

I hugged my knees to myself. "I like being alone, and I am not very hungry."

"Because you are sulking."

"I'm not! If you came out here to scold me, pick something that I've actually done."

"Like being mouthy?"

I groped on the ground until I found a leaf. I shredded it and sprinkled the pieces beside me. "What do you want?" I was being inexcusably disrespectful, but in a way, it felt good, like letting out a cloud of steam from a rice basket.

"I brought you a snack. But since you're so grouchy, I'll take it back inside and eat it myself."

"Fine. I didn't ask for a snack."

She was silent for a moment. I could feel her looking at me, probing me. "I'll give it to Auntie Yang. She's worked hard this afternoon. She hasn't been sitting under cherry trees sulking."

"I am not sulking!" I paused for a few moments. "What is the snack? Maybe I am a little hungry." I let my feet slide away from me until my legs stretched flat on the ground.

I thought I heard a smile in her voice as she took my hands and placed something cool and damp in them. "Sliced fresh pears. Eat them before they brown."

I bit into a slice. It was perfect. The juice was sweet, and the flesh soft but not mushy. The skin had just a bit of tang to it. And as I swallowed, my stomach rumbled.

Auntie Helen laughed. "I can see you are not hungry at all."

"Thank you, Auntie Helen."

"You're welcome. I brought you something else." She placed something heavy and flat and hard on my lap.

"What is it?"

"A book."

I shoved it off my lap. "I can't read. You are mean to tease me."

She reached over me to retrieve the book, and this time she slapped it quite forcefully on my legs. "Stop feeling sorry for yourself! There are people trying to help you, but if you keep being so ugly toward them, they'll want to stop."

"So people only want to help pretty, sweet girls?"

I think she may have growled softly. "You are a sweet, pretty girl, Wen Ming. And very smart. But you are angry and bitter, and that will make you become ugly and mean—and stupid. Because smart people know that being angry will ruin their lives. Smart people never give up, no matter how hard life is."

I didn't want to like this English foreigner. But she was tough. And when I pushed, she pushed back. It felt good. It made me feel alive again for the first time in weeks.

"What is this book?"

Instead of answering, she opened the book and put my hand on the page. "Feel it."

Tiny bumps, all over the page. "What is that?"

"What do you think it is?"

I traced the bumps. They were arranged in patterns. In rows. I turned a page, and there were more bumps, more rows. "Are they words?"

"Very good. You really are smart."

"What language?"

"Chinese."

"Chinese writing does not have bumps."

"This Chinese writing does. It's called Braille. I've been studying it. I helped students learn Braille English back home. I can help you learn Braille Chinese."

I sat up straight, my breath coming in little puffs. I caressed the book. These tiny bumps—could they open the world to me again? "I could read? Lots of books? I could go to school?"

"There are not many books written in Braille Chinese. As you can see, it makes the book very large because you can only put the bumps on one side of the page, and the symbols take up a lot of room. But I have a few books I can use to teach you, and then we can work on finding more for you later. They are rather expensive. But we will do what we can."

"So could I go back to school once I learn this Braille reading?"

"I'm sorry, but no. But I'll help tutor you as much as I can."

It was much, much better than nothing. I hefted the book to my chest and hugged it. "Thank you. I would like that very much."

"There is a condition. A few conditions, actually. First, you must eat your food. Second, you must be polite and kind. And third . . ."

"What is third?" I had no problems with the first two.

She placed her hand on my shoulder. "Third is you must forgive Auntie Yang and make friends with her again."

I slowly laid the book on my lap again. Forgive Auntie Yang? "I can't. I don't know how." I didn't want to. Being angry hurt less than being sad.

"I want you to try. Or else I will not teach you Braille."

It was as if she were poking me with a stick. Poking and poking, prodding and pushing. She didn't care about me. She was doing this for Auntie Yang. I threw the book down. "Then don't teach me! You don't know how it feels to have your home taken from you. To have your foster mother say she doesn't want you anymore. Don't tell me to forgive. You don't understand anything! You're just a stupid foreigner with yellow hair and a bad accent. You can't teach me anything."

I tried to run from her across the courtyard, but there was a bench in my way that should not have been there. I smacked into it and fell over it. My legs stung, and my elbow throbbed. I couldn't stop myself from crying.

Auntie Helen scooped me up and sat on the bench. She examined my legs and elbow and told me I'd have bad bruises, but otherwise I was unhurt.

"I haven't had the same experiences as you, dear one," she told me. "But I have been greatly hurt, by people who should not have hurt any child. For too long, I did not forgive. At last, I learned that by not forgiving, I was only adding to my pain. It's one thing for some-one else to hurt you, but why should you do it to yourself?"

I rubbed my bruised shins. She had a point. "I will talk to Auntie Yang. But I can't promise to forgive. At least not right away. But I will think about it."

Auntie Helen hugged me. "That is fair enough. Starting tomor-row, we will have Braille lessons. You, me, and Auntie Yang." She set me down and then I heard the grating sound of the bench being moved. "I had better put this back. I moved it when I came out. A well-placed bench is always useful."

I sighed. This foreign auntie was possibly more stubborn and manipulative than I was.

And for that, I had to admire her.

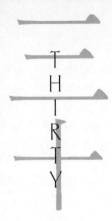

THIRTY

Meg Lindsay, September 2009

I saw a documentary on the Learning Channel recently about how many times surgeons accidentally leave their tools inside the bodies of their patients. They sew the poor folks up, leaving gauze or tweezers or even clamps and wires. The patients go home, and when they have searing pain or an unexplained infection, no one thinks to check for what might have been left behind. So they get sick. They're in pain. They set off security alarms at the airport. Some die.

Eva had been my daughter for three and a half years. In all that time, she had never said "I love you" to me or Lewis. Only to Wen Ming. *Wo ai ni, jie jie.* The phrase was lodged in my mind, in my heart, like a scalpel, and whenever I heard it, a slicing pain ripped through me.

Was it so much to ask—just three words? I tried to be patient. Tried to give her space and tell myself I could wait. But I hungered for it regardless.

It became an obsession to me. I analyzed every expression, every intake of her breath, her words, her gestures. The pressure of her hugs, the wattage of her smile—looking for clues, for a gauge of whether she was coming closer to me or pulling farther away. I measured my words, I worried about each one of them, and whether I had infused every touch and every tone with love and acceptance and affection. And when I failed, I berated myself for failing, for setting us back and making it harder for her to come to love me.

I was losing. By my measurements, she was moving away from

me, not toward me. She had friends now—chiefly Jolie—and activities in school. Tutoring improved her grades, and her therapist was helping her work through her anger and grief.

But still the nightmares continued, and still Wen Ming held a place of primacy in her life that no one else could match.

She had her own obsession—China.

I went to her school one Friday afternoon. She was giving a big presentation to her class about China and about being adopted. She'd worked on it for weeks, nearly to the exclusion of everything else. I had asked her if she wanted me to come, half expecting her to say no. But after she hesitated a bit, she said yes.

She introduced me to her class with "This is Meg Lindsay. She's my mom. Well, not really my mom. Sort of my fake mom. My real mom lives in China, but we don't know who she is."

And what was I supposed to do? I smiled brightly, as if my only daughter had not just denounced me to her entire fourth-grade class. I bit my tongue to stem back the tears. I wanted her love, and if this was what I had to go through to get it, I would.

I'd be glad never to hear the word "China" again. It was too bad, really. I had so many positive feelings toward the country, but it was hard to recycle the same good memories when it was driving a wedge between me and my daughter.

After school, she had a violin lesson, and after that, we returned to an empty apartment. Lewis had his own obsession these days—his research. He was in Switzerland . . . again. He might remember to call me, but more likely he would forget, lost in his world of particles and atoms and the haunting desire to earn his mother's love.

I'd already decided I could either be alone all evening, trying to coax some sort of affectionate response from my distant daughter, and feeling depressed when I failed, or I could reach out and try to focus on someone else. Fight the obsession. Ignore the ache.

So I had invited Li Shu for dinner. I wasn't a party person. One friend would be plenty to bring into the refuge of my home. I didn't let people into my home very often. It was my private place.

Li Shu was the least invasive of all my friends, and yet still able to chase away the loneliness.

She'd promised to teach me how to cook Chinese food. We'd been meaning to do it for ages, but it took me that long to let her in. Not just into my home, but into my life. I'd known her for so long, but somehow in the last three years, she'd become more than just my stand partner—she'd become my friend.

I opened my door to her, and she came in, arms loaded with reusable canvas bags of groceries. I gave her a hug.

"I told you I would buy all the ingredients." I slid the bags from her arms and walked them into the kitchen.

"There were some more items I thought we might need. I didn't think you would know what to look for, so I got them myself."

Eva barreled into the kitchen and flung herself at Li Shu. "Li Shu! Did you come to speak Chinese with me?"

She smiled broadly and nodded, responding in Chinese. We had started taking family Chinese classes after Eva's second cleft palate surgery a year ago, and I was amazed how well she was doing. Much better than Lewis and I.

I followed some of the conversation, but not a lot. If I wanted to hold my own against Eva's love of all things Chinese, I was going to have to work a lot harder on my language studies. Being left out like this was no fun.

The three of us chopped and stirred and poured, and soon the entire apartment smelled gloriously of rice and fresh spinach and the earthy warmth of green beans and leeks. We pulled out chopsticks and the usually reserved Li Shu even giggled at our awkward attempts to use them.

After dinner, and after Li Shu had taught Eva a child's game in Chinese, it was Eva's bedtime. I told her to say good night to our guest. She threw her arms around Li Shu.

"I wish you were my mom, and that I could live with you."

The pleasant evening ground to a painful stop.

This must have been how the Trojans felt when the Greeks popped out of their beloved horse statue. I'd let this woman—my friend—into my home, and she'd stolen my daughter's affection. A more rational part of my brain reminded me that she hadn't done it on purpose, but it didn't lessen the sense of betrayal.

She stared at me, horror and embarrassment on her face. "Eva . . . you have a lovely mother, and a beautiful home."

The moment was so awkward that even Eva must have noticed, for she giggled nervously and said, "I was just teasing you!"

Li Shu forced a laugh, but I could not. I herded Eva into her bedroom and shut the door.

"Why on earth would you say such a thing, Eva?" I was trying so hard to keep my voice low, but my words came out as a menacing hiss.

She stepped backward, but her chin was set in that determined way I'd come to dread. "I didn't say anything bad."

"All day long, you've been telling everyone who will listen how I'm not your real mom, and how you wish you had a different mom. Why would you do that? Don't you know how that makes me feel?"

Her lips trembled. "You never talk about my China parents. You get mad at me when I talk about them. Why do you hate them?"

"We can't talk about this right now."

"You never want to talk about it!"

I glanced at the door. "Keep your voice down. We have company."

"You hate my parents! You hate that I'm Chinese!" Now she was crying.

Part of me wanted to take her by the arms and shake her. "Where did you get such a ridiculous idea? That's not true."

"I just miss them. I want a real family."

"You have one!" I forgot to keep my voice low. "You have a mom and a dad who love you. Your China mom and dad left you! Is that what a real family does?"

I could have killed myself for saying that. Of all the things to throw at her.

She squeezed her eyes shut. "They couldn't help it."

"You don't know that."

She threw herself across her bed. "I hate being adopted. I hate having American parents."

It was like a giant fingernail had pierced open my heart. The pain overwhelmed any other thoughts I might have had. I gripped the doorknob behind me and leaned against the door. I wanted to scream.

Instead, I left without saying anything. I couldn't deal with it, not with my friend waiting for me.

I returned to the living room, where Li Shu sat stiffly, hands tucked underneath her, in the armchair. "I am very sorry, Meg. I should go home now and not bother you anymore."

I couldn't be mad at her. It was my fault, not hers. Somehow, I wasn't enough for Eva. I wasn't what she needed, as much as I longed to be. And once again, she'd taken my heart and devoured it. But Li Shu wasn't responsible for that.

"You're not a bother."

"I made trouble between you and your daughter."

I sat on the corner of our sofa, as close to her as I could come. Tears clogged my throat. "No, you didn't. She says that to almost every Asian woman I am acquainted with. I should have been expecting it—I wasn't thinking. I am sorry. I should have warned you, or talked with her before you came. It's my fault for not being better prepared."

"Why does she say that?"

My shoulders slumped. I gave her the rationale the therapist gave us, but it was harder and harder to keep believing it. "Because she's confused. She has some attachment problems—problems bonding with us as her family. She's always searching for new parents because she can't believe or accept that we are her parents forever."

"I am very sorry. That must be painful."

"Thank you. It's not what I wanted for her. For any of us."

"You are a very good mom, to love her even when she hurts you like that."

If only she knew. I groaned. "Sometimes, I'm so angry about it. I should be able to forgive—it's not her fault. She doesn't mean to hurt me. But it's over and over and over." I stumbled to speak around my tears. "A mom should always forgive and forget, but I don't think I can."

Especially not after tonight.

"Is it like that for all adopted children?" There was a sharp, desperate note in those words.

"No." I sniffled and reached for a tissue from the box on the end table. "It depends on their experiences when they were younger. Most children adapt very well to their new families. We don't know why some children have more problems than others."

"Are you okay?"

I started to say yes. But then my head drooped. "No. Not really. We've been working with a therapist, and so I understand what is going on. But . . . it doesn't change how hard it is. I feel like I've failed being her mom. I can't let it go. I can't forgive her. I thought all I'd have to do is love her enough, but there are some things that not even love can heal. She won't even call me her 'real' mom."

"You are her real mom, even if she doesn't see it."

A mangled quality to her voice made me look up. There were tears in her eyes. I waited for her to continue.

"You are the one who is there for her, every day, even when she doesn't want you. You have made her more important than your career, and put your dreams on hold for her. You hold her when she is sick and you go to her school presentations. And you love her even when she doesn't love you back. That's what a real mom does."

She meant well, but it was all the same platitudes I'd been telling myself for years. They angered me now because they had no strength left to give me. "And how would you know?" I gasped at the harshness in my voice. "I'm sorry. I shouldn't have said that."

She mashed her hands together in her lap, wouldn't look at me. Tears dripped onto her hands. "You are the sort of mom I should have been."

My own thoughts ground to a halt. "What are you talking about?"

"When I was twenty-three, I had a baby. A boy. I was not married, and it is not acceptable to be a single mother in China. I thought about having an abortion, but my best friend and her husband could not have children. So I told her she should adopt my baby. I went to another city for nine months and worked, where no one would know me. My friend wore pregnancy pillows for the last several months so all her friends would think she was pregnant. When I had the baby, I told everyone the baby had died. They came for a visit to pick up the baby, and when they got home, they told everyone my friend had gone into labor while they were visiting me. I met my husband shortly after that, but not even he knows the truth."

"You have his picture on your music folder."

She nodded. "My friend sent me pictures at first, but then she got scared that someone would find out the truth, so she told me she never wanted to see me again. That's when I auditioned for the Nouveau Chicago Symphony. I've heard nothing from her since that time. That photo is the last one I have of him. He is twelve now, and I always try to imagine how he looks, what he likes, what kind of boy he is."

What do you say when "I'm sorry" is so weak, so inadequate? What do you say when you realize that your problems are nothing compared to the pain in another person's soul? What do you say when words are profane compared to the sanctity of sorrow?

I said nothing. Just handed her a tissue and squeezed her hand.

"I should have been braver. I should have kept him. He was beautiful. Perfect. A real mom would have done anything she had to do to keep him."

"You were brave, Li Shu. You did what you thought was best for him. You acted like a real mother."

She gripped my hand and we sat in silence together, and yet alone with our private obsessions. We didn't speak because really, what do you say?

After Li Shu left, I washed up a few remaining dishes and tidied the living room. I was just heading into my own room when I heard the soft slide of Eva's door.

"Mom?" Her voice cracked, like she'd been crying.

I turned to her, and the naked fear and desolation in her eyes wrung the air from my lungs.

And I knew what I had to do. Even if I didn't feel like it. Even if I wasn't strong enough.

It had to be done. And I wanted to be the one to do it. I was the only one who could.

I ran to her. I wrapped my arms around her and rocked her like a baby. She was getting so big, but still—I needed to hold all of her at once. I pressed my face into her hair, the sweaty dampness like perfume to me. "I love you! You can hate me. You can tell the whole world I'm not your mom, but I still love you. I will always love you. I will not leave you. I'm staying. I'm staying. I'm staying."

I held her and rocked her, murmuring all the things to her that I wished I'd been told when I was her age, all the things I'd dreamed of telling her.

She'd been so stiff earlier, but now she was like dough, kneaded and punched down, and soft.

Finally, she gave a moaning cry and threw herself closer against me. "I'm sorry! I don't hate you. I love you, Mommy. I love you."

I stopped rocking her. She'd said it. Those precious words I'd wanted to hear. I wanted, needed to grab on to them, hold them, savor them. But they rushed by before I could scarcely register that they'd been said.

And somehow, it didn't matter so much. What was important was what she needed from me, her mother. I wouldn't always get it right, but there was grace for right now. This one time. I reached deep inside for the words she needed, even though I was still bleeding inside. "I know. I forgive you. I love you too."

Because that was what a real mother does.

THIRTY ONE

Wen Ming, December 2009

My whole life had been measured by how much I could see. I was always nearsighted, and my vision was like looking through a hole in a black sheet. When I was two and came to the orphanage, the hole was the size of a soccer ball—with only a small black ring around the edges. When I was three, it shrank to the size of a dinner plate. Six—the size of a grapefruit. By the time I was eight, it was the size of my fingers forming a circle. When I was ten, the hole had shrunk to the size of a yuan coin. When I turned eleven, it was only the size of a tiny fen coin. I knew it would not be long before the hole disappeared completely—there isn't a lot that is smaller than a fen.

I did not worry about it or fear the dark. After all, my sight had always been bad and I'd known for years it could not be repaired. I had learned to read Braille and how to listen and remember what I heard. I knew people by their smell and the sound of their walk.

I did not think that becoming blind should matter. Seeing was only one way of knowing the world. The world was rich in sensations and fragrance and sounds and tastes. Those four ways remained open to me. I felt I should not mourn the loss of the fifth.

I woke on a chilly December morning, before the other children in my ward were awake. I did not know what had woken me, but then I heard a low, growly voice call my name.

"Wen Ming," it purred. "Come."

Sitting in my bed, I saw shiny black and rippling silver scales flash in front of me. I could see them clearly. In my joy of this miracle, I got out of bed and did not question where this creature was taking me. I simply followed.

I followed its beauty and compelling voice through dark hallways and out to the courtyard. Although it was winter, I did not feel the cold. The strange creature settled under the cherry tree's naked branches.

The creature slithered and curled into the branches of the tree. "Come up here, Wen Ming," it said.

"I will stay here, where I won't fall."

"Then you will miss a beautiful sight."

"I cannot see. So I will miss it anyway."

"What if I promised you that you would be able to see clearly all the way to where the earth and heaven join?"

I peered up at it. When I looked at it, I saw clearly. When I looked away, all was dark again. But I had not lived my life as an orphan for nothing. I did not give my trust easily. "Why should I want to see that?"

"Why should you want to miss it?" The creature scolded me with a hiss. "You are asking the wrong questions, Wen Ming. You have not asked who I am or why I call to you."

"I think you are an evil spirit."

"Or I might just be your imagination. Since your world is so small, I suppose you don't have much else to do other than create monsters in your mind."

"If you were my imagination, you'd be a lot more interesting." I turned from the insulting, arrogant creature.

It laughed at me. "You are surely right. Since you are so clever, tell me why I am here."

"It's cold and I want to go back to my bed, so don't waste my time with your riddles."

It dipped its head—which was like a dragon's, only without horns. "I'm here to take your sight. All of it. Forever."

"I won't give it to you."

"You have no choice."

I gave the creature the most obscene hand gesture I knew. "My sight is only the size of a fen coin. Everything else has been taken from me. Why do you want my sight?"

"I don't want it. I'm only here to take it."

"You are a demon."

He looked sad to me. "If your sight is so little, then why should you mind the loss of it?"

"Because it is mine."

"What if I told you that losing it would bring you a life more wonderful than you ever dreamed?"

"I'd say you were lying. There is nothing wonderful in a life of blindness."

"Come up here, Wen Ming. Let me show you a beautiful thing. Let me give you a gift, to make up for having to take your sight."

"I cannot trust you."

"I have not lied to you. Be brave and see something wonderful before you go blind."

Stay on the ground where it was safe, or climb the tree and take my chances? If the beast did not lie, I could at least taste the independence of climbing a tree before losing my sight entirely.

I would take the chance.

I climbed the tree, and the tree climbed into the sky. I chased the strange creature higher and higher until I caught him on a limb at the top.

"Brave girl. Now watch." It held me in its grasp, turning me to face out. I caught my breath—the world lay stretched below me, its colors shimmering and misty in the first light of dawn. There was no black sheet to block my view.

"You've seen so much ugliness in the world," the creature said. "I wanted you to see its beauty too."

A large white crystal floated in the air—a perfect, glittering snowflake. It spun delicately in front of me, preening and showing off its points and facets. Another one joined it, and they danced for me. Soon the sky was full of dancing snowflakes, draped in diamonds. They balanced on my fingers before diving into the air. I held out my arms, as if to dive with them.

"Never forget—the world is full of beauty. Remember the beauty, Wen Ming. No matter what happens."

The diamond snowflakes swirled around me. "Who are you?" I asked the creature.

"I am The Thing That Happens."

"That makes no sense."

"I usually don't. There's never a good reason for me or an explanation. I just am. I'm not a demon, Wen Ming. It's how you respond to me that makes me good or evil. Do you see?"

"I think so."

Its touch on me turned regretful. "Good. It's time, then."

Its black-scaled hands slid around my head, covering my eyes. I did not fight it. I took one last look at the beautiful snow and leaned into the creature. A crushing pressure, and then . . . nothing.

I cannot say it was black, because black is color, and now there was no color. There was no light. There was no dark. Nothing.

And then there was something. The biting, wet flavor of snow. The way each flake prickled against my skin. The muffled hush of falling snow. The fresh, clean perfume of the cold.

But my sight was gone. Forever. Tears fell from my dead eyes. They froze into pellets that rolled off my skin. I flung my arms out to touch something, anything. But it was nothing but air. I was falling . . .

"Be brave, Wen Ming . . ." The creature's voice was a whisper on the wind.

Wen Ming.

Wen Ming.

"Wen Ming!" Director Wu's voice stopped my fall. I sat up, feeling the rough bark of the cherry tree at my back. My clothes were wet with snow. I trembled with cold and with knowledge. She wrapped a blanket around me and helped me stand. "You must have walked in your sleep. You should be very grateful that Ling Mei woke up and noticed your bed was empty, or you might have frozen to death."

"I am blind, Director Wu."

She hustled me inside. There were no shadows or light to guide me. I slipped on snow and stumbled over the threshold. Director Wu caught me.

"What do you mean?"

"I have no sight left. It is gone."

I sensed the weight that dropped on her shoulders. She sighed heavily. "You are being very brave about this."

She made me some hot tea and gave me almond cookies. She seemed very worried about me.

"Don't worry, Director. This is just a thing that happens."

Be brave, Wen Ming.

Part Three
LION DANCE

"I have found the paradox, that if you love until it hurts,
there can be no more hurt, only more love."

—*Mother Teresa*

THIRTY TWO

Meg Lindsay, April 2010

We were in Switzerland, chasing Lewis's high-energy dreams. I'd dubbed his experiments "the Big Higgs Dig," and this one was the pinnacle of all his work for the past two years. He was one of the team leaders, though I wasn't sure what he actually did. My impression was that it was a high-tech version of playing with Hot Wheels—crashing them into each other until all the pieces flew apart. Only these mad-scientist boys and girls were crashing pieces of black holes and particles that had more energy than an atomic bomb.

As long as it made him happy.

They were so close to the prize. Lewis had so much confidence, he invited me and Eva, for the first time, to travel with him. So we took Eva out of school—thinking this would be a better education than anything her fourth-grade teacher could come up with—and we moved into apartments on the CERN campus for three weeks of carefully controlled chaos and drama.

Lewis had warned me not to expect him to play tour guide while we were there. It was rather like living with a medical resident—he worked thirty-six- to forty-eight-hour shifts, tumbled into bed for a few hours, and then rushed back to the lab. Eva and I had to fend for ourselves.

So we took day trips into Geneva, rambling through the promenades along the lake—Eva wanted to try out the amusement rides—and touring the European UN headquarters. We explored flea markets and cafés tucked in out-of-the-way corners on cozy side streets, and our personal favorite was the botanical gardens.

And we talked. I learned more about my elusive little girl in those few days than I had in the years we had been living together.

"Mom, do you know what I like best about you?" she asked me one afternoon over fondue at a little café.

My heart did a happy dance when I heard that there was something about me she liked. "What?"

"Your hair. The color is so pretty. I wish my hair was like yours."

I reached across the table to stroke a lock of her glimmering black hair. "Oh no. Your hair is perfect. I always wished I had shining black hair like yours. It's like satin threads."

"Well, yours is like . . . like sunshine threads."

I grinned at her. "Maybe we should switch hair? You give me yours and you can have mine."

She giggled. "I think we'd look silly." Then her smile faded. "I wish I looked like you, though. Do you think my China mom looks like me?"

I tensed, as I always did when the subject came up. Even though Eva had finally accepted me as her mother, I still struggled against old hurts and insecurities. I did my best to ignore it. I was the one who wanted fresh starts, right? "I bet she does. I bet she has the same little dimples in her cheeks, and the same cute little nose." The thought made my chest tighten.

"Maybe I have my China dad's nose."

I pretended to study her nose. "That adorable thing? On a man? Impossible. It's way too sweet to be a guy's nose."

We laughed, even though a part of me still ached.

Lewis's experiment ran for five days. After the third day, I stopped asking how it was going. All I got was a blank stare and mutterings in a science language I didn't understand. But the manic light in his eyes made me think it must be going well.

A few hours later, the light was gone and bleak worry coated his face. "One of the superconducting magnets isn't calibrated properly. We can't get the energy we need in the beam." He slumped into a sleek metal dining chair in our sparsely furnished apartment, murmuring more geek-speak.

I held his stubbly face between my palms and kissed his lips, even though his breath smelled like stale coffee. "You'll get it to work. I know you will. It's going to succeed. I believe in you."

He hugged me tightly, and I knew his tension was caused by more than just the historical experiment. There was so much more at stake for him.

They got the magnet to work, and in a few more days, the light was back in his haggard eyes. They were data crunching now, and he disappeared into the lab for two and a half days, while Eva and I did more sightseeing. About four o'clock on the third day, he burst into the apartment.

"Meg! Meg!"

I looked over the edge of the loft to the wood floor below. His clothing and hair was rumpled. He was jumping and waving a piece of paper.

"We found it! The Higgs! We found it!"

I ran down the stairs, and he shoved the paper in my face. "See?" He jabbed at a peaked line on the graph. "It's right there. You are looking at something no one has ever seen before. We are making history. History, Meg! This will be in every physics textbook for the next century."

I peered at the very ordinary-looking spiked line. "That's it?"

"That's it. Beautiful, isn't it?"

His face was what was beautiful. It shone with rapture of mysteries revealed, the ecstasy of knowing the secrets of the universe. I threw myself at him and tasted his beatification. It was still a mystery to me, but I was part of it because I was part of him.

We took Eva and went to the lab, where the rest of his team was celebrating. They were disheveled, exhausted, and I didn't understand even half of what they were saying—much less than half once they'd had a few rounds of drinks. But their excitement was common language enough.

Later, even though Lewis had been awake for nearly three days, we went out to eat in Geneva, just the three of us. Lewis bought Eva and me the largest box of Swiss chocolate truffles he could find to mark the occasion.

"Are you going to be famous now, Daddy?"

"I don't know. Maybe. How would you like that?"

"Well, just don't come to my school to sign autographs. I don't think you'll be famous with kids my age. We're sort of Disney-type people, not science people."

Lewis laughed. "What if I'm on Disney?"

"Then you can come. When will you know if you're famous?"

"We have to publish a report about our experiment. That will take a few months. When that report comes out, then we might be famous—only not, of course, with fourth graders."

It would end up being three months, and it did bring a new level of fame. Even my parents gave grudging admiration when they saw the news reports about it. There were lecturing requests, more data to study, and interviews to be given.

But that night, still flush with his breakthrough, my husband went back to the apartment at CERN for the first time in three days. He tucked his daughter into bed, took a shower, brushed his teeth, and opened his laptop.

"What are you doing?" I massaged his back and his neck and peeked over his shoulder at his computer, where he had pulled up the website for MIT. "You need sleep."

He clicked to a listing of the physics department professors. He studied their bios, occasionally adding their e-mail addresses to an open e-mail message he'd started. I read what he'd written so far:

> I'm Dr. Lewis Lindsay, professor of physics at the
> University of Chicago. I'm writing to see if you have
> any information on Dr. Naomi Ricci. I know as of 1999,
> she was a professor at MIT. I need, if possible, her current
> location and contact information.
> I am her son.

Over the next several months, we learned a few things. We learned that Eva's love for us hadn't cured her nightmares. It hadn't improved her grades, either. And we learned that fame couldn't ensure tranquillity, or lure a long-lost mother out of the shadows of the past.

September brought speaking-engagement requests for Lewis—most of which he turned down; he said he had traveled away from us enough the past two years. And it brought another less-than-encouraging progress report—the first for fifth grade, but the story was all too familiar.

"I'm sorry, Mom. I'm trying my best."

"I know you are. I'm not mad. I'm really proud of you for working so hard." Those sorts of encouragements came much easier these days. I found myself reverting back to the biting, critical words of the past only when I was extremely tired, or upset about something else. I was trying hard, so it seemed to me that Eva deserved some credit for her efforts, as well.

"I'm just not as smart as you and Dad."

"You are plenty smart. Smart has nothing to do with this. Do you know how smart you have to be to learn a whole language in only four years? You're brilliant."

"Tell that to my progress reports, please."

Lewis stormed out of our office. "Do you have to talk so loudly? I'm expecting a phone call." He disappeared back into the room.

Eva frowned at me. "Daddy is grumpy tonight."

"I know."

I left her to do her homework and I slipped into the office. "You're Professor Perky this evening."

"Sorry." He balled up a piece of paper and threw it at the trash can, knocking it over. "The science world is not that big. Where is she?"

None of the MIT professors had any information. They said their understanding was that she took early retirement at the end of 1999. She'd mentioned guest lecturing at places like Harvard, Stanford, Berkeley, and Caltech.

Lewis had been working through that list, trying to find someone in each of those departments who knew what seminars and speakers they'd had up to a decade ago. So far, none of them recalled Naomi Ricci speaking there.

"She can't have just vanished. There's one guy who was at Stanford about that time. He's supposed to be calling me back in just a few minutes."

I kissed the top of his head. "I'm sorry. Is there anything I can help with?"

"Thanks, but I want to do this."

Whenever we did find his mother, I had some choice words for her. They were not words a good Christian girl like me was supposed to know, much less use. They were the only words I could think of that were fit to describe what I thought of the woman Lewis was so desperate to know. I couldn't bring myself to hate my mother, but I had no problem hating his.

Lewis's cell phone rang. He almost answered it without looking at the caller ID, but at the last second, he glanced at it and stopped. "It's from China."

"Wen Ming? Why would she be calling on your phone?"

"No. It's not her number." He answered it. Grabbed a notepad and a pencil. Wrote down "guest lecturer." Scribbled some physics jargon. "October. 4 wks."

After he hung up, he turned to me, grinning. "How would you and Eva like to come with me to Shanghai for a month? That was Zhou Wei. The physics department at his university wants to host me in October."

Shanghai. Yang Hua. Eva.

Wen Ming.

I didn't know whether to say yes or no. Eva and I had reached a fragile peace. Would visiting her past destroy that? But how could I deny her this chance?

She needed to go back. It would be okay—we'd be with her. It would be our chance to show her that she could have her family *and* her country. And Wen Ming too, I supposed. It would be my chance to show Wen Ming that Eva belonged with us. She would have to let go.

"Eva, darling!" I ran out of the office and into her bedroom. "We're going to Shanghai!"

THIRTY THREE

My Zhen An smelled like cherry blossoms when the bud breaks open in the spring. My Zhen An walked with delicacy and smoothness, like the sweet lightness of lotus paste in moon cakes. My Zhen An's voice was the hush whisper in the grass, the velvet of steam rising from jasmine tea.

My Zhen An was coming back to me today.

Director Wu and Auntie Yang had warned me for weeks that it was only for a visit. That I must not expect or hope for her to stay. Her adopted baba had made a great discovery for science, and Uncle Zhou had persuaded his university to invite him to come talk about his work. My Zhen An, who had left Shanghai as an unwanted orphan, was returning as the daughter of a highly honored guest of the nation.

She was like Ye Xian, the beautiful fairy-tale orphan who became a princess. But I would be the mother—the one who became a fish and who watched over Ye Xian even after the stepmother killed the fish and ate it for dinner. It was, after all, not Ye Xian in her cloak of kingfisher feathers and her golden slippers who was the hero of the story. It was the mother, who—even in death—took care of her daughter and provided for her.

I waited for her in a meeting room at the Children's Home. Director Wu said I could take Zhen An and her American parents on a tour of the orphanage. I was proud that I'd be able to show them around even though I could not see.

The door opened, and I recognized Auntie Yang's steps. "Wen Ming, they are here."

I held my breath and listened for Zhen An. I heard the movements of many strangers, but nothing that sounded like Zhen An. Someone approached me—the walk sounded confident and energetic. Young. Even cocky.

Then the steps slowed. A hesitancy crept into them. A trace of fear.

"Who is it?" Maybe Auntie Yang hadn't meant that they were *here* in the room. Maybe she'd just meant they had arrived in the building. Maybe this person in front of me was going to take me to them. But who was it?

"Wen Ming?" I knew her voice, but it did not sound like blades of grass or steam curling from tea. It was more like one of Auntie Yang's bath towels—soft and pleasingly abrasive. And tall—my height at least. "I'm . . . Zhen An."

This couldn't be. I leaned toward her and breathed her in. My Zhen An did not smell bad, like this foreigner.

She touched my hand. I turned it to hold hers. Her hand was so much bigger than I'd remembered.

This Zhen An was a stranger to me.

"Are you afraid of me?" I asked her in Chinese.

"Yes, a little."

My Zhen An had never been frightened of me. For the first time, I felt blind. Horribly, darkly, hopelessly blind. "I am me. Just like always." My fingers crept up her arm. She pulled from me.

"But you can't—you're . . ."

"I can't see. But I can still smell. And you smell like onions and sour milk."

"That is rude!"

"So is being afraid of me because I'm blind." I smiled. "We will make a deal. I will ignore your American stink, if you will not fear my blindness."

I hoped she could tell I was teasing her.

After a moment, she giggled. "I won't be afraid anymore. But you should know—Chinese people stink too."

Then she hugged me, before the significance of her statement sunk into my mind. Chinese people. As if we were a different group from her. I squeezed her tight. She'd come back to me, but everything had changed.

She was still my Zhen An, wasn't she?

She introduced me to her American parents, and I was as polite as I could be. They did not like me—especially the mother. I felt her distrust in the touch of her hand when I shook it. I heard it in her voice, even as she said in careful Chinese, "It is nice to meet you."

"Come see the Children's Home," I said in English. I'd been practicing with Zhen An, and she gave my hand a pat of approval.

"Do you need any help?" Zhen An held my arm when I stood.

"Not really. But here, do this." I positioned her arm at an angle so I could take it. "Walk normally, only pause at doorways or steps. I will tell you which direction to go."

"Didn't we used to walk this way when we lived with Auntie Yang?"

I smiled. "You remember."

"Of course."

"I didn't know if you would. You were very small."

"I try to remember everything about you, *jie jie*."

The warmth of the sun filled my heart. She was still my Zhen An.

My Zhen An. A starving, ravenous dog woke in my belly. So many years of not having her, and now for a few days, anyway, I would feast. It was too much. I couldn't take another step.

"Are you all right?" She slipped her arm around my waist.

It didn't matter what she smelled like, or sounded like. Her spirit was still the same. I gripped her. Hard. Until I felt her ribs struggling to expand and her heart surging.

"I am good. You're here. I am wonderful!"

THIRTY FOUR
四

Meg Lindsay, October 2010

I didn't expect to fall in love with Wen Ming. Pity, perhaps, like the feeling one has for a stray cat that is torn and disheveled. Your daughter might plead to keep the kitty, but as much as you feel sorry for its homeless condition, you cannot stand the thought of it in your house.

Wen Ming, however, was impossible to pity. She thought she was ugly, but she was too young yet to understand the beauty of a strong mind and the elegance of a determined spirit. She loved with a reckless stubbornness that attracted me in spite of my feelings of inadequacy.

Before that first day was done, my fear of her faded. She'd been such a looming shadow over Eva for so many years, it disoriented me to discover that—despite her intelligence, her perception, and her willful enthusiasm for life—she was only a child after all. A child hungry for attention. For love. A child hungry to learn and experience the entire world in one great leap.

At the end of our visit to the orphanage, the two girls stood together, clutching each other's hands.

"You will come back tomorrow?" Wen Ming said.

Eva looked at me. I nodded. She gave a little bounce. "Yes, tomorrow."

Wen Ming threw her arms around Eva, burying her face against my daughter's neck. It was almost like seeing a mirror image of how

I felt about Eva. A sort of pain-filled joy and desperation and wonder. It hurt to see it.

I turned to Lewis, and I could see she'd won his heart too. I had begun to suspect that his heart was much more easily won by children than he wanted to admit. He leaned to whisper in my ear, "Let's ask if she can stay with us."

"Stay the night?" I murmured, so Eva wouldn't see.

"Stay the whole trip."

I hesitated. I no longer resented Wen Ming, but sharing my daughter with her for the entire stay? Being in a foreign country was hard enough without a stranger invading my personal space.

Lewis saw my ambivalence. "If you're not comfortable with it . . ."

Memories of years ago flashed in my mind: begging my mother to let some friend or another stay the night. Or the time when one of them invited me to go with her family on vacation. My mother always said no. "We don't know that family," she would say, as if that made it clear to me. Or, "They don't share our *values*," which I later realized meant that they either weren't Christian or weren't Christian enough to satisfy her. Sometimes, it was simply "Our evenings are family time, not friend time."

I could count on one hand the number of times she let me have a sleepover. Maybe she was as uncomfortable with strangers in her house as I was with them in mine. Maybe we were actually alike in that way.

I blinked away the musings and shook my head. "No, I'm fine with it. Let's ask."

After we secured permission from the orphanage director, Lewis extended the invitation to Wen Ming.

Eva shrieked and bounced around her friend. "It'll be like an extralong sleepover, Wen Ming!"

Wen Ming hung for a second between exhilaration and panic. I read it in her unseeing eyes. I saw the hungry way she responded to Eva, the desperation in each longing touch. Was it kind to let her stay, let the girls bond again, only to tear Eva away once more?

She chose to accept our invitation. I couldn't help but admire her courage.

Lewis had to travel to Beijing to give lectures there, and the three of us went with him. We stayed in a huge hotel and visited the Great Wall again. I could almost hear the voices from the past and feel their presence brushing against me again, as they did the first time I stood here. I thought of the line of women in the sky that I'd seen that first night with Eva, so long ago. I hoped they approved of the job I had done with Eva so far.

Lewis came to stand next to me, the wall at our backs. He shook his head at the girls as he watched them climb on a two-thousand-year-old cannon. "They're really something else. I didn't expect them to get along so well. I mean, you hear how hormonal preteens are."

"It's like they were made for each other." Tears pricked my eyes. I'd always wanted to be able to say that about Eva and me, but I was starting to doubt I ever could. "Look at them, arms around each other, always together, always touching. I've never seen Eva so happy."

Lewis studied me. "She's happy with us too."

"Not like this. It's her. It's Wen Ming. It's always been her."

"You aren't jealous of a twelve-year-old, are you?" He slid his arm around me.

I leaned into him, trying not to let my sudden gloom ruin the day. "Maybe a little."

"I think it's not just Wen Ming. I think it's China. She hasn't had any nightmares since we arrived, has she?"

I thought for a moment. "No. I guess not."

"Strange."

"Did we make a mistake—in adopting her?"

Lewis glanced down like I'd poked him. "Why would you think that?"

"She's at peace here. She adores Wen Ming. This is where she belongs."

He heaved a sigh. "I don't think it was a mistake. We're a family now. That can't be a mistake. A friend can't take the place of a parent. She needed us."

I swept my arm in front of me. "She needs this too."

After a moment, he said, "I know."

But what to do about it, we had no idea.

He kissed my ear. "It's been good for me too. I didn't know I needed to come, but now that we're here, I wish I'd done it years ago."

He was waiting for me—to see if I felt the same. I couldn't give him the answer he wanted. I wished I could, but I wasn't the same naive woman I'd been the last time I had traveled here. Then, China had been the setting for the most amazing adventure I'd ever had. I didn't know all the pain that lay in store for me. I wasn't quite strong enough to be adventurous now. I wanted to be safe. "I'm happy that you and Eva are happy. I'm glad for the peace."

When we returned to Shanghai, we turned it into a playground. We snapped copious pictures—Wen Ming and Eva, arms entwined, choosing flowers from a street vendor in Shanghai, piled together in a bicycle rickshaw, having their faces made up at the Clinique counter in the department store. Always together, always touching, always smiling.

Toward the end of the month, one night after the girls were sleeping sprawled on a foldout couch in our suite, Lewis took my hand and tugged me to the chair in our bedroom. "I've been thinking."

"About?"

"About Eva, and how worried you are that she's unhappy with us."

"I'm not—" I started to deny it, but he gave me a don't-even-bother look, so I amended my words. "Okay, I'm a little worried. Especially about what's going to happen when we take her home. You weren't there the first time—you didn't see how lost and broken she was. I can't handle going through that again."

"I know. That's why I was wondering . . . what if we adopt Wen Ming?"

I could do nothing but stare at him. "Another child? You would do that?"

He shrugged. "For Eva, anything."

That made my throat tighten. "Do you think she'd want to? It would be a huge change, not to mention her being blind. Could we handle it?"

"I think we could. My question is—would *you* want to?"

A weary weight pressed on me. Opening my heart and my home to one child had turned out to be the most painful, yet rewarding, thing I'd ever done. Could I do it a second time? I wasn't sure I had the strength, but it would make Eva so happy. Couldn't I do this for her? For both of them? Was it possible Wen Ming was meant to be part of our family too?

Too soon, the end of the month arrived. Two nights before our departure, we dined with Yang Hua, Zhou Wei, and their three-year-old daughter on soup dumplings and crispy chicken at a restaurant that overlooked the Pudong River.

"We have an important announcement," I said in English, my throat feeling a little dry. Yang Hua translated for Wen Ming. "We have grown to love you, Wen Ming, very much. We know you love Eva . . . Zhen An. And we are wondering if you could love us as well?"

Wen Ming waited for the translation and then grinned. She responded in Chinese.

Yang Hua smiled at us. "She say that her love for Zhen An is big enough to include Zhen An's American family."

I took a deep breath, hoping I was strong enough. "Wen Ming, we would like you to be part of our family. Forever. If we can get permission to adopt you, would you be our daughter?"

I didn't know whom to watch. Eva's face flooded with every happy color in the world. She caught her breath, turning to Wen Ming with a heartbreaking look of pleading and hope. Wen Ming's sightless eyes widened, and she became very still.

"I would . . . go America. With you?" She said it in slow English.

"You wouldn't be able to go with us when we leave in two days. It might take many months. But eventually, yes, we would come to Shanghai again and bring you to America to live with us."

Yang Hua provided the translation. She shot me a tremulous smile, but I caught a glimmer of worry too. Wen Ming frowned and bowed her head, chewing her bottom lip. Maybe she didn't want to come. I now understood, after all we'd gone through with Eva, the earthshaking change we were asking her to make. I wouldn't blame her if she said no. A tiny part of me hoped she would, but it was very small.

"I go school?"

"Yes. There are many more options for education and jobs for the blind in the United States."

"I think about it."

Eva's eyes grew so wide, I thought she would sprain them. She clearly wanted to say something, but I shook my head at her. "Fair enough. But no matter what you decide, I want you to have something." I slid my jade dragon bracelet off my arm. Strange to not feel its cool weight there anymore. I placed it in Wen Ming's hands. "There were two bracelets. One I knew was for Eva. But I didn't know who should have the other one. Now I know. It was for you."

She traced the carvings. "A . . . dragon?"

"Yes. And it is for you to keep, even if you decide you want to stay here in China."

There was a whisper of tears in her eyes. "Thank you." She slid it on her wrist and sat a little straighter in her chair.

We continued our meal, but I could see the struggle playing out on her face. Toward the end of dinner, Lewis's cell phone rang. He excused himself to answer it. Several minutes later, he returned, his color high, his eyes shining.

"That was one of the profs at MIT. He said that he might know someone who would have information about my mom."

The news gave him an added urgency to return home. The next day, we said our final good-byes. Wen Ming hugged me and took both my hands in hers. "I want you adopt me. I want to live with you."

Eva screamed and tackled Wen Ming. They fell over in a heap of giggles and excited chatter. I grinned at Lewis, a burst of excitement smothering my remaining misgivings. We were going to be parents—again.

THIRTY FIVE 三十五

Meg Lindsay, January 2011

A phone call can change everything. It can reunite a son and a mother. It can bring a family together. It can bridge the gap of a million miles. Calls like that you wait for, long for, dream about. Every time the phone rings, it makes you jump inside. That's the ever-burning hope reminding you it's still there, ready to answer the right call.

My phone was on vibrate because I was in a symphony rehearsal. I checked the number. "It's the adoption agency," I murmured to Li Shu. "I'll be right back."

She nodded over her viola and winked at me.

I slipped into the hall and answered the phone. The call we'd been waiting for since we returned from Shanghai. The more we'd talked about it, the more we'd dreamed about it, the more confident I was—Wen Ming was meant for us. Our family wouldn't be complete without her. Already, she was growing in my heart, like Eva had. I couldn't wait to have her with us.

"Mrs. Lindsay?"

"Jaime! I was hoping we'd hear from you soon. Did you get any information back from the CCAA? Can we start on adopting Wen Ming?"

"We did hear from the CCAA. They very much appreciated your letter explaining why you would like to adopt Wen Ming. Most parents don't want to adopt children who are already so old, especially if they are handicapped."

"She's very special. She needs a family. So can we start the paper-work?"

"Mrs. Lindsay . . ." There was a gentleness in her tone, a pulling back.

I didn't want to be pulled back. I already knew what she was going to say—there'd be challenges to bringing in an older child, a blind child. I didn't care. We'd been through it before. We could handle it.

I was on the brink of telling her so, but she let out a little groan. It stopped me cold. "What's wrong?"

"I'm sorry. I'm so sorry."

A phone call can change everything.

I don't remember driving home. I know I picked up Eva because that's the only way she could get home from school. And she was there. So I must have gotten her. But I went to my room, closed my door, and sobbed until Lewis came home.

I told them both what our agency said.

Wen Ming was not eligible to be adopted. By anyone. Ever.

Eva had often wished she knew something, anything, about her birth parents. But in Wen Ming's case, if we'd known nothing, if there had been no information about her past, she could have easily been ours.

She'd been left at a police station by a woman who had claimed an intention of adopting her, until she realized how bad Wen Ming's eyes were. That was in 2001. In early 2006, police arrested the woman in connection with the baby-trafficking scandals in Hunan. To her mind, she had only been acting as a matchmaker of sorts, an undercover adoption agency. She found women who were poor or otherwise unable or unwilling to care for their babies. She persuaded them to give her the children, and she paid the mothers a modest fee—enough to ease whatever crisis they were in. Then she found families to adopt the children or she transferred the children to an orphanage. Either way, she was paid a substantial amount for each child she moved.

When the trafficking scandal broke, she was arrested and ques-tioned. She had to give names and dates for as many babies as she could remember. Wen Ming was one of the babies. In her case, however, the woman had truly meant to keep her. It was her eyesight and the resistance of the woman's in-laws that prompted her to leave Wen Ming at the police station.

Even so, the fact was that Wen Ming had been "purchased" from her birth mother—who was still untraceable. The orphanage and the China Center of Adoption Affairs were not willing to risk their reputations by allowing a trafficked child to be adopted. Not even someone as in need of a home as Wen Ming. They'd had her in the waiting child program in 2005, at the same time as Eva, but they'd pulled her shortly after arresting the woman.

When I finished my explanation, Eva whimpered. "You—you said . . . you promised . . ."

"I'm sorry, honey. There's no way we could have known this."

"Auntie Yang knew, didn't she?"

My eyes felt like wool. I rubbed them but it only made them sting worse. "I don't know." But there had been that hint of concern in her eyes that night at the Shanghai restaurant.

"You promised!" Her face twisted in injured fury. "You promised us both!"

"I can't help it. There's nothing we can do."

She raced into her room. Lewis and I chased after her, and we stood in the doorway, Lewis's arms supporting me, holding me. I felt the dull weight of his sorrow, smelled it on his skin. Eva grabbed her clothing and flung it on her bed.

"What are you doing?"

"I want to go back to China! I'm going to live there. I'm going to live with Wen Ming."

Lewis and I could only look at each other. What could we say? What was the right thing to do? Finally, he said, "We can't go back to China. Not right now. Your home is here with us."

She threw a jacket on the floor and her face was tight and red. "I don't want to live here. Not without her! I don't want this home. I don't want you. I want my *jie jie*!"

It was just the grief talking. I had to believe that. We'd come so far with her. She loved us. This was a huge blow to us all, but especially her.

"I know you're disappointed—"

"I'm mad, Mom. You took me away from her. You took me away from China. It was you. You did it. And now she doesn't have anybody. And you say it's not your fault. It is! It's your fault she doesn't have anybody, because you took me away."

"That's not true."

Only, it was true in a way. She'd been on the same waiting list as Eva just a few photos up from her. If I'd chosen Wen Ming instead of Eva . . . the adoption would have been final before they'd discovered her story. She would have been ours. Wen Ming would have been my Eva. And Eva would have . . . not been in my life.

God forgive me, but I could not regret my decision. As much as I had come to care about Wen Ming, she was not yet my daughter. Eva was. I could never be sorry we chose her.

Lewis stepped gently around me and over to the bed. He calmly folded her clothing and returned it to her closet and dresser. "Would you like to call Wen Ming and talk to her?"

"Do I have to tell her?"

I shook my head. "No, Jaime said the orphanage director talked with her and explained it all early this morning. I know she would want to talk to you. You may call her."

She nodded, her face hard and fragile, like blown glass.

I handed her my cell phone and kissed her. She didn't respond. I closed the door and fled to my own room. I couldn't play the strong, compassionate mother any longer. I didn't have any strength left to give.

Three days later, another phone call pulled me from rehearsal. Maestro Chelsea shot me a perturbed look but I didn't care. It was Bree, and she wouldn't have called during my work hours unless it was important.

"Jolie just called me from school. She was in tears."

"Is she okay? What happened?"

"She's pretty shook up. She said she's been keeping a secret from me for a couple of days, and she was scared to keep it anymore."

Darkness gathered at the edges of my vision. I leaned against the wall of the corridor outside the practice room. "A secret?"

"She said Eva is planning on running away during afternoon

recess. Jolie said Eva thinks she's going to travel around doing odd jobs and chores for people so she can save up enough money to buy a plane ticket to Shanghai to be with Wen Ming."

My lips tingled and the lights faded and flickered. The floor tilted under me. I stammered a grateful, horrified response and hung up. I grabbed my purse and fled to my car. I didn't bother following the speed limit. If I got stopped, maybe the officer would help me keep Eva from her idiotic, foolish, terrifying plan.

I slammed the car to a stop in a parking stall in front of the school and sprinted to the main office. "Where is Mr. Compton's fifth-grade class? I need my daughter, Eva Lindsay, right now."

The secretary barely glanced up at me. "If you'll just sign in right there, Mrs. Lindsay, I'll have your daughter paged."

"I need her now! I need to know where she is!"

I was losing control. Yelling. They'd call security if I didn't watch out. I held my breath a moment and then tried to steady my voice.

"I just got a phone call from the mother of one of her friends. My daughter is planning to run away during afternoon recess. I need to find her immediately."

The office burst into a flurry of movement. We found out the class was at recess at that moment. The security guard called the police while he escorted me out to the frozen playground.

"Do you see her?"

I scanned the yard while the principal rushed over to Mr. Compton to explain the situation. Eva was not on the playground. There weren't many places a child could escape to, but I finally found a small hole in the chain-link fence, partially obscured by bushes. "Eva!"

Fifteen minutes of unspeakable terror, and then a police officer found her several blocks away, hiding under a neighbor's porch. I didn't know if I was furious or brokenhearted when he helped her out of the patrol car.

Teachers hurried the rest of her class inside, out of the cold. We went into a meeting room where the officer could take a formal report. I hated this. Neither Eva nor I were criminals, but there was a suspicion and a hardness in his demeanor that made me feel filthy. I knew he was just doing his job, but the process was humiliating.

She didn't say anything or even look at me until the officer finished with me. Then he started questioning her. I had to leave the room, and my last glimpse of her was her pale, frightened face. I felt sorry for her, but a voice in my head was saying, "Let her be scared. Maybe she'll think twice before pulling a stunt like this again."

In a few moments, the officer stepped out of the room and closed the door behind him. "Mrs. Lindsay, Eva claims you aren't her mother."

What? "I've been her mother since she was six years old. She's adopted from China."

"I know. All your information checked out just fine. And she says there's been no abuse. She's not scared of you. She just says she won't go home with you and that you aren't her mother."

The room swayed. The officer grabbed a chair and shoved it under me. I sank into it and covered my eyes. I explained to him about Wen Ming.

We called the psychologist. She left her office and came to the school to speak to Eva. By this time, school was out. I had left four messages for Lewis, but he hadn't come yet.

The counselor pulled a chair alongside me. "Mrs. Lindsay—"

"Please, call me Meg. Everyone has been saying 'Mrs. Lindsay' all week and none of it has been good. Just say my name."

She gave me the sympathetic therapist smile. "Meg, Eva is very confused right now and upset about not being able to be with Wen Ming. I'm concerned that if you try to force her to leave with you, she'll only look for another chance to run. That would be dangerous for her."

I wanted to scream. Did she think I was stupid? I knew what the stakes were here. "What are my options?"

"We could try a residential program where she'd be under constant surveillance, but I think that would do more harm than good in the long run. Is there another family she could stay with temporarily? I think if she promised not to run, she would keep her promise."

We talked to Eva about that. She didn't want to go to Bree's, since Jolie had tattled on her. And she didn't want any of my relatives.

"What about Li Shu?"

She perked up. "Will she take me to China?"

The counselor cut in. "I think that will totally depend on whether or not you can be trusted not to run away again. What you did was very dangerous. We want to help you, but we can't help if you are determined to put yourself in harm's way."

"I don't want to run away. I just want to get to Shanghai, and *she* won't take me."

I didn't even have a name anymore. I swallowed my tears, shoved them down into a tight box at the pit of my stomach. I couldn't deal with them right then.

I called Li Shu, and she came right away. I filled her in on the problem. "Her therapist thinks it would be safe to let her stay with you, as long as she promises not to run off. From there, I don't know where to go next."

Li Shu looked a bit ill.

"I'm sorry. I know this is asking a huge thing of you. But she won't go home with us, and I don't want her to end up in a foster home or residential center—which are our only other options. Please. I know you understand how I'm feeling. Please help me."

Her shoulders tensed. She nodded. "I'll take her, if she'll go with me. But what happens if she runs away again?"

"Then you call the police. I don't think she'll run. She's terrified. That officer was big and scary-looking, and he scolded her pretty hard for what she did."

"Are you okay?"

I clenched my fists. "Don't ask me that! Not right now. I'll collapse if you do. Don't give me any pity. Don't give me any sympathy. I'll deal with myself later. I just have to get through this."

She nodded again. "Okay."

After getting Eva to sign a written statement promising to stay with Li Shu, to go to school, counseling, and nothing else, I watched Eva follow Li Shu to her car, climb in, and ride away without looking at or speaking to me. I knew the pain was going to kill me, but I had to drive home first.

Lewis didn't arrive until later that evening. "I'm sorry—I had my phone turned off and was staying late working on a paper."

"You didn't come. I had to go through all that myself."

"I'm sorry."

I was standing in the middle of the kitchen. I wanted to be angry with him, to scream horrible things at him. At least it would be someone to blame. At least it would make me feel alive a few minutes longer. But when I opened my mouth, all that came out was a long, keening wail. I fell to the floor, the horror of the afternoon crushing the breath from my body. I wanted to die.

Lewis sat beside me, holding me, crying with me. I gripped his shirt, but the grief wouldn't allow me the comfort of another human being. It surrounded me, swallowing me down to a cavern under black water, where it consumed me bite by bite, until I was nothing but bones worn smooth by the deadly caress of the waves.

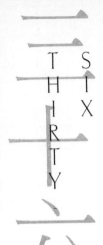

THIRTY SIX
一三六

Meg Lindsay, January 2011

One week went by without her—a stinking, walking-corpse sort of horrid week. My grief dulled to an aching fatigue in my chest, like pneumonia of the soul. Li Shu took her to counseling every day, and at the end of each session, she would ask Eva, "Are you ready to go home yet?"

And Eva would say, "Yes. Home to China, with Wen Ming."

I tried to call Wen Ming, but she would not talk to me. I received an e-mail from her:

> *You are kind person, Mrs. Lindsay. But you have*
> *Mr. Lindsay and your family. I only have Zhen An.*
> *If she want to live here with me, I cannot say no.*
> *I am sorry for trouble you.*

And I'd trusted her. I'd set aside my suspicions and jealousies and embraced her. I'd been willing to make her my own daughter. I didn't understand this kind of betrayal. It made no sense.

The crazy thing was that we adults were at the mercy of the grief-stricken fantasies of an eleven-year-old. There was no way Li Shu or any of the rest of us were going to take my daughter to China and leave her there, no matter how hard she begged or what hateful things she said or stupid things she did.

After a week of her immovable determination, I grew more frightened. What if we couldn't get her to come home? What if we had no choice but to put her in foster care, or in residential care?

Was I losing my daughter?

Those questions had the power to immobilize me, and I couldn't afford to be incapacitated. Lewis and I couldn't take time to grieve, to fear, to panic. We had to be the grown-ups. The strong ones.

Bree was my refuge. She let me cry and rant and rage to her, so I would spare Lewis, who was suffering too. She never judged me, even when I said the most horrible things, which I knew I wouldn't mean an hour later. And when I woke in the middle of the night thinking I heard a sound from Eva's room and ran in, only to be attacked by the empty silence, she didn't complain when I called her at one thirty in the morning, incoherent with tears.

Li Shu was my rock. I hoped God was planning a special reward in heaven for her, because she was the only thread keeping Eva from being lost to me. It cost her—she and her husband weren't used to children. Her husband didn't understand why she wanted to get so involved in our troubles. She finally had to tell him about the baby she gave up years ago. He was angry at first that she'd kept such a secret from him. But having it out in the open would be good for both of them—eventually.

Into the middle of all this came another phone call. This one was made by Lewis to a man he had been trying to track down ever since the professor at MIT had mentioned him. A man named Cary Dressler, Naomi Ricci's longtime romantic partner. We suspected that he was still with her, and we'd finally found a phone number for him in New Mexico. Things with Eva were at such a wretched standstill—we needed something else to think about.

One evening, Lewis dialed the number and pushed the speakerphone button.

"Hello?" He had a thick New Jersey accent.

Lewis glanced at me and then leaned toward the phone. "Hello. I'm Dr. Lewis Lindsay, with the University of Chicago. I'm acquaintances with your friend Jeremiah Davies. He gave me your phone number."

"All right."

Lewis looked a bit startled that the man wasn't more receptive.

But I prodded him to continue. "Um . . . I was told that you know Naomi Ricci."

There was a pause. "Why do you mention it?"

Lewis briefly closed his eyes. "Because I'm her son and I want to find her."

"Naomi has no children."

Has. Present tense. From his quick release of breath, I gathered Lewis had noticed too.

"She does. I know she claimed otherwise, but I can provide her marriage certificate to my father, Liam Lindsay, as well as my own birth certificate with her name on it."

"What do you want, Dr. Lindsay?"

"She left when I was seven. Her last words to me said to look her up if I ever found the Higgs boson. Well, I did, sir. And I want to bring it to her."

Silence on the other end lasted so long, I thought he'd hung up.

"Higgs, you say?"

"Yes, sir."

"What's your name again?"

"Lewis. Lewis Lindsay."

Yet another long pause. "I think you should come to New Mexico. But before you do, there's something you need to know."

"What's that?"

"Naomi—your . . . mother—she has Alzheimer's."

"I'll go with you."

Lewis jammed more clothes into his suitcase. "Someone has to stay for Eva."

"She's safe with Li Shu—who also thinks I should go with you."

He'd requested family leave from the university, and they'd been happy to grant it. He was going to drive because last-minute airline tickets were far more than we could afford.

At first, I'd agreed with him that I should stay. It seemed unimaginable to leave town when everything with Eva was such a mess. But I would never forget the awful, stricken look on Lewis's face when he hung up the phone after his talk with Cary Dressler.

And I knew—my place was with him. Yes, I was Eva's mother. Yes, she needed me, but Lewis had been my best friend, my family, long before we became parents. And long after this crisis was past, Eva would go out on her own, create her own family, and forge her own friendships. But Lewis would be mine to care for, mine to love, until we died. I belonged with him on this journey. He needed me.

So I packed my suitcase too, regardless of his protests. Then, when he was loading the car, I walked into Eva's room and listened to the silence. I threw back my head, staring through the ceiling, past the building, into the expanse of stars hidden by the sun.

"Where are the ladybugs now?" I shouted. "The red threads? The mist and music?" I thought I was dry of tears, but I found more on my cheeks. "Where is the mysterious woman and the crane?" I picked up my old teddy bear that sat on her bed now. "I am leaving town without my daughter! Where are you? Why did you abandon me? I just wanted a family. Was that too much to ask?"

I'd trusted. I'd had faith. Enough faith for myself and my unbelieving husband. I had submitted to the painful process of becoming a mother. I'd done my best.

"Is this your best?" I shot my whisper to the heavens.

I understood then why people give up on faith. Why it's easier to say there is no God. A crossroads opened before me. Lewis stood in one direction, my God stood in the other, like two propped-up, life-sized cutouts. Lewis's way offered no hope, but no disappointment either. Things happen because they do. No reason to get angry because no one promised anything different.

God was more of an all-or-nothing proposition. Faith meant seeing beyond reality, but it also meant disappointment, pain, and the wrenching question of where God was when it hurt.

It was an unfair choice. An overwhelming choice. So I huddled with my teddy bear in the space between the two, closed my eyes, and waited for the pain to go away.

THIRTY SEVEN

七

Eva Zhen An Lindsay, January 2011

I feel trapped. I don't know why I do the things I do. I don't understand why I feel so angry. Why I don't want to go home.

Li Shu is a very kind person. She has been good to me this past week, but I see that she is getting tired. So am I. I don't like who I am. I don't like being in trouble. I don't like being away from my parents.

But I am so afraid. I know—it's stupid of me to be afraid. I feel so stupid most of the time. I'm afraid to be their daughter. I don't want to be left alone again. What if they leave me? What if I'm so bad that they don't want me anymore?

Like I said—it's really stupid. They've stuck with me longer than anyone else ever has. They put up with a lot of crap from me.

But there's something about Wen Ming. Maybe it's because she's not a grown-up. She's not a mom. And she knows just how I feel. I don't want to lose her. I don't want her to be alone. I wear a bottle around my neck that has her crane feather in it. But there's more in there than just the feather. In that bottle is Wen Ming's voice, the happiness of her smile, and her love for me. All I have to do is hold that bottle, and I feel the warmth of her in my hand. I never told my mom and dad this. I don't think they would like it. It's a big secret.

There's no way to have my family and Wen Ming. I had to choose. Wen Ming needs me. I need her.

I thought I knew the right thing to do. I'm not sure of anything anymore. Only that I hurt, that everything in me feels broken. And heavy, like a huge backpack full of rocks, or really boring books.

I tell some of this to my counselor. She's very nice about it. She doesn't judge me or make me feel bad. She says I do that to myself far more "efficiently" than she ever could. I always feel better after I talk to her, but it doesn't change anything.

We talked about that today—about feeling trapped. My mom used to come with me to my appointments, but I haven't let her come since I tried to run away.

I miss her. She has the lovingest eyes in the world. Even when she's mad at me, her eyes spark little love beams at me. She has a bad temper, but so do I.

I know I can't get to China—even though no one has come right out to say it. I can't be with Wen Ming, but I can't bring myself to go home, either. It would kill Wen Ming. It would be turning my back on her, and I can't do that.

But part of me wants very much to go home. I hate myself for that.

I had a nightmare last night. I dreamed an airplane dropped me right in the middle of the Pacific Ocean, between China and America, and that my parents and Wen Ming and all my friends and Auntie Yang and Uncle Zhou stood in the airplane and yelled at me that since I couldn't make up my mind what world I wanted to belong to, I'd have to swim in the middle until I chose. Then I'd have to swim to whichever country I wanted to live in. There were sharks and nasty fish and stinging jellyfish in the water, and I grew so tired. The waves dragged me down, and I started to drown.

I woke up screaming, but since I was at Li Shu's house, my mom and dad weren't there to calm me down. Li Shu stuck her head into the room and asked if I was okay. I could tell she was worried about me, but she didn't know what to do. Bad dreams are kind of private. I couldn't tell her about it, and I don't think she really wanted to hear.

Li Shu and I have just returned to her house from my counseling session. She tells me to do my homework, and she checks the voice mail on her phone. She gets a sickish, I-just-drank-sour-milk look on her face and clicks her phone shut.

"There was a message from your mom and dad. They've had to go to New Mexico for a few days. You're staying with me until they get back."

My world stops at the word "go." It means they're not here. It means they're gone.

It means they left me.

"Why did they leave?" I am trying not to sound freaked out. I don't think Li Shu would know what to do if I did, and if my parents aren't here anymore, then I can't risk it.

"Your dad finally found his mom."

I'd heard them talking about that. My sort-of grandma, I guess. Dad wanted to find her really bad, even though she left him when he was a kid. I didn't blame him—if I could find my China mom and dad, I would.

"She's in New Mexico?"

"Yes."

I picture the map of the United States in my classroom at school. New Mexico is a very long way from Chicago. "They didn't even say good-bye." There's a big hand squeezing my throat and lungs. "They left without me." I am not going to cry.

I'm not.

But it's scary to think of them so far away. What if I need them? What if they don't come back? What if something happens to them, and I never see them again?

I want . . .

I need . . .

I can't breathe. I'm just a kid—and everything about this is growing way too big and scary for me.

Li Shu's jaw gets very tense. She stares straight ahead, like someone who is counting to ten so she won't lose her temper. Finally, she looks over the top of my head, not at my eyes. "Why do you care? You don't even want to live with them. Why shouldn't they take a trip without you?"

She has a point, and it's terrifying. "I'm their daughter. They shouldn't leave their daughter."

"Really? No one would be able to tell by the way you act toward them."

This fear is really choking me now.

I feel it filling me up, black and strong. "You can't talk to me that way! You're not my mom."

"No, I'm not. But you left your mom and dad. You left them just the way your grandma left your dad and your China mom left you. So now you're stuck with me, and I'll talk to you the way I feel I must."

"I didn't mean to leave. I didn't know what else to do!" The tears are forcing their way out of my eyes, no matter how hard I try to stop them.

"What else to do? What are you talking about?"

"Wen Ming. She needs me. She thought that if—"

Oh. I wasn't supposed to tell anyone. I clamp my mouth shut and wipe the tears from my eyes.

But Li Shu is pretty smart. She narrows her eyes at me, until they are like blades piercing me. "She thought if what?"

"Nothing."

"Eva Zhen An Lindsay! You are not going to get up from that chair until you tell me what Wen Ming said to you."

Whoa. For not being a mom, she does it pretty well.

A mom. Moms know how to make things better. Moms are safe—they take care of kids even when kids are bad. I need . . . suddenly, I want to tell. Somehow, I know, I hope that telling will get me out of this mess.

"Wen Ming said if I ran away and if I was mean enough, my parents wouldn't want me anymore and they'd send me back to China. Then she and I were going to get our own house and be each other's family forever. She says no American parents will ever love me as much as she does."

I can breathe again. I gulp the air, and I don't even try to stop the tears anymore. Everything is wet—my nose and mouth and eyes. I can hardly speak. But I know what I want.

I want to go home. To my real home. To my parents.

I'm so sorry, Wen Ming. But when I tell what you suggested, when I say it out loud, I see how really dumb it is. How childish. I need a mom. And you aren't grown-up enough to be that for me. You need a family too, and I'm sorry you don't have one. I'm sorry I couldn't give you mine. I tried. But you can't ruin what I have.

I don't want to swim in the ocean until I drown. I'm scared to choose, but I have to.

I choose them.

"I want my mommy!" The wail escapes me before I can change the baby word to a more grown-up one. But I don't feel grown-up at all. I feel like a baby. I want to suck my thumb and wear a diaper and drink from a bottle.

And I want my mommy to hold me.

Li Shu is staring at me like I've turned into a big sewer raccoon—cute but dangerous. And what do you do with one who is sobbing all over your kitchen table?

"Wen Ming is wrong."

My head is on the table now, my arms shielding it so I can't see her. "I know."

"No, you don't know."

I peek at her under my arm. "It was a stupid idea. She shouldn't have said it, and I shouldn't have listened." My voice has that wailing, sobbing note in it again. I feel like such a brat. No wonder Li Shu doesn't look very sympathetic.

"What I mean is that Wen Ming is wrong about loving you. She doesn't love you."

That brings me almost to my feet. "She does! She does love me!"

"No! Anyone who would tell you to do such a horrible thing doesn't really love you. Anyone who is so selfish that she wants you to run away from your family to be with her is not loving, is not a good friend. A real friend isn't so manipulative and selfish."

I grab the bottle of Wen Ming around my neck. I squeeze it. But there is no warmth there. It is cold and hard. I look through the painted surface to the feather inside.

It is not Wen Ming. It is only a feather.

Li Shu is right. I've been such an idiot.

I yank the bottle. The string cuts into my neck a little and then snaps. I race to Li Shu's front door and pull it open before she can stop me. I stand on the concrete steps that are just off the curb and throw the bottle as hard as I can into the street.

It shatters on the pavement. A car rushes through the debris, and the feather gets stuck in a tread on the tire.

I turn and find Li Shu behind me. She's not a mom, but she's the only thing I've got. I wrap my arms around her and bury my head against her breasts. "I don't know what to do."

She breathes in slowly. "You should talk to Wen Ming, then you should call your parents."

She's right. She would have made a great mom, I think. "Okay."

I thought I would miss the feather bottle. But I don't. I feel lighter without it. More complete. Less confused. I don't feel like I'm drowning in the ocean anymore.

I feel free.

THIRTY EIGHT

Meg Lindsay, January 2011

The closer we came to Albuquerque, the more withdrawn Lewis became. I realized he was going on a journey, like my first trip to China. The trappings of the world he knew, the ties that held him to his old life were snapping with every mile. I was with him physically, but the journey a soul goes on is undertaken alone.

And I was only partially with him. A large piece of me was still in Chicago, with my daughter. She wouldn't know it, of course. It was yet another thing no one warns you about: when you become a mother, you are never whole again. Pieces of you lodge in your child's heart, and you become scattered across the world—wherever your child is. There's a certain pain in that, but there's also a beauty to it, a becoming one with something far greater than you alone.

Cary Dressler had given us directions to the facility where Naomi was living. It was called the Cottages, and with its small group-style homes and antique furnishings, wide green lawns, and winding paths for Alzheimer's patients to wander, it appeared idyllic—at least as idyllic as could be expected under the circumstances.

He met us there at the administrative building. Short, bald, over-weight, with puffy, peachy jowls and a hooked nose—he couldn't have been more different from Lewis's attractive, slim father. Introductions were muted, awkward. I don't think any of us really knew what our roles were or how to breach the decades-high wall Naomi had con-structed between us.

Lewis stuck his hands in his pockets and walked to the window overlooking the lawns. "How long has she lived here?"

"Since 2000. She got the diagnosis in 1998, when she was fifty-eight. We'd been together for over ten years by then, and I wanted to marry her, but she . . . she said she wasn't the marrying sort."

"And she wasn't." He couldn't keep the bitterness from his voice, and I shot an apologetic glance at Cary.

He rubbed the back of his neck, and I felt sorry for him. It wasn't fair for him to be caught up in Naomi's first family's drama. "Anyway, she'd been having memory lapses for a few years, and it was starting to affect her work. Her last paper was published in '99 and was written mostly by her graduate students. She couldn't remember how to spell the words she needed. She retired after the paper was published, and I helped her settle her affairs in Boston and find this place."

Lewis pivoted to face Cary. "Why the secrecy? Why didn't any of her colleagues know anything about this?"

"She was a proud woman. She didn't want the physics community to know what was happening to her. Can you blame her? One of the world's smartest people—losing her mind? We knew what the outlook was. I remember one night, she cried in my arms because she couldn't remember some formula. She couldn't do the math anymore. She wanted to disappear so no one would know. So that's what we did."

Lewis slumped. He looked old and tired. "I want to see her."

"She's pretty far gone. You know much about Alzheimer's?"

"Enough to not have any expectations. I just want to see her."

He took us to the cottage she shared with a group of other women. The living area had soaring ceilings and skylights—bright, airy under the New Mexico sun. Cary entered Naomi's room and returned a moment later. "She doesn't want to come out. She doesn't know me today, so just—" His voice broke. "Anyway, I'll let you go in. Don't stay long. Visitors tire her quickly."

Was this the infamous Naomi Ricci? This small, old-before-her-time woman hunched over a desk piled high with scraps of paper? She was scribbling on a sheet of paper when we went in.

Lewis felt down my arm for my hand. I took his and squeezed.

"Uh . . . Dr. Ricci?"

She didn't look up.

"Naomi Ricci?"

She mumbled something, head bent low over the paper. What I could see of her scribbles, they looked like mathematical problems.

"Mother?"

Her head snapped up. "I don't have children!" She swore and then scratched out her writing in dark, violent strokes. "What am I missing? Why doesn't it add up?"

"What is it?"

"Feynman diagrams."

"Let me take a look at it." Lewis bent over to read what she had written. "Here, try this." He made some calculations for her.

She barely glanced at them. "Are you stupid? That's not how you do it. A child could do it better."

I braced Lewis around his waist. Before he could respond, she crumpled the piece of paper and threw it on the floor, which was dotted with similar clumps.

"I used to have a child," she continued, her gaze unsteady and restless, never looking directly at us. "But I lost him. I lost my son. How can you lose a child? I went away and never came back and he was gone. I should have stayed with him." Her words and her mouth grew soft, loose, distorted by her own self-hatred, and she didn't have the mental capacity to hide it or make it more palatable.

Lewis's eyes shone with tears. "It's me, Mom. Your son. Lewis."

His name sent a shudder through her. She bent over her papers again, muttering, "I used to have a son named Lewis. But I lost him. I went away. I was a bad mom. A good scientist, but a horrible person."

I could feel the overwhelming sludge of emotions rising in Lewis. This was decimating him and there was nothing I could do. He'd known the diagnosis, but knowing hadn't destroyed the dreams he'd cherished for a lifetime. But this—this brutal reality—had the power to destroy.

He tensed, then relaxed his muscles. "Mom," he said, stopping her hand from its scribbling, "I am your son. I am Lewis. And I . . . I forgive you for going away." His cheeks were damp with tears.

She yanked her hand away. "Shut up! Shut up! You always want something from me. You're thirsty, you want a hug, you have to go potty. I'm working! Leave me alone. I have to find it. I have to find the Higgs. I don't want to see you again until you can bring me the Higgs! Find me the Higgs, Lewis, and then we'll talk."

Lewis was shaking. This was torture. I pulled over a side chair and guided him into it. He set a black leather folder on her desk. "I'm grown-up now, Mom. I'm not a little boy. I found the Higgs."

She looked up again, her face hollow and sad, desperate. She put her hands on his cheeks, looking straight through him to the child he used to be. "You did? What a good boy! You're a good boy, Lewis. Mommy's sorry for yelling. Mommy doesn't mean it. You should have a better mommy. You're a good little boy."

He'd waited his whole life to hear that. He let out a strangled noise. I put my hands on his shoulders, praying, begging God to make him strong. He took a deep breath. "That was all in the past, Mom. I'm an adult now, and I found the Higgs. Let me show you."

He pulled out the graph and showed it to her. She studied it, and for one moment, she seemed almost lucid. Lewis explained it all to her, and she listened, her eyes shining, her mouth parted. He stopped speaking, waiting for her response. There was so much hope in his eyes.

So much faith.

And for a moment, I thought it might be rewarded. A warmth crept into her eyes. Just for a second.

Then her inner light shut off, and she turned aside. "Go away. I'm busy. I have a lot of work to do. I have to find the Higgs."

THIRTY

NINE

二十九

Wen Ming, January 2011

I did not think anything could be worse than losing Zhen An to America. But being told I could never be adopted—that I'd come so very, very close to my dream of being with Zhen An and being a family—it was a pain that goes beyond the words I know to describe it.

I did feel guilty about encouraging her to run away, to come home to me. To China. But I knew she would never do it. It was a stupid idea. It wouldn't work. I just wanted so badly to have one last thing to believe in. It made me feel better, even for a second, to imagine that we children could find a way even when all the grown-ups said we could not.

So I was not expecting her to call in the middle of the morning. Director Wu was very busy—more babies to send out for adoption that day, and everything was in chaos. Director Wu let me use her office and told me not to stay on the phone very long. Then she left.

"*Ni hao*, Zhen An."

"I'm not good today, Wen Ming."

Her voice was hard, like ice. A shiver swept through me, like a wind that is lonely. "What is wrong?"

"You are wrong. I was wrong to listen to you. You are a very bad friend to tell me to run away. I did. I did what you said! Now my parents are gone and I can't go home, and I am not coming back to China."

I couldn't breathe. I felt like she was slicing chunks of my skin away with every word. She was so upset, she was mixing Chinese and English together, but I understood what she was saying. "You . . . ran away?"

"Yes! For you. I did it for you. You are selfish and mean, and I might have gotten hurt or killed because I was stupid enough to listen to you. But my mom came for me. She found me. And then I wouldn't go home with her, and now she's gone with my dad."

My hands started shaking. My breath came in shallow bursts. "I am sorry. Very, very sorry."

"I have a family. I love them. And you can't take that away from me."

"I'm not—"

"You don't love me. You're not my *jie jie*, and I don't want to talk to you or hear from you ever again. Never, okay?"

"*Mei mei* . . ."

"Don't call me that! Good-bye, Wen Ming."

There was a click, and then silence.

She was gone and it was my own fault.

I felt my way around Director Wu's desk. I knew somewhere behind it was a door to the courtyard. I didn't really think about what I was doing. I just had to get outside where I could breathe. With shaking hands, I pried open the door.

I ran into the January deadness of the courtyard. There were no sounds other than the trembling rhythm of my heart. I tripped, the pavement biting and stinging my hands.

I found the cherry tree by falling over it. The tree that would always mean Zhen An in my mind. "I hate you!" I kicked it and hit it with my bare hands until they were bloodied and numb. "I wish I'd never met you! I wish I never trusted you. I wish I never loved you!"

I ran through the courtyard entrance and into the street. I could still hear her voice in my head: *You are a very bad friend. You're not my* jie jie. *I don't want to talk to you or hear from you ever again.*

"Shut up!" I screamed. I had to keep running. I had to get away from her voice. So I ran. And fell. And got up, and kept running. But the voice followed me. People yelled at me for running into them, but I didn't stop to apologize. I almost hoped I'd find a busy street where a bus or car could run over me. I was already dying. Being run over would make it end faster.

Finally, I couldn't run anymore. I leaned against a building, its rough bricks biting into my already damaged skin. I still had air in my heaving lungs. That was not right. I should not have air. I didn't deserve it.

I listened. There were no people whom I could hear. I walked ahead several steps until I felt another building in front of me. A ruin of a wall with rubble all around. I was in an alley of some sort, but I didn't know where. It was cold and I had no coat.

I groped along the brick and concrete until I found a place where the wall seemed to have collapsed on itself. I huddled under the broken bit of wall and cried. I was going to die, alone and in the dark. And my *mei mei* would never even know. It was only what I deserved. She was right—every word.

It was all my own fault.

FORTY

Meg Lindsay, January 2011

"That wasn't my mother."

We were walking down the gentle, wide curve of the concrete path, away from Naomi's cottage. I had a wild urge to comment on how green and well trimmed the lawn was, and gush about the sparkling white paint job on the picket fences, or make some other inane remark on a trivial detail. Anything to avoid the deadness in Lewis's eyes.

But his observation compelled a response. "No, it wasn't."

I heard people say that before about loved ones with dementia or mental illness. That it's not the same person they knew. I suppose it's our too-human way of denying the loss, easing the pain. Trying to make sense of it all. Like children, playing make-believe.

We had said good-bye to Cary Dressler, who had waited for us in the cottage's living area. He seemed like a good man, who loved Naomi greatly. Lewis asked if there was anything we could do for her, but Cary said that everything was in order. Naomi had done a thorough preparation for leaving this time. She wasn't going to storm out of life like she'd stormed out of her marriage.

I knew Lewis wouldn't be back. He talked about it with Cary, but the older man thought it might be more upsetting for both Lewis and Naomi. He told Lewis he was welcome back at any time but not to feel obligated. He also asked for our address. Said that Naomi had several physics books and notes she had made about her work. He had no use for them so he offered them to Lewis. Even though Lewis said he'd have to think it over, I knew eventually those things would find a home with us.

We found a hotel in Albuquerque, and it wasn't until we'd checked in and ordered room service that he said anything more about the visit. He was so tense, I was afraid to touch him for fear he'd burst.

"I owe you an apology, Meg." He leaned against the pillows on our bed, arms folded across his chest, ankles crossed. Closed, inaccessible. Protective.

This was not the response I was expecting from him. Everything else about Naomi Ricci had brought out the strongest, most wrenching emotions, not this tightly controlled, nearly philosophical demeanor.

"Here I thought that I was more rational, more reasonable than all you religious people chasing your God fantasies." His mouth twisted into a smirk. "And all the while, I was chasing a fantasy of my own. That was not my mother—she only existed in my head. So go ahead and fill Eva's head with whatever stories you want about Jesus. While you're at it, let's spin some nice fairy tales about her grandmother too. Let's all be delusional."

It stung like a slap in cold weather. There were so many different directions I could go from that remark. Most of them would take us someplace bad. I flipped through my options and settled on saying nothing at all.

He stared at his feet pointing in front of him on the bed, bitterness dragging his mouth and eyebrows down. I recognized that look now—it was from his mother.

At once, I saw her, hunched across her desk, caught in the hold of her two greatest failures—her son and her life's work. Only this time, she was young, at the height of her success. Same regrets, same prison, only dressed and covered up. In a way, the dementia had merely made naked what had always been there.

"All these years—my whole life—and it comes down to the fact that she can't even write her own name anymore. I've spent an entire career trying to win the approval of a woman who can't control her own bladder."

His tone was harsh, but he looked small and lost. Just a boy, really, putting up his fists to cover a broken heart.

"At least you know now that she feels badly for what she did. I think she did love you — in a way."

Agate eyes trained a glassy, hard stare on me. "That's supposed to make me feel better?"

Forget this. I wasn't going to be his verbal punching bag. "Fine. Sit here and feel sorry for yourself. I'm going to get some fresh air."

He didn't try to stop me.

I headed for the pool. As I pushed open the double glass door, my cell phone rang.

"Hello?"

"Mom, it's me — Eva."

My hand clenched with such a jerk that I nearly dropped the phone. Her voice — it felt so good in my ears. And still, a shiver of apprehension shot through me. So much heartache today, I didn't think I could bear any more. "Hi."

"I wanted to tell you . . ." Her voice sounded thin, scratchy.

"Yes?"

"I want to come home!" The words were broken and running with tears. "I'm sorry I was so stupid. I don't want you to be gone anymore. Please come home."

My legs couldn't hold me. I grabbed for the nearest pool chair and sank into it, shaking. I didn't know what had brought her around, but it didn't matter. I just wanted to wrap her in my arms and never let go. I opened my mouth to say so.

And the words wouldn't come. A sickeningly sweet smell filled my nose, tangy, like blood — the fragrance of fear. My fear. Here she was, apologizing and begging to come home, and all I could think was that she'd hurt me once too many times. I couldn't take any more.

How many ways was it possible for a child to break a mother's heart?

"Mom?"

I had to say something. I couldn't say no. I couldn't tell her what I was actually feeling.

"Mommy? Are you there? Mom?" She sounded breathless, choked, pleading.

"I'm here. I . . . forgive you, darling. We'll be home tomorrow, and you can come home then, okay?" I fought to say each word. It wasn't that I didn't mean it, because I truly did, but that nauseating, suffocating fear fought me with each syllable.

"I love you, Mom." Relief slammed her voice into a flat puddle.

"I love you too. I'll call tomorrow."

I flipped the phone shut and huddled against the back of the chair, my knees to my chest, trying to breathe.

I couldn't trust her. My own daughter. She frightened me.

Love always trusts.

Love always perseveres.

Love never fails.

But I had failed in every way. Years ago, I'd made a vow to always accept, always encourage. Forgive, forget. Be patient, selfless. Be there for her no matter what.

It had all seemed easy. I didn't want to be like my mother. Wanting to be different had seemed like all I needed. It should have worked. If desire had been enough, I would have been the perfect mother.

Yet over and over, I'd fallen so short. All the times I'd lost my temper. The cutting words I'd said. The way I'd put my own interests ahead of hers. I thought I had conquered it. I thought I'd improved.

I thought I'd learned to love, despite the pain.

Maybe, if things had turned out differently with Wen Ming, maybe that would have been enough.

But now, at the final test, I couldn't do it. She was like the prodigal wanting to come home. And in my heart, I couldn't find the strength to trust her again.

I was empty.

My phone rang again. My mother. A sound burst from me—something between a groan and a growl. I didn't *have* to answer it.

But something in me wanted to. It was her fault, after all. Her fault I didn't know how to love, that I was failing as a mom. I'd been just as bad as Lewis—living my whole life trying to please a mother who—

"Your daughter called and told me you and Lewis are in New Mexico?"

—who didn't deserve it. What was wrong with me?

"Hi, Mom."

"What are you doing there?"

"Visiting Lewis's mother." I briefly explained the situation to her.

"I can't believe you left your little girl to go chasing some woman across the country who can't even recognize who you are. I wouldn't have thought even you could be so irresponsible. You didn't even tell me where you were going. I had to find out when Eva called me just a while ago."

A burning ache twisted in my stomach. My hands started to shake again. "I wasn't irresponsible. Eva was with Li Shu. She was fine."

"She's *not* fine! She's a troubled little girl, and you left her with someone not even her family. You know, I'm really disappointed in you, Meg. I didn't think you and Lewis would still be so self-absorbed. This is my granddaughter we're talking about!"

And where was this woman when her own daughter had been *not fine* all those years? The words almost escaped, and I shoved them back down, dense and sickening.

Two girls scampered into the pool enclosure and jumped into the pool. They splashed each other in the shallow water. One looked older, with a ponytail. The younger had blond hair divided into pigtails.

"Let's play house," Ponytail Girl said to the younger one. "I'll be the mommy and you be the baby."

"I'm *always* the baby. I want to be the mommy."

I watched the younger one and felt the ever-tightening mass of resentment in her. But she adored Pony too. I read it in her eyes.

Pony stuck her hands on her hips. "I'm older. I know more about mommies than you do."

Oh, Pony Girl, don't do this to her. Can't you see she just wants to play with you?

"You're too bossy." Pigtails cradled her doll.

"You're a big baby."

The words cut through me, as if they'd been directed at me.

"I'm not playing!"

"Yes you are."

Pony yanked on the doll, and Pigtails yanked back. Predictably, the doll's arm dislocated with a sharp pop and floated on the surface of the water.

My mother was still talking. ". . . Moms are supposed to be there for their kids. You can't just pick up and leave."

A shriek tore through me. I couldn't hold it back anymore.

"Meg?"

"So where were you for me, Mom? All those years, when all I wanted was your approval and support and affection? You left me for five years, just because I married someone you didn't like. You left me!"

Silence. I couldn't believe I'd said it. I'd never said it before. I'd let Lewis say it for me in his letter, while I crouched behind him, not speaking.

Pigtails was crying.

Finally, my mom found her voice. But instead of the normal coldness, it had a punctured sound to it. Fragile. "I did everything for you. And you never appreciated it. You always wanted something different. Anything. As long as it was something I didn't like. You went out of your way to defy me. Don't gripe to me about approval. It would have been nice to have some from you too."

I curled into a tight ball on my chair. I should have known it was no use trying to explain to her. "I loved you! I did everything I could to be what you wanted me to be, and it wasn't good enough. So I gave up. Why try so hard if I was just going to fail?"

More silence. Then, "You have a weird idea of what love is."

"I wonder why."

A woman walked into the pool enclosure. She wasn't particularly beautiful, except her dark hair that rested in glossy waves across her back. But she had grace and dignity. I couldn't help but notice her.

She knelt in front of the girls, who both clamored for her to hear their side.

I watched her talk to them, and it was as if I could see into her spirit. Everything about her was transparent, like her whole life had been downloaded into my mind. Here was a Real Mother. So different from me. So different from my mom or Lewis's mom. Looking at her, I saw that all we were in comparison were children. Children playing house. We were too broken, too needy to really love each other. We were too busy trying to survive, to protect ourselves.

But this one. She was wisdom and nurture, patience, strength, and love. They streamed from her, like points of light, settling on everything around her in layers of peace. I could see it, feel it seeping into me. She was a stranger, and yet the longer I watched, the more I felt like I'd always known her.

She loved her children, and they adored her. I adored her. How did she do it? Here was a woman who would not be desperately terrified that her child would hurt her. She wouldn't be so paralyzed by the fear of that pain that she couldn't give her daughter what she needed.

She couldn't possibly be someone who would cower for years, afraid of losing her own mother's approval, or spend her whole life trying to find the one thing that would win her mother's love.

She was strong, complete. Whole. I knew in my spirit that when she loved, it was a love borne of freedom, of excess. Not want. Not desire.

She took the broken doll in her hands and said a few words to the older girl, who apologized to the younger one and scurried back into the hotel. Then the mother turned to Pigtails.

"You and your sister need to treat each other with love." She sounded serious, but I felt a smile in each word.

"I try! It doesn't work." Pigtails ran her hand across her runny nose. "She doesn't love me."

"Of course she does."

"She doesn't act like it."

"Neither do you sometimes."

"It's too hard. I'm not good at it."

She took the broken doll arm and eased it back into the socket until it snapped into place. Then she handed it to the girl. "Loving someone is never easy. It means you have to grow up inside."

My mother had been saying something, but I'd been distracted.

Now her words arrested me. ". . . You whine at me like you're still a child. Grow up, Meg."

Grow up.

It sounded so different coming from my mother than it did from this other mother. From my mom, it was an indictment of my failure, but this other mother made it sound reassuring, like a promise.

What would growing up look like? Would it make me like this woman?

How did one grow up inside?

"Come, Meg," the mother said.

I jumped at hearing my name, but she was looking down at Pigtails. Then she glanced up, straight into my eyes. And she smiled. She led the little girl around the pool, toward the glass doors of the hotel.

"Look, Mama!" The child with my name pointed at the pool water. "I see other kids in the water."

"Do you?" The mother didn't look at all surprised or put off by her daughter's imagination. "What are they doing?"

She frowned at the water. "Uh-oh. They're not being grown-up either."

"Probably because they're children." She took the child's hand. "Let's go."

They disappeared into the hotel corridor.

"Meg?" My mother's voice cut sharply into my ears. "Are you listening to me?"

"Sorry, Mom." The words came out of my mouth almost before they formed in my mind. "You're right. I need to grow up."

"You always want me to listen to you, and then you don't— What did you say?"

"I said you're right."

Silence.

"I have to go, Mom. I'll call you tomorrow sometime."

I ended the call and walked to the pool edge.

Looked into the water.

And I saw myself.

Just a child. A little girl who'd only been playing house. Trying to live in make-believe.

"I'll be the mommy and you be the baby."

No wonder I kept failing. A child wasn't capable of loving the way a parent must love.

More reflections, more children. Lewis, Naomi, my mom, my dad, even my sister and my brother. Adam. Wen Ming. And Eva. All of them striving with one another, trying to fill their own needs, protect themselves, get what they want. Trying to trade love as they barter for toys.

The reflections wavered, wrinkled. Aged. Until we all became like Naomi, children trapped in an elderly body, still trying to get what we needed and angry that we couldn't.

I knelt by the pool and reached my hand to those sorrowful figures. I couldn't hate them. I couldn't be angry. They were suffering, and they were alone.

I watched and watched them, unable to look away. I didn't want to be among them. If, God forbid, I ever ended up like Naomi, I wanted my mind to be able to find only the best, most memorable moments in my life and abandon me there. I didn't want to be trapped by regret. I didn't want to be a child forever.

But was that possible for me?

I leaned over the water and stared down my reflection.

"Grow up, Meg."

Be like the mother.

How?

Her reflection joined the others, so calm, so mature. She held out her arms to me, inviting me to come.

The pool was full of pain. Their pain and my own. I could not jump in.

But her eyes told me it was the only way to grow. Only way to become who I wanted to be. I had to trust her.

I dove into her reflection.

It shattered around me, and the water closed over my head.

I had to love.

I had to forgive.

I had to trust.

But it hurts so much, Mommy.

Burning lungs. Seizing muscles. Frantic heart.

The answer flowed around me in caressing waves. Love anyway. Let the pain stretch you, fill you. Stop fighting. Stop using love to meet your own needs. Give up. Give in.

Float.

But I'll die.

Trust.

I listened. I stopped fighting and let the pain take me. All the tears. All the disappointments. The wounds they all carried around, unseen and unstanched. I floated in it, letting the weight press me to the bottom. I opened my eyes, and I could see them—my mother, my daughter, my husband, Wen Ming, and all the others. Little broken, hurting creatures hovering in the water.

Through the gathering haze in my mind, a mother's compassion shot through me. They were so small. So helpless. I wanted to catch them in my arms and hold them. Comfort them. Nurture them. Did it really matter what they'd done to me? They were just babies. They didn't know any different.

It's okay, Mommy is here. Mommy loves you.

I was almost out of time. I spread my arms to them, wanting the last few moments to be for them, to comfort them.

My vision went dark.

Live.

Cool arms closed around me and shoved me up to the surface of the water. I broke through, the air crashing into my lungs.

Flooding out of me, like a fountain, came a willful, fully aware, defiant mother-love—the sort that would shake its fist, stick out its tongue, and say, "You are a mess, but I'm going to love you anyway and you can't stop me." It gushed from me to my mother.

This was love. At last. No expectations, no conditions. No self-protection. The pain had killed all of that.

All that remained was this life-creating love, powerful and ancient, and it was in me, surging through me. More than I could ever hold. How could that be?

My mom would carry the brokenness of her own life with her to her grave, and even if she never showed it, I now knew it was there. I couldn't hate her for being broken. I was broken too. We all were. But she didn't live in me anymore. I was free.

Finally. A love that overwhelmed the pain and left only itself in its wake. "I forgive you. All of you."

I forgive myself.

And my darling Eva—I wasn't so afraid now. She might hurt me again, but I thought . . . I hoped that now I'd be strong enough to take it. To trust and accept her, even with her problems. I couldn't wait to be with her again, to see if things really could be different now. Maybe we could have our new start after all.

My clothing floated heavily around me, and water streamed into my eyes. The hotel staff would think me insane, splashing in the pool like a little child. Only I knew the truth—that I was finally, for the first time, truly growing up.

And in the air, a mother's voice shimmered. "Good girl, Meg."

FORTY
ONE

Wen Ming, January 2011

I have never been a person of impulsive action. I make plans. And backup plans. And plans beyond that. Without them, I am Wen Ming, Doer of Stupid Things. Like running away from the orphanage when I cannot see.

The cold of the alley, having already conquered my backside, was invading the rest of my body. It made each noise loud and crisp—a crunch here, a pop there, a thud somewhere else. My ears throbbed with the beat of my heart. Anything could be out there—a stray animal, a homeless person, a criminal, or a man waiting to assault me. How could I fight what I could not see?

I should move, should try to find someone to help me, but I was as frozen as the air around me. I banged my head against the wall behind me. I'd acted like my head was full of rice instead of brains. I, Wen Ming, of plans and actions, had no idea what to do and was too frightened to move, too frightened to scream.

"Are you trying to smash your head?"

I screamed.

"And I thought you were scared speechless."

A woman's voice. Not high, but roundish, like a glass ball. I smelled a cigarette. The odor of tobacco always disgusted me. I made a show of coughing. "Smoking is bad for you."

"Bad for me and the half of China that does it. Hitting your head on a brick wall in an alley in the winter is bad for you too, but I only see you doing it, and no one else. So you win a prize for originality."

"Who are you?"

"What are you doing here, Wen Ming?"

"How do you know my name?"

"Why are you sitting here?"

One of us had to answer a question, and I was too tired to wait her out. "I did a very bad thing and lost the only friend I have ever had. She was like my *mei mei* and now she is gone."

"And this is your way of fixing your mistake?"

I struck the wall with my fist. "I wasn't thinking! If you just want to mock me, go away."

"Why don't you ask for help?"

"No!"

She must have squatted down beside me, for the smell of her smoke grew stronger. I scowled and waved my hand in front of my face.

"Don't be such a snob. So why won't you ask for help?"

"I don't need help. I can manage on my own."

"Yes. Obviously."

"Go away."

"Is this how you treated your friend? No wonder she doesn't like you anymore."

I snarled and leaped for her. I knocked her off balance and fell on top of her. I had never hit anyone in my life, but I swung my hands, slapping and hitting whatever I could. She wrestled me until she restrained me from behind. For a moment, I was sure I was going to die. The smell of her smoke filled my lungs, making me want to retch.

But then she rocked me in her arms.

She sang to me. It was a song about family, about love, about loyalty and truth. Even though I didn't mean to, I soon found myself relaxing against her. A tight knot loosened in my chest. I felt small, safe.

"I wanted a family," I said when she stopped singing.

"And who says you don't have one?"

"I live in an orphanage."

"Don't you think of them as your family?"

"No! They leave. They always leave me."

She slowly let go of me. I soon smelled smoke again. "You think a family never leaves?"

"Of course. A family would stay with me forever."

I felt a warm touch on my face. Her hands didn't seem cold. I wasn't cold anymore either. "Dear child, what you are describing is a prison, not a family."

"But—"

"In a family, love doesn't depend on physical location. Love can travel the world in a single heartbeat. Love lets go, and then bridges the distance. You would put those you love in a cage, but that's not love. Love sets free."

No control? Letting go? The very thought was like a knife to my throat. "I can't. It would hurt too badly."

"I never said you had to. That's the problem with you, Wen Ming. You always think you are the only one who can do anything. You don't trust."

Trust was definitely not safe. "I only trust myself."

"And who was it that ruined your friendship and got you lost in the city?"

Tears wet my eyes. She was right. I had proven that I couldn't even trust me.

"Ask for help, Wen Ming. Ask me to help you."

"No." I rubbed my eyes with my palms.

"Trust me."

"No."

"Give me your hands."

"Why?"

"Just do it."

I held my breath and stretched my hands toward her. She took them and turned them over, palms up. "They are scraped and bleeding."

"I . . . fell."

"I know."

She moved her fingers—to touch the raw skin. I felt the movement and jerked away. "Don't touch!"

"Trust me."

My hands trembled, but I forced them to stay open. She placed her palms flat on mine, and my skin felt like it was on fire, but I didn't pull away. I didn't cry out.

She removed her hands. "Touch my hands."

I ran my fingers along her palms. The skin was torn and raw. I heard her suck in her breath and quickly withdrew my touch. I flexed my own hands. They no longer hurt. They were no longer scraped. They no longer bled.

"Love takes on the burdens and pain of other people, child. I love you."

I held out my hands toward her voice until I found her face. Her skin was soft, smooth, but with the first traces of wrinkles around her eyes. I felt a small bump, like a mole, on the left side of her chin. "You don't even know me."

"Not as I wish I did. But still, I love you." She pulled me back into her arms. "Rest awhile."

I did. Tears flowed out of my eyes, like a stream. It wasn't exactly crying. It was more like being washed. I felt her love seep into me, opening me. It felt good, safe, strong. I could feel it shifting things around inside me, putting things in their proper place, mending parts that were broken. It was the first time I'd ever let someone else love me. I'd always tried to be the giver, never the receiver.

Suddenly, I wanted to go home. Home to the orphanage. I wanted to see Director Wu, Auntie Yang, and everyone else there. I still was frightened of them leaving me, but maybe not so much as before.

"Will you help me get home?" I didn't even know her name.

She cupped my cheek with her hand. "Come." She took my arm and guided me down the alley. Only a few short steps, then she stopped.

"Wen Ming!" The joyful, relieved voice belonged to Auntie Yang. "What are you doing outside the courtyard? We were terrified about you! We've been searching for hours."

She pulled me into her arms. Her hands touched my hair, my cheeks, my back, my hands—frantic and desperate.

"How did you find me?"

"What do you mean?" She tugged me through the courtyard entrance. "You were standing right here. Though I don't know where you thought you were going. You could have been killed!"

I hugged her, the newly open places in my soul soaking in her love for the first time. "I am very sorry, Auntie. It was wrong of me to worry you. I won't do it again."

I stopped and turned back the way I'd come.

"Where is the woman who was with me? She helped bring me home."

Auntie Yang's touch on my arm tensed. She seemed confused, worried again. "There was no one else there, Wen Ming. Only you."

I let her guide me back into the orphanage. For the first time, I felt it open loving arms to welcome me in. Had it always been this way and I never let myself feel it? I didn't know.

I only knew I was home.

FORTY
TWO

Meg Lindsay, January 2011

Eva came back to us a half hour after we arrived home. She walked through the door and slid her backpack to the floor, then just waited—somber, young and old all at once. I'd been creating this moment in my mind since she called us in New Mexico. We'd driven home, stopping only when both of us were so tired that it would have been dangerous to continue.

And now, I thought there would be music or mystery, but there was only the sweet calm of rightness, of completeness. The midmorning sun filtered through the windows of the living room, highlighting the dusty motes that had moved in like squatters during our absence. There was only breath, and the pulse in my throat that quickened at the sight of her.

There was only the tentative hope in her eyes.

And then there was only she in my arms. The silk of her hair against my face, the tremor of her arms as they wrapped around my neck, the sagging relief of her body giving itself fully over to the care of her mother for the first time. Shudders of moist breath against my neck, the wordless whispers of solace and reconciliation.

I only gave her up to Lewis's embrace because he needed her too. His long, wide hands spread across her back, his head buried against her neck. He breathed her in, and I saw with each breath a strengthening, a confidence in his hold on her, as if she were steadying him, giving him a new frame for the remaining years of his life.

"You aren't going to get sick like your mom, are you, Dad?" She tightened her hold on him, and I understood she was still broken in many ways. But she was here. She'd found the courage to come home, to let us love her. It would take a lot of work from all of us, but she could—would—find healing yet.

Lewis raised his head. "None of us knows what will happen in the future. But I promise you—I am not like my mother. I will not be like her."

His eyes met mine and there was so much resolve and purpose in them. He would be all right too.

I stretched my arms around both of them. I looked up at Li Shu. "Thank you," I mouthed.

She smiled, but it was a hollow expression, standing as she was—an outsider, appreciated but no longer needed. She nodded, a sort of little bow, as if she was summoning again that Asian reserve, smoothing out her emotions under the polite mask of it-is-no-bother and do-not-thank-me. She slipped out, closing the door behind her.

Wen Ming, April 2011

The peach blossoms spread their hopeful fragrance across the Nanhui District of Shanghai, and at the Children's Home. Our own cherry tree burst into bloom with the perfume that will always remind me of Zhen An.

Auntie Yang told me in January that Zhen An had returned to her parents. I was happy for that. At first, in my selfish child-way of thinking, I expected that now all would be well between us. I called her once. Her mother, Meg, answered. I had been working very hard on learning my English from Auntie Helen, and I was able to understand Meg's words.

"I am so very, very sorry, Wen Ming. But Eva says she isn't ready to talk to you."

It was true sorrow in her voice, and I was sorry too, for causing them pain.

"I was bad. To you and to Mr. Lindsay, and to Zhen An. I mean . . . Eva. I am sorry."

She didn't say anything right away, but when she finally said she forgave me, the sincerity was so strong it washed over me even though she was so far away.

"Will Eva ever forgive me?" The American name felt strange on my tongue, but I didn't have the right to use her Chinese name anymore. She was no longer my *mei mei* and I had come to see I must honor her new life by respecting her new name. It was what she had chosen.

"I don't know. I wish I could say yes. But I don't know. I hope so."

"May I call again?"

"I think you had better not. I will stay in touch with your auntie Yang, though."

Auntie Yang said that I had to wait, had to stay out of Eva's life so she could grow strong without me. I had to let her go so she could make a good life with her family.

It seemed to me like saying, "Let go of breathing," or "Let go of heart beating." How do you do that? How do you survive?

But that was the price I had to pay for not letting go earlier; for interfering, for thinking only of myself. And though the first few days I thought my lungs would stop breathing and my heart would stop beating, they did not. Even though it seemed the days would stay short and darkened forever, they did not. Even though I thought the pain of missing her would make me sad the rest of my life, it did not.

And with each breath and heartbeat and few seconds more of sunlight, I grew stronger, more confident in my ability not just to survive, but to create a life for myself that was good and joyful and full of the very best dreams. Dreams that did not depend on others always being there for me, always being dependent on me so they would never go away, but dreams that relied on my being there for other people and yet standing on my own as well.

Finally, the air warmed and blossoms returned to the trees. One cherry-scented afternoon, Director Wu and Auntie Yang took me into the director's office. I felt little pulses of excitement jump between the two of them.

"Wen Ming, there is an organization called Half the Sky Foundation. They have programs to help orphans who cannot be adopted."

Auntie Yang was too excited—she interrupted Director Wu, which was rude of her, but the director did not seem to mind. "They have a program called Big Sisters that helps provide education to older girls in orphanages. They want you to be in their program!"

"I don't understand."

Director Wu took my hand. "They are funded by donations from all over the world, and they want to use some of that money to provide you with a tutor and special equipment so you can learn and go to college. You are too smart to not go to college just because you are blind."

I felt a little dizzy and held on to Director Wu. Education . . . for me? University . . . for me? It was like telling me to hold all the cherry and peach blossoms of Shanghai in my two fists—it was so much more than I could grasp. "What may I study?"

"Anything you want," said Auntie Yang. "It's completely individualized. Of course, if you want to go to the university, you'll have to complete the required courses, but they'll help you do that."

"Why? Why me?"

Auntie Yang giggled, and I felt the warmth of the director's smile. Director Wu squeezed my hand even tighter. "We may have contacted them and told them about you."

Zhen An (I mean, Eva), in her American exuberance, would have thrown herself at them in a huge embrace. But I was Chinese. And young womanhood was within my grasp. I channeled the rising tide of joy inside me into a smile, a smile that felt like the heat of the sun. I nodded my head at them both. "Thank you. Thank you very much."

I would make them proud of me—these women who believed in me and loved me enough to bring help to me. There would be no more running away or moping because of past sorrows I could not change. I would not waste their goodness and generosity.

The world was opening up to me, like the view from on top of an old cherry tree. And I would launch myself into the air and fly like snowflakes, like blossoms, like all that is happy and lucky and strong—to honor the truth that I was not alone. That I was loved.

FORTY FOUR
四十四

Meg Lindsay, January 2012

"Mom, I can't find the box with my clothes in it!" Eva clambered around stacks of boxes in the living room of our new apartment.

Our new apartment in Shanghai.

Yes, *Shanghai.* I still could barely comprehend it.

"Can you wear something from your suitcase?"

"It's all dirty."

I sent Lewis to ferret out the missing clothing box. The job offer had come from the university in October. They wanted Lewis to expand and retool their high-energy physics program. It was hubris for them to even ask—he'd already turned down offers from some of the most prestigious universities in America. But after our visit to China, the university administrators knew we had a personal connection to the city, so they must have figured they could make it appealing enough. And they did. They helped with all our moving expenses, found us a beautiful apartment near an international school for Eva, and even casually mentioned that they would be offering Zhou Wei a promotion for having connected them to Lewis in the first place.

Our shipment with all our belongings had come in a week later than we'd anticipated, and now we were scrambling to unpack as much as we could before our guests arrived for dinner.

The apartment was beautiful and spacious—much too fine in my opinion, but the university had chosen it for us as part of the relocation package, and we already felt the first stirrings of home-love for it.

We had been in Shanghai for three weeks full of every sort of shopping, of meeting other expats, of getting acquainted with the university faculty and administrators whom Lewis would be working with. When I closed my eyes at night, all I saw were Chinese characters and countless to-do lists: get transportation cards, enroll Eva in the international school nearby, find where to shop, find out how to get medical care, set up bank accounts, buy furniture, buy kitchen supplies, buy groceries . . .

Lewis returned, carrying the box of Eva's clothing. She dug through it until she found what she wanted and hurried to her bedroom to change. I wrapped my arms around Lewis's waist and surveyed the mess.

"Do you think she'll be okay?" I said.

"The therapist thought so. And she'll adjust. It's not like it's totally new for her as it is for us."

"I just wish she'd at least write to Wen Ming. There's been too much not-talking in my family. It's no way to handle a problem."

He kissed my hair. "I know. But we can't force it."

"We're going to be happy here, right?"

"I think so. I hope so." He moved from me and sat on the edge of a sturdy box. "I've spent all my life chasing the one member of my family who happened not to be Chinese and rejecting the rest of them who were. Argentine culture fascinated me because my mom grew up there. I always felt like my Chinese heritage was being shoved down my throat."

"Your relatives understand that." We'd stopped in California on our way to China, and Lewis had taken the opportunity to clear a lifetime of miscommunication away.

"But I want to know China. I want to understand that part of myself. I want Eva to understand it too. This could be the only opportunity we'll have to do that."

"I want that too—for all of us."

"What about you? Will you be happy here?"

It was a bit late to be asking these questions, and we'd already talked about it anyway. But now that we were here, it was as if we couldn't help taking a moment to reassess, reassure ourselves that we weren't crazy for doing it.

Could I be happy here?

Eventually, the newness would fade, and I would wake up one morning and not be able to do anything but cry for my lost home of Chicago. There'd be days when I would hardly be able to face the world outside the apartment because the unfamiliarity of it all was too exhausting. I would cry over e-mails and phone calls to Audra, Cinnamon, Bree, Li Shu—and even my parents. It would be many months before I'd be able to walk out of my home without giving my-self a pep talk first. Many months before the city felt a little smaller, a little less like a giant dragon and more like—oh, maybe just a very large dog.

But right now, this moment, hope fluttered in me like a banner. Hope that I could make my peace with this country. Hope that the lingering soreness in my heart would eventually fade. "Yes," I told him. "I think I can be very happy here." I gave him a long, tango-worthy kiss.

"Aw, come on! Can you two go suck face somewhere else al-ready?" Our daughter, in full command of sixth-grade slang, stood to our side, making fishy lips at us.

The kiss ended in an explosion of laughter. "Don't be rude." But giggles ruined any force my admonishment might have had.

Today was Chinese New Year's Eve, and tomorrow was Eva's birthday. It was her birth year too: the Year of the Dragon. We were determined to celebrate, even if there were boxes everywhere and I hadn't been able to find the kitchen utensils I needed to make a birth-day cake. In the end, the boxes were mostly stowed, and Eva found clothes to wear. Yang Hua and Zhou Wei and their daughter were coming to help us have our first Reunion Dinner in China. It meant Zhou Wei had to tell his family why they would not be at the annual family gathering this year. If his mother was anything like mine, he would not hear the end of it for years. I appreciated the sacrifice.

They were to arrive several hours before we were supposed to eat in order to help me prepare the food. That's what Yang Hua said, anyway. We both knew the reality would be that she would do most of the work and I'd be looking on rather helplessly. But I had a few American tricks up my sleeve, taken from my favorite Christmas recipes. Yang Hua and her family would be getting an introduction to cranberry salad and my favorite potato soup, which we always had on Christmas Eve. Plus chocolate chip cookies, since I hadn't been able to make a birthday cake.

East and West, coming together to celebrate a New Year, a new life, a new home. It seemed—in the way of Chinese thinking—very auspicious.

"They're here!" Eva sprinted to open the door. She never walked anywhere anymore. It was hard to believe that six years ago, she'd been shy, timid, terrified. Now, of the three of us, she was the most intrepid about going out and getting reacquainted with her city.

Yang Hua had her arms full of grocery bags, and for a moment, it felt like Li Shu coming to our Chicago apartment to cook Chinese food with us. The first longing for home twisted in me, and I was glad that in the general chaos, no one noticed me blink back tears.

Zhou Wei carried bags in one arm too, and his free hand was wrapped around his daughter's hand. She was four now, and proudly showed us with three fingers. Her mother gently lifted the fourth, a covert smile around her mouth.

Once they were through the door, Yang Hua and Zhou Wei stopped together, looking toward the door and back at us with hesitant expressions.

"We are sorry to bother you, but . . ." Yang Hua gestured to a figure standing outside the door. "We brought one more guest."

"That's okay. I'm glad—"

A slim, petite teenager walked through the doorway. She reached her hand out and felt until she found the doorframe.

"Wen Ming!" I shoved past Yang Hua and skidded to a stop in front of Wen Ming. "It's me, Meg." I tapped the top of her hand, and then offered her my arm. I noticed she still wore the jade dragon bracelet I had given her. It fit on her wrist now. I looked into her unseeing eyes and felt nothing but a sweet and wistful tenderness for this child who had almost been mine.

"I am sorry to intrude on your home, Mrs. Lindsay."

"You are never intruding. You are welcome anytime."

She nodded her head politely. "Thank you."

Yang Hua and her family stepped back, giving Eva a clear view of this unexpected guest. I tried to read the expression on my daughter's face, but there were too many conflicting emotions flickering past—sadness, anger, joy—I couldn't identify them all. We silently waited—to see if Eva could walk through this final test of healing.

Wen Ming waited too, not shifting her weight, not fidgeting. Just waiting. There was a calmness, a peace over her, as if she had found the strength to accept whatever Eva's reaction might be.

Eva glanced at me, looking suddenly very young and unsure. I smiled and nodded at her. She could do this. I had confidence in her.

She lifted herself tall and walked toward Wen Ming. "*Gong xi fa cai, jie jie.*"

Jie jie. Big sister.

Wen Ming's composure collapsed like an imploded building. A gasping sob escaped her, and the next I could see, the two girls were in each other's arms, so tightly that they seemed to melt into one person. None of us adults could understand the mangled tangle of English and Chinese phrases gushing from them, but the meaning was clear enough.

There is probably some terrible taboo about crying on New Year's Eve, but I didn't care. There couldn't have been a more promising start to a year than witnessing such a miracle, and tears seemed the most appropriate response.

Even Yang Hua's eyes looked extra sparkly. But she tightened her mouth into a secret sort of smile and said, "Meg, we should start preparing the food."

Chinese are not huggy, but I embraced her anyway. "Thank you. That is the best birthday present you could have given her."

She gave me a little squeeze in return, and we toted the bags into the kitchen.

Hours later—after we ate our first real dinner in our new home—we heard the popping and crackling of fireworks. We rushed to the street and joined the revelers.

Drums pounded, and a troupe of lion dancers paraded down the street. Two lions—one black, one white—wove and bobbed to the rhythm of the drums. The white one came to a stop in front of our little group. He blinked great glittering eyes at us, the eyelashes wafting like downy feathers. He curled his head toward us, like a cat wanting to be scratched under its chin. He leaned close to Eva and Wen Ming. Eva guided her big sister's hand to pet the lion's head. He bent his mouth toward their hands, as if to breathe on them, but instead, two shiny objects fell from his mouth—one to each girl.

Tiny painted bottles on red ribbons, each with a red crane's feather inside.

The girls blew kisses to the lion and placed the bottles around each other's neck.

The lion's dance grew ever more acrobatic, and the air grew thick with smoke from the firecrackers and dense with the sound of drumming. The lions leaped into the air and mounted invisible steps to the stars, which danced with them and spread their well-wishes throughout the centuries. Their joy rained on us like the ash from a hundred million fireworks.

The lions were dancers no more. They swooped down around us, swirling like exotic comets, wrapping us into the embrace of the celebration on the street. And suddenly, we were not foreigners. We were not strangers. We were not rivals. This was our family.

China had adopted us. We had come home. Everything we'd gone through—it had been so that we could have this moment.

Lewis looked at me with a puzzled frown. "Did you see . . ."

I grabbed him and swung him around in a dance of our own. "Yes! Yes, I see."

I see everything now.

EPILOGUE

Wen Ming, September 2013

I sit in a padded theater seat in the Shanghai Concert Hall. Eva tells me that everything around us is golden luxury and elegance, like heaven. I am with my family—Baba Lewis and my *mei mei*, Eva (who will answer to either Eva or Zhen An now that she lives in China). The fourth one of us, my mama Meg, is on stage, performing. That is enough heaven for me.

I have lived with them for more than a year now. It was a birthday present to me, from Eva. I didn't realize that birthdays are so important to Americans, but this family chose to honor my fourteenth birthday by inviting me to live with them.

I am still a ward of the state, but I now attend the Shanghai School for the Blind thanks to Half the Sky and my new family. I don't need a document saying I am part of the family. You cannot document the heart's truth—it is more binding than any paper, any court, any government.

It is an odd thing to have someone in my life to call "Mama" and "Baba." I was not certain I could do it at first. But I grew tired of having only aunties and teachers.

I turn my attention back to my Mama Meg. She is performing a solo with the entire orchestra at her back.

The melody is fast, furious, passionate. Sorrow and longing joining hands with exuberant joy and spinning until it's all a blur of sound. It makes me feel things I cannot put into words. Like being part of a family.

I shift in my seat, distracted by the sore muscles in my calves and thighs. We've become very active in the Tango Shanghai group, and my only complaint is that there are no boys my age that go there. My baba says that I will have to wait until I'm older to find boys who enjoy dancing, but once I do, he is going to make us dance with a two-meter wooden pole stuck between us.

He says the most ridiculous things sometimes.

We are not a perfect family. Eva is as strong-willed as I am, and her ways sometimes seem brash to me. So unlike the timid little Zhen An I thought I knew. But her heart is as it always was, and I cannot help but love her.

I sometimes forget that I am not alone anymore, and that I do not have to twirl the world on my finger to keep it from plunging into chaos. I am still trying to grow used to having parents. It is a very strange feeling. I mostly like it very much.

My mama's music wraps around me, like the warmth of her arms. She is not frightened to play anymore. She is confident and strong and beautiful, and I think my heart might break as I listen to her.

After the concert, we wait for her to join us. Then it is the four of us, close together, as one unit. And I hear again the music of my parents, and it is joined by the melody of my sister's heart and my own. There is a wash of scents around me, each one precious and distinct—my mama's resin for her viola bow, the musty fragrance of my baba's thick books, the echo of cherry blossoms that autumn can't diminish. There is the foreign pungency of America too, but I have grown familiar with it, and I will miss it if it ever fades completely. Curling through it all, around and above us, is a thin, faint trail of smoke.

It is sweet like incense to me now.

ABOUT THE AUTHOR

Author Meredith Efken believes all people have a created purpose—something that they are born to do, that brings deep meaning into their lives. "Some people," she says, "seem to know from the time they are small what that is, and other people search for it their entire lives without finding it."

She believes hers was to be a writer. "It just took me a while to figure it out." Apparently, though, she should have recognized the clues. Her mom made "Book of Life" books to use as birth announcements for her, and some of her earliest memories are book related. "My dad intentionally messed up bedtime stories in increasingly obnoxious ways to see if I'd correct him," she recalls. "Books were treated as precious treasures in our house, and being read to was one of my favorite activities." Even before she could read, she tried to write letters. And when she did learn to read? "I don't remember actually learning to read. It just happened sometime before kindergarten, and suddenly a new and enchanting world opened for me."

She wrote her first story when she was eight—"The Flower and the Bee." She says it was meant to be an entire chapter book, co-authored with her younger brother. "He lost interest after the first sentence: 'Once upon a time, there was a flower and a bee.' Hmm . . . can you blame him?" Despite her sibling's defection, Meredith was happy to finish the rest of the two-page tome herself. After that, she enjoyed journaling or writing stories or poems. "Not brilliantly," she points out, "but at least consistently."

She rewrote the endings of novels if she didn't like how the author ended the story. She says she couldn't go for more than a few months without having the nagging urge to write something. In eighth grade, she finally completed a novel-length book. She sums up her juvenilia by stating, "It's so unbelievably bad, it makes me laugh."

Meredith says her childhood friends were Aslan, Charlotte and Wilbur, the March sisters, Black Beauty, Anne Shirley, Bambi, Jane Eyre, and all the other characters residing on her bookshelf. Her first crush was not on a teen heartthrob. It was on a fictional hero from a novel.

Meredith says that, like so many people, she had a lot of misconceptions about professional writers. "I thought that it would be impossible for a 'nobody' like me to ever become published. It seemed like winning the sweepstakes or becoming a movie star—something that happens to only one in a million." When it came time to choose a career, she decided to try something that seemed more realistic. Both her parents were teachers, and she loved school. With a high regard for education and learning and a love for kids, she decided to get her degree in elementary education.

"There was lots I enjoyed about teaching, but it didn't stir my heart the way writing did." When she left the education world to adopt her oldest daughter from China, she finally paid attention to what she now says she should have known all along. "Writing novels was and always had been the desire of my heart."

As she started getting involved in the writing community, she learned that—like most careers—becoming a published author is a combination of talent, hard work, being teachable, understanding how the industry works, a bit of luck, and being persistent. It took five years for her to get her first contract.

"I thought that I'd finally achieved the prize, but I quickly realized it was just the beginning. Four published novels later, I still can hardly believe I have the privilege to be an author."

It's not a life of glamour or leisure, however. She describes the great amount of time she spends alone with a blank computer screen. "I have lots of time to confront my own insecurities, to wrestle with the language and to push harder to understand not just myself but other people and to force myself to be more honest and vulnerable in what I write." Despite the challenges, she says, "It satisfies me in a way few other pursuits can, and I love it."

As a novelist, Meredith believes she has a responsibility to her readers and to society as a whole. She says that novels, like other art forms, reflect our culture and serve as a time capsule. "I feel like there's a deal being made between me and the reader—they enter into the story and allow it to impact them, but they expect in return that the author will be authentic and honest in how she writes. I take that expectation seriously." Whether her story is humorous, serious, realistic, or tinged with fantasy, her aim is to ground it in some core truth about the human experience.

She hopes her readers come away from each book with a better appreciation for who they are and their purpose for being here on the earth. She says that these questions of "Who am I and why am I here?" keep finding their way into her stories. "As I grapple with them in my books, I learn more fully how to answer those questions for myself." The process of becoming a writer has taught her that in order to find that created purpose, "we have to have the courage to dream and take the risks necessary to see those dreams become reality."

Q&A WITH THE AUTHOR

For this Q&A, Meredith turned to good friend and avid reader Amy Bettis, to find out what questions she had about *Lucky Baby*. A mom of three and director of children's ministries at her church, Amy also has personal experience with the world of adoption and foster care, making her the ideal reader to chat with about the story.

What inspired you to write Lucky Baby?
Ever since we adopted our daughter Jessamyn from China, people have asked me, "So, when are you going to write a book about it?" The problem was that our adoption experience is so close to my

heart, so emotional for me, that I couldn't easily write about it. I was determined to not even try until I felt that I had a story that could do it justice.

I love the international adoption community—from the agencies, orphanage workers, and foster parents to the adoptive parents and the children themselves. I care so much about the birth families too. I wanted to write this book as a sort of loving testament to the adoption experience. When you think about it, international adoption is a totally new phenomenon (new in the context of human history)—at least on the scale that it is now. It was unheard-of even a century ago. And with it has come so many new kinds of blessings and challenges. It's taught us much about families and about child development that we simply would not have understood any other way. It's a historical development as much as it is a personal journey, and I wanted to pay tribute to this experience.

That's a lot to tackle in one book. Do you feel you accomplished your goals?

Yes and no! In many ways, I tried to take on way more than I could actually handle. I'm so emotionally close to the subject that it's hard for me to keep a good perspective on it. It was a huge struggle to write the book because I wanted it to be "perfect"—for my daughter, for the other adoptive families, and even for the Chinese people. The truth is, no book will ever be perfect. There are flaws in this book, and I had to get to the point where I could accept that and be satisfied that I'd done the very best that I could do at this point in my career.

I do I feel my story provides a good snapshot of some of the trials and joys that many adoptive families face. I feel it also is a respectful and compassionate portrayal of birth parents and of the orphanages that care for our children until we can be united with them.

I also wanted to convey the sense of "magic" and wonder that I felt during the process of adopting, and then bonding with, my daughter. The way to do this in the story eluded me for months, until I came across the idea of using a technique called "magical realism." Once I made the decision to incorporate this into the story, everything seemed to fall into place, and I am so happy now with how the book turned out.

So what is "magical realism"?

It's actually a literary technique developed by South American writers several decades ago. Some of the more well-known authors in this genre are Gabriel García Márquez, Isabel Allende, Salman Rushdie, and Joanne Harris.

Magical realism incorporates fantastical story elements into an otherwise realistic setting. It's used to draw attention to different aspects of the human experience—both the physical and the spiritual. In the original South American writers' works, it had a political and revolutionary aspect as well, which I chose to downplay in my work.

There's no actual "magic" in magical realism, which is what separates it from fantasy. It just blurs the line between supernatural and natural, so that we can come to a deeper understanding of both worlds. In *Lucky Baby*, you'll notice that Meg and Wen Ming never question the supernatural things that happen to them—that's a feature of magical realism. The supernatural is accepted as being part of the world. The true wonder comes from the truth about the human experience that the characters gain through the story.

As I am a Christian, this approach excites me because I believe that the separation between the spiritual and the supernatural, and the physical and the realistic, is not as wide as we think it is. I think that God is always crossing that line into our world, and we can see it if we are paying attention. Incorporating this technique into *Lucky Baby* allowed me to explore both worlds and how they interact to affect our lives and our choices.

How much research did it take to write this book? Where did you find most of your information?

I started with my own experience adopting my daughter. I also drew from the experience other adoptive families have had. I did need to do some research even beyond that, however, since my story was set about ten years later than when we adopted. A lot changed in that time, and I needed to have accurate information for the time period I wrote about. But it was easy to talk to other families, get news from our adoption agency, Great Wall China Adoption, and stay current through e-mail loops and e-zines.

The most challenging part of the story was how to accurately portray the characters living in China, especially in the orphanages. Chinese culture tends to not be as open with information as American culture, so I couldn't just call up an orphanage director and start asking questions. I used the limited experience I'd had touring my daughter's orphanage, as well as the stories of other people who'd worked with Chinese orphanages, and I did a lot of digging for personal experiences online.

For other parts of daily life in China, I read blogs, watched personal videos on YouTube, and talked with some of my Chinese friends. As an American, I can't capture the Chinese experience as authentically as someone who has been immersed in that culture can, but I hope I came close. It was important to me to give a respectful and appreciative portrayal of the Chinese people, out of love for my daughter and her heritage.

So how much of this story was autobiographical?
Not a whole lot, actually. The most autobiographical part was the scene where Meg receives Eva. My husband was with me, whereas Meg's was not, but we were in a government building, and the way Meg felt as she waited for her child and the way the receiving took place was pretty much the way it happened for us. Our daughter was much younger than Eva, but she did start screaming when we took her. The scene following that, with Auntie Yang in the private room, was totally fictional.

Some of Meg's despair about not being a good enough mother is similar to how I've felt about some of my own failures as a mom. The exact circumstances are fictional, but the emotions are the same.

I wasn't willing to make the story very autobiographical because that story belongs to my daughter, and I don't have the right to take it for my novel.

Can you separate some of the other details into fact and fiction?
Sure! I think it's safe to say that the details on the actual adoption process are accurate. I skimmed over most of the paper chase because it's so tedious, there's not much I can do to make it exciting for a book.

I think that the depiction of Wen Ming's orphanage is fairly true to life as well, though the orphanage itself is fictional. All orphanages are not the same—there are good ones and not-so-good ones. Wen Ming and Zhen An lived in a really good orphanage, and in some ways I made it similar to the one my daughter came from. The workers are kind and dedicated, the building is clean, and the children are as well cared for as they can be in an institutional setting.

I mentioned one real-life organization in the book—Half the Sky Foundation, which is devoted to helping the orphans in China who aren't adopted, through building schools and providing medical care and other important projects. You can find out more about Half the Sky at the foundation's website, which I included in the Resources section.

Several of the shops in Guangzhou that I mentioned are, or were, real shops. I've heard that Shop on the Stairs closed a couple of years ago, which saddens me.

The tango restaurant Meg and Lewis frequent, as well as the tea shop, are both fictional. So is Meg's church and the Bible college she attended. Her symphony, and its unusual focus, are fictional, but are inspired by a real symphony in a different city.

Lewis's university—University of Chicago—is real, and so is Fermilab and CERN, but his mother is not and neither are her contributions to the physics world. The search for the Higgs boson is very real, but that breakthrough hasn't happened at the time of this writing. The way I portrayed that breakthrough is based on the conjecture of some of my physics friends, so we'll have to see how that plays out in the future.

The supernatural elements in the story are whatever you make them out to be. Real or fictional? You choose.

How do you develop the characters in your books?

I think every author develops characters based on her own experiences and a combination of different people and types of people she knows. I usually have a general mental picture of the type of person I need for a certain character—rather like a director getting ready to conduct auditions for a play. I use my experiences with different people and my own understanding of human behavior to help me shape each character. I borrow aspects of personalities or individual quirks and put them together to create a unique, fictional character that is based in human reality.

Do you base your characters on real-life people?
There's a T-shirt I want that says "Be careful, or I'll put you in my novel!" I used to tease my friends' dates that if they hurt my friend, they'd end up my next villain. Here's the secret: I'm just bluffing.

In reality, it's very rare for me to base a character entirely on one real person. It's too difficult because fictional people have to be shaped to an extent to fit the parameters of the story. Since real people are more complex and their lives rarely follow the structure of a novel, it's more useful for me to create entirely fictional people.

The other issue is a respect for privacy and compassion for the people I know. In a novel, it's necessary for characters to behave badly and make poor choices at times. I wouldn't want to hurt anyone or damage his reputation by basing a character on him and then having that character act wrongly. If I ever did base a character on someone I know, I would use only the most positive and noble aspects of that person. All the "bad stuff" would be strictly fictional.

I did use one of my daughter's teachers in the book—at least his name. But it was a very minor character and I did it to amuse her and the teacher. You *were* amused, right, Mr. Compton?

Why did you choose to make the relationships between Meg and her mom and Lewis and his mom so tense?
It was a thematic decision. One of the things I wanted to explore in the book was that there is more than one way to be abandoned. The Chinese orphans were abandoned in a traditional sense. But in an indirect way, so were Meg and Lewis. I wanted to explore the effect that might have on them as they try to all come together to form a family when none of them had a good model to follow. Given the number of broken and dysfunctional families for those in my generation and younger, I think it's an important question to explore. And since Meg was my main character, and this story is also about her

journey to become a mother, it made sense to focus on the mothers in the story as a way to tie the themes together.

Is it usual for adopted children to have the sort of attachment problems that Eva had? Doesn't that make adoption a bit more scary?

That's a delicate question. Parenting itself is scary—regardless of how the family is formed! There are no guarantees that any child is going to sail through life without problems. But there are some challenges adoptive families face that most nonadoptive families don't have to deal with.

First of all, I want people to understand that when an author sits down to plot out a book, she fully intends to make life for her characters as difficult as possible. A novel without conflicts, without challenges for the characters to overcome, is boring.

So you can't judge the adoption experience on the basis of a novel: fiction requires levels of conflict that real life does not. The same can actually be said of most news stories about adoption. Bad news sells. Good news doesn't. That means you will hear far more stories of difficult adoptions or problems than you will about all the many, many adoptions that are virtually trouble-free. Unfair, but that's how life is.

On the other hand, there is an aphorism in the adoption community that *every* institutionalized child is a "special needs" child. This includes those in foster care and those in even the best orphanages. At the very least, every adopted child has to heal from the wound of being separated from her birth mother. This affects each child in a different way, but adoptive parents have to understand and be equipped to deal with that very deep loss and the grief it often brings.

We've only learned about attachment disorders in the last twenty years or so. There's a lot we don't understand, but we've made tremendous progress. Not every adopted child has attachment problems, and it's not entirely clear why some do and some don't. Even nonadopted children occasionally have attachment disorders. But it's not the end of the world—there are a growing number of techniques and therapies that have successfully helped children heal and learn to bond with their families. There is always hope and healing.

I used to conduct adoption information seminars as part of my job as a regional officer for Great Wall. My advice to prospective parents was to educate themselves about attachment disorders and to be prepared to love their child and be committed to that child no matter what difficulties arose. I also assured them that the majority of children adjust to their new families with few or no problems at all.

At the end of the book the relationships are still quite fragile in their healing process. If you were to lengthen the book, how would you help the characters develop strong and deep relationships?
I think counseling is always a good place to start, especially when the problems are caused by trauma that happened to children before they were old enough to process or understand.

I also would love to have explored Lewis's faith journey in more depth. I firmly believe that God heals not just our bodies but also our emotional wounds, and I think that if Lewis could come to even a point of acceptance about God's existence, he would find the path to healing much easier.

For the family as a whole, I would focus on their consciously and deliberately defining for themselves what a family is, and what their family is going to look like. I think they'd need to be very protective of their family space and time together. The girls would need direct instruction about how to be part of a family, and they'd need lots of reassurance that they are loved by their family no matter how badly they behave or how angry they might feel. Lots of communication, lots of forgiveness, lots of patience—these are what I would "prescribe" for them. And I'd also want them to take it in baby steps and not expect everything to be perfect overnight. It's a process, and it might take years, but in my mind, they do make it.

DISCUSSION QUESTIONS

THEMES

1) There are several different mother figures in this story. Discuss the strengths and weaknesses of each one and the effect they had on their children. How did each character show a different facet of motherhood? (Hint: Look for a few characters who have mother attributes even if they aren't actual mothers.)

2) In what ways were each of the four main characters (Meg, Lewis, Wen Ming, and Eva) abandoned by his or her parents? How did this affect them personally? How do you think this contributed to their struggles in becoming a family? Were there other instances of abandonment in the story? How did these events affect the characters?

3) Each section of the story is prefaced by a quote from Mother Teresa, who dedicated her life to serving orphans in India. Discuss the first two quotes: How do these pertain to that part of the story? How did the characters typify the idea in each quote? What do these quotes mean to you? How do you see the truth of each quote played out in real life?

4) Discuss the final quote: "I have found the paradox, that if you love until it hurts, there can be no more hurt, only more love." Do you think this is true? If so, how do you think this can be possible? How did Meg and other characters in the story discover or exemplify this idea?

5) Journeys are a recurring theme in the story. What different references to journeys did you notice in the story? What kinds of journeys were the characters on? Do you think they reached their destinations? What unexpected turns did they take on the way?

6) The color red signifies luck and happiness in Chinese culture. What role does the color red play in the story? What objects are red? What effect do these objects have on the story? What other images in the story represented luck? Wen Ming placed a great deal of value on the idea of luck. Do you think she was lucky? What symbols of luck and happiness do we have in our culture?

7) What do you think was the meaning of the two crane feathers? What role did they play for the characters? What was the significance of Zhen An (Eva) finding the feather and giving it to Wen Ming? Was there a connection between the two feathers?

8) In your opinion, who was the chain-smoking Chinese woman with the mole? In Chinese culture, it's considered unfeminine for women to smoke, and moles are considered serious flaws. In what other ways was the woman flawed? What were her strengths? When Wen Ming says, "You don't even know me," the woman responds, "Not as I wish I did. But still, I love you." What do you think she meant? Do you think she will show up again in the lives of the Lindsay family?

9) How was food and food-related imagery used in the book? What was the significance of food for Wen Ming? For Meg? What was each of them truly hungry for? Do you think they found it?

10) What was some other Chinese-related imagery in the story? What did these images mean to you? Several of them are based on Chinese folklore. If you have time, it might be fun to find more information about some of them and discuss how that information helps you understand the story further. You can also compare the modified versions of the symbols that were used in the story with the original folklore images.

11) Meg draws a distinction between having a child and becoming a mother. Do you agree with her on this distinction? Describe the steps she went through to finally feel like she was truly a mother. Is becoming a mother a process or an event? Why?

12) Discuss Meg and Lewis's relationship. What were its strengths? Its weaknesses? What do you think the effects were of the differences in their religious beliefs? What did each of them do to work around that for the sake of their marriage? What do you think of their compromise about taking Eva to church? Do you agree or disagree? Why?

13) Describe Lewis's conflicted feelings about his mother. How could he be so angry at her and yet desire her approval so strongly? How will he feel about physics now that he knows it is impossible to earn her approval? What do you think will happen to him now that he has moved to China?

14) Some readers have said that Meg's parents weren't all that bad, and that Meg didn't have reason to be upset with them. What do you think? How did Meg and her parents each contribute to the conflict between them? What do you think her relationship with them would be like if the story were continued?

15) Discuss Wen Ming's relationship with Zhen An (Eva). In what ways was it positive and healing? In what ways was it detrimental to both of them? Do you think it was good for Eva to get rid of Wen Ming's feather? Was she right to blame Wen Ming for encouraging her to run away? Why or why not? What do you think their relationship will be like going forward?

16) Did Wen Ming really hate America and adoption? Why or why not?

17) How did Zhen An/Eva change throughout the story? Do you think being adopted was overall a positive thing for her or did it hurt more than help? What effect do you think Meg's motives and expectations for adoption had on Eva's adjustment to the family? Why do you think Eva's nightmares and other problems were lessened when she visited China?

18) How were Meg's expectations about adoption different from what she actually experienced? If you are a parent, how did your expectations about becoming a parent differ from the reality of it? What did you think about her motivation for having a child—good, bad, neutral? What do you think are good reasons to have children—whether by birth or by adoption?

19) What were the positives about Zhen An being adopted? What were some of the negatives? How important do you think one's culture and heritage is? Eva lost her Chinese culture to a large extent—do you think having a permanent family was a worthwhile trade-off?

20) How did the story change your view of Chinese orphanages or of the situations surrounding abandoned children in that country? What new understanding did you form about China? What new understanding did you form about international adoption?

21) What's your opinion on the "magical" elements of the story—were they really happening or were they just some sort of vision? Why do you think so? What did they represent in the story? Do you think Meg and Wen Ming will continue experiencing these sort of things in the future? What about Lewis? Will he come around? We only had one scene from Eva's point of view, so we don't know if she experiences the same sort of supernatural things. What do you think—does she? What are the differences between what happens to Meg and what Wen Ming experiences? What do you think is the significance of these differences?

22) Discuss Meg's experience by the hotel pool at the climax of the story. Who was the mother she saw? Who were the children? Were they just random strangers or did they represent something more? What happened to Meg in the water? How did she "grow up" in the way she viewed her parents and others who had hurt her? How did her way of loving them change, and how did that help her overcome the pain?

RESOURCES

Great Wall China Adoption: www.gwca.org

Half the Sky Foundation: www.halfthesky.org

Shaohannah's Hope: www.showhope.org

RainbowKids.com: www.rainbowkids.com

NOTE FROM THE AUTHOR

I'm a big fan of book clubs, and I'd love to chat with your group either in person, by speakerphone, or online chat. If you go to my website, www.meredithefken.com, you can download a book club kit that includes the information here plus additional discussion questions, ideas for creating a Chinese theme for your book club meeting, recipe for Chinese dumplings, and a fun Chinese calligraphy project for your group members. Information is there on how to contact me to speak to your group.

You can also e-mail me at Meredith@meredithefken.com; follow me on Twitter: http://twitter.com/meredithefken; and friend me on Facebook: http://www.facebook.com/meredithefken.